Helen Salsbury is a published short story writer, spoken word performer and community journalist, who has been longlisted for the *Mslexia* novel competition and shortlisted for the Impress Prize for New Writers. She's the founder of environmental writing project Pens of the Earth and a director of the Portsmouth Writers Hub.

www.helensalsbury.com

Mark & Stacey,

Thanks for coming to see The Bookshop.

And good luck with your books!

Helen xx

sometimes when i sleep

HELEN SALSBURY

Matador
9 Priory Business Park,
Wistow Road, Kibworth Beauchamp,
Leicestershire. LE8 0RX
Tel: 0116 279 2299
Email: books@troubador.co.uk
Web: www.troubador.co.uk/matador
Twitter: @matadorbooks

ISBN 978 1 8004 6478 0

British Library Cataloguing in Publication Data.
A catalogue record for this book is available from the British Library.

Printed and bound in the UK by TJ Books LTD, Padstow, Cornwall
Typeset in 11pt Aldine401 BT by Troubador Publishing Ltd, Leicester, UK

Matador is an imprint of Troubador Publishing Ltd

For my sisters

ONCE

"Once there was a princess,
dreamed from a drop of blood,
with skin white as snow,
with hair black as jet;
with her future carved in stone."

From the album *Faerie Gothic,*
by Dark Island

ONE

'The University of Eden,' Harriet murmurs. Despite the tension in the car, the post-fight chasm between her and Dad, she has to say it out loud. Their car has been crawling over the vast shoulders of the Pennines for what's felt like hours, gradually climbing, gradually descending, and then finally this last turn in the road and there it is, nestled deep in the Eden Valley, all walls and buildings and green grass and well-trodden paths. 'Eden University.'

The taste of apples and the slither of serpents and the promise of something different, something better, something brighter. Harriet fights her seatbelt to crane forward; last time she'd only been a visitor, here for an interview. This time she belongs.

The road is narrow, twisting, and Dad has been hunched forward over the steering wheel for pretty much the entire journey: arms tense, shoulders bulked like a bull's.

She's kept a wary eye on him, unable to keep out of his way like she normally would after one of their fights. Now, she senses him turn his head briefly to look at her.

'You chose it for the name?' he says.

'No, I didn't! You *know* that.' She drums her trainers against the car floor, rakes a hand through her short hair.

It's not easy to let the anger, the resentment go. Never is.

She leans forwards, glares through the windscreen. In the distance, the sunlight is striking the white tops of Eden's residential halls creating a clean brilliance. And that lightens her mood.

There are no shadows there. It's a reinforcement of the Dark Island lyrics she'd heard for the first time this morning. "*You're leaving the shadows.*" That's what Medea had sung, that's what she keeps replaying in her head.

I'm leaving the shadows! She hugs the promise to herself, turning her head away to look through the side window so that Dad won't spot what she's thinking.

The free DVD of Dark Island's new song, "Bleeding for Strangers", had arrived in the post this morning, attached to the front of Harriet's goth mag. The timing was immaculate! Even though they were meant to be leaving straight after breakfast, Harriet hadn't been able to resist sneaking away to play it, using the excuse of ordering more library books for Mum to justify unpacking her laptop; only Dad had caught her watching it and been furious, their row so much more menacing for being conducted at low volume so that it didn't disturb Mum.

Harriet can still hear the words he'd snarled at her, can still hear the names he'd used for Dark Island. He'd called them "Ghouls". He'd called Medea a "grief harpy".

He'd not even tried to understand, even though she'd wanted him to; *really, really* wanted him to.

Dad clears his throat. 'You chose Eden for Dr Drake then?'

This is safe ground.

'Absolutely,' Harriet says. She hesitates, but the desire to get past their argument is strong. After all, how many chances has she got left to speak to him? She'd been looking forward to this journey, to having him to herself for once. 'She excites me every bit as much as she terrifies me.'

'Hmm.' It's a half laugh, encouraging.

'The way she grilled me at the interview,' she says, 'making it clear she's after brilliance, passion. She'll make me the best I can be. She'll teach me to build bridges.'

Then you'll be proud of me.

Again Dad clears his throat, an awkward sound. His fingers are clenched round the wheel, knuckles white. This journey can't be easy for him.

A sudden tightness in her chest, like someone has stuck her in a corset and pulled tight. She exhales rather noisily.

'You didn't have to choose civil engineering just because that's what I do,' Dad blurts. 'You're allowed to make your own choices.'

Harriet widens her eyes. Dad doesn't really do analysing stuff or heart-to-hearts.

'It's what I want,' she says.

And yet, she knows it's more complicated than that. It's what Stephen would have done. But to tell him this would bring them too close to what she fears is unsaid in every fight they have, the reason why they don't bounce back, the reason why no argument ever resolves things.

Dad and Stephen used to have epic rows. But there was never this awkward terrain of afterwards to negotiate, this smouldering half-life of anger, resentment, bitterness. Their rows always cleared the air, nothing was left unhurled, they'd emerge from their titanic clashes as bouncy as ever.

Bouncy. It's a funny word. Not one she'd use for Dad these days.

She looks out of the window into the distance, where the sharp peaks of the Lake District flirt with the blue sky. They are far less serious than the dour humps of the Pennines. It's another reminder that not everything has to be sullen-shouldered, hunched.

She immediately wants to visit them, and longs for her bike which just wouldn't fit into the car. She'll get it at Christmas when she goes home, bring it back on the train.

Dad thinks it will be easier for Mum to cope if Harriet doesn't keep coming and going, and Harriet hasn't argued with his conclusion, wasn't even sure she wanted to. She bites her lip, frowns. Will Mum be okay?

Surprisingly, what hits her is anger, rather than the usual guilt.

She clenches her fists and stares hard at the mountains until she's found a way to push it under, make like she never felt it. Impossible to feel anger with Mum, she'd have to be a monster to do that. And she's not. Doesn't want to be. Is intent on proving that she isn't.

She watches the mountains until the descent into the valley blocks them from view.

Nearly there! She rubs her palms on her jeans to dry them. She's nervous, inevitable perhaps, but it's all going to be okay.

I'm going to be a new person here. Not "the sister of the boy who—"

No. Not that. Not even *close*.

There's no one here from Harriet's school, no one here from her hockey team. It's the way she chose it. She's on her own, and she can make this hers. She can be whoever she wants to be.

Dad steers the car through the entrance to the walled campus and along its "fifteen miles an hour" roads, turns into a space in the car park, kills the ignition.

He stays sitting there, while the engine ticks. He looks tired, edgy, and there's a crease of frown just above his eyes. His hands are still locked to the steering wheel.

Finally, he lifts one hand. 'This is it. Genesis Hall.' He gestures at the square white building, with its splodge of red climbing plant. 'I'll start getting the boxes out while you pick up your room key.'

*

Every step is new; every face is new. Harriet does a fair bit of nervous smiling and saying, 'Hi'. Everyone's busy, either laden or returning empty-handed, like this group clattering down the stairs and past where the two of them are standing, checking Harriet's instructions on where to go.

'Top floor,' Dad says. 'Wouldn't you just know!'

Harriet hoists her hockey bag, with its clacking sticks, more securely onto her shoulder and shifts her grip on the huge box she is holding.

The stairs are currently clear; she gets a sudden impulse, acts on it.

'Race you,' she says.

It's an old game between them, but one they haven't played for a long time. He glances at her, a funny questioning look in his eyes, then says, 'You're on.'

They take the stairs two at a time, shoulder to shoulder. Harriet begins to edge ahead, then drops back. Dad is breathing hard, Harriet also, but more easily. She's been at hockey-club boot camp all summer, training and competing with the mixed seniors. Whereas Dad, who she always thinks of as fitter than her, has been stuck in the house when not at work. She slows her pace, lets him edge ahead. But then he too slows, and they arrive on the top floor together, shoulder to shoulder. A draw.

A couple of girls, who've been standing back waiting for them to arrive, grin at Harriet and Dad, then head off down the stairs. Another pulse of nervousness. She concentrates on finding her room, telling herself it will all be easier once she's on her own, unpacked, settled in. But she's really nervous now.

What if no one likes her?

But there's hockey, and there's class – no, she means *lectures*. There're lots of things she's good at. It occurs to her that she's never had to forge a new path. She's always been known – not always the way she wanted to be, but known nonetheless.

Her room is near the kitchen with just one other numbered door between her and it. There are voices in there, muffled by the thick door, people, floor mates.

Gulp! Not just yet. Got to unload first.

She unlocks her door and swings it open. The room is narrow, with bright yellow blinds concertinaed at the window, and a dense carpet, nubby and ungiving, under her feet.

Dad dumps his first load and heads back down the stairs, but Harriet lingers, assessing the room.

The desk is large and functional with deep shelves above it, just the place her Role Playing character sheets could go – her paladin, her trickster elf, her grenade-tossing princess – *if* she'd brought them. She'd wanted to, like a security blanket. Her gaming groups were another place she fitted, another place where she knew how to belong.

But there was no point in coming to university and doing *all* the things she'd done at home. And this was one sacrifice she was intent on making. If only because she'd always been convinced that Stephen would call her "sad" for holing up with the other gamers for hours and hours, for creating imaginary selves and existing in imaginary worlds, for wasting so much time inside. Impossible to think of Stephen sitting still for that long, letting his character do his fighting, his exploring, his roof-climbing for him. He just wouldn't!

She flushes, and turns to check out the pinboard on the wall. It's well used: covered in graffiti, embedded with drawing pins. She starts reading one of the jokes, *Why do lecturers...*, then breaks off as Dad comes through the door with her suitcase in one hand, her favourite pillow in the other.

'That's nearly it,' he says. 'You can pick up the rest as you see me off.'

Dropping the suitcase, he tosses the pillow onto the bed and walks to the sink. She watches as he splashes water over his face, then turns.

A thick stillness. There's nothing more to keep him. Unless –

'Do you want coffee before you go?'

He hesitates, then nods. 'You make it, while I give Mum a quick ring. Check she's all right.'

Mum!

The way she felt when I hugged her goodbye. So insubstantial – ghostlike in her fragility. As if I were already gone or as if Mum was. Nothing to hold.

Mum had stood just inside the open front door and Harriet could feel her longing to retreat.

'I just can't—' Mum had said.

Dad, pressing a hand briefly on Harriet's shoulder, had said, 'Get in the car,' and he'd turned back and taken Mum inside, and then they'd driven off.

Harriet hadn't looked back. So she doesn't know whether Mum was at the window waving, or whether the windows were as blank as usual.

And it's there again, that flicker of anger, resentment. She hefts the box of crockery and walks away.

'Coffee,' she says, as she leaves the room, takes the paces necessary to bring her to the kitchen, and pushes the door open.

*

She'd forgotten about the voices she'd heard, is unprepared for the two girls already occupying the kitchen, wants to walk out and walk back in, smile in place.

Fortunately, both girls are preoccupied, the nearest perched on a counter, texting, the other unpacking crockery into a cupboard. They have matching lengths of dandelion-blonde hair, falling across their shoulders and shimmering down their backs.

Harriet heads over to the kettle, which is steaming gently, and puts her box down. She rummages self-consciously.

'Is she back?' The girl texting doesn't look up.

'Nope, it's someone new,' the other says. 'Hi, I'm Jenna.' She closes the cupboard and smiles at Harriet, 'and that's Marcia. Are you moving in?'

Harriet nods, then hesitates. It's not just the hair, it's everything about them. Their cute, baby-doll T-shirts, immaculate jeans and most of all the similarity of their gestures.

'You're twins!'

'No shit, Sherlock.' Marcia's tone is more sarcastic than friendly.

Jenna laughs. A softer sound. 'Do you want a coffee? I was just about to—'

'I'm making one for Dad.' Harriet gestures with the mug which she's finally managed to unearth. It feels weird saying this, like she's caught between two worlds.

Just then he walks into the kitchen, pocketing his mobile.

'How is she?' Harriet asks in an undertone.

'Bearing up, but I ought to get back.'

'I know.' Her voice feels scratchy. She focusses hard on making his drink, splashing in plenty of milk so he can down it quickly. Tiny bubbles rise to the surface as she stirs.

A strike of heels.

'Iquis!' Marcia exclaims, sounding pleased.

It's an unusual name. Harriet passes the coffee to Dad, then turns.

And it's like Iquis has stepped out of one of Harriet's goth mags. She's framed in the doorway and her presence is huge. Maybe she's stopped there deliberately, for maximum impact.

She is vivid in her darkness: hair too blue-black to be natural, heavy-white face paint which contrasts sharply with the tar-black tyre-tracks round her eyes, a wide burgundy slash of mouth. A skinny ankh pierces her right eyebrow like an exclamation mark. She's high-fashion goth, very cutting edge, very modern.

Wow! Harriet wants to get to know her.

Harriet's never actually spent time with goths. She can't dance, freezes into red-faced immobility if she gets anywhere near a dance floor, so hanging out at Sheffield's one goth nightclub was always out of the question. She'd just have felt awkward, out of it.

It's surprising that Iquis is who Marcia has been waiting for; she is so opposite to the twins' shiny prettiness, so extreme. She's wearing a cropped PVC top and matching shorts from which squares of black mesh are suspended on tiny silver chains. Her skin gleams pearly pale through the fine mesh holes. She's tall.

Probably as tall as Dad. Glancing at him to compare, Harriet spots the forward jut of his chin. It's a bad sign. Given their recent fight over Dark Island, he's not going to be pleased about this girl.

But that's too bad. She grins at Iquis. *This* is her soulmate, the person she wants to spend time with, listen to music with – perhaps even share some of that black make-up with. *Anything* is possible.

Except that there's no response. Iquis regards her without expression. Her high cheekbones and razor slash of hair give her an arrogant look, a cold, detached appearance.

Harriet's grin lessens. Rebuffed, but determined not to show it, she gazes defiantly back into stormy grey-blue eyes.

And they get stuck like that. Neither giving an inch.

Harriet sees a brief, unforgiving snapshot of herself: her short hair, thin shoulders, too-big man's shirt and narrow face. Perhaps it's not surprising that Iquis doesn't recognise that Harriet belongs in her world. That she always has.

But she will, in time.

'Do you want to come to the bar with us, Iquis?' Marcia asks, but neither Harriet nor Iquis acknowledge this interjection.

Dad clatters his mug into the sink.

'Come on, Harriet, time I went.' He moves, steady and tanklike, towards the door, a collision waiting to happen.

'Okay, Granddad. Don't let me get in your way.' Iquis turns sideways to allow him room to brush past her. Although unsmiling, she seems amused. Harriet isn't. Dad is not fair game.

He says nothing, just moves to pass Iquis so that they are both in the doorway. Harriet can see the familiar anger working under his skin as he half-twists to look back.

Don't lose your temper, not here, she silently begs.

Iquis kisses him.

It's that sudden. That unexpected. He's there on the threshold, inches away from the goth girl's scantily clad skin, when she leans forwards and presses her lips into his.

For a moment they are frozen like that, their mouths welded together, and then he throws himself off her. Hands slam into the wood of the door as he powers himself away and storms down the corridor, the muscles of his back bulging in outrage.

Impossible at first to react. The whole encounter seems unreal. Only the faint smudge of lipstick above Iquis's lip convinces Harriet it really happened. She starts forward: angry, disappointed.

'Why?'

Why did you do that? We could have been friends.

Iquis shrugs. There's the faintest hint of a smile playing at the corner of her mouth.

'Harriet! Are you coming?' Dad calls.

The girl winks at her and then with a sweeping gesture clears the doorway. The action disarms Harriet. She hesitates briefly, unsure what to do, then obeys her father. She will deal with Iquis later. As she sprints down the corridor, she is dimly aware of heavy perfume settling against her skin.

She catches up with Dad by the stairs. There's a burgundy smear, tangled in the black hairs of his hand, and a fresh awkwardness between them. Harriet is aware of a flicker of jealousy, as if Iquis has reached him, has touched him, in a way she herself has been unable to do. She pushes the thought away in disgust.

The incident makes it even more difficult to find a decent way to say goodbye. Dad puts the final suitcase on the pavement and Harriet piles her loaded rucksack on top. The car boot gapes empty, then he closes it. There's a brief hug – more awkward than usual – a quick exchange.

'I know you'll work hard,' he says, 'you always do.'

She nods an acknowledgement. 'Safe journey.' She thinks of the long drive ahead of him back across the Pennines to Sheffield and Mum. Strange to think of him "going south". Sheffield's always been the north until now. Cumbria has become the new north.

'You'll do well here,' he says. 'The Eden Valley's a good place.'

'I know.'

He hesitates, then adds. 'Stephen would have liked it.' He climbs quickly into the car, without waiting for her reply.

TWO

"Dark child we're losing you.
You're leaving the shadows,
Reaching for the light."

Medea is singing the "Bleeding for Strangers" lyrics. Even though she's not visible in the video, Harriet pictures her: a white streak flashing from her forehead down through her long black hair, hooded eyes, the tightness of pain in her clenched stance. She always looks like that, tends to linger in the darkness at the back of the group. She's an alto, and her harsh saxophone voice is as rough and melancholy as ever.

'Grief harpy,' Dad had called her. Harriet is still simmering about that, can't help it. Doesn't he realise –

He doesn't, of course.

Medea sounds nothing like Mum, and yet Harriet has always made that connection, right from the first time she heard Dark Island, as if Medea can give voice to the things Mum doesn't say.

Harriet, cross-legged on this strangely firm bed with the laptop open in front of her, reaches forward and pauses the video.

This is where Dad had caught her, one stanza in, hardly started.

'This is not what you're meant to be doing!' His voice had been taut with anger.

She'd not appeased him the way sometimes she did, hadn't been able to, something angry in herself rising up to meet him.

'It's Dark Island,' she'd said, 'and it's just arrived. It's synchronicity. It's like a message.'

You see, Dad, she'd thought, *someone cares that I'm going away.*

She sucks in her breath.

Of course he hadn't understood anything. Dad had this huge hostility to Dark Island, an unreasoning dislike.

He'd told her to stop the DVD, and his voice had been flat, but the tell-tale muscle in his forearm twitched. He always thought with his arms.

'At the end of the song,' she'd said.

'NOW!'

She'd paused it, with the screen full of Circe's face – those china-blue eyes, that orange-red hair, that gothic-heroine look. 'You don't understand...'

'You're meant to be ordering Mum's books.'

'Yeah, I'll do that next. It's not exactly urgent, is it?' And then the *something* had driven her to utter the unsayable. 'It's not like she's going anywhere!'

His bicep had bulked as his fist clenched. She'd thought briefly that he was actually going to hit her – and some part of her had been pleased. As if, perhaps, it would explode once and for all that unrelenting tension. But he hadn't. Instead, he'd slammed the laptop shut and headed out of the house with it, saying he was going to lock it into the car boot, seeing as Harriet couldn't be trusted.

Left empty-handed in her room, aching to hear the rest of the song, Harriet had vowed that one of the first things she'd do when she got to uni was fire up the laptop and watch the whole video without interference, without anyone telling her to stop.

And now she can, as many times as she wants.

She restarts the video.

> *"Dark child we're losing you.*
> *You're leaving the shadows,*
> *Reaching for the light."*

Circe, clad in a Victorian nightdress, is running to escape the other members of Dark Island. She's trapped inside a turreted mansion and, as she flings herself through the maze-like passages, her blue eyes are wide with horror, her pouting red lips open wide in a scream which invades the music.

The running and the cornering is hypnotic, as repetitive as the drumbeat pound. The shaky hand-held footage makes Harriet's pulse race, and her headphones drive the sound deep into her mind.

Circe rounds the corner, slams to a halt and tries to back pedal. Sauron is there, wielding a bass guitar like a blood-axe, his face contorted.

✳

'You're obsessed with that band.' Dad's words from the fight. Why can't she get them out of her head?

'It's about me,' she wants to tell him. 'It's like I'm Circe – we're both going away. And I just need to find out...'

What they have to tell me.

How it ends.

*

The house begins to split apart, walls cracking and rupturing, slabs of ceiling raining down. Dodging falling masonry, Circe breaks out of the house and hurls herself down the long, shadowed drive, until she slams to a halt, stopped by the vast, wrought-iron gates.

She yanks at them, but they are held shut by heavy chains, wound round and round and secured with a huge padlock. The sound of her struggle crashes and clanks into the music, as the gates sway and shudder. Then, with both hands – and superhuman strength – she breaks the padlock apart and hauls the chains through the gates, unwinding them, their heavy length clattering down into a heap at her feet.

> *"Dark child, when you're bleeding for strangers,*
> *remember the darkness that gave you the light."*

The gates swing open. As Circe steps through, the sun hits her flame-red locks and turns her into a blaze of light, burning her image into the screen until there is nothing but brightness, a magnesium glare which fills the entire screen.

Something about the brightness – the nothingness of the brightness – unsettles Harriet. It's too intense, it's like Circe is burning up in front of her.

She starts the video again, hoping for a different ending.

*

Later, when she sleeps, she dreams she is Circe.

The Victorian nightdress is tight across her shoulders, trapping her arms. It smells of oil and steel and when she looks down she's tightly wrapped in chains. They cross and recross her chest, pinning her arms and clanking. They hang heavy and cold. She feels shorter, like she's being dragged downwards, compressed.

What about the gates? Where are they? And Dark Island? Circe? She'll have the key. Or just... break the chain open with her hands.

The gates.

Yes – the gates. Harriet sees them now. Sees –

It's not Dark Island behind the gates. It's Mum and Dad; Stephen. Stephen's reaching out to her through the bars, his fingers curling to beckon, to summon.

Heavy with chains she shuffles towards him, dragging her way, obeying him, like she always does.

Then the shadows behind Stephen bulge and Stephen's best friend, Graham, steps forward. She can't meet his gaze. He's pushing forward to stand next to Stephen and she can't look into his face – but if she looks down she'll see his trainers, a gash like a wound across one instep.

And she'll know.

*

She wakes up.

She tells herself it was only a normal nightmare. Not the one – not the recurring one, which has haunted her for years, and been particularly bad in the last few weeks, so that she never wants to go to bed, because she's so terrified of encountering it.

Someone pushing her... forcing her to dig... the scratching sound of soil... the smell of decay... the opening earth...

No! Not that nightmare. But this one –

As bad. And somehow too close – As if the two nightmares are connected, and if she falls asleep now...

Well, she'd better not!

She pushes back the duvet, rolls out of bed. Nubby carpet, small room. Alien, really. Not yet comforting.

She doesn't dress, just puts on a sports-bra under her pyjamas, adds a fleece coat and trainers, then wends her way through the silent corridors and stairwells. On the ground floor she hears the faint sound of music travelling along the corridor and hesitates. There's someone else awake. But it would be impossible to knock on a stranger's door, with the fellowship of the night as her only excuse. And besides, she might say things she regretted, tell things which are better left in Sheffield, on the other side of the Pennines.

She shakes her head, continues towards the exit.

Outside she starts to run. She picks up speed rapidly, jettisoning her usual warm-up routine.

As she leaves the university behind, she loses the artificial light and runs on into darkness. Gradually her eyes adjust. There's a faint light from the crescent moon.

She's on a curving road, between walls. The night air hurtles towards her full of imagined obstacles. She speeds up, lowering her head to butt against them. She runs at this pace for some time, her body warming as her muscles relax.

The trees sneak up on her, solitary sentinels that draw closer together until they surround her, the tops of their branches reaching out to each other far above her head. They eat the light.

As the darkness thickens, her footsteps falter until she stops.

The wood creaks and whispers, and trapped pockets of cold air drift slowly towards her like ghosts. Her heart sounds uncomfortably loud.

'Who's there?' The words emerge without volume, disappear into the dark gaps between the trees as if swallowed by a great mouth. It increases her sense that there is some presence out there paying too much attention to her.

She swallows.

It's the dream. I ran away from it. But it's followed me.

The ground beneath her feet seems precarious. It could so easily crumble, give way, pitch her forward. She wonders if she is really awake. She presses her thumbnail into the palm of her hand, struggles to feel it and slowly backs onto safer ground.

For a moment she hears laughter – or thinks she does – then, just as her hand begins to throb in delayed reaction, the loud snap of a twig spins her around and she's running, faster than ever, back to the safety of the walled campus.

THREE

Having fun shouldn't feel like hard work, but by Wednesday it's beginning to. Harriet has a sneaky longing for Freshers' week to be over so she can stop performing, stop introducing herself over and over to new people, settle down into the safety of lectures.

At least the blur of events has pushed that eerie experience in the woods to the back of her mind. And she's discovered beer. Not the big brand-name cans that she occasionally drank during role-playing games back home, but proper beer; locally brewed Cumbrian stuff with depth and bite. Lovely stuff, relaxing stuff, it makes everything fuzzy round the edges, even the nightmares.

Tonight she's nursing a pint of Coniston Old Man in a flexible plastic cup and trying to ease her way through the press and jostle of bodies in the vast student bar. The canteen-like ambience and public swimming pool noise has become a familiar backdrop to her nights.

'It's Harriet, isn't it?'

She halts, creating a bottleneck. It's Paul, the friendly second-year from the hockey stall, yesterday. He'd been all right, not like –

She'd been intent on speaking to the coach, wanted to

tell him she'd been playing for the mixed seniors at league level all summer. Getting into mixed teams was tough, and she hadn't wanted to leave it all to the try-outs. Things can go wrong. He might be looking in a different direction and miss seeing her. But the mixed coach had been preoccupied by some arrogant fucker who took up all the space.

There's always one!

Paul, however, had been kind. He'd ignored the giant ego performing close by, and expressed interest in Harriet and her match experience. They'd been at two of the same tournaments over the summer and once they'd discovered that, conversation had become easy, pleasurable.

'Hi,' she says.

He grins at her. 'Still trying out for us tomorrow?'

'Can't wait!'

She's yearning for the familiarity of the stick in her hand, the ferocity and focus of action. She knows who she is when she's playing hockey.

Paul smiles and lifts his hand to brush back the lock of hair which has fallen across his face. As Harriet watches, it slides slowly back towards his hazel eyes.

'I've forgotten what position you play,' he says.

'Centre Forward or Right Inner.'

'Of course, should have been obvious.' He eyes her appraisingly. 'You look dangerous. I bet you're fast.'

Her blood thumps. Is he...? Could he be...?

'I better go,' she says. 'The others...'

'Sure. Catch you later.'

She's halfway back before she starts to regret her flight. *Why* does she always run away? But it's too late. She can hardly go back.

He'd taken her by surprise. She wasn't ready.

She reaches the table where the other girls from her floor are sitting. There's a gap next to one of the twins, she doesn't know which. Tonight they're wearing identical skinny-rib T-shirts, so no clues there. She decides to wing it, sits down.

The twins are popular and confident. At school Harriet would have considered them out of her league, however here the order is all shaken up and anything could happen. She doubts if they'll ever find much in common though. Their speech is noun-heavy with boys, make-up and the sort of music Harriet can't find a pulse in.

The twin turns to her. 'Fast work. I'm impressed.' She makes a tiny gesture with her head towards where Paul is still standing.

'Hardly,' Harriet says. 'He's just one of the hockey organisers. He was being friendly.'

'Well, of course. It's FAF week, isn't it?'

Her knowing tone leads Harriet to conclude she's talking to Marcia. Jenna would have been preferable.

'What's that?' she asks dubiously, not sure she wants the answer.

'Fuck a Fresher week.'

Harriet goes red. He didn't seem like that.

'Stop it, Marcia,' Jenna intervenes. She turns to Harriet. 'She's just showing off. Pay no attention.'

'Just telling it how it is,' Marcia says.

Harriet senses tension between the two sisters, quickly hidden.

'Are you going to the Enrica Iglesias concert on Friday, Harriet?' Jenna says. 'She's not bad for a tribute act.'

'Not sure yet.' Harriet doesn't fancy it much. 'It depends.'

Marcia grabs Harriet's arm. '*Who* is that? Talking to your boyfriend. Do you know him?'

Harriet can only see the boy's back, which is solid with smooth curving shoulders. Tawny, sun-bleached hair curls onto his shoulders, the ends straw-fine and split.

He needs a haircut, she thinks. It's a relief to find a fault.

She can't help but know who he is: Mark Collier, the arrogant fucker from yesterday. The one who had screwed up Harriet's chances of making an impression on the mixed coach.

Mark hadn't just been grabbing all the attention in person, yesterday, either. It hadn't been enough that the coach was beaming at him like a proud father, hanging on his every word, Mark's image had also been splayed across the hockey-stall backdrop: a two-page spread from the local newspaper which pronounced him "Eden's rising star". He'd been pictured riding high on his teammates' shoulders, stick held aloft, hair darkened by sweat, eyes triumphant.

Yesterday, the coach's arm had been flung over Mark's shoulder; today, Mark's arm is flung casually over Paul's shoulder. He's leaning forward, dominating Paul's attention. As he talks he bounces lightly on the soles of his feet, reminding Harriet of a predator ready to attack. His shirt is red, like the mixed hockey shirts, but far finer. This shirt is silk and moulds to his back, showing off his muscles.

What a poser.

'Well?' Marcia sounds impatient. 'Do you know him?'

'No.'

And yet, even yesterday, there had been a nagging familiarity fuelling her antagonism.

Marcia has managed to catch Mark's attention. His gaze dips to her lacy top, lingers there, before returning to her face. He winks. Marcia chokes off a giggle. Jenna frowns down into her drink.

As Mark turns back to Paul his gaze passes straight over Harriet, just like it had yesterday.

Marcia swivels towards Harriet and leans in, as if Harriet has suddenly become the most interesting person in the room. 'What was *that*, with Iquis and your dad in the kitchen?'

Harriet wriggles uncomfortably.

'Does he know her?' Marcia says.

'Iquis? No. He doesn't.'

'So what did he say after she—?'

'Not a lot.'

Marcia is clearly performing for Mark. No way is Harriet talking about Dad. Instead, and despite herself, she asks, 'What did you think of Iquis?'

'Unusual.' Marcia pings her wine glass with one nail. 'Maybe even a bit dangerous.' Her eyes gleam.

'She was totally out of order,' Jenna says, shooting a sympathetic glance at Harriet. 'If it had been my dad...'

Harriet always found sympathy hard to handle. Today is no exception. Dad's abrupt departure is back in her mind, the churning emotions too close to the surface.

There has been no sign of Iquis since then, and it feels like unfinished business. Yet Harriet has no idea what she'll do when she meets her.

Marcia nudges Jenna and gestures towards Mark. 'Has he been watching?'

Jenna shakes her head.

'Hey, Harriet,' Marcia says. 'I bet you could introduce us. After all, you've got the in.'

No way, Harriet thinks. And yet, as with that newspaper article about Mark which she ended up reading in full, she is drawn against her will. So that if Marcia presses it...

'It's too obvious,' Jenna says. 'Let him come to us.'

'That's sooo last century,' Marcia dismisses, 'and besides, he might not.'

'Then he's not really interested.'

'Or he's shy.'

'Hardly.' Jenna's tone is caustic.

'Go on, Harriet. Pleeease.' Marcia drags the word out. 'Why don't you go and talk to Paul and then we'll just kind of bump into you?'

Harriet wants to resist, starts to shake her head.

'You don't dare, do you?' Marcia says.

Stephen taught Harriet never to turn down dares. Marcia is playing dirty, even if she doesn't realise it.

'All right,' Harriet says, pushing abruptly to her feet.

As she reaches them, Paul starts laughing at something Mark's said. He throws his head back and doesn't notice her arrival. Mark, however, is looking straight at her, just like he had at the hockey stall. And just like then, she feels like wallpaper, something that exists, but is of no interest.

There's no gap in Mark's flow. He's talking about waxing his surfboard, his biceps bulging as he demonstrates the sweeping action. 'The best wax is...' Harriet doesn't catch the name, wonders what's so special about any wax, then finds out. 'The grip,' he's saying, 'is second to none. That's how I managed to ride down that tunnel wave... All the way! You cannot imagine the sensation. Better than sex. Better even than a threesome!'

This is getting embarrassing. Retreat is not an option. Harriet tugs on Paul's sleeve.

'Paul. I've something to ask about tomorrow's try-outs.'

Mark does not stop talking. But Paul looks down at Harriet's face, then holds up a halting hand.

'Mark,' he says. 'This is Harriet. She's one of us. You'll see her on the pitch tomorrow, trying out for the mixed.'

'Right,' Mark says shortly. 'But you're not on duty tonight, mate.'

He directs a fleeting glance at Harriet. 'Get it asked, then. He's got partying to do. You newbies, honestly!'

Harriet flushes, anger rising, the way it sometimes does on the pitch at home or when she's been benched unfairly.

But not *here!* That's another thing she's left behind, getting in trouble for shooting her mouth off, for throwing a... Dad-sized tantrum.

'What did you want to ask?' Paul continues to be friendly, despite Mark.

'Whether you're playing the new penalty-corner rule.' It's a lousy question, not one which justifies this interruption. But it's the best she can come up with.

'Still in discussion,' Paul says. 'No one ever decides things until—'

Mark grabs his arm.

'What?'

'You know that blonde who was watching earlier?'

Paul nods.

'Well, there's two of them.'

'You're pissed.'

'I am not. Look for yourself.'

Jenna and Marcia are heading towards them. Paul gives a low whistle. 'You're right!'

'When am I not, mate? Come on.' He grabs Paul's shoulder, steers him towards the two girls. Harriet follows, a spectator.

'Are you a double act?' Mark says.

'Are you and your friend?' Marcia ripostes.

'We could be,' Mark says, suggestively. 'If that's an offer.'

Marcia's smile dies. 'It wasn't.'

Mark turns to Jenna, touching her arm just below the shoulder. 'I'm Mark. And you're...?'

'Jenna,' she mutters. She points at her twin. 'And Marcia.'

'Right. I've already been assigned, have I?' He laughs, turns towards Marcia.

'We don't share,' Marcia says. 'That's a ground rule.'

'What, never?' He's laughing again.

'You got it.'

'In that case,' he turns to Jenna, 'you'd better meet Paul.'

Hey, Harriet thinks, *he was interested in me – you can't just reallocate him.*

But it seems he can. Paul is smiling at Jenna, Jenna's smiling back.

Harriet is caught between disappointment and relief. She was feeling out of her depth. She hasn't really had a lot of experience: a few popcorn-flavoured kisses in a cinema with one of the boys from her gaming group, before they concluded that they fitted better fighting trolls, side by side, than clashing teeth. It had been more awkward than exciting.

Paul would be a huge step up from that. She knew that immediately, when he said, 'I bet you're fast.'

That's why I ran. And maybe that was sensible. It kept me safe. And yet...

She can't help drifting off into a fantasy of what might have happened earlier, if she'd stayed.

'No way did I say that!' Mark's voice yanks her attention back to the conversation.

'Yes, you did,' Paul argues. 'It's true. He boasted that his step-mum's a MILF!'

'I wasn't boasting, I was complaining. It's what my friends think. They don't have to share a house with her!'

'Come on,' Paul says. 'I saw the photo. She's really something,' he says to Jenna, 'you know, very Hollywood.' He twists a smile at Mark. 'It would be typical of you to want the one woman you can't get.'

Briefly, Mark looks uncomfortable, then he laughs. 'Yeah, well – she's not so bad,' he says. 'It's her skinny nine-year-old daughter that's the real problem. She worships me. Stupid little insect. Always following me and my friends around, can't seem to realise she's not wanted.'

As he says this his gaze settles on Harriet.

She doesn't stop to consider whether it's deliberate, for already she's identifying with the stepsister. The reaction comes from so deep within her that she has no control over it. 'I'm surprised she'd want to be near you,' she says and her voice is shaking. 'If I was your sister I'd keep out of your way. You're a complete wanker!'

Mark looks surprised. 'Who rattled your cage?'

'Go fuck yourself up your own vast egotistical bum,' she says. Then stops, horrified. Paul is staring at her with a puzzled expression; Jenna looks startled.

What am I doing?

'I'm out of here.' She turns, starts to shove through the crowd. Behind her, Mark utters a comment. She hears Marcia laugh.

Bitch!

Outside she pauses, feeling a bit sick. *What happened? Why did I let myself do that?*

But there aren't any answers. She's still holding her pint. She sips at it slowly, watching the breeze push the branches of a nearby tree. By the time it's finished she's calmer, but not calm enough to go back inside.

She puts the empty on a nearby table and walks away.

*

For once it's not the nightmare which jerks her awake, but the sound of knocking.

'Who is it?' she calls.

Silence.

She lies waiting. No one knocks again. The room is freshly alien. Nothing is where she's used to. The thin veil of familiarity which has spread across it during the last few days has been ripped away by the darkness, by the pounding of her heart.

She twists in the bed, trying to reclaim the last shreds of sleep, trying to ignore the muggy residue of beer in her mouth, the dull ache across her temples.

Water would make a difference. But she stays put, still not sure what – *if anything* – has jerked her awake. The uncertainty maroons her in the bed, prisoner to the frantic workings of her imagination.

She lies there, listens for movement. She had been

playing Dark Island before she slept. Now she longs to turn it on again, but doesn't dare.

Instead she waits.

Finally, just as she's beginning to feel safe, a soft, rhythmic thudding starts to emerge through the wall which borders Marcia's room. At first the sound is soft, only just perceptible, then it gathers force, becomes the knocking that woke her.

For some reason the memory of a bucket of fish, freshly caught, invades her head, until it's all she can see. It's a fragment. The bucket is red. The fish are a mottled browny-green, slimy and iridescent, with pinpricks of warmer pink and gold. Their mouths are torn where the hooks have been removed. Their tails beat against the side of the bucket, a rhythmic, battering sound which has the music of desperation in it.

They are dying.

She cannot place the memory.

The noise from Marcia's room reaches a crescendo and then stops. Harriet lies locked into position in the bed, a long line of frozen muscle. Only when she hears the bass rumble of regular snoring is she able to move. She's sure it's not Marcia, so it must be Mark.

Desperate not to be heard, she climbs carefully out of bed, shrugs on a jumper and pads silently towards the kitchen. She'll make a hot drink, for comfort.

Marcia's room borders the kitchen. Harriet concentrates hard on easing the door open and then, once through, on releasing it slowly back into its frame. Mark's snores continue undiminished.

The kitchen is dark, an obstacle course of shapes.

Harriet begins to pad her way around them to reach the kettle. A sound jerks her head to the far corner where a silhouetted figure lurks.

Harriet sucks her breath in, a small gasp, and backs away, straight into the wall. Whoever it is, is unnervingly still. Harriet's heart is so loud she feels like it could be heard. She windmills her arm along the wall until she finds the light switch, clicks it on.

Iquis! Sitting on a stool, pressed back into the corner like a wary spider, dusty black legs trapped inside the stool's bars.

Harriet exhales. 'What are you doing here?' The rush of adrenaline dissipates, leaving her weak, shaky.

Slow blink of those storm-cloud eyes. Tiny pinpricks of black where the light has startled.

Iquis is different tonight. Muted.

The make-up is missing. Without it she looks colourless, less arrogant, more bleak. Her pale face is all angles. Even her hair is curiously flattened, its blunt ends drooping.

'What are you doing sitting in the dark?' Harriet repeats. 'Couldn't you sleep?'

Another shrug. Iquis's answer to everything.

Harriet heads for the kettle. Iquis's head turns to watch her move. The attention is too much, too strong. Harriet spins round, about to say, 'Stop looking at me,' but the expression in those eyes stops her.

What do you want? Harriet doesn't say it aloud. A pulse in her neck starts ticking. She swallows.

Iquis just might be the loneliest person in the world. That's the sensation she's broadcasting. A starvation, a vast need; like a sharp-set wolf looking for a hand to be held out.

Like she's hungry, and I –

There's a compulsion, like I – Harriet – could fill that void if I stepped forward.

'Stop it!'

Iquis twists away, into the corner. And Harriet feels – *guilty*? Like she's rejected Iquis. Only she doesn't know what she wanted. She really doesn't get Iquis; nothing she does makes sense.

A disturbing thought surfaces. If Iquis has been here for –

'How long have you been here?'

The goth girl turns back into the room, her gaze pinned on the wall between the kitchen and Marcia's room. A wry smile sneaks onto her lips and with it there's a touch of her previous defiance, her power.

'What are you doing here?' Iquis says.

The wall seems to bulge towards them, its blotchy magnolia spreading out and invading, choking Harriet, who – in order to escape from dying fish – spits out the first alternative that occurs.

'I get these dreams. Nightmares really...'

She stops, aware of what she's said.

She's never told anyone.

Impossible to snatch the words back. They hang in the air, leaving her more exposed than ever.

But there's no attack. Iquis just nods, thoughtfully. 'Come for a walk,' she offers.

Harriet hesitates, drawn by the apparent simplicity of the offer. But there's too much she doesn't want to talk about, too many raw feelings close to the surface. She's afraid of what may escape. And besides, Iquis's encounter with Dad is still vivid in her memory, still unresolved.

'No.' Her voice is abrupt. Yet Iquis seems to take it as normal, just nods.

Harriet backs out of the kitchen, dragging herself away from Iquis's gaze, retreating to the not-quite-safety of her room.

It's a long time before she sleeps.

FOUR

The rain began just after Harriet went back to bed, and has kept up its constant drumming all morning. The hockey pitch is sodden. Even though it's no longer raining, the sullen yellow-grey clouds hang motionless overhead. The air is dense with pressure.

Mark's stick crashes into Harriet's, sending the white ball spinning into the mud. He barrels his shoulder against her as he retrieves it and flicks it to Loli, the slender Spanish girl who'd arrived walking side by side with him.

Harriet's wrist aches. 'You complete tosser.' She says it in a steady enough voice. Even though he's deliberately targeting her, playing dirty and getting away with it, she is *not* going to lose her temper.

Mark doesn't seem to hear, too busy watching Loli pat ineffectually at the ball which is taken away from her within seconds. Loli giggles, like losing the ball doesn't matter.

What an air head!

'Ignore them,' Harriet coaches herself in a mutter. 'Regain your focus.'

But it's been smashed to pieces by Mark. And it's not just his nasty tactics on the pitch; she's still unsettled from last night's abrupt awakening, still worried that he knows that she overheard him and Marcia *doing it*.

Loli's giggles intensify as the ball moves down to the other end of the pitch and the players at Harriet's end relax. Mark and Loli are mouthing words at each other, the flash of their teeth white against the tan of their skin. Loli's arms dance patterns when she speaks.

Harriet tries to distract herself from them by contemplating the faint but definite sideways lean of the pitch.

'It's levelled every couple of years,' Paul had told her, 'but it always resumes its slant.'

A raindrop falls onto the hot skin of her cheek. A gust of wind sways the line of slender alders just beyond the goal, quickening Harriet's determination, feeding her imagination.

Maybe it's him.

For years, ever since she started taking hockey seriously, Harriet has had a fantasy that she is playing for someone – an imaginary watcher who is there on the sidelines, his eyes intent only on her. It gives her something to aim for. It's to please him that she pushes herself so hard. Sometimes she's convinced that if she could only play perfectly he would become real.

But today, just when she needs him the most, she's losing her sense of him. So that this rustle of movement behind the goal seems like a last chance.

Aware of the ball's progress towards her, she feints to the left and Mark follows. Then, as the ball cracks into Julie's stick, she moves with a burst of speed, not forwards but back, grabbing at the opportunity of surprise, feet churning up mud as she turns and sprints towards Julie.

Send it to me, she wills. *Don't write me off. I'm going to do it this time.*

Perhaps Julie reads the determination in her face, for she hesitates, then, with a short punching jab, pushes the ball in Harriet's direction.

Harriet traps it clumsily, feels it bump against the wood and spin, and then she's off, forcing it through the wet grass, beginning to form a rhythm. *Faster,* she goads herself, hands clenched tightly round the stick.

I can't blow this.

She risks a glance beyond the goal. The trees are still swaying, just like someone has moved forwards, intent on watching her. She begins to believe in it. This time, in this place, he will be real – if she can only make it to the goal.

Mark hits her like a wall, crashing into her from the side, jerking her off her path. She's painfully aware of the ball spinning away from her, as a shaft of sunlight picks out the individual trunks of the trees, reveals the empty space between them. There's no one there.

Before she realises it, Harriet's stick is swinging forward, heading for Mark's chest, weighted with her anger. Somewhere inside, there's the pleasure of letting go, a rush of blood as he steps back too slowly. Contact seems inevitable. It's only the whistle that stops her.

They stand suspended. Harriet's arm trembling. Briefly, she is rewarded by an uncomfortable, surprised look on Mark's face, before he slicks back his usual don't-care smile.

'Foul,' the mixed coach utters just the one word.

It breaks the tableau.

Harriet is about to protest hotly, the way she would at home, that she hadn't actually done anything, that she'd stopped! But Mark is mouthing silent swearwords and Harriet realises it's being called on him. Finally! Relieved, she dares to glance at the halted players surrounding them. Maybe they hadn't seen. No one is looking at her.

The mixed coach walks over, pauses beside Harriet, speaks quietly, so that only she can hear, 'And you, watch that temper.'

She goes bright red. 'But he...'

She stops herself. She'd sound pathetic, like a girl. Mixed hockey's a tough game – it's why she likes it. But you have to be able to take the knocks, not complain.

She walks forward to take the penalty. But there's no joy in it. The sun is still on the alders, highlighting the empty space between them and the river. The fantasy is childish, stupid. She's always known that. Underneath.

There never was anyone there. Dad never came. The game doesn't matter.

She raises her stick and ploughs the ball straight into the pads of the keeper.

*

The half-hearted cries of sympathy are still ringing in Harriet's ears as the whistle blows for half-time a minute later. Mark is first off the pitch, walking ahead of her, laughing, his arm slung across Loli's back.

Harriet is still seething. He gets away with everything! And she's not going to let him.

'Mark!'

He and Loli turn in tandem.

'What happened to Marcia? I mean... last night?'

Mark narrows his eyes at her, a "Shut your mouth" look, instantly familiar. But she's not taking it from *him*.

'Yeah,' she says. 'Marcia. What about her?' She's flushing, but she doesn't care. It will pass as a match flush.

'Who is Marcia?' Loli's decorated fingernails tattoo the question along Mark's forearm.

'The girl he was... in bed with last night,' Harriet says.

'Oh grow up, Harriet.' Mark looks contemptuous. 'It's none of your business.'

'Maybe not,' Harriet says, 'but you're still an absolute shit.'

'Thanks.' He tries to laugh it off.

Loli's grip on his arm says different. She yanks him back towards the deserted pitch.

The sound of their fight follows Harriet as she walks towards the changing rooms. She glances back. Loli's arms are beating the air for emphasis, her voice rising to a crescendo, '*Cabron*! *Gilipollas*! Bastard!' She slaps his face, then turns and stomps away, her stick slung over her shoulder like a weapon.

*

'Hey, Cabroney!' Mark's voice booms across the bar-room of the run-down Albatross Hotel. Situated on the narrow crossroads just beyond the campus, its large rooms are crammed entirely with students. A couple of tourists, who'd been hesitating in the entrance hall when Harriet arrived, had quickly retreated.

'Don't call me cabraney,' the student behind the bar says, twiddling the gold band in his nostril. 'What's it mean, anyway?' It's a poor simulation of annoyance which doesn't fool Harriet. He's clearly pleased Mark's taking notice of him.

'What a tosser,' Harriet murmurs.

'Yeah.' Julie, next to her, must have overheard. 'Arrogant fucker, isn't he?'

'He so is!' Harriet's voice gains confidence. 'Glad I'm not the only one. Is he always like this?'

'Always.'

Mark looks up, straight at Harriet, and she jerks her gaze away, then immediately returns it, determined not to cede ground. But he's staring across the bar-room.

She follows his gaze, and the day changes.

There's four of them, two girls and two boys, all dressed in subtle shades of black. The lack of colour soothes Harriet's eyes, eases the sullen ache behind them. They are encamped in a square-sided alcove at the far side of the room.

Their movements are stately, their abstraction from the other students total. They are separate, archaic, complete.

Harriet doesn't immediately recognise Iquis. She's different again, camouflaged by the company of the other goths, and by her clothes, which are far more trad: a long flowing cloak, the hem of an equally long dress showing where the cloak parts at the front. There's a soft gleam to the dress, which suggests velvet. She looks *settled*: that restless hunger, that isolation, which Harriet had sensed in the kitchen, is nowhere to be seen.

She belongs. And Harriet is jealous.

They're curled into two immense, saggy-looking sofas. The scuffed soles of their boots peep from the folds of their clothing. They look like they've been there for centuries.

Harriet can't look away. She's hooked by the intense

concentration with which they are conversing, like nothing exists beyond their group.

'Harriet.' A booming voice, a clap on her shoulder.

It's the women's captain, beaming good will and patronage at Harriet. Her timing couldn't be worse.

'You enjoyed today's game, then?'

Harriet forces a nod, a smile.

'Good. That's what I like to hear.' A big, solid slab of a woman, she leans over Harriet, making her feel trapped. 'We'd like you to train with the women's team.'

Harriet is not surprised. 'What about the mixed?'

And does she even care? A dull throb somewhere, composed as much of resentment as anything else. What's the point? That tosser is all over the mixed.

'Perhaps later,' the women's captain says.

Harriet could still prove herself, prove them all wrong, work her way up, and then be the thorn in Mark's side until he takes her seriously, until she finally wipes that smug grin off his smug-git face.

And yet, does she even want to play any more? Absurd to be driven out by Mark, but maybe it is time to move on, try something different.

Despite herself, she looks towards Mark. But he's not at the bar any more.

Where is he? Has he gone?

No. There's no mistaking his laugh. She follows it. He's standing near Iquis, in the middle of the goth enclave.

No way! You don't get that too.

Julie and the captain are discussing a forthcoming match. Murmuring an excuse, Harriet quietly slides from her stool and heads towards Mark.

As she approaches, she studies the faces in front of her.

Iquis looks intrigued, the other goths don't. Their settled look has gone. The red-headed boy next to Iquis has moved forwards on the sofa, blocking Mark's approach. On the other sofa, the boy with long black hair has his arm protectively around his girlfriend. Her face is turned into his chest.

Mark looks uncomfortable. But he's ignoring the unspoken hostility, concentrating on Iquis, who is leaning forward, gaze intent.

As Harriet nears them, Iquis's gaze jerks towards her.

Mark turns, and groans theatrically. 'Not you again.'

Iquis looks curious. 'You know each other?'

'We're beginning to.' He's being deliberately light, charming. It doesn't fool Harriet.

'Are you trying to go through the whole campus?' she says, unblushingly. She's too intent on unseating him to feel embarrassment. 'Marcia, last night, Loli, this afternoon, and now, Iquis.'

'Marcia.' Iquis's eyes are on Harriet as she drawls the name out. 'So he's the one.'

And they could be back in the kitchen, the two of them looking at the magnolia wall behind which Marica and Mark had –

'You make a lot of noise,' Iquis says. The look she turns on Mark is forensic, a paint stripper peeling away his layers. But underneath there's that same hunger which Harriet had sensed last night. It's equally compelling. Mark looks wary, uneasy, almost mesmerised. Victory has never felt closer, even though Harriet can't quite explain why.

But there's something wrong about letting this play

out in front of the goths. Iquis is unpredictable. She could do something shocking, alienating; like what happened with Dad. Until Mark turned up, she had looked so safe, so contained. There has to be another way.

Instinctively, Harriet starts to laugh. Mark flinches.

Of course, ridicule; the one thing he wouldn't be able to stand.

She looks at Iquis, glimpses what might be relief, and then the corners of Iquis's lips flash upwards. She laughs hard, like it's jerked out of her. But it sounds enough like amusement to have the desired effect.

'I'll leave you to your gloom merchants,' Mark comments, with a disparaging gesture to the settled goths. 'Call me when you get bored.' And he's gone.

Harriet watches him all the way to the bar. He doesn't look back.

'That what you wanted?' Iquis says, her unblinking stare turned onto Harriet.

'I guess.' Another staring match imminent; narrow pupils, like before. Pinpricks, even though there's not much light in here.

'Are you staying?' Iquis challenges. 'Or is it time for you to storm off, now that you've worsted Mark?'

A split second of choice. And Dad? The conflict is still there. But it's possible to allow it to slide out of her grasp and down to wherever the undertow takes it.

'I'm staying.'

FIVE

Harriet presses the mouth of the bottle against her lips. The hot spiciness of the red wine is thrilling against her tongue. She swallows, then passes the bottle on. A warm hand brushes against hers as it is taken.

She's lying on her back, wrapped in Iquis's cloak, gazing at the sky through tendrils of trees. Now that the clouds have lifted, the air is achingly clear. The ground is surprisingly dry, and the thickness of the cloak protects her from any remaining dampness.

Tonight the wood is friendly, the menace of her previous visit missing. The small rustles and creaks only enhance her sense of well-being, of connection.

The bottle circles back to her, and arrives with a faint click of nails against hers. She drinks.

Her head bumps softly against another. The five of them are lying, a head-centred star, fingers outstretched almost to touch. The moon gleams behind a smudge of mist. The breeze strokes gently across her face.

It's late, very late. She presses her finger against the button on her watch and releases a tiny cloud of light into the night: 3.30 a.m. She revels in the lateness. She wants the night to last for ever.

She's drifting on a tide of new memories. The night's experiences have burst the bounds of conventional time. Everything has changed since she crossed the carpet, even her; especially her.

The goths are fabulous. It's the way they talk, full of imagination and curiosity and an unusual seriousness. Somehow their rhythms are hers, their language one she is fluent in. And they really like her. There's none of the hostility and defensiveness they displayed to Mark. It's like they've adopted her. And somehow Iquis's cloak is the symbol of that adoption.

Harriet's smiling, reliving yet again that moment on the walk into town when Iquis released the cloak from her shoulders and handed it to Harriet.

'But won't you get cold?' Harriet had protested, even as she longed to retain that comforting presence across her shoulders, that sense of being wrapped up and held.

Brief shake of Iquis's head.

'I love it!' Harriet had said, feeling the sweep of it against her feet as she walked, enjoying the way it bounced on the pavement, noticing the silvery dust it was gathering around the hem.

'I look like one of you now. Like I belong.' And she'd outstared the people they passed with the same don't-care look which the others gave out: moody, collective – apart.

'We walk alone like cats in the night,' she'd added, and Lucien had laughed.

Iquis hadn't reacted to Harriet's enthusiasm or thanks. She remains abrupt and mysterious. And yet, Harriet is convinced that the loan of the cloak means that she has been accepted. Even, she dares to hope, that for some reason Iquis wants her here.

Iquis is studying psychology which sounds like a heavy subject – how people think – and makes Harriet wonder what Iquis knows that she doesn't. That sense of somehow being understood by Iquis without words, is that to do with her studies?

And yet, Iquis is just a first year like Harriet. Except that Iquis doesn't seem like a first year. Not sure what she seems like. Whether she's at the front of the group, leading a powering wedge of them through the town centre or largely silent as she is now in the woods, letting the others converse, she exudes a certainty which Harriet envies.

'How long have you known her?' Harriet had asked the second years earlier.

'Since Monday,' the softly spoken Beth had replied. It had been impossible to hear Beth in the bar, but outside the night gave her a voice.

Three days, Harriet thought. *Such a short time.*

Richard slipped back to wrap his hand round Beth's. 'We recognise our own.'

Harriet hadn't been sure whether to take him seriously. *A bit pretentious*, she'd thought, when he first said it. And yet, she's beginning to think it really is that simple.

All these years I've been trying to fit in, trying to be normal, undetected. What a waste of time! It's actually great to be different. Once you've got the right company.

So yes, she too recognises her own.

Iquis is not quite in sync with the other goths though. Harriet detects awkwardnesses, as if they, like her, don't entirely get Iquis. She's entertaining and dazzling and kind of fun in her unpredictability, yet she doesn't have the easy intimacy with Lucien, Richard and Beth which they have among themselves. She's not quite one of them. At least not yet.

Whatever. Harriet settles back into the present, not wanting to miss it in the ramble of her thoughts. She wants to capture and record this moment: the solidity of the ground underneath her, the sound of the others breathing, the stops and starts of the conversation.

Lucien's head bumps briefly against Harriet's, as he wriggles into a more comfortable position. He starts to sing.

> *"'All men hate the wretched,*
> *How then must you hate me,*
> *My father, my creator;*
> *My primary rejector.*
>
> *You make me what I am.'"*

It's Dark Island's "Monster Song". How fabulous! How appropriate; how perfect.

Lucien gives voice to Frankenstein's creature, aiming his tirade of frustration and loneliness at the oblivious scientist. Lucien doesn't quite capture the underlying menace of Loki's delivery; but his voice is soft with melancholy and Harriet is moved.

She touches the wine bottle to her lips and drinks deeply, letting the spicy wine boost her confidence, so that as Lucien draws the narrative to an end she adds the half-whispered conclusion, Circe's lines, which echo the plaintive underlying melody. She concentrates on getting that catch in her voice, that lost note which always rakes the back of her neck with its sound. She imagines herself as Circe. The wine bottle microphone butts her lips softly with its glassy nose. Her voice carries out into the night, swirling and weaving between the trees.

> *"Is this how it must end*
> *in iceberg isolation*
> *where only the inhuman*
> *can survive?"*

In the silence she is aware that Iquis has turned her head to face her, and flushes with pride. She knows she sang it well; the sound still echoing in her head. She hears Iquis's hand shift, as if she is restraining an impulse to reach out, and holds her breath, waiting to see what will happen.

But nothing does.

'Wicked,' Richard says.

'What would Mary Shelley think, if she could hear *that*?' Beth says, wistful.

'She'd totally love it,' Lucien says. 'It captures the essence. Unlike that play they put on last year which focussed on the killing and totally missed the subtle psychological stuff.'

'Too right,' Richard says. 'To be fair, it was a student play, but even so. I just couldn't see the point. I mean, look at the things they excluded!'

'Yes,' Lucien says. 'Like the bedroom scene, where he wakes to find the monster leaning over him. How could they cut that? It's the heart of it. His need for acceptance totally misunderstood, taken as a threat.' He shakes his head sadly, turns to Harriet. 'Have you read it?'

The question startles her. 'I read my brother's copy,' she says. The memory is vivid. 'I used to sneak his books out of his room...'

The room which was both his and not his; too tidy, his smell missing. Mum would be downstairs cooking something complicated. Harriet would stealthily sneak out the book she'd chosen and slot another into its place – a doppelgänger, which she'd usually picked up from some car boot sale, its spine similar enough to pass unnoticed on the shelf. The next time Mum went into his room, to sit on his bed or to do whatever it was she did do in there, she wouldn't register the change.

'I read it under the duvet,' Harriet says, now, 'with a torch in the middle of the night. He'd written comments in the margins. It made me feel like he was...' Dangerous. What is she doing? She doesn't want them to know, does she? 'Like I understood him better,' she amends. 'He was five years older than me. I was always trying to catch up, but it never seemed possible.'

She thinks of the other stories she could tell them. The way he'd climbed onto the school roof and stood there laughing as the crowd gathered. The way, when the teachers arrived – like they always inevitably did – his best mate, Graham, had been the one to drag her away. "He wouldn't want you to get in trouble."

'Stephen,' she says. 'My brother's name is Stephen.' Some instinct, which overrides her natural caution, has her reaching out to Iquis, as if to say, this is important. Yet after she has snagged Iquis's hand she regrets the impulse.

'God, your hand's cold,' she exclaims.

She rubs it briskly, the same way Mum used to do for her. 'You shouldn't have lent me your cloak.'

Iquis tenses, then reclaims her hand, like a wild animal sensing danger.

'It's okay about the cloak,' she says. 'You keep it.'

SIX

'Dedication.' Dr Drake's pale, ice-blue eyes skim over her tutorial group. 'Standards. Responsibility. Research.' She makes every word stand out. 'Memorise these terms. Put them on your screen savers. Tattoo them on your wrists. Recite them every day.'

Harriet is struggling to keep her breath inaudible. She doesn't want Dr Drake to know that the only reason she's not late is because she's run all the way. It won't make a good impression.

Dr Drake picks up the projector remote control, crosses the room and switches the light off.

In the darkness, the last golden threads of Harriet's dream wrap round her like seaweed. She struggles to recall details; but there is nothing tangible left of the dream that kept her too entranced to hear her alarm clock. Just a sense of warmth and a lingering happiness.

The image of a suspension bridge appears on the wall. Beneath the bridge, dark tips of trees angle upwards from a steeply sloped valley. The image looks familiar.

I ought to know this.

She's staggeringly tired. She's had about two hours

sleep, and would have been better with none. When she'd finally got in, just before dawn, she hadn't been able to resist lying down, if only so she could stare at the ceiling and relive the whole night. She'd slept.

The image on the wall changes. A film of the same bridge in a storm is displayed. The trees shake and bend, yet their movement is insignificant compared to the centre of the bridge, which flexes like a trampoline.

Harriet gasps in recognition. She knows what's coming next. Dream forgotten, she leans forward, rapt.

The camera angle changes. The white line at the centre of the bridge's road twists, buckles and then snaps.

It happens so fast it's stunning. Like a flimsy toy the suspension rears up and tears. The road breaks into sections which fall, fragmenting further as they crash down into the sea.

The light snaps on.

'Name it.'

Harriet's arm is in the air.

A small quirk of smile crosses Dr Drake's face.

'We're not at school now, Ms Johnson.' It's clear by the way she says it that the *Ms Johnson* is ironic. Harriet jerks her arm down, flushing.

'Go on.' The pale emotionless eyes are still on her.

'The Tacoma Narrows Bridge.' The pleasure of certainty is in her voice. She can hear Dad talking – partly to her, partly to himself – analysing the mistakes made on the bridge.

'Year?'

Easy. '1940. Four months after it opened.'

'Why?'

At last something worth answering.

'It was too vulnerable to aero-dynamic forces, both because the bridge was too narrow giving it too much flexibility and because the use of stiffening plate girders failed to absorb the turbulence.' She snatches a breath, continues fast before she can be interrupted. 'They should have used web trusses instead. It was a landmark failure in engineering history and they abandoned the use of plate girders in suspension bridge design as a result.'

She tries to read Dr Drake's expression.

'How many killed?'

'None. The bridge was already closed due to previous oscillation.'

And then it's over; Dr Drake flashes her a tight-lipped smile and turns away to switch the light off. The wall show resumes.

A thin tower creaks and shudders, then leans beyond recovery and breaks low in its structure, begins to fall.

Dr Drake pauses it mid collapse. A brick suspends in the air. Falling figures freeze like tiny screams. The impact is like a shock wave. Even though it isn't the Twin Towers on the screen, that's what everyone is thinking of; those TV images burnt into collective memory. Then the light floods back in, and everyone is blinking, looking sobered.

This is real. This is about people dying.

'A reconstruction.' Dr Drake's voice breaks through the tension and there's a collective sigh, just audible. But they don't escape that easily. 'How many died?'

This time no one answers. They just keep their eyes on the faded silhouettes of falling figures in suspended animation against the wall.

'Look it up. It's never too soon to know your disasters.'

Harriet finds herself nodding.

'Dedication. Standards. Responsibility. Research.' Dr Drake gives each word its separate space. 'It's time to stop playing and start concentrating. The work you do here could make the difference, between this...'

On screen movement resumes. The brick hits the ground. The piles of dust settle.

'And this...'

A different tower sways in a storm but doesn't fall.

'Ask yourselves why you chose this course.' The tower's creak harmonises against her voice. 'Be sure it's what you want. And then, be sure you do it well. Failure kills.'

Harriet shivers.

'And if you don't know, ask. That's what I'm here for. That's what we're all here for. To make sure you learn everything you need. Right, tutor group introductory meeting over.'

She pauses, sweeps her eyes over them.

'Don't think I don't know what you're thinking.'

They gaze back at her innocently.

'You're thinking that other tutors take their groups out for a drink when they first meet. So that they can get to know them in a relaxed environment. I'm giving you something more important. I'll take you out for a drink when you pass. Until then, you've got work to do.'

And with a blink Harriet is back out in the maze of corridors, glancing at her watch in bewilderment. The whole thing has taken twenty minutes and not the hour scheduled.

As her trainers squeak down the corridor, she hears the

rumble of falling masonry emerge from the empty lecture hall and spares a thought for the small, upright form of Dr Drake watching over and over again the destruction caused when civil engineers fail to outthink nature.

And terrorists? Dr Drake hadn't mentioned them, but Harriet suspects that it's not just nature that she's going to have to consider. The weight of the responsibility seems huge.

She's not sure whether Dr Drake's more or less scary after today's lecture. Knowing her better makes her more understandable. She's not going to be easy to please though. *And* – Harriet thinks, as she heads towards the library – *one thing is certain, civil engineering definitely seems more scary, more real.*

*

As the afternoon light dims Harriet sleeps. As she sleeps she dreams.

She's back in the woods. It's strangely factual. She's just lying in the star, the way it was. Except that this time she reaches out and as she does so she can sense the others doing the same.

Hands meet. Smooth skin to smooth skin. An instant circuit. The contact burns. A wave of energy pours through the group, ignites; like a power surge or a water spout it rises upwards with a magnesium-burn brightness.

The star is connected.

It is so vivid that she wakes and opens her eyes, expecting to be bathed in light. Instead dusk has fallen.

Harriet's gaze goes immediately to the dark shape of

Iquis's cloak which is draped over the back of her chair. It's a confirmation of everything that's happened. The cloak's skirts are spreading out over the floor, half-concealing Harriet's mobile phone, which is lying there, vibrating against the carpet.

How long has it been ringing? She rolls off the bed and grabs it.

'Hi.'

'Harriet?'

'Dad!'

'I thought you weren't going to answer.'

'Yeah, sorry.'

Does she sound sleepy, like she's been awake half the night and is just catching it up?

There's a silence. This talking on the phone thing is tricky. When Mum phoned, two days ago, Harriet had had to do lots of the talking and it had been really hard. Mum kept sighing, and Harriet, who felt she could read the thoughts behind each sigh, found it impossible to give voice to them: *It should have been Stephen, not me. He should have been first.*

She couldn't say it. With the goths she wanted to talk about Stephen. It brought him closer. With Mum it was the opposite. Mum's version of Stephen and Harriet's were so different that Stephen seemed to slide further and further away whenever they talked.

Dad clears his throat, but still doesn't speak.

'How's Mum?'

'She's fine.' Dad has never won any prizes for communication. Engineering, yes.

'Did you get back okay?'

'Yes, thanks. It was quieter on the way back.'

She half laughs, to hide a sudden twist of sadness.

'Are you getting settled on the course?' he says.

A safe subject. She rolls over onto her back on the carpet and crooks her arm over her head to hold the phone in place as she tells him about the bridge, about knowing the answers for Dr Drake.

He has questions, suggestions, at least until the subject is exhausted, marooning them back into silence.

What would they be doing if she was at home? Probably something practical – either that or arguing.

'So what else have you been doing?' Dad says.

Lying in a head-centred star in the woods, feeling a glorious sense of connection, of kin.

'Playing hockey.'

'Nice.'

It hadn't been. 'I'm no longer into it. I'm giving it up.'

'Oh.'

Is that it? Is that all he's going to say?

'I suppose there are more exciting things to do there,' he says.

Her fingers tighten around the thin rectangle of phone.

'It would have been *different* if it was *football*.'

'What do you mean?' He sounds bewildered.

'You *never* came to see me.'

'I couldn't. You know that. I couldn't leave Mum. Not when she'd been on her own in the house all week. She needed me. It was only the weekends that kept her going.'

'No, I suppose.' What else had she expected?

'How is she *really*? Can I talk to her?'

'She's, um... in a funny mood today. Probably best not.'

Quick beat of panic.

'What's wrong? Is she okay?'

'She's fine. I said she was, didn't I?' He sounds impatient, familiar ground.

'Well, give her my love.' It feels over-formal, inadequate, as if there should be something more.

He grunts in reply. 'I better go.'

'Okay.' And she's left listening to the silence of the line.

*

Later, a knock at her door. She leaps to open it.

A little crowd of darkness clusters in the corridor.

'You came.'

Like an escape artist she follows them into the night and feels it close over her, blocking out the day she's just had.

SEVEN

Three weeks later this particular stretch of wood has become their special place; they always come back here at some point of the night. Even the rustle of animals in the undergrowth, and the creak of trees shifting, have become familiar sounds.

Earlier, they'd walked along the riverbank and Iquis had dared them to leap from boat to rocking boat. Then, inevitably, when they'd attracted angry shouts she'd wanted to stay and fight it out. But the rest of them had fled, even Harriet, who was laughing so hard that she couldn't run straight.

These mellow times in the wood, after the action, are what Harriet loves best. This is when she tells them about Stephen, unearthing memories she'd kind of buried. 'When I was very small,' she'd told them, earlier tonight, 'he used to spin me round and round in the back garden.' Her words brought the memory alive. Stephen holding her wrist and ankle, the world whirling, green and bright, while she screamed with the thrill of it.

And now she's quiet, just enjoying her sense of his presence. He's become part of this group. Somehow they've taken not just her but Stephen, too, into their hearts.

Her new family.

The contentment these weeks have brought is heightened because her recurring nightmare has disappeared. This happens from time to time, and whenever it does she relaxes and becomes less driven. She always hopes it's gone for good, even though she never knows what makes it go, just as she never knows what makes it return.

She's rarely in bed before dawn. Could that be the reason? It's not a cure she's tried before and although it's rather radical, and she has to fight to stay awake in lectures, she wouldn't change a thing. She loves this secret night life. It's so different from her studious, daytime existence.

Iquis, however, is still a mystery. Harriet has grown close to the others, knows that Lucien writes poetry, knows that Beth and Richard met when he nerved himself to stand up to the girls who were bullying her outside her school, that he'd never fought anyone before and he'd been terrified. But he'd had to, because of her: Beth. 'Because I knew as soon as I saw her that we were forever,' he'd said. Beth and Richard are always telling Harriet about their dreams, dredging up as much detail as possible, then asking, 'What do *you* think it means?' And Harriet does her best to answer, even though Iquis is the one studying psychology, the one with all the textbook knowledge.

Oh yes, she has *that* all right. Harriet suspects she hides behind it, talking in depth about psychological theory to avoid having to confide anything. She speaks like an observer, a detached examiner of human nature. Not like a friend.

And yet Harriet is keen to break through, convinced there's more if she can just get Iquis to trust her.

Last night, she'd thought she was on the cusp of this breakthrough. The two of them had been walking through the campus, on their way to meet the others. Iquis had stopped abruptly to examine a poster on a lamp post: a missing student. The girl in the photo was slight, with bright eyes and an eager face. Tragedy tugged.

'Do you know her?' Harriet said.

'No.'

Yet Iquis had lingered there, her gaze travelling the length of the poster, reading everything. Rereading it. She'd been very still, quiet. Yet Harriet sensed tension, was reminded of finding her backed into the corner, in the kitchen, in the dark.

'Whatever it is, you can trust me.'

No answer.

'Does it remind you of something? Did something happen before you came here?'

This last was pushing her luck. Iquis *never* talked about where she'd come from. It was like she'd been dropped here, fully formed.

'No.'

'I might be able to help.'

Iquis turned away. 'It's nothing. Let's get out of here.'

She wasn't entirely pulling it off. Her mood was sombre, and she spoke even less than usual for the rest of the night.

This afternoon, Harriet returned to the lamp post for another attempt at understanding. The poster was no longer there.

She hasn't told Iquis this yet. She's waiting for her to settle. It takes Iquis time to adjust to being in the group each evening. She's edgy and abrasive when she joins them, burning with energy and wild suggestions. By the time she's ready to tolerate the quieter moments it's usually late.

The bottle of wine is passing from hand to hand, mouth to mouth. It's reached Iquis. She holds it out to Harriet, waits for her to grasp it, then tugs. There's something intent in her manner.

A beat of excitement. Is she about to mention the poster?

'How did Stephen die?' Iquis asks.

Harriet wrenches her hand away from the bottle and jerks backwards. 'How did you know he was dead? I never said. I never told you.'

'The way you talk about him. The stories you tell. They're in the past tense. There's nothing about what he's doing now.'

Harriet is winded.

I knew I was talking about him too much. I haven't been able to resist it.

'None of your business,' she manages.

'Fair enough.' Iquis dumps the bottle at Harriet's feet, sits back.

'Wait!' Harriet finds herself saying. She thinks of the keep out signs which are plastered all over the door to Iquis's room. In the face of such discouragement, Harriet's never dared knock for Iquis, has always waited to be collected.

There are no keep out signs on Harriet's door and yet, there might as well be.

I've spent years shutting people out. It's engrained in me and I've never questioned its necessity. I do understand her. Trusting people isn't easy. Maybe I have to show her the way.

'Stephen died nine years ago.' The words are hard to force out because he's been alive here, with them.

Iquis nods, quiet.

'We ought to be over it, but somehow we got stuck.'

'What happened?' Iquis's voice is lower than usual, less demanding.

'It was an accident. He was where he shouldn't have been. The disused boarded-up quarry two miles from our house.' Harriet is prey to a curious detachment. 'He fell into the pit and although it was full of water and he might have been okay, he wasn't. He and Graham – his best friend – were there together. My parents blame Graham. But Stephen was always the ringleader so I don't know. All I know is that it was Graham who got him out of the quarry and called an ambulance. It didn't do any good, he died on the way to hospital, but at least he tried.'

She has no emotions. It's like she's telling a story.

'I was never allowed to talk to Graham again after it happened.'

She feels the bottle pressing against her thigh. Her other hand is jamming it there. No one else is saying anything.

'You remember what I told you last week, about how he climbed on the school roof and sat there with his legs hanging over the side laughing down at us? I try to imagine that is how he was just before he fell. Not frightened but ecstatic, thrilled with his own daring and blazingly alive.'

Beth's hand gently covers Harriet's.

Harriet snatches her hand away. She can't stand sympathy. It's always been too dangerous. It makes things more real, shakes her self-control, and she doesn't like that. There has always been a frozen feeling attached to the memories of Stephen's death. It's like the incident has been paused in mid-frame, exactly the way Dr Drake had paused the video of the collapsing tower.

'And afterwards? What happened afterwards?' Iquis asks intently.

'What do you mean?' Harriet demands, rattled. *I can't remember that! I was only nine.*

But something is forming in her mind.

She's cycling as hard as she can along a road, past a red van. The sun is blazingly hot and she's dusty and scratched. There's grit pressing between her palms and the handlebars. The wail of an ambulance passes behind her. She lowers her head, keeps cycling. She tastes fear.

Where did that come from? It's a fragment of memory and she can't slot it into place.

'Well?' Iquis demands, dragging her attention back. 'What happened afterwards?'

'That's such a weird thing to ask,' Harriet says. 'Why do you care? Why focus on the fallout?'

She sees that inevitable dart backwards, as if Iquis feels she has revealed too much. But she's revealed nothing.

EIGHT

When Harriet wakes up the following afternoon she's in no mood to work. Last night has left her raw and vulnerable, struggling with an anger she can do nothing with. It's Saturday, so there aren't any lectures. She sets off on the five-mile walk into town, intent on outpacing her thoughts.

They prove hard to shake. Iquis should have given something back last night, even if not immediately, once they were alone. It's not fair to expect Harriet to peel off so many layers, without –

She feels fragile.

She'd told herself Iquis was just waiting until they were alone to say something meaningful, helpful. Even *if* it came from textbooks. It would at least show that she cared.

So, once it was just her and Iquis, walking back to halls, she'd waited.

Nothing.

So she'd steered them via the lamp post with the missing, missing-girl poster.

'It's gone,' she'd said.

The light had poured down on Iquis's face; Harriet had watched intently. *Nothing.*

'So it has.' Iquis barely hesitated before striding on. Harriet, lingering, was left behind, had to run to catch up.

She'd simmered all the way back to halls, biting back words. If she said anything, she'd say too much. Judging by the amused look Iquis had given Harriet when they parted outside Genesis Hall, Harriet's emotions had been far easier to read than Iquis's.

'Fuck you, Iquis!' Harriet spits at the trees she's stomping past.

She'd bitten those words back last night. Had punched in the entrance code, headed inside with a muttered goodbye. Had left Iquis to disappear off back into the night. Iquis never came upstairs with Harriet, never seemed to want to call it a night, no matter how late. That restlessness always there under the surface.

'What is it with you?' The trees listen to Harriet's frustrations. They don't answer, but it helps, and by the time she arrives in town she's ready to let it go. At least for now.

She heads for the bookshop cafe and orders a double espresso and a wedge of chocolate cake, carries it over to an armchair and settles, tucking up her legs. She's surrounded by blue-painted shelves containing books. She scans them casually, comforted.

'Hey!' A familiar voice grabs her attention. One of the twins is walking towards her, holding a stack of paperbacks. But which twin?

As usual, she can't tell. 'Do you work here?'

'No, Jenna does. I'm covering for her.'

That makes it easy, which might be why Marcia said it. There's something else, though. Harriet senses mischief. She says, 'Do they know you're not Jenna?'

Marcia shakes her head and gives Harriet a conspiratorial look. She looks around, checks she isn't being observed and then lowers her stack of books onto Harriet's coffee table.

'Do you like Dark Island? Tell me you do!' Her eyes are glittering with excitement.

'Of course I do. Why?'

Marcia punches the air. 'I *knew* you had to. You and Iquis and the other goths.'

'What's this about?' Harriet senses something major. But if so, Marcia is taking her time, enjoying the journey.

'I've only been into them since *Lost Soul Blues,* on MTV. That bit with Loki getting drenched with the fire extinguisher and all the foam melting against him.' She grabs a breath, her eyes shining. 'He's to die for!'

Marcia's got her *I'm with Mark* look on: all mesmerised and enchanted like she can't believe her luck.

Harriet, who frequently passes Mark draped around other girls, is relieved to discover that Marcia is not entirely obsessed by him because he's going to hurt her. Also, it might just wipe that smug, entitled "I'm the centre of the universe" look from his face.

Harriet's been struggling to decide whether to tell Marcia about Mark's other girls. It's tricky. She suspects Marcia would rather not know.

Anyway, it's not the moment for that dilemma. Not when there's news about Dark Island.

'What is it? Tell me.'

'They're doing a limited tour of the UK early next year. They're only covering four venues, but one of them, on the 14 February, is Newcastle.'

'For real?' Harriet's voice rises to a squeak.

Marcia nods.

'Unbelievable! They hardly ever do live stuff. How do we get tickets? Are they already on sale? They'll sell out quick.'

'Not yet,' Marcia says. 'Next week.'

She holds up a hand as if to halt Harriet, who has half risen from her chair.

'It's not quite the whole group,' Marcia says. 'Circe won't be there, apparently she's working on a solo album, but the rest will. And really, as long as Loki puts in an appearance...'

Harriet shakes her head vigorously. 'It won't be the same without Circe.'

She hopes that this is a temporary thing, not a permanent split. For some reason, she remembers Circe bursting through those gates, the sunlight and the magnesium flare.

'So you don't want to go?' Marcia says.

'I didn't say that. Of *course* I still want to go. I have to go.'

There's a small fantasy starting up inside her: Dark Island looking down from the stage and seeing her and knowing at once that she belongs with them.

She knows all Circe's lyrics. She's practised her intonations until you couldn't hear the difference. Singing with Lucien in the wood. The intensity of Iquis's unspoken attention.

Harriet would be up there on the stage and Iquis would be watching her and it would all be different. For once, Harriet would be the one with the mystery and glamour. And Iquis would be the one trying to break through to her. There'd be no more amused glances!

'Absolutely,' Harriet says. 'I am so up for this.'

'And Iquis?' Marcia says. 'And the others? We could go as a group. What d'you reckon? Oh, and – there's a piece I found about Dark Island.' She digs into her pocket, pulls out a folded page and presents it to Harriet like a bribe.

It's rather good to have something Marcia wants.

'I don't see why not. Jenna as well?'

'Nah. She's not a fan, says they're too dark. But that's the whole point, isn't it? That sinister edge is so thrilling, makes me feel so alive. It's like the adrenaline kick of walking through a wood and feeling that there's someone out there, following you.'

She swallows, her eyes bright.

'The woods around here are good for that,' she continues in a rush. 'Very edgy. I could swear there's a presence there – something dark and old and watchful.'

She's too excited. Harriet quivers with the memory of that first night when she'd run out to the woods and heard someone laughing at her – or thought she had. Of course she'd imagined it. And it's never been like that again. Not when she's been there with Iquis and the group. But she does know what Marcia means.

Anyway, Dark Island! 'How do we make sure we get tickets? You say, next week?'

'Monday,' Marcia says. 'And we go in person. Have to go in person! There's no Internet or telephone sales. So we head up to Newcastle on Sunday, spend the night in the queue, and we're *practically guaranteed* to get them. You up for it?'

'Totally!'

'Fab. Fab. Fab.' She glances across the shop. 'Gotta go.

The owner's watching. Jenna will do her nut if I get her sacked. You'll ask Iquis?' She's already moving away.

'Sure,' Harriet says. She crams in a mouthful of cake, washes it down with coffee and scans the article. She hardly tastes anything in her eagerness to finish and be on her way back.

She has news to share.

The Mysterious Dark Lords of Goth

Who are the elusive quintet of musicians who form Dark Island? What do they look like under their painted masks? Do their real names match up to their stage names? And where did they come from? Our reporter, Serena Dayton, goes looking for answers and finds... not very much.

Dark Island is the latest in a long line of goth bands to break into the mainstream. They seem unlikely candidates. The casual brutality of their lyrics and performances leaves a macabre echo long after the music fades, a sinister half-life reminiscent of the uneasiness felt when Frankenstein's monster wandered off into the ice, leaving Mary Shelley the option of a sequel she never wrote.

Perhaps she scared herself too much to want to go near it. Because what does it take to write such gothic horrors? And what might it do to the people who scribe them? These questions were close to the surface when I started off in search of answers.

I began with Dark Island's alter-egos, the names and adopted identities they prowl around under: Sauron, Medea, Loki, Kali, Circe. Like many, I had a vague familiarity with these creatures of story and myth: Sauron – Tolkien's Dark Lord, reigning over a blackened land where nothing good can grow; Medea – betrayed by a lover, her revenge bloody and terrible; Loki – a trickster, in love with chaos, not always on the side you think he's on; Kali – Indian goddess of death; Circe – island enchantress who turned greedy men into pigs.

They're a miscellaneous bunch of mixed heritage and antiquity: Greek, Indian, Roman, English, Norse. And yet, their manager's term for them is, "the family". (About all I managed to get out of him!)

I'm following the pattern of so many articles, aren't I, telling you about the myths and not about the people?

Well, acquit me. It's not for want of trying. The truth is, it's far easier to find out about their alter egos than about them. There's far more of a trail, far more words, far more facts.

Perhaps it's because Dark Island emerged when goth had gone underground, in the mid-nineties, that we know so little. The spotlight of the press was turned elsewhere when they slithered up from the shadows. By the time we noticed them, they were immense and reclusive: impervious both to questions and requests for interviews. They didn't have to please us, and they didn't try. They chose to be defined only by their music, their videos, and their rare stage appearances.

Protected by their ferocious guard-dog-like minders they retain their mystery. The only available quotes come from their manager: a stocky, middle-

aged man who passes out comments attributed to the group with the stoical expression of one being well paid to spout nonsense.

The latest gem is the explanation for Circe's absence from the tour.

'She doesn't like islands. It reminds her too much of her past.'

And when pressed, 'She says there are enough pigs in the world already, and that she couldn't be answerable for the consequences of being surrounded by water once again.'

My talk of her disappointed fans achieves nothing. He has used up his array of quotes and remains silent, unmoved.

I try one final question, 'Are they really a family?'

He smiles. Nods. Raises his eyes to heaven as if to converse, then gestures us out past a stray Dark Island minder who lurks growling in a corner, watching us under lowered black brows.

*

Harriet, who's run the whole way back from town, hammers on Iquis's door. The painted nuns – "Communing with God. Do not disturb." – quiver. The humour in the flying nuns makes them less irritating than the other do-not-disturb signs on the door. But Harriet's intent on ignoring them all. And perhaps Dark Island gives her permission, but it's also about last night, about that amused look, about that permanent "keep out" sign Iquis wears on her face.

'What is it?' Iquis sounds startled.

'The most exciting news *ever*. Open up.'

Iquis opens the door partway and steps into the gap. She's partially blocking the threshold but Harriet can see past her. Not that there's much to see. There are no posters, no pictures, not even any scattered belongings. Apart from furniture and a pile of text books on the desk the room is bare; a nun's cell.

'Let's go outside,' Harriet says, giving up. 'I'll tell you there.'

'Right.' Iquis exits quickly, locking the door behind her.

They race down the stairs, burst out into the early evening and head for the shelter of the weeping willow tree. Pushing through the fronds, Harriet grasps its trunk and turns to face Iquis. She spills everything out: the meeting with Marcia, the miracle of the Dark Island concert. 'It's for real!' Even Iquis will react to this. 'And we're guaranteed to get tickets, if we—'

'I've already seen them.' Iquis picks at the bark of the willow tree. 'They were okay. But no, I don't want to see them again.'

Harriet stares in disbelief. 'You're winding me up. Of *course* you want to go. What about that first night in the woods when Lucien and I were singing and we were all so close? Imagine what it would mean for the five of us to go, together. I know Marcia will be there as well, but that's not a problem. Is it?'

Iquis shrugs. 'It's not a problem. I just don't fancy it.'

'But... But... You have to! For me, for us. It just wouldn't be the same without you.'

'I don't really like them. They're overrated and a bit over the top. I'd be bored.'

It's like Iquis has thumped her in the stomach. 'You never said any of that when we were singing. I thought you were with us. I thought you were listening...'

If I got that wrong, then maybe I got everything wrong. Perhaps there is nothing between us.

'Did Stephen like them?' Iquis asks. 'Is that why it matters so much?'

Harriet laughs. A short, choked-off explosion. 'What's that to you?'

Iquis shrugs. 'You loved him.'

'Is that your psychology course talking? Stop treating me like an experiment! Why should I tell you stuff when you never tell *me* anything? That's not friendship. Friends are meant to share things. It doesn't count if it's only one way.'

Iquis steps back. Perhaps she's going to turn and leave. If she does Harriet won't even try to stop her.

'Well?' Harriet says.

'I had a brother who died,' Iquis says, but she says it passively with no emotion, and Harriet is convinced that she's lying, saying the one thing that –

'Did you? Or are you just saying that to get me off your back?'

And then she sees it. There's a crack in Iquis, and it's like a broken mirror.

It's happened to her, too. She's not lying. There's something terrible in her face. She's lived through... Lived through the same thing Harriet has. That's why she doesn't talk. And why her room's so devoid of personality. She's shut off. Just like... Harriet has.

Then Iquis's face returns to its pale, impassive norm.

'You know nothing about me, about the things I've come from,' she says quietly, 'and you'd never understand them. So don't try.' She strips a long piece of flesh from the willow-tree. 'I have to get away now. This campus presses in on me.'

She walks to where the low curtain of leaves is almost touching the ground and sweeps aside a huge swathe.

'I thought you were different,' she says. Then she's gone.

Harriet doesn't try to follow.

NINE

Next day, Harriet is on edge. Something's scratching at her mind. She thinks she can hear the scrape of metal on stone. She's failing to work, just doodling tendrils around the edges of the force diagram she's meant to be analysing.

She has a horrible feeling that the dream was there last night. Just the first flicker, the opening moments. The presence behind her. The sweat from her tightened grasp bleeding into the handle of the spade as she pushes down, lifts up. The shifting sound of falling soil. The building suspense. That terrible momentum towards...

It's surfacing from her subconscious with that slippery, unreal feel of dreams in daytime. Yet, despite the sun shining through her window, previous repetitions have made every detail horribly clear.

Did I really dream it last night? Or am I tricking myself into thinking I did? And if I did, why didn't it continue? I must have woken up. Something must have happened. Maybe a noise from the corridor or something.

But even though it was only the beginning of the dream the threat is still there and with it that sense of isolation.

It's coming back. I can't bear it.

Someone knocks on the door and she tenses. Iquis?

'Who is it?'

'It's me, Marcia. Let me in.'

Marcia. Harriet lets out her breath in a sigh and walks over to open the door.

Marcia bounces in. 'Did you ask them?'

'Sort of.'

'What do you mean?'

'I asked Iquis. She wasn't interested. I didn't bother asking the others.'

'Shame,' Marcia says. 'Are you sure she doesn't want to go? Perhaps you caught her in one of her awkward moods.'

'Don't be ridiculous,' Harriet snaps, and then after a moment, 'Sorry. Slept badly.' The dream sneaks closer. 'I'll come with you to the concert,' she says, suddenly determined, 'and to get the tickets in Newcastle. It would be good to get away for a night.'

'We don't actually need to go to Newcastle any more,' Marcia says. 'I asked Mark and Paul.'

'Oh shit!'

I can't face Mark.

'What is it with you two?' Marcia asks, then continues without waiting for an answer. 'Mark's got a friend in Newcastle who can get the tickets for us. He was dubious about getting them for a big group, but if it's just us four there should be no problem.'

'Does Mark know one of the tickets is for me?'

'Yes,' Marcia says. She hesitates then continues with a grin. 'He actually said, he supposed he could cope with you for one evening as long as I kept you under control. Why do you two hate each other?'

'Long story,' Harriet says.

'But you've only just met.'

'Some things don't take time. You believe in love at first sight, don't you?'

'Yeah.'

'Well then!' A thought occurs to Harriet. 'Mark wouldn't just say he'll get me a ticket and then accidentally only get three, so I can't go?'

'No, he's straight. If he says he'll do something he will. He prides himself on never promising anything that he doesn't deliver. Believe me, I should know.' There's an ironic edge to her voice. It makes Harriet think that Marcia does know about Mark and the other girls, after all.

TEN

Harriet walks with Lucien. Somehow, in the last three nights without Iquis, it's always been Harriet and Lucien, Richard and Beth.

'Recite it again,' she says.

He coughs self-consciously, glances over his shoulder.

'Are you sure?'

'Yes. I liked it,' she says, then adds tentatively, 'maybe a little slower.'

Lucien's pace drags to a near stop. The others catch up and bottleneck behind them as his shoulders hunch forwards. Over their narrowed shape, Harriet watches the gleam of the river through the hedge. She's trying not to think about whether she finds Lucien attractive. If she starts down that path she'll totally blow it, the way she did with Paul in Freshers' week before it became obvious that he was far more interested in Jenna.

Lucien catches a vast mouthful of breath, and rapid-fires the words out. The form of the poem only just survives in tiny catches of space between each line.

"i am that minefield
you talked of.

so, watch how you walk
i am confused as to the enemy
and anyway
perhaps i don't care.

you come here with your smiles
and expect me to glow,
eager in your light.

but i am mud
and glisten only in the rain."'

He slams to a halt. Looks out along the lane, his pose indifferent.

I am mud, Harriet thinks, *and confused as to the enemy*. It makes her think of Iquis and stops her from saying, 'It's me, I know what it feels like.'

None of the goths knows the reason for Iquis's prolonged absence. She's been gone three nights now, and Harriet's mood has gradually grown bleaker, so that even though Lucien has written a poem that Harriet can identify with, it doesn't make her feel closer to him. Instead it just highlights her inability to connect.

She's felt like this before all too often back at home in Sheffield. Usually she would turn to Dark Island for relief. Putting on headphones and turning the volume up high, lying for hours on the floor of her bedroom staring at the ceiling; letting their lyrics tell her that they know what she's feeling, that they've been there too.

Often she doesn't know what triggers these moods, but once they're there she can't control them, just has to wait for something to happen to pull her out of them.

But this time she can't play Dark Island. It's too entangled with what happened with Iquis, so that each time she tries to play a track she finds herself reliving their argument and has to switch it off.

'Isn't that Iquis,' Lucien says, 'up there ahead of us on the path?'

Yes. A jolt of pure nervous energy. Iquis's figure is unmistakable. She stands perfectly still, waiting for the others to approach.

Harriet is reminded of how arrogant and indifferent Iquis had been during that first encounter in the kitchen. Because that's how she looks now, not like one of the group, but like an outsider. She's wearing close-fitting leather which looks like body armour.

What do I say?

But Iquis isn't looking at Harriet, she's focussed entirely on Beth and Richard.

'Where have you been?' Beth says.

'Away. I'm back now.'

'Away *where*?' Lucien sounds different, less relaxed than he is with Harriet, more guarded.

'Nowhere important,' Iquis says. 'Come on. Where're we going?'

'Nowhere in particular.' Lucien matches Iquis's brusque delivery.

'Right.' Iquis shrugs. She turns to talk to Beth and Richard, falling in behind Lucien and Harriet as the walk is resumed. Harriet is struggling to find words to bridge the gap, but she can't come up with anything neutral because what she's hearing is, "*I had a brother who died*".

It's easier to respond to Lucien. 'It's really good, your poem,' she says. 'I feel like that sometimes.'

He grunts, but she's sure he's pleased.

She glances behind her at the three silhouettes. In the centre of the path, Iquis dominates the skyline and overshadows the softer bell shape of Beth on her right. Richard, on Beth's other side, is lost in the overhang of the hedge.

Iquis's head is tilted towards Beth. She seems to demand Beth's full attention. Richard's hand, still attached to Beth's, is the only thing that draws him into the picture.

'Why don't you recite it to Iquis?' Harriet suggests.

But Lucien looks awkward. 'I'd rather not,' he says, quietly. 'I don't always share it with people. I just felt that I was ready to let you hear it.'

Harriet is touched. Sharing his awkwardness, she mutters, 'Thanks.'

Iquis creates an interruption. 'Hey,' she says, 'the hedge is weak here. Let's break through and go down to the river.' She sticks her arm into the hedge and starts to yank branches aside.

'I don't think that's a good idea,' Lucien says. 'They keep sheep in that field. If we make a gap in the hedge the sheep will get out.'

'So what?' Iquis's voice is too loud.

Beth intervenes. 'It's only another ten minutes' walk until the path comes back to the river.'

'But we've been to that part of the river before,' Iquis says. 'Let's do something different.'

'Like what?' Lucien says. 'I'm happy with the river. The water is always different. And it's peaceful – I like peaceful.'

'Well I don't!' Iquis says.

'Tough.'

'Let's go to Decadance. I want to dance.' Her eyes glitter.

'But that's miles away,' Lucien says, 'and besides, we wouldn't get in. You have to know someone, be introduced.'

'You do know someone. You know me.'

Before Lucien can respond, Beth squeals with excitement. 'You can get us into Decadance?'

'Wow!' Richard, too, is excited.

'What's Decadance?' Harriet asks. She doesn't like the sound of dancing, not if they all hit the dance floor and she has to stand by the side watching, or worse, needing to find excuses about why she... *can't*.

'It's *the* goth nightclub,' Beth says. 'We've never been, but we've read all about it.'

'It's legendary,' she continues, 'set in the middle of nowhere – in this really cool Victorian Gothic folly – and it goes on all night. Closes down just as the first light of dawn filters through the windows.'

She turns to Iquis. 'Can you really get us in?'

Iquis nods. Beth grabs Lucien's arm. 'What are we waiting for? Come on, let's go.'

*

Lucien drives, directed by Iquis, who sits in the front and speaks only to give terse directions. They seem out of sync – like strangers. Harriet, Richard and Beth share a different mood in the back. The couple are excited and – despite her qualms about the dancing – it spreads to Harriet. The journey leads them further and further into enchantment, as the roads grow narrower and the hedges crowd closer.

It's like travelling through the Sleeping Beauty forest, Harriet thinks, enraptured by the scrape of branches against her window.

'Turn here,' Iquis says, abruptly.

Lucien twists the wheel, slewing them into the beginnings of a driveway. Just ahead of them a set of immense gates are planted wide open, revealing a long driveway headed by a turreted building, which pulses with colour and noise.

But it's the wrought-iron gates which snatch Harriet's attention.

'Stop!' she yells.

Lucien brakes hard. Everyone jerks forwards.

'What is it?' He turns an alarmed face to Harriet.

'It's the gates!' Her voice is high with excitement.

'They're open. There's plenty of room.'

'Yes, but don't you get it?' In the beam of the headlights, the long spokes and twisted tendrils are clearly visible. 'Surely you recognise them from *Bleeding for Strangers*? Circe runs out of the house and down through *those* gates. Look at the dragon with the tongue of flame surrounded by brambles.'

She yanks the door open and tumbles out, stumbles over to the gate, touches it.

Cold metal surfaced with a crumbly coating of dirt. Near the gate's latch the paint has been scraped away. *Circe hauling those chains through and through.* Damaging the paintwork? Harriet's convinced. The gate's base is embedded in a pile of earth and stones. A tangle of weeds has taken root. The top hinge is broken.

It wasn't broken in the video. She pushes hard but the gate won't move.

'Harriet's right!' Lucien exclaims.

She turns to see him reaching for the door handle, but before he can open the door Iquis's hand is on his shoulder. He jerks to a halt.

'We want to get to Decadance,' Iquis says. 'What's so exciting about a set of gates?'

Is she for real?

Harriet's in a different world. At the top of the long drive shifting lights spill from tiny, Gothic-arched windows to stain the sky with a haze of purple, red and blue. The house stands silhouetted against its turbulent aura. The last time she saw it, it was cracking up, falling apart stone by stone.

She doesn't understand why the others are still in the car. But perhaps it's because this is for her; just for her.

'You go on,' she says. 'I need to be alone with this.'

She hardly registers the protests, hardly hears the engine rev or the car head up the drive without her. She's deep in the past, caught in a memory so vivid that it's like a hallucination.

*

Her fingers are flicking through a line of CDs in her local music shop. She's meant to be buying a present for her friend Lisa's twelfth birthday party, but she's been distracted away from the new releases to search through the second-hand section, cruising for something different, something novel. And then, out of a silence between tracks, she hears Dark

Island emerge. Their sound already somehow known and significant – so that she freezes, until only her blood is moving, pulsing with their beat.

Then the lyrics start. The woman's voice, telling the story of a lost child in a wounded jazz-rasp of pain, dizzies her. It's as if Mum is finally trying to communicate with her from over the silences and the denials and the petty terrors that have kept her locked away. She finds herself dragged across the room towards the speakers – wanting to enter them, wanting to hold her hands out to this woman – and then, strangest of all, she finds herself mouthing the concluding lyrics moments before the singer reaches them, as if she has known them all along.

'*Whose hand pushed you?*'

Half question, half accusation – the words terrible in the static air of the music shop – her mouth tightening to the tiniest mumble, so that no one will see.

'*Whose hand pushed you? Is hell too far to fall?*'

She never makes it to the birthday party. Instead she finds herself buying the Dark Island CD and hurrying home to play it feeling that she is clasping a secret to her chest. Her mind racing as she invents the first of the many scenarios that has her reaching out to Dark Island, has them reaching back, ends with her joining them, becoming whole.

*

Medea's voice fades into silence, as the memory slips away. Harriet is shivering. She's searching for something. Leaning against the broken gate – she's trying to understand the significance of actually, physically being where Dark Island have been.

The outpour of music from the house masks the night sounds. Could they be out here?

No, ridiculous. And yet, this discovery has the same power as the one when she was twelve. It's too much of a coincidence.

'What is it?' she asks the night. 'What are you trying to tell me?'

The hedge creaks and crackles, its tall fronds swaying.

'Are you out there?'

Her voice sounds nervous, not the way she'd expected to sound. But it's cold, and all the light is up at the house, very little where she's standing. In her mind, there's the echo of a laugh. But nothing happens. No figures come striding towards her as she waits.

The metal against her back leaches warmth. She shivers.

The others must have reached the house by now. Should she go after them? She is torn between the reality of the others and this earlier yearning for something she can't even find words for.

She slips her arms through the curlicues of the gate, hugging the crusty metal against her face and body until it is imprinted in her physical memory. Then she lets go, turns and runs towards the people and the music.

ELEVEN

Harriet climbs the wide stone steps towards the swarming entrance hall, reaches the top and hesitates. The doorway is flanked by two alert bouncers in black jackets and white shirts. One of them steps towards her, holds out a hand. 'Invite?'

'No, I—' Is she going to be able to get in? 'I'm with—'

Lucien's red hair appears behind a couple of black-haired goth girls. 'It's all right,' he says, 'Harriet's with us.'

Richard and Beth are close behind him, looking awed. And yet, they shouldn't. They belong in this beautiful chaos of milling goths and dancing lights.

'Isn't it stunning?' Beth's face is bright with excitement.

Harriet nods. 'Where's Iquis?'

'Buggered off with the owner,' Lucien says, 'after ordering us to wait for you.'

'She knows the owner?' she says.

He nods.

'How typical of Iquis! What's he like?'

She pictures some kind of uber-goth, though she can't quite dress the image. For some reason what comes to mind is Frank-N-Furter from *The Rocky Horror Show*. She raises one eyebrow.

'He's not what you'd expect,' Lucien says. 'Kind of...
normal.'

'Friendly though,' Beth says. 'I liked him.'

'Yeah well,' Lucien's expression is definitely resentful,
'as much as we were allowed to see of him.'

'How d'you mean?'

'Iquis snatched him away before we could say anything
more than hello.'

Beth rests a hand on his arm. 'That's because she wanted
us to dance, to make the most of it as we're not going to be
here long.'

'No,' Lucien says, with emphasis, 'it's because she wants
to keep him to herself. And anyway, we're only tight on time,
because *she* took one look around and decided we shouldn't
stay. I really don't get her sometimes.'

'We're not staying?' Harriet is both disappointed and
bewildered.

'Not according to Iquis. She says the scene has gone
downhill.'

'Leave it, Lucien. Let's just go and enjoy it for as long
we can,' Beth says. She's beginning to sound tense.

'Sorry,' Lucien says, 'you're right.' He turns to Harriet.
'Come and dance.'

Can't, Harriet thinks, but she holds off from saying this
any sooner than she has to, just follows them silently as they
push their way inside.

✳

Confusion. A wall of noise, physical in its presence. The
press of strangers intimate one moment, left behind the

next. The heat and scent of bodies and perfumes, of dusky clothes, velvets and silks. Deep drifts of light bulge over them as they plunge deeper. The colours switch back and forth across their hands and faces; dancers all around them; a labyrinth of slow, twisting figures, transmuting the music into fluid patterns.

Harriet can feel the essence of this place sneaking into her, making her part of it. A woman's voice slides out of the music, curls around her, snags her. She follows it deeper into the maze, looking for Circe, for Loki, for Medea.

They could be here.

She starts to laugh, starts to sway unthinkingly in time with the music. A slow, steady, unselfconscious movement. They are halted, but it's not like a queue, more like belonging. She wants this, wants this feeling.

Lucien grabs her hand, starts to pull her deeper into the pattern of moving figures. 'Come on,' he yells, 'let's join them.'

'No!'

She freezes. The spell slips out of her fingers.

He's looking at her, questioning.

Perhaps she should claim a sprained ankle, done between the gates and here. But no, that would be pathetic, unworthy of Stephen's standards.

Stephen. What would he say? There's a funny buzzing in her ears – *"Just say, I don't want to dance."*

But the words won't come.

Lucien's grasp loosens.

'Where's Iquis?' Harriet yells. 'I should find her.'

She has to repeat it, close to his ear. Then he's gesturing, pointing to a place of calm beyond the dance floor. There's more space there. People are sitting, resting. She can only grab glimpses of it between shifting figures.

'Thanks! I'll see you later, then.'

He nods, touches her lightly on the shoulder, then he's slipping away from her. Moving with the others onto the dance floor. She sees them, sees the way their faces ease and lighten, the way they seem to effortlessly belong and feels a fierce envy.

But there's no point in that emotion. She turns, and starts to forge her way towards Iquis.

*

Emerging from the dance floor is like crawling out from rough sea onto a beach. The music recedes, the lighting softens and space opens up. She's separate now.

She hears a faint, conflicting melody, and glances at the far wall where a rounded tunnel-like opening is leaking music and cinematic images. Intrigued, she draws closer, until she can see a little way inside, just far enough to pick out the edge of boots, the partial outline of legs.

There are people in there lying down.

It makes her think of the rabbit hole, of Alice sliding and falling into another world. She wants to be Alice.

Inside there, anything could happen.

But it looks full. And there are people surrounding it, waiting their chance to go in. A mixture of shyness, and the recollection that she's looking for Iquis, causes her to retreat.

Moments later she sees her. She's sitting at a table in the far corner, facing a middle-aged man who looks like he's come here by mistake. He has thinning blonde hair caught back in a twisted ponytail, and is dressed in a white T-shirt and blue jeans.

He can't be the owner. He looks too normal.

He's shorter than Iquis. She's leaning over him in a slight curve with her arm resting on his shoulder. He listens intently while she talks. Harriet can't help feeling that he has the closeness with Iquis that she has been striving for.

She remembers their argument, and realises that getting out of the car and disappearing on her Dark Island quest wasn't the most conciliatory action.

Yes, but – it meant something to me. I don't see why that should be such a problem for her.

Feeling self-righteous, and therefore far more sure of herself, she marches over to them. 'Hi!'

Iquis looks up and for the first time tonight meets Harriet's eyes. Unreadable. Not hostile; not friendly.

'I'm sorry about what I said last Saturday,' Harriet says. 'About your—'

Iquis jerks one hand up and presses her fingers across Harriet's mouth, slightly too hard. There's an impasse.

The man with Iquis breaks it. 'Hello. I'm Glyn. You must be Harriet.'

There is something infinitely safe about him. She doesn't usually trust people quickly, and yet something about how content he looks and how naturally he smiles at her makes her feel peaceful.

'Iquis's best friend,' he says and rests his hand – warm, faintly calloused and steady – briefly against hers.

She glances at Iquis whose expression is unfathomable.

Glyn pushes himself up from his chair. 'Have my seat. I'll get another glass.'

For the first time she notices the bottle of wine and the two full glasses on the table. Then, as Glyn moves away, she tries once more. 'I really didn't mean...'

'I know,' Iquis says. 'It's over. Forget it.'

Harriet hesitates, wanting to say more.

Iquis's fingers touch Harriet's lips, fleetingly this time. 'Leave it. Come and dance.'

I thought I'd escaped that.

'I don't dance,' she says, turning it into a statement, a choice.

'Why not?'

'Just don't.' Stiffness in her voice. 'I'm awkward. *Okay?*'

'No, *not okay.*' An unusual softness in her voice. Her fingers touch Harriet's, tug gently.

'You *don't* understand. I'd make a fool of myself.'

'Not here, you wouldn't. It would be different here.'

'Would it?' A tingle of excitement. Briefly, it feels like Iquis could change even this about her. Then the feeling fades.

There's a silence. Harriet can see the music pulling at Iquis.

'It's the only place I come alive,' Iquis says. And there's yearning, hunger in her tone.

Then Glyn looms over them and Iquis affects disinterest.

'So, Harriet,' Glyn says, lifting the bottle from the table and glugging wine into the new glass. 'What do you think of my creation?'

'It's beautiful,' Harriet says. 'I've never seen anything like it.'

He grins. 'I wanted to make people happy.'

He hands her the wine glass and she takes a mouthful. It's good – rich. Her attention is caught once more by the rabbit hole.

'What's that?' She gestures.

'The vibe room.' He tucks his hands into his T-shirt. The action lifts the hem and reveals a glimpse of dense, softly haired belly.

'That sounds like something out of the sixties.'

'Cool.' He laughs. 'That's what I was aiming at. You know, something psychedelic.

'Picture yourself entering an igloo,' he continues, 'only one that's warmer and carpeted with mattresses. There's a stem in the centre with a fish-eye lens which projects the music video all around you. I wanted to create a 3D effect, to make people feel as if they were part of the video, so they'd lose themselves in it. It's really intense. You'll have to try it before you leave. Isn't that right, Iquis?'

But Iquis is watching the dancing. So much hunger there.

Just because I can't, I've no right to stop her. It would be like me not going to the concert.

'Go dance,' Harriet says abruptly. 'That's what you came for.'

Iquis hesitates. 'You won't discuss me.'

It's hard to tell whether this is a question or command.

Don't be so arrogant, Harriet wants to say. But actually Iquis is right, that is exactly what she wants to do. There are so many questions and Glyn might have the answers.

But it would be cheating and she wouldn't forgive me. No matter how frustrating it is I have to wait until she's ready to trust me.

'Not a word,' she promises. 'Go on. The others will be pleased if you join them. They've been feeling left out.'

Richard, Beth and Lucien are closer now. They have the same rhythm as the other goths, their movements slow and self-contained. They are solitary dancers sharing an experience.

Iquis hesitates, casting a quick glance at Glyn. Then with a shrug she's gone, forging through the dancers towards the others.

The scene changes. Her tall leather-clad figure stands out. She is wild where the other dancers are contained, crackling with brilliance, throwing out a challenge with the speed and ferocity with which she translates the underlying drumbeats.

'It's like she belongs to a different tribe,' Harriet says, then adds, 'She moves like she owns the music.'

'Perhaps she does,' Glyn says idly. He's watching Harriet with the same intent expression he'd watched Iquis with earlier. He shows no sign of moving away, and Harriet is flattered. This is also, she realises, her chance.

'Why are the gates broken?'

Glyn looks startled. He raises a questioning eyebrow.

'Dark Island,' she says. 'I recognised the gates from the video.'

He holds his hands up in a gesture of surrender. 'Loki broke them.'

Harriet wants to thrust her hands into the air in triumph. 'Why? Was it a symbolic act? What did it mean? What was he trying to say?'

'He didn't confide in me.' His voice is flat.

It's disappointing. 'When did he do it?'

'After they finished filming. Just before they left.'

It's like trying to lever up a limpet. 'And he didn't say anything?'

'Not to me.'

'But you have met them?' A hint of exasperation in her tone. Why isn't he excited?

He nods.

'What are they like?'

He hesitates, looks over to where Iquis is dominating the dance floor. Not content with her own space, she is now hurtling out from the others like a flung yo-yo or a dervish. She treats the other dancers like a vast puzzle, an obstacle course to be crossed.

She's found the maze.

A ripple of disturbance follows Iquis as she moves. Like the Sleeping Beauty prince gone rogue, she awakens people as she passes them. Glazed looks are swept away, replaced by edgy, excited awareness.

Glyn hasn't answered the question. Harriet repeats it, trying to sound casual. 'What was Loki like?'

'Put it like this, if I had a daughter I wouldn't let her anywhere near him.'

Not you as well, she thinks, reminded uncomfortably of Dad. 'I don't see why,' she objects hotly.

Glyn is silent. Dad would have exploded.

'It's not fair,' she says to Glyn, 'you all make these pronouncements, but you won't justify anything. Why don't you like them?'

He looks surprised, then rakes a hand into his hair disarranging the effect of the ponytail. 'There was just something about them,' he says slowly, 'as if they'd swallowed their own myth, forgotten how to mix with ordinary people. As if people were only there for their convenience. What's the word I'm looking for? Callous. Indifferent.'

Hideously disappointing. 'No! They're not like that, you just didn't get them... didn't understand where they're coming from.' She stops herself. Difficult to claim greater knowledge than he has, after all he's met them – she just *knows* them. She changes direction.

'What about Circe?'

Dangerous, what if he says similar things about her? Well if he does, it just goes to show how little he understands.

'She was different.' His fingers are worrying at his hair once more. 'She never seemed to quite fit with the rest of them, but I couldn't tell you why.'

'You mean like in the music videos, the way she was always fleeing from them?'

He hesitates. 'Not really, but...' His expression changes – there's something almost sly in it. 'You know,' he says abruptly, 'I bet there's one of their music videos which you've never seen.'

Harriet catches her breath. 'You mean *Cold Ethel's Lover*? The one that was banned. The one that no one can get hold of.'

'I've got a copy.'

'I don't believe you. That's incredible. *Please* can I see it?'

Glyn looks at her. His expression is intent, his eyes crystal blue. 'Are you sure?'

'Of course I'm sure. Why wouldn't I be?'

*

He walks with her to the Alice in Wonderland tunnel. 'I'll get them to play it next,' he says. 'As soon as you're settled.'

It's a different experience approaching with him. Everyone knows who he is and because she's with him, she too is special. He crouches at the entrance, says something she fails to hear and the bodies shuffle apart to make space for her.

Like Moses splitting the Red Sea, she thinks, as he springs up and turns to her.

'There you go.'

Then, just before she kneels to crawl in, he places a hand against her arm – fingers warm through the fine mesh of her shirt, their imprint friendly against her skin.

'Iquis needs you,' he says.

She gazes dubiously into the clean blue eyes – at the faint traces of smile lines, currently unused. Then, before she finds a reply, he turns and eases his way back through the club. Briefly she considers following him and asking him what he means. But she's too consumed with what she's about to see.

She crawls through the tunnel and onto the freshly vacated patch of body-warmed mattress. The people either side of her are quiet and still. She feels their heat and inhales their perfume as she wriggles onto her back and gazes upwards at the domed ceiling. The sound vibrates up and through. The current music video is playing all around, so that she is engulfed by it. The feeling grows as she allows herself to relax into it, letting the movement and thick music hypnotise her, until there is nothing other than this heady buzz of anticipation.

TWELVE

The music – when it starts – doesn't sound like Dark Island. Growing out of the brief silence left by the previous music video, it has the hurdy-gurdy sound of fairground music, so that it takes her a while to recognise the tune as a wedding march.

The sky is overcast. The bride's heavy veil conceals her face. She stands, an isolated figure, in the foreground of a church. In the background tiny humps of stones look like scattered teeth, embedded in moss.

Is it Circe?

It must be. She's always the one in white. It would be good to be sure though. Harriet wants to know.

As if in answer to this wish, the bride lifts her hands up to the veil. But she doesn't remove it. Instead, she grinds her fists into her eyes. It looks like she's rubbing furiously at a flood of tears. Emotion snags at Harriet's throat.

Then she drops her hands, revealing two black tar pits where her fists have been.

Harriet starts to feel uneasy.

Snatches of what she has heard about the banned music video come back to her, *"depicting the act of necrophilia...*

inspired by the Alice Cooper song... obscene... designed to shock, to gain notoriety... tasteless..."

But that's not why I'm watching.

The cheerful music seems to mock. Where are the guests? Why is the bride so alone?

Harriet scans for some hint of movement, of people. She finds only a shadowy distorted image, positioned low down on one curving wall. The stillness, the way he is watching, disturbs her. *Like... like the dream figure, behind my back... in my nightmare. No – mustn't think about that.*

The scenery starts to move, and yet the figure stays located in the same place, hovering just above the moving ground. The motion is disorienting, a bit like travel sickness. Harriet turns her head and the ground spins faster, until she finds the bride and everything halts. The rush of movement, like the effect of a landslide, has achieved a rearrangement: the scene has changed.

Harriet focuses on the open grave first, and then on the bride standing right at its edge with a spade in her hand. There's mud on her dress, streaks of it on the edge of her veil.

Harriet's attention is sucked inexorably back to the gaping, rectangular hole.

The sick feeling strengthens. Inside Harriet's head there's a shifting sound, then that scrape of metal on stone. She can feel the spade in her hands, the blistering of her palms...

No. This can't be happening – I'm not asleep.

"Why have you woken me?"

Medea's harsh saxophone accusation makes Harriet's body jerk.

Not my fault! She wants to cry out in denial, but the bride's black mascara-stained eyes impale her with their lifeless stare and she is too afraid to speak.

> *"I was out with the stars*
> *cold, bright, distant*
> *nothing hurt"*

The bodies on either side of Harriet press towards her – hostile-shadowed strangers who trap her in place.

Flash of silver in the bride's hands...

> *"I took the knife*
> *spilt out*
> *the burning hope*
> *rejected life*
> *as it rejected me"*

... slashing at the cuffs of the dress.

And then the blood spurting, the knife falling from her shaking hands towards the open grave. Bright silver flashing, taking the light with it, taking her with it. The whole screen widening. The vast mouth of the grave yawning, reeling her in, sucking her down.

'No.' Trying to stop herself. Feet scrabbling on the surface.

But it's inevitable... she can't...

That familiar, all-consuming terror...

THIRTEEN

Outside Harriet inhales deeply, feels the cool night air soften the inside of her lungs, feels it spreading, the panic lessening.

I've made a fool of myself.

Embarrassed memories: fighting her way out of the vibe room, pushing through the club, white faces seeming hostile, everything closing in.

She feels the itch of sweat drying on her face. The night chill is more extreme after the heat of the building.

Then it hits her again.

The shifting sound... the watching figure... and then... falling...

That was my nightmare in there. Only it wasn't in my mind – it was played out in front of me. As if they knew what's inside my head.

Her breath snags.

No! I must have imagined it – overreacted. After all, that stuff about the bride slashing her wrists isn't in my nightmare. The other stuff – the stuff I recognised – can't possibly have happened... it would be supernatural, terrifying. I must have been hallucinating or something. Perhaps someone put something in my drink.

She does feel pretty weird: hot and cold, heart racing. And yet, she doesn't really feel like she's drugged. Everything looks pretty real out here... and that cold breeze, pulling up goosebumps on her arms... well, there's nothing strange about that.

I just can't think about this any more, she decides with fierce resolution. *It didn't really happen.*

It hits her then, as it had earlier, that she's on her own again; outside the party, separated from the others.

Why can't I be normal? she thinks, and wonders about going back inside. But she's still too shaky, so instead she walks round the building – taking in the turrets, the sheep-like hump of parked cars, the vast shadow of the house against the tufted ground. She drifts past the occasional groups of people, some smoking, some walking towards the cars.

When she reaches the front entrance again, she finds Lucien, Richard and Beth waiting for her. She approaches them slowly.

'Are you okay?' Beth asks.

They saw, then. How do I explain?

'I'm okay. It was just...' sudden rush of inspiration, '... the vibe room. It was too small. Crowding in on me.'

She hates admitting weakness, even fictitious weakness. But it's better than the truth.

They'd think she was mad.

'Claustrophobia.' Richard supplies the word, saves her the effort of pronouncing it.

She expels a breath, feels immediately safer.

'Where's Iquis?'

Richard shifts uncomfortably, glances at the others.

None of them looks at Harriet. 'Lucien pulls a face at Richard, takes over. 'She went, just before you did.'

'Went?'

Silence. They look awkward, guilty even.

'What did you do to her?' she finds herself asking.

'Nothing.' Lucien is indignant.

But there's something. The night is sullen with it. Something they're not saying. Lucien breaks the impasse, begins to speak.

'It was disturbing... She totally lost it. How much did you see?'

'I saw her dancing.' She hesitates. 'It looked a bit wild, but surely...?'

'You mean "typical Iquis"? Listen, Harriet, that was only the start. Okay, so she didn't fit in – disrupted the whole dance floor – so what's new? It was far more than that. There was this group close to us. Lovely people, we'd been kind of dancing with them before she turned up. Not really speaking, just... well, sometimes you don't need words to make friends.'

'I think it was the music,' Beth says. She sounds close to tears. 'They put on that Nick Cave song about the wild rose and the river, and him bashing her head in with a stone. Well, it's pretty sick really when you start to think about it... but the music's compelling. Before then, she'd been kind of predatory, banging up against people, invading their space.

'One of them in particular – he was kind of exquisite: willowy and fey, with these beautiful, flowing arm movements and hand gestures.

'I mean...' she grabs Richard's hand, 'not my type at all. But I could see why Iquis singled him out.'

'I still don't understand why what she did was so out of order,' Richard says. 'I mean worse than normal. Wasn't she just trying a bit too hard, the way she does with us?'

'You didn't really see,' Lucien says.

'I saw her pin him against the wall, looked like she was trying to get off with him. She's never been any good at subtlety.'

Harriet has a brief memory of Iquis in the kitchen at the start of term, that sudden dart forward, kissing Dad.

'No,' Lucien says, 'I think she was going to hurt him. I think she went a bit crazy, and that if Glyn hadn't appeared and pulled her off...'

'Don't be ridiculous,' Harriet says.

'He's not,' Beth says, with a catch in her voice. 'It was the words of the song, "*all beauty must die*", it was like I could hear her singing it. Like she was acting it out. Like she got so lost in the music that she couldn't remember who she was. It makes me wonder what we're doing, listening to that sort of stuff.'

'Beth,' says Richard, putting his arm over her shoulder, 'calm down. It was all just too intense in there. It's okay, you're okay, you have to stop feeling responsible for everything. You did nothing wrong.'

Her face crumples and she starts to sob. He pulls her into his arms, starts stroking her back.

Harriet looks in bewilderment to Lucien. 'I don't understand.' But she's thinking about the nightmare, wondering what the hell it is about this place.

'Look, Harriet, I don't know what I saw, all I know is that there was a violence in it that's hard to explain. Okay, maybe we all overreacted, we'll never know, but I'm not sure it matters. She keeps on doing things that are out of order. I've had enough.'

'Of what?' But she knows.

'Of her. Of Iquis.'

Harriet expects the others to argue, but Richard just nods, and Beth sobs harder but doesn't protest.

'It's this place,' Harriet says. 'Bad things happen here. I mean, I didn't tell you what happened to me. It will all seem different when we get away from here.'

'But it's not just tonight,' Lucien says. 'I liked it the way it was, the way we were before her. I've realised that in the last few nights. We're more comfortable, more relaxed.'

Their feet shift in the gravel, a sound of tiny stones scrunching.

'But you can't...'

'Not you,' he adds, reaching a hand out to Harriet. 'You're always welcome. Always one of us. You know that.'

She jerks away from his hand. 'It's not that simple.' She can't abandon Iquis.

'There are reasons,' she says, 'for the way she acts.' She pauses, struggling for words. *I had a brother who died*, she thinks. But of course Iquis wouldn't want her to say this.

'Finished discussing me, then?'

Iquis's voice makes her jump. She turns, to see her shadowed in the moonlight. 'How long have you been there?'

'Long enough.' Her voice is clipped, devoid of feeling, yet it makes Harriet ache. She doesn't know why. Just that she sounds so distant, so starved of contact.

There's an awkward hiatus. Beth shifts from foot to foot.

Harriet expects Iquis to turn away and storm off into the night, something dramatic like that, but instead she says, 'Come on, let's go back,' and her voice sounds old.

They drive back in silence, the car full of the cold night air, the pre-dawn chill.

FOURTEEN

'Failure kills!'

Dr Drake's glare has invaded Harriet's dream. It hangs there, as disembodied as the Cheshire cat's grin. 'People died because of you.'

Harriet twists restlessly, almost surfaces, but can't quite make it.

'I can still see you.'

'But I can't see you.'

'I'm still here.' Again that mad giggle. Then suddenly her face is in front of Harriet, distorted into caricature – the Queen of Hearts passing judgement.

'Off with her head!'

A line of students, like a well-trained army, move towards Harriet – but she can hear music. She chases the sound, knowing it's an escape route.

She rolls over and one flailing arm scoops up her alarm clock. But that's not the source. She half remembers switching it off, falling back asleep. And anyway the music's wrong.

It's her mobile, the new tune not yet familiar.

As usual it's abandoned on the floor. She crawls to the edge of the bed and picks it up, glancing at the display. It's

Dad's work number and, worried he will somehow know she ought to be in a lecture, she considers not answering. But he rarely phones from work. Something might be wrong. 'Hello, Dad. Is everything okay?'

There's a gap, like a hesitation, then his voice. 'Harriet. Yes, everything is fine. I just had a few moments free and thought I'd call you. Is now a good time? You're not on your way to a lecture?'

'Now is fine.' Stephen always said that the best way to lie was to keep it simple, not to fall into the trap of explaining too much. She pulls herself upright, taking care not to rustle the duvet, and tugs the curtain open. Outside it's raining.

It will be wet in the woods tonight, she thinks, with a familiar ache of loss. Because it no longer matters whether it is wet in the woods. She and Iquis haven't been back there since what happened at Decadance a week ago. They are going out of their way to avoid the other goths.

Harriet still doesn't understand what happened. The group had seemed so strong, had felt like a family. How could it all go wrong in one night?

If only she and Iquis could discuss it. But Harriet can find no way to broach either her own or Iquis's experience of that night.

Dad's taking a long time to respond. She wonders what he wants.

'So how's things?' he asks at last, in his carefully neutral work voice. 'What have you been doing?'

'Working,' she lies.

'That's good.' He sounds distracted, taking it for granted as usual, as if all these years of conscientious study have served only to make her invisible.

She's tempted to say, "I missed a lecture today", then, when he fails to get the point, to add with a laugh, "Deliberately, just to see if I could". But of course she doesn't.

'How's Mum?' she asks instead. 'Is she any better?'

And again there's that hesitation, long enough for her to feel uneasy.

'Things have been strange,' he says. There's an awkwardness in his voice which is not sufficiently explained by the office background.

Harriet feels a lurch of anxiety. 'What do you mean? Is she okay?'

'She's fine. It's just that she's...' He coughs. 'It's difficult to explain... It's small things...'

'Like what?'

'I keep finding windows open.'

Harriet has a sudden vision of the sky on her last day at home. Remembers Mum's reproachful glance at the window that Harriet had placed ajar. There had been a relentless nature to the sky that day. Empty of clouds, its high, motionless blue had seemed pitiless.

But what can she say? It's not as if they've ever acknowledged the problem. The shuttered windows. The locked doors. Mum's hand clenched round Dad's fist on those few occasions when she couldn't avoid going out.

'Last week,' Dad continues, 'when it was raining really hard, I caught her holding her arm out of the window. She had the sleeve of her dress rolled up, but the material was still drenched.'

'Oh.' This is weird. This is not something Mum would ever do. It's wild, unconstrained. It makes Harriet think of

Cathy Earnshaw, running out onto the moors and getting soaked after Heathcliff had gone. And no one could be less like Mum than the turbulent heroine of *Wuthering Heights*.

She lifts her hand and touches her hair, shocked again by its dry texture. She and Iquis had dyed it black the previous night, and she's not yet used to the change in how it feels, or to the shock of her appearance in the mirror.

I wouldn't have done that six weeks ago, she thinks, and wonders for a moment whether this new mother might understand her better? She feels a pulse of excitement, a kaleidoscope whir of things changing, spinning. But it's too fast. It reminds her of the spinning ground in the Dark Island video, which had happened just before things got out of hand.

'Is she okay?' she asks again. 'You don't think she's ill?'

'No,' he says. 'Not ill. But there's other things... Things out of place...' He sounds bewildered. She's used to him sounding strong, sure of himself, in charge. Her throat feels dry. 'The storage jars in the kitchen, you know how they're placed on that shelf in a particular order?'

'Yes,' Harriet says, 'the order's very important to her.'

'Well, she keeps getting them down and not putting them back. They're spreading all over the work counter, right up to where the kitchen door swings open.'

Harriet pictures the jars lined up like prisoners trying to escape, sees them edging closer and closer to the exit, sees Mum's fragile hand putting them there, placing them precisely, then shifting them, inch by inch, day by day, closer to the edge.

'She smashed a plate yesterday.'

It's as if Harriet's silence pushes him to drag out larger and larger things in an attempt to force a reaction

'Dad, everybody has accidents, even Mum.' She's trying to deny what he's saying.

'Deliberately.' The word hangs there. 'And when I asked her why, she shouted at me.'

'She shouted?' Harriet is stunned. 'She never shouts.'

'She did yesterday. She sounded really angry.'

'I don't believe you.' Harriet's mum is never angry, only ever soft like soap left too long in water.

'Suit yourself.'

That's better, he sounds more like himself. It gives her the opportunity to retreat. But something stops her.

'Would you like me to come home for the weekend?'

It's a spur of the moment offer which she immediately regrets, afraid of its implications, of risking the clash of her two worlds. And also of leaving Iquis when so much hangs in the balance.

This last week it's like we've both been wounded, like we're both a bit stunned, crawling out of the wreckage of Decadance, and I don't know where we're going. We're in a funny kind of limbo and I want to wait it out.

But I also want to be in Sheffield. I want to see the windows being flung open. That house has always been so closed up, and if Mum needs me, if there were a way to break through to her, to understand her...

No, it's too scary. I wouldn't know how to act.

'No, don't do that,' Dad says. 'You've got your lectures to think of and your coursework.'

Is she relieved? She doesn't know. She hears a man's voice, muffled, talking to Dad, hears Dad mumble a reply, then he's back talking to her. 'Harriet, listen, I've got to go. They need my input in a meeting with the customer. It's all fine,' he says, 'don't worry about it. I shouldn't have phoned you. I was just having a funny half hour.' As he's saying it, she can hear him shrugging on his business persona. 'You take care now,' he says, 'and let me know if you've got any case studies you want to discuss. You know I'm always happy to help.'

And then he's gone and Harriet, glancing at the time on her mobile, realises that if she rushes she'll make it to her structures lecture.

It's not guilt about missing the lecture that drives her into action – for missing lectures, the way she has for the last week, has become a positive act, a gesture of rebellion which she finds curiously satisfying.

No, what motivates her now is a need to give her mind over to analytical thought. Because that way she will be on familiar, unemotional ground. And that feels suddenly very necessary.

FIFTEEN

The corridor is filled with dust motes which float under the buzzing strip lights and brush against her face as she surges through them. The air is heady with some smell that makes her think of wide steps in sunshine, a smell that nags at her memory, but fails to connect.

She knows she ought to recognise the smell. It's distinctive, individual and unmistakable, yet it's so out of place here, so atypical of the usual student smells, that she can't unlock the correct memories.

She reaches the white painted wood of Iquis's door. Eager now, her knock sounds urgent in the temporary quiet of the corridor. Sometimes, when she has called for Iquis recently, there has been no reply.

Iquis opens the door and a thick wave of the buttery smell escapes and surrounds Harriet. The light of the corridor fails to penetrate the room. Instead, it settles on the pallor of Iquis's face.

'I went to some lectures,' Harriet says.

'Am I supposed to applaud?'

It's the answer she's been waiting for. She examines the disinterest in the other girl's face and feels comforted.

There's something odd about the darkness which surrounds Iquis. But Harriet can't quite capture what it is. She can see the curtains flapping at the window – and the campus lamps stretching out along the path she has just walked along – but the room itself has the essence of a black hole. No. That's not quite right. It's not empty – the way she imagines a black hole would be – it is perhaps more like standing at the entrance to a cave filled with hidden treasure; for there's a gleam of colour shot through the darkness, jewel-like glints of ruby and green.

'Why have you got the light switched off?'

However, even as she queries this, she begins to understand what's different.

It's the walls. *That's* what the light isn't reaching.

'Iquis?'

She eases a hand into the gap of the door, splays the pads of her fingers against the nearest section of wall.

A tacky texture, not yet dry.

'Fuck!'

The smell makes sense now that she has the evidence.

'Oil paint!'

Iquis switches on the light and Harriet registers her self-satisfied cat expression. Then, the enormity of what Iquis has done hits her. The walls and ceiling glisten, and almost drip, with the heady hues of oil paint. It's like being trapped in a painting.

Vast thunderous clouds, swollen with rain, roil across the ceiling's sky.

But the walls are where Iquis has really gone mad. It must have taken hours. Little curls of colour twist into each other with a decadent abandon, forming almost shapes, but escaping translation at the last minute.

Tiny vortexes, drawing Harriet towards them.

'So this is what you do when you're not with me,' Harriet says with relief.

'Amongst other things.'

Harriet stares hard at the dense tapestry – then does a double take – as she remembers where she is. For the very nature of this room has been changed. It no longer fits with what is outside the door. It's crazy, surreal. For some reason it makes Harriet think of Mum and the storage jars.

'Dad phoned,' she says, desperate suddenly to confide. 'He sounded different. Less sure.'

Suddenly, clearly, she sees the Dark Island house splitting apart and again she is Circe, running from the cracking, falling stones.

'What are you afraid of?' Iquis says.

Harriet is surprised that Iquis gets it so quickly.

'Of it all falling apart, falling out, like a nightmare. Maybe I won't be able to wake up. Maybe there won't be a way for me to go back.' It sounds stupid when she says it. Meaningless.

And yet, Iquis is nodding, as if she understands.

Reassured, Harriet continues.

'I never expected it to change. Them to change. He says he's worried about her, as if there's something wrong with her, something needing fixing. It sounded to me more like she was breaking out. I found myself thinking, how will he cope, how will we cope, if she does?'

She shakes her head again. It still doesn't make sense.

The smell of oil paint invades her – she's getting high with the fumes.

'I don't know why I'm so scared. But I don't want it to change. It can only work the way it was.

'She never changed when I was at home. It's as if by changing now she's announcing that I was what was wrong all these years. That I was what was holding her back. As if now that I'm not there...'

The sour taste of exclusion threatens to choke her.

'She has to change. You have to let her,' says Iquis.

'I thought you'd understand.' Harriet feels betrayed. 'I thought you were on my side. I thought you'd believe me, not them.'

'I do. I am.'

Iquis doesn't look at her. Instead she crosses the small distance to the far wall, her back square to Harriet. She scrapes the flat of her hand rapidly along its surface, smudging the paint.

As Iquis's hand moves, Harriet finally sees the pattern. Twinned pinpricks of red erupt through the black-green swirls to stare out at her like maddened eyes.

Watching me.

Surrounding me.

'You should be glad,' Iquis talks into the wall, 'that they can change. Without change there is no hope.'

Her words resonate and yet it's too much for Harriet to take in.

'Imagine what it's like to be stuck – stagnant – to be eternally locked into who you are, what you are,' Iquis continues. 'Unable to grow, unable to allow anyone else to grow. That's far worse than what you're afraid of. That's terrible. That's damned. You don't know what you're wishing for.'

But you don't know what I'm afraid of, Harriet thinks. She feels attacked and snatches at a change of subject.

'The cleaners will have a fit when they see this,' she says. She pictures the stridency of their response, as they travel the halls spreading a miasma of outrage from room to room.

'The cleaners never enter my room,' Iquis says sounding smug. 'I have an arrangement with them – a financial understanding if you like. I prefer to sleep undisturbed in the mornings.'

'You've bribed the cleaners!' Harriet's shocked. 'You can't do things like that.'

'Yes, I can. I did.'

'And they accepted?'

'After a certain amount of discussion. They'd probably prefer it if you kept quiet about it.'

'Sooner or later someone will discover that you've done this. They'll probably throw you out of halls.'

Would we survive that? Would Iquis even stay around if that happened? I don't want to lose her.

I don't know what this is between me and her – this sense of fate, this feeling that she holds the answer to something within me. But having come this far, I can't let it slip back into mystery. Not without an attempt to solve it.

'So what?' Iquis says. 'I can't stay in this room much longer anyway. I hate the closeness of it. The way I'm surrounded by other people. The way their breathing presses in on me. I'll go mad if I stay here much longer.' As she speaks, the detachment that she usually hides behind ripples, and once again Harriet glimpses the turmoil underneath.

Like last time, it makes Harriet uneasy and rather scared.

Dark currents, she thinks, and is relieved when Iquis, with a gesture of impatience says, 'Let's get out of here. I need to be by the river. None of this matters. The authorities have no power over me, and they only have it over you because you let them.'

Harriet wants to argue. But she also wants to get back to the safety of not speaking about anything significant. She's beginning to discover that her relationship with Iquis is easiest when they stride silently, side by side, through the night.

SIXTEEN

Three days later Harriet finds a padded envelope in her post slot. The size and shape of it are familiar – it's obviously a CD or DVD – but she hasn't ordered anything recently, and anyway there's no company logo on the envelope. A present then? She's intrigued. The handwriting is unfamiliar: big, rounded and rather boyish. The address itself is incomplete.

Harriet Johnson,
Student,
Eden University.

It's surprising it reached her. There's a delicious anticipation in peeling the flap up, sliding her hand in. She pulls the contents out slowly to prolong it. The disk is in a thin case without a sleeve. It has not been labelled, but comes with a note – a torn-off page from a reporter's notebook which has been folded once. The imprint of the same large scrawl presses through it.

She opens it, scans for the signature first.

Glyn

That's a surprise. She reads on, prey to a mixture of feelings.

Harriet,

It was good to meet you. I enjoyed talking with you, and hope that Decadance was all you believed it would be. I thought you might like a copy of "Cold Ethel's Lover" as a memento of your visit. Unless you object to pirating in which case my apologies. You are more moral than I and of course totally right. The artist deserves their tribute. However, in this case as it's no longer possible to buy it, I hope you'll forgo your principles and accept this gift. I'm rambling, aren't I? A bad habit. I'll draw to a close and who knows, maybe I'll see you and Iquis again sometime?

But if not, or until then, enjoy yourself...

Despite the sunlight blasting through the windows the night-time terrors are surfacing. Why did Glyn send it? Didn't he see her running out of Decadance? Surely he wouldn't want to inflict...

No. She's being ridiculous, letting her imagination run riot.

Even so – 'I don't want it!'

She shoves it back into the envelope and presses the flap down. There's a bin by the doors but that's not far enough away for her. She has to destroy it, take it out somewhere rocky and jump on it until it's just bits.

Then something stops her.

She can't outrun this. She shivers, doesn't know exactly what that means – just that this has to be faced one day. She can't get rid of the DVD. The sick feeling rises further up her throat.

What is she going to do?

With dragging steps she walks up the stairs and into her room. Yanking the window open, she stares out across the campus, then turns and looks at the room. She can feel the heat of the sun against her back. The room seems smaller than ever.

The wardrobe. She crosses to it, shoves the package behind it. A spider darts out, runs across her hand. She screams, and the package falls away from her and into the gap.

Harriet shakes her hand frantically until the spider falls off. She can still hear the soft thud the package had made. But it's out of sight and it can stay there.

Now, to get out.

She locks the door behind her, thinks, *Iquis*, and bypassing the stairs heads towards her room. Iquis won't be awake. But Harriet's seeking comfort, can still feel the tracks where the spider's feet have crossed her skin. She isn't normally scared of spiders, but it's the coincidence. It feels creepy.

Everything feels creepy.

*

Harriet rounds the corner and freezes. The two middle-aged cleaners who clean her floor every Friday are standing with another woman outside Iquis's door. The stranger has an air of authority, a large chain of keys and a badge that says *Supervisor.*

'We don't usually like to disturb her,' one of the cleaners says. 'She tends to sleep late.' She sounds nervous.

Shit! Harriet thinks. *Not this as well.*

'All the rooms have to be cleaned,' the supervisor pronounces. She raises her hand and knocks sharply on Iquis's door.

No response.

The supervisor hardly waits for one, she just selects a key and slides it into the lock.

'Stop!' Harriet cries, starting forwards. She can't let them see Iquis's artwork. 'You can't go in there.'

The woman turns and looks at her in amazement. 'Why ever not?' She takes a closer look at Harriet. 'Are you all right?'

'Yes. I'm fine.' The woman's perception jolts Harriet and she answers fiercely. The supervisor's face hardens and her fingers start to twist the key.

Hell! Harriet thinks. She has to shake off what's just happened and concentrate on keeping the secret of the painted room.

'It's the sky,' she says. 'The sky and the sun and the fear of going out. When it's really bad she has to control everything about her environment. Nothing can be out of place. You going in there would be an invasion. She's terribly bad at the moment. You have to leave her alone.'

'What do you mean?'

'My mother suffers from it. That's why I recognised it in her.' She's lying proficiently now, but at the same time she isn't lying at all. She's spilling out the things she's always known and never put into words.

'She's agoraphobic,' she says and stops to let the word speak for her, then hurries on. 'If you're worried about mess you shouldn't be. Her room is spotless. That's one of her control mechanisms. Her way of coping. Please leave her alone, leave me to deal with this. I've had the experience, you see. Years of it.'

She's shaking slightly; she's not over the thoughts of the spider and the DVD. She imagines the envelope already covered in cobwebs and crawling creatures and she wants to be sick. She knows that the others can see some of this – and she hates that – but it's having an effect.

The supervisor removes the key from the lock. 'There must be procedures for this,' she says, bouncing the keys in her hand for emphasis. 'Somebody ought to be doing something.'

'No. You mustn't interfere. You don't realise how fragile... You can't go pushing in... invading... You have to leave it with me.'

'But surely the college counsellor...? You shouldn't have to... you don't look strong enough... you're too young...'

They are regarding her as a human being for the first time.

The next time they clean my room they're going to see me, Harriet realises, and wonders if that will be worse.

'I've always been too young,' she says.

As she speaks they've been edging away from the door by common consent, their voices lowering.

'But didn't her family know? What were they doing sending her here in this state?'

'She was better than this when she first came here. They thought she'd be okay.'

'We can't just leave it,' the supervisor says. 'We won't do anything today, but I expect this to be sorted out before my next visit. The rooms *have* to be cleaned.' She looks at her watch then turns to the other cleaners. 'We'd better leave this floor for now. You can come back to it later after I've gone. There's just time to go through the storeroom issues.'

They start to move off, but then she turns back and looks at Harriet. There's a terrifying kindness in her eyes. 'It's not your job to solve this,' she says. 'You might think about talking to a counsellor yourself. About your mother, I mean.'

Harriet wants to lash out, but she forces herself to keep her face neutral, even to jerk her head slightly in what could be taken as a nod.

Then they are gone.

Harriet waits for a minute – staring rather blankly at Iquis's door – then, when she can no longer hear their voices in the distance, rushes down the stairs. She needs to get away from here and out into the open. She needs to run for mile after mile, until she is hot and sweaty and exhausted.

SEVENTEEN

Harriet is just starting her third mug of brandy and Coke when Iquis stalks into the kitchen. She makes a half-hearted attempt to straighten up, then decides she can't be bothered. She's in what she thinks of as *Iquis's corner* and the wall is providing most of her support. Iquis glances at Marcia and Jenna who are cooking, then wanders over to Harriet and studies her.

'You're drunk,' she concludes.

'No,' Harriet says, 'just numb. Just – comfortably numb.' As she drawls it out she hears the shearing roughness of the recent Scissor Sisters cover. Their music is hard to mimic so despite the mix of brandy, cooking heat and post-run exhaustion she's not quite detached enough to sing it out loud.

'You weren't in your room,' Iquis says.

'You weren't in yours earlier.'

'I know. But that's different.'

Harriet nearly laughs; what a typically Iquis thing to say. 'You're not the only one who can't stand these rooms.'

Iquis gives her a *watch what you say* look. By now Harriet is adept at reading them.

'Shall we go?'

Iquis hesitates. 'Wait a bit.'

'For what?'

'I don't know.' She glances at Marcia and Jenna. 'What are you up to?'

'Making party food,' Marcia says. 'There's a party in the town tomorrow night at one of the student-share houses.'

'I see.' Iquis moves to the table where Jenna is rolling out pastry and starts to draw a pattern in the scattered flour.

She's trying to be friendly, and yet – how hard she makes it look.

'Harriet's helping drink up the cooking brandy,' Jenna adds, directing a conspiratorial smile at Harriet. 'It's a tradition we have. I'd offer you some, but we've poured it all out now.'

'That's okay,' Iquis says. She pinches some of the flour between her fingers and lifts it from the table, before sprinkling it like snow. Some of it drifts over Jenna's rolling pin and onto the pastry.

Jenna brushes it off.

'Do you want to come?' Marcia asks. 'We mentioned it to Harriet earlier but she said you wouldn't be interested.'

Iquis dusts her hands together and steps back from the table. 'Could do,' she says.

'Wicked!' Marcia looks both surprised and triumphant. She pulls a pen out of the back pocket of her jeans and, turning over a receipt which has been lying on the counter amongst the other shopping, scribbles the address down.

'We made this one earlier,' Jenna abandons her pastry-rolling to proffer slices of an oven-warm tart, 'to enjoy tonight. We never get round to food at parties.'

Iquis wards off the plate. 'I'll share Harriet's,' she says. 'What is it?' Again that slightly awkward friendliness.

It's the right question, playing as it does to Jenna's obvious enthusiasm for cooking. 'It's our own invention,' she says, and Harriet can hear the pride in her voice. 'Beef, mushroom and brandy quiche, made with lashes of cream and egg. It's got a mustard and poppy-seed pastry base.'

Iquis hooks a piece of meat out of Harriet's slice with one long fingernail and sucks at it thoughtfully. She pulls a slight face, but only Harriet sees it.

'It takes forever to make, but it always goes really quickly,' Marcia adds. 'And Mark loves it.'

Harriet tenses at the mention of Mark's name, then takes another swig of the brandy and Coke and settles back into numbness. She just hasn't the energy to react to anything else today.

Marcia slides a glance at Iquis. Like Harriet, Marcia is on her third brandy and Coke. It might be this which encourages her to wink at Harriet and say, 'Iquis, there's a spare ticket going for Dark Island. Mark's Newcastle friend has had to pull out. If you've changed your mind and fancy joining the rest of us, it's not too late.'

Iquis stills, then shifts her gaze to stare hard at Harriet. 'Just exactly who do you mean by "*the rest of us*"?'

Harriet shifts uncomfortably. It's not that she was keeping it from Iquis, just that she hadn't wanted either of them to recall the events which had been triggered by the Dark Island concert.

'Well, Harriet of course, and me, Mark and Paul.'

'Right,' Iquis says.

There's a long silence. Iquis discards the piece of meat

she's been toying with on the edge of Harriet's plate. 'We should go. Come on, Harriet.'

Marcia looks crestfallen. 'Is that a "No"?'

'It is.' Iquis turns to sweep out of the kitchen, then hesitates. She glances back. 'Till tomorrow,' she says, and flaps the receipt at Marcia before departing.

She's learning, Harriet thinks, as she hides a smile at the bemused expression on Marcia's face.

*

Harriet catches up with Iquis downstairs, by the exit door. 'I saved you from the cleaners today,' she says, 'but they'll be back.' She's feeling aggressive now. There's no way she's going to apologise for the concert. She has every right to go. It's Iquis that's being unreasonable.

Well, if Iquis wants a fight she can have one, but Harriet is going to choose the ground.

However, Iquis doesn't react. 'I know. I heard.' She stops and studies Harriet under the door-lamp. 'That means you're complicit. Do you like that?'

Harriet feels a thrill, a buzz of adrenaline. It's such a sexy word. Complicit. She thinks of the painted walls – the frightening beauty of them. 'I don't know. Should I be?'

Iquis shrugs. They surge through the door. Outside the night air is rough and hints of rain. Harriet's momentary aggression has gone. They aren't going to fight about the concert. Good – she hadn't wanted to fight, not tonight.

'You told them I was agoraphobic!' Iquis starts to laugh. 'How did you come up with that?'

'It's not funny,' Harriet snaps.

'Few things are when you examine them closely,' Iquis retaliates.

Silence. Harriet broods for a while, but the brandy is warm in her blood and she's tired of being alone with her thoughts. 'My mother's agoraphobic,' she says. 'It started when Stephen died.'

Iquis keeps quiet. It's the right response. It gives Harriet room to manoeuvre.

'We've never admitted it,' she says at last. 'Just skirted around it as if it wasn't there. I don't know why – don't know why we couldn't discuss it – except that we never discuss anything.' She feels the usual sadness welling up and tries to push it away.

Iquis's shoulder is close to hers. They are moving in rhythm. It's comforting.

'I don't really want to talk about it.'

'Okay,' Iquis says equably.

For a long time they walk in silence. A splatter of raindrops falls across them, leaving a pattern of sensation on Harriet's skin. Under their feet the path is a churned mess of mud. The edge of her cloak will be soaking it up. Tomorrow, when she glimpses the crust of it during the day, it will remind her of her night-time life.

Gradually, the walking sinks her back into the comfortable zone of familiarity and habit.

Then Iquis breaks the silence. 'My mother never changes,' she says, startling Harriet with this unlooked-for confidence. 'She's never going to change. She just waits for me to come back. Sometimes I can feel her gaze on my back, boring into me. She will never let me go. She needs me too much. She wants to live through me.

'It makes me feel trapped.'

Harriet tenses, this too is a new direction, Iquis confiding. She has to respond carefully. 'But she let you come here.' Not quite a question. If Iquis doesn't want to answer it she doesn't have to.

But Iquis does answer. 'Yes, but only because she couldn't do it herself. She's living vicariously through me. I feel like she's still watching me. Sometimes I think that if I turned round quickly enough I'd catch her behind me, just ducking out of sight. In fact, sometimes I feel like they're all watching me. It's hard to believe that they've really let me go.'

That sounds rather paranoid, and also unfamiliar – not something Harriet can match with her own experience. She doesn't know how to respond. 'I see,' she says at last.

'No you don't.' Iquis laughs. 'But that's okay.

'Hey, feel the air,' she says, changing the subject. 'The storm's about to break. Shall we go to the boathouse and take shelter amongst the canoes? Or shall we just get wet?'

'The university boathouse,' Harriet votes. 'Otherwise I'll end up getting cold and we'll have to go in early again and I want to stay out as long as possible tonight. You still haven't told me how you came by a key for it,' she adds casually, hoping to take advantage of Iquis's confiding mood.

'I know,' Iquis says, and again she laughs. 'Come on,' she adds, 'let's run.'

They take off, flying through the night, and soon Harriet is hooked once more by the exhilaration of escape, as everyone and everything falls away, far, far behind them.

EIGHTEEN

It's after midnight when Harriet and Iquis – booted and cloaked and in full goth armour – arrive at the student house. The party has that intense, speeded-up sensation which comes from being well advanced. The lounge is full and people are spilling out into the corridor in a hectic barrage of shouting voices and swaying bodies.

Harriet can recognise nobody. 'Where do you think Marcia and Jenna are?' she yells at Iquis.

Iquis shrugs. She's standing watching the crowd, one shoulder hitched against the wall. Now that they have arrived she seems strangely purposeless.

Harriet, scanning unsuccessfully for the silver white drift of Marcia and Jenna's hair, becomes aware that she and Iquis are attracting sidelong glances which scuttle away each time her gaze reaches a face.

They are watching us the way they would a curiosity, she realises. Yet nobody approaches. Nobody meets their eyes.

We don't fit here. These are not night people. They're tourists from the day. Safe on their pleasure boat. Protected from the realities of it. Its senses and dangers. When we walk in carrying the reek of the night with us, lingering like woodsmoke on clothes and skin, they retreat from us.

'What are we doing here?' she asks Iquis. 'Surely these aren't our people?'

Iquis shrugs. She is still watching. Still waiting? The hint of a frown on her face, as if she too has expected something else.

It's this slight sign of uncertainty that causes Harriet to take control.

'Let's go through to the kitchen,' she shouts, 'open our wine and on the way see if we can find Marcia and Jenna.'

*

The kitchen is less crowded. A boy and girl sit and talk intently in one corner, their lips edging gradually closer as they speak. A noisier group of boys clusters against one counter, hands casually trawling at the remains of a plundered feast.

The sink is partially obscured by a girl. Glimpsing pale hair, Harriet thinks she's found Marcia. She draws closer. The girl's face is pressed into the jet of water which spills from the cold tap, her hands grasp the central stem of the tap and the trailing edges of her long sleeves are getting drenched. Her mouth is open, her face coated and distorted by the torrent. Caught in the current, her Marcia-length hair is dragged like waterweed round a rockery of discarded grimy cups and spent teabags.

Harriet has the same fastidious reaction to this as she has to the cigarette stubbed out in the bowl of whipped cream, which lies abandoned next to the sink.

'I forgot the corkscrew,' Iquis says to Harriet. 'See if you can find one.'

Her voice disturbs the girl at the sink, she pushes away from it and turns to cross the room.

Harriet does a double take. 'Hey, you're the girl from the missing poster. Aren't you? I'm so glad you've turned up. Where were you?'

The girl staggers to a halt and gazes blearily at Harriet. 'Not again,' she slurs. She's clearly very drunk. Her hair has been bleached since the poster and the eager look is gone. 'Do I know you?' she demands.

'No, but...' Harriet looks at Iquis expectantly.

The girl follows her gaze. 'Oh it's you. What do you want this time?'

'Nothing.' Iquis says. 'I only ever wanted to know you were all right.'

'Well, I'm fine. Okay? Just because my picture was up on campus, doesn't make me some kind of fucking celebrity.' She lurches out of the room, her hair dripping down her back, her sleeves leaving a trail of drips.

'Thank goodness she's okay,' Harriet says. 'Why didn't you tell me?'

'Timing. She turned up the night before we went to Decadance.'

'So what happened? What's the story?'

'It's a non-event. She went missing for a couple of weeks and her parents panicked.'

'That it?'

Iquis shrugs. 'It's a typical rebellion pattern. Convent school upbringing, overprotective parents. I wanted to case-study her for my course. But, as you can see, she wasn't agreeable.'

'That doesn't explain why you were so caught by the poster.'

'I guess I thought something worse had happened. That's all.' She turns, starts to rummage in a drawer. 'Are you going to help?'

'What sort of worse?'

Iquis throws Harriet an impatient look and shoves the drawer closed. 'Use your imagination.' She turns to the counter and starts to sweep food, wrappers and abandoned cups onto the floor.

'Creating chaos as usual, Iquis.'

It's Mark. There's something proprietary about the amusement with which he addresses Iquis. It short-circuits the last few weeks, during which Harriet hasn't seen him, and her fists clench.

'Indeed. Isn't that what fascinates you?' Iquis says.

'It's one of the many things that fascinate me about you, Iquis. I'll tell you the others one day.' He pulls a bulky penknife from the front pocket of his jeans. 'Here.' He holds his hand out for the bottle.

Iquis hesitates, then allows him to take it from her with an ironic smile.

What game is she playing?

'I thought you always carried a bottle opener with you.' Mark wedges a thumbnail beneath the tip of the penknife's corkscrew attachment and levers it up.

'Normally.'

Their familiarity is disturbing. They must have met again since that early encounter.

As Mark works the spiralling metal deep into the cork, Harriet studies him with a scowl. His hair is careless, even more unkempt. He retains summer in its lengthening sun-bleached curls, the still golden tan of his skin. But for how much longer? It can't last; even he will have to accept winter soon.

He's put on weight. The muscle definition remains, but there's a softness, a roundness to him which is new. It ought to lessen his appeal, but instead increases his physical presence. He looks well fed and contented like a spoilt cat.

'Let me have about me men who are thin,' she misquotes, sneaking the words out below the music. 'Mark Collier has a brash and fleshy look. I do not trust him.'

Her mutter draws his attention. His gaze traverses her face.

She wonders why he isn't ignoring her the way he usually does.

Perhaps he's waiting for me to thank him for the Dark Island ticket. Well, tough! He can wait all night. She remembers what Marcia had repeated. "He said he could cope with you for one evening as long as I kept you under control."

Patronising bastard!

Mark turns back to Iquis, hands her the bottle.

He watches her as she lifts it to her lips and drinks, head tilted back, throat moving as she gulps it down. There's a frisson of excitement in the air which Harriet hates. It announces too clearly their mutual fascination.

'Hey, Mark, mate!' One of the boys who had been grazing the party leftovers strolls over and drapes a casual arm over Mark's shoulder. 'Where's the decent beer hidden?' Surreptitiously, he flickers an interested eye over Iquis.

He's trailed by the other boys, who cluster noisily around them.

'If I told you, it wouldn't be secret any more,' Mark says, then grins and gestures to a cupboard. 'Chuck us one, will you?'

As he twists to catch the flung bottle, Harriet scans the slogan on the back of his T-shirt.

"If you're not living on the edge, you're taking up too much room."

An appropriate slogan for this party, she thinks, as the rapidly growing group presses her back against the counter. Funny how with Mark's presence the kitchen is starting to fill. He's like a magnet.

The boys proceed to talk about football with great enthusiasm. They appear to take no notice of the girls, yet Harriet senses that they're being performed for.

We're being assimilated. I'm not sure I want to be.

She looks at Iquis for a similar reaction, but Iquis seems to be content, enjoying the party forming around her. She's at the centre once more, the way she was with the goths.

But that was different. That meant more.

One of the boys, a flake of pastry still riding disconcertingly on one lip, speaks to Harriet. 'What's your name?' He's eyeing her hungrily. Taking in the dark flow of her clothes, the kohled stare of her eyes, the stark black of her hair.

Harriet doesn't fancy being a snack for a friend of Mark's.

Besides, it's more important to listen to Mark and Iquis talking. Harriet can't hear everything that they're saying. But what she does hear disturbs her.

'Decided yet?' Mark to Iquis.

'Nothing to decide.'

They're circling each other like duellists.

'You haven't changed your mind?'

'I don't change my mind,' Iquis says. 'You'll have to change yours.'

What does she mean? Harriet dislikes the shorthand feel of this conversation. She tugs at Iquis's sleeve.

'Let's go to the river. It'll be really turbulent after last night's storm.'

Iquis hesitates. Harriet notices Mark's eyes on her face again. She glares at him, and sees his eyes tighten in thought.

'You hate me, don't you?' he asks.

'Yes.'

'I thought so.'

She doesn't know why her answer pleases him, but senses that it does. There's a calculating look on his face. Then he grins and tosses his penknife into the air, with the deliberate ease of one who has finally decided on a move. 'Later,' he says to Iquis.

He slides the knife into his pocket and departs.

Left behind, the party deflates, its centre gone. The small group of strangers eye each other uncomfortably. The boy with the pastry flake raises a hand to his lips and dislodges it. He casts an uncertain glance at Harriet.

'Wanker,' Harriet murmurs to Iquis for the comfort of it, gesturing to the open door through which Mark has departed.

Iquis eyes her wordlessly, then drains the bottle of wine in one long swallow.

'Come on,' she says.

'Where?'

'The river. Isn't that what you wanted?'

'It certainly was.' Though she can't help feeling confused.

Why is Iquis ready to leave now? They haven't seen Jenna and Marcia and they've only been here a short time. Is she bored?

Or has she already got what she wanted?

NINETEEN

'Given the coefficient of expansion for concrete, what's the rebar measure for a singly-reinforced beam?' Dr Drake's gaze sweeps the front bench like a searchlight. As Dr Drake pauses to consider Iquis's outré appearance once more, Harriet resists the urge to run. Then, those steel blue eyes are on her.

'Harriet?'

Fuck!

She was supposed to have done the calculations as coursework. They should be resting in Dr Drake's pigeonhole along with everyone else's, but they aren't. She senses Iquis shifting to watch her and is momentarily distracted by the sheer absurdity of her presence. *Why the hell did I agree to let her come?*

'Well?' Hard to ignore the sarcasm in Dr Drake's voice.

She already knows I haven't done it. Otherwise she'd have picked on someone else.

'The steel bars should have... 10 millimetre diameters,' – it's a wild guess – 'and 300 millimetre centres.'

'10 ml diameter, 300 ml centres.' Dr Drake's gaze pinions her, making it impossible to look away.

'Yes.' Harriet swallows uncomfortably.

Dr Drake turns to the board and obliterates the row of circles (representing the steel bars) which occupy the centre of the pictured beam. She writes down Harriet's measurements, then draws a new line of smaller, further apart circles within the beam.

She pauses, one eyebrow raised, as if waiting for a reaction. Then, with swift pen strokes, she adds jagged black cracks in between the circles.

'With such timing she should be a comedian.' Iquis's comment is too loud. Dr Drake's eyes narrow as they halt on her for a second.

Turning to the class Dr Drake holds her pen out level in front of her and rests its ends on the opposing forefingers of her two hands. She pushes down with her thumbs on its centre until it comes to resemble the concave vaulting horse currently pictured on the board.

'Too far apart for that diameter of bar.'

Slowly, as she applies more pressure, the plastic casing of the pen starts to split squirting ink out onto her hands. The class watch in silence as the pen snaps.

Dr Drake eyes the broken pieces thoughtfully, then raises her voice.

'Anyone tell me how to put this back together again?'

It's clearly impossible. Harriet, familiar with Dr Drake's dramatics, is well aware that this is her point. Mistakes can't be undone.

Suddenly, Iquis stands up and eases herself past where Harriet is sitting. She walks across to the shelf of supplies on the far side of the board.

'Here.' She picks up a pen and tosses it to Dr Drake

– who retrieves it from the air with a displeased snatch.

Iquis smiles at her. 'It might look more interesting with a bit of red in it anyway,' she says, as she returns to her seat.

There is a collective holding of breath as Dr Drake stares hard at Iquis, who gazes back calmly.

Finally Dr Drake breaks her stare.

'Of course pens are easy to replace,' she says, 'and nobody gets hurt.' She looks at Iquis once more.

'We seem to have acquired a stray.' She scans Iquis, taking in the heavy make-up, the orange tinted glasses, the mesh clothing edged with black fur. 'A visitor from some – *arts course* – no doubt. Come to see what life is like on the other side.'

She pauses, waiting for confirmation, but Iquis is silent watching her appreciatively.

'Well, let me tell you about it. It's hard. We don't pretty things up with red pens here. Things aren't,' – pause – 'open to interpretation.

'Here it's about right answers and wrong answers.

'And there's no room for wrong answers.' Her gaze returns to Harriet.

'Why does it matter so much to you?' Iquis asks quietly.

Harriet exhales, aware of a giddying mix of fear and excitement. Where is this going to end?

'Why does it matter?' Dr Drake repeats, turning to her students. 'Somebody enlighten her.'

'Because failure kills.' Several voices volunteer the answer.

'Exactly. Failure kills. Now if you shut up you might learn something.'

'Is that a guarantee?' Iquis doesn't say it sarcastically, but with the analytical air of someone who wants to know whether it's worth her effort.

'No. I don't make promises. Only you are capable of making sure that you learn. All I can do is provide the opportunity. It's your choice what you take from it.' And again her gaze sweeps the lecture room, to make sure that it's sunk in. Another learning point.

To Harriet's surprise, Iquis grins at Dr Drake.

'Okay. I'll give it a go,' she says, and leans back in her chair, ready to be educated.

*

'Dr Drake ought to get a life,' Iquis comments afterwards.

'You can't say that!' Harriet is startled into laughter.

'Yes I can. What's so important about bricks and metal that she wants to dedicate her entire life to it?'

'She's intent on making sure that nothing goes wrong,' Harriet explains. 'She's trying to save lives.'

'So she's living her whole life looking over her shoulder expecting disasters. What a waste. What's the point?'

'But surely it's vital. What could be more important?'

'Living. She's obsessed. It's sad. She's throwing her life away.'

'You don't know that.'

'I can guess. You think she has all the answers, don't you?'

'No I don't.'

'Yes you do.' Iquis leans back, under the shelter of one of the trees, with a cocky grin. Something about the confrontation in the late afternoon lecture seems to have pleased her. So much so that, for the first time since the break-up with the goths, they have returned to the woods.

'I don't know why you wanted to attend anyway,' Harriet says.

'Just a whim,' Iquis shrugs. 'It was something different to do. Besides, I was curious. You talk about her a lot.'

'No I don't.'

Iquis laughs.

'Oh shut up.' Harriet is wrongfooted, but trying not to show it. Until now she's kept the two halves of her life separate. Allowing Iquis and Dr Drake to meet has brought disruptive thoughts to the surface. And having Iquis question Dr Drake's motivation is disquieting.

I told myself I was having a small rebellion by missing the odd lecture and the occasional assignment. I was tired of being the good girl all the time – of it being taken for granted – but I fully intended to get back on track just as soon as somebody noticed. I never fundamentally questioned whether the goal was worth having.

She changes the subject.

'It's getting cold. How much longer will we be able to spend our nights outside?'

Until now, they have ignored the falling temperatures, refusing to acknowledge the hastening of the year – the departure of autumn. But here in the woods the cold seems concentrated – embedded deep in the ground and lurking in tight pockets between the stark, all-but-naked trees.

'Did I ever tell you about the first time I came here?' Harriet says, reminded for some reason of that initial, panicked visit.

'No.'

'I felt like someone was watching me.'

'What?'

'The first time I came here. I thought I heard, sensed, someone in the woods watching me.'

Iquis turns her head and searches between the trees. A slow scan.

When she doesn't turn back to Harriet, Harriet finds herself tensing. There's something in her shoulders, something about the way she's staring into nothing.

'What is it?' Her eyes seek out the pale glimmer of Iquis's face, absorb its stillness, its stiffness.

Iquis continues to study the gaps between the trees.

Harriet lies back and gazes up towards the stars – which scatter between the skeletal fingers of the trees – and waits for Iquis to speak.

The announcement when it comes is abrupt. 'I'm leaving Genesis,' Iquis says. 'Moving out to the edge of the town.'

Harriet sits up. 'Because of the cleaners?'

'Hardly!'

'Then why?'

'Mark Collier's dad bought him a house there as an investment.'

Which doesn't answer the question.

'It's got a basement room which is totally separate, has its own key and everything. He's offered it to me. He says I can paint it. He says I can do whatever I want. He says you can come too.'

Iquis still isn't looking at Harriet.

'Come with me.'

'You have to be joking!' But Iquis is too tense for this to be a joke. 'You better be joking.'

Iquis shakes her head.

It's taking time for the outrage to surface because Harriet's so stunned. But it's coming.

'You're a fake,' she says. 'You're just like the rest. Like Marcia and Loli and all the other pathetic girls who hang around him.'

'Am I?'

'I should have realised at that stupid party last week. Those dumb boys. The way you acted around Mark and them. I thought you were so different and all the time you were just looking for a chance to fit in.'

I'm going to lose you, she thinks, and it sears.

'How could you do this to me? You know I can't stand him.'

'You can't hate him that much. You're going to the concert with him.'

'*That's* what this is about!' Harriet exclaims, aware of relief. 'To punish me for arranging to go to the concert and not telling you. Don't you think that's a bit petty?'

'It's not about the concert,' Iquis says slowly. 'It's just that there's so much I need to know, so much I need to do. I have so little time, Harriet, I have to cram it in. And Mark, I don't know, there's something... I have to explore it.'

Worse and worse.

'Then you don't need me.'

Iquis opens her mouth to say something, but Harriet gets in first.

'I could have stayed with the others, with Lucien and Beth and Richard. They didn't turn away from me, just you. But I couldn't do that to you. I couldn't let you be that alone, that rejected.'

She stops, wanting to see the response to her words in Iquis's face. But she can't see it – can only imagine the pain that she is trying to cause – but this is enough. She doesn't want to destroy Iquis. 'Don't I mean anything to you?'

'Of course you do.' Iquis's response is immediate, fervent. 'I need you, Harriet. I need you more than you will ever know. I told Mark I wouldn't come without you and I meant it. It's just a different direction, Harriet. It's still about us.'

At any other time these words would have moved her, stunned her even. But now, they just slow her down a little.

'It's impossible anyway. Mark doesn't want me. We'd fight the whole time. Or worse – he'd just ignore me – and I'd be tagging along behind the two of you. I can't do it.'

'I told you. It's a deal. He can't have me without you. That's what we were discussing at the party.'

Her words add fuel to a simmering fire. 'When you said he would have to change his mind, because you wouldn't?'

'That's right. You see, I was thinking about you.'

'No you weren't.' Harriet jumps up. 'Not by discussing me in front of him. Like I was your *toy*. How could you? I'm *not* your puppet.'

She storms off, but is so angry that she blunders straight into a tree. The pain makes her turn round. Iquis is still sitting there. She looks puzzled. As if she doesn't understand why what she's done has annoyed Harriet so much.

'You can't treat people like that,' Harriet yells in exasperation. 'You can't treat me like that. Not and call me your friend.'

Then – not waiting for a response – she turns and runs, head down through the trees.

TWENTY

'Open the coffin.' Harriet leans forwards.

'The lid creaks slowly open to reveal the brittle white bones of a long dead skeleton,' the gamesmaster (Andrew, from civil engineering) intones. 'A shrivelled shank of steel wool hair curls into itself, a mummified reminder of what once might have been beautiful.'

'Anything else?' Simon asks. In the crowded confines of Andrew's room, his knee is pressed against Harriet's.

'On the pillow beside the skull lies a red rose.'

'I pick it up to examine it further,' Harriet says.

'Its heady perfume greets you. You notice a drop of dew nestled in the folds of the petals. The leaves of the rose are cool and fresh against your finger. Before you have time to replace it a sudden draft blows out your candle and a disembodied voice gusts against your face. "I don't think you should have done that," it says.

'Then the laughter starts.'

*

Unfortunately, the game of Call of Cthulhu can't go on forever. Walking back to halls at three in the morning, Harriet has run out of distractions. She feels wretched. It's forty-eight hours since the scene in the woods, and she hasn't seen Iquis since. Indeed, has deliberately been unavailable, staying away from her room until as late as possible. Avoiding Iquis, as much because she doesn't know what to say, as because she's too angry to say anything.

In the meantime, the arguments keep going round in her head.

Of course, at some level, betrayal by friends when boys come on the scene is normal. She's seen it happen enough times. But Iquis has always been so different that Harriet had never anticipated such behaviour.

What she can't work out is whether there is any future with Iquis now that this has happened. The thought of Mark's house is just as raw, just as impossible, as it had been two nights ago.

She has no answers. Just a seething mass of contradictory arguments.

She is almost at Genesis when Iquis steps out from the willow tree and onto the path in front of her.

It's an abrupt move, making her jump. She is aware of a startled relief.

'Were you waiting for me?'

'Yes.'

That's something. 'Do you still plan to go to Mark's house?'

Iquis tightens her lips and nods.

'Right.'

There's a long silence – a stand-off. It gets increasingly awkward as they look at each other, look away, look back. In the end they fall into step, a wordless compromise. They head past Genesis, towards the edge of the campus.

'I've had a great night,' Harriet says. 'Been playing Call of Cthulhu. You know it?'

No response.

'It's a horror-based role-play game. I used to play it back at home; but it's a whole different level here. The group I was with are amazing – and Andrew, the gamesmaster, well he came up with some truly terrifying scenarios. We've been killing vampires. Hordes of them. There was a point in the graveyard where there seemed to be one behind every gravestone.

'Honestly, Iquis, it was so real I forgot where I was. And the adrenaline rush...'

She's getting very little response from Iquis. Doesn't really expect one. Even so, she keeps talking. It's something to say, and it demonstrates to Iquis that she can do very well without her, if she has to.

'... round about two o'clock we limped into a safe house, covered in blood and injuries. We were so low on sanity points that we couldn't afford to fight any more. The head of the vampire clan was outside, on his own – we'd killed his family – and we just needed to sit it out, wait for daylight.

'Anyway, Simon – who's a loose cannon – was exchanging insults with the vampire for the hell of it. He was standing on the bed by this stage, swaying from all the beer he'd been drinking, and his eyes were glittering with excitement. It was intoxicating. I was tempted to join in, but it would have been crazy.

'"Your father robs graves for a living – I should know." The head vampire was really getting into it. "Your mother suckles werewolves!"

'Then Simon blew it. "You come in here and say that!" he yelled, bouncing on the bed.

'And of course... you know that thing about inviting vampires in – that they can't come in unless they're invited, but once they are...

'All hell let loose. We only survived because the head vampire headed straight for Simon. Ignored the rest of us. We left him to his fate. But later we had to kill him because he'd been turned. I didn't like that, Iquis... We drove a stake through his heart and all the time he was pleading with us, pretending he was still our friend. I still felt like he was our friend. But it had to be done.'

She hesitates. Retelling it, she's got caught up in it again. But now, looking at Iquis, she sobers. She wonders whether she isn't coming across as a bit sad. Getting this excited about a game.

This is what has always worried her about role-playing. That it isn't real life, even though while she's playing she often feels it is. That the sense of accomplishment she feels always slides away from her afterwards.

Besides her, Iquis is unreachable. A silent figure striding purposefully, her face set towards the way they are going.

'Where are you leading us?' Harriet asks, suddenly needing reassurance.

No answer.

The road they are on is unfamiliar to Harriet. Yet Iquis walks it with such certainty that Harriet is convinced she knows exactly where she's going. They reach a path leading upwards past a small, shuttered building. Pale grey shapes loom at them from behind black spiked fencing. Iquis presses forward towards the spikes, runs her hand along them.

'Here.'

Harriet joins her. Iquis has found a gap in the wrought-iron fence where three of the spikes have broken away leaving little stubby iron feet embedded in the concrete base. At the top of the fence the broken spikes still thrust upwards, held in place by the iron crossbar. The gap in the middle is small. They would have to crawl through, if...

'In there?' Harriet is shocked. The shapes have gathered form. Most have rounded tops. There are some which have sharper shapes, angles, peaks. The odd tree crests them, shadows them with even darker night. 'You want us to go in there? Into the graveyard?'

'Why not?' Iquis asks. 'It's what you've been doing all night, isn't it?'

'So maybe I deserve a break.' Harriet doesn't want to go in. But doesn't want to admit the contradiction, that though she'll rampage through them in games, in reality she hates them.

'I thought you wanted scary,' Iquis says.

'Did I?'

Iquis grips her arm briefly. 'You shouldn't get all your kicks from board games. You should get out, make it real, make it believable.'

'It's not a board game.'

Harriet is trapped. After all her talk there's no way out.

TWENTY-ONE

Inside the graveyard the night is dense and dangerous. The gravestones seem to stretch out forever. As Iquis leads her deeper, Harriet concentrates on keeping to the indistinct path, terrified of stepping off it onto one of the swollen mounds.

Iquis stops at an oblong tomb. There's a life-size sculpture reclining on it, a girl with blank eyelids and hip-length hair. She's been cracked and eroded by time, her nose is eaten away and one arm is broken.

'Meet Lucy Westenra,' Iquis says, reaching down to grasp the figure's hand. 'Here's where she rose from – until they destroyed her.'

'I know the story,' Harriet says. 'I've read *Dracula*.'

Iquis ignores this. 'Her friends cut her head off,' she continues, 'stuffed her mouth with garlic and thrust a stake through her heart. They'd given their own blood to her, yet in the end they killed her. Just like *you* killed Simon.

'Here,' she takes Harriet's hand and lays it on the cold body, presses it to the rigid chest. 'This is where her heart was.'

Harriet is silent. Despite herself, Iquis's words and the cold touch of the stone are drawing her in.

'That's a hell of a lot to go through in exchange for a soul.'

Harriet nods.

'But I forgot.' Tugging Harriet with her, she moves rapidly through the stones. 'You'd rather have risen vampires, for the thrill of killing them.'

She stops at a large stone which leans out over a hollow. The dark shadows it, making it look like a raised tombstone. She releases Harriet's arm, pushes her forwards. 'This one's walking.' Her voice is a soft whisper.

'You can wait here to ambush her on her return.'

Harriet stretches her arm out to touch the stone. Despite its weight it shifts under her hand with a creak. Startled, she jerks both hands onto it, leans her body to steady it. Then, realising how much momentum it would take to actually make it fall, she laughs and turns towards Iquis.

But she's disappeared.

'Not funny,' Harriet calls. 'Get back here.'

The night eats her words. The cold stone seeps the warmth from her fingers. It shifts again, a shudder which reflects her panic. Because now, the idea that the stone has been levered from the ground by hands far stronger than hers is all too believable.

'Iquis!'

In the silence her voice is too loud. It seems to draw the night creatures towards her. There's stealthy rustling, a soft pad of what could be footsteps. Surely those noises weren't there a minute ago?

The soft brush of air on her cheeks is like a ghost's fingers.

What if there is something here? What if Iquis has left me alone with whatever is out there?

She starts to back away, trips over a gravestone and falls.

She thumps down onto her back, and freezes. Something just moved to her right.

Was it that tree bent by the wind? Yet the movement had seemed swift, rapid, like... Isn't that a figure in the branches? A white face with black eyes, the shape too small to be Iquis.

Lucy?

The eeriness of that first night in the woods when she'd heard laughter is back.

'Iquis!' she yells, panicked.

There's a rushing sensation – the wind? Something white swoops towards her. She screams.

Then Iquis is next to her. A powerful silhouette. 'Get out of here!' she roars. Anger and defiance burning out of her.

And whatever it is, was, it's gone.

And even though Harriet's half-convinced she imagined the whole thing, something has changed.

Iquis can save me.

The thought is in her mind and it can't be shaken now.

They walk uphill together until they reach a bench with a view right across the graveyard.

They sit and Iquis lights the ancient oil lamp which she sometimes carries with her at night. It sparks and smokes, then settles into a steady flame; the scent of hot oil suffuses the air.

The blood slows in Harriet's veins. She watches as Iquis uncorks the bottle of red wine.

'Why did you disappear on me?' she says.

'I was angry.'

'*You* were angry?'

Iquis doesn't answer immediately. Instead she takes a long swallow of wine, then presses the neck of the bottle into Harriet's hand. 'Why shouldn't I try to be normal? Why is that so wrong? You make a religion of me being different. But I'm not a god. I don't want to be a god.'

Harriet tilts the bottle until the wine flows thick and fast down her throat.

'I never said you were.'

Both girls are silent, looking out over the graveyard. The view is spectacular. The flatness in the foreground is broken by the peaks and domes of gravestones; the mountains in the distance are a jagged silhouette against which the sky shifts hues from indigo to dense black.

'I often come here,' Iquis says after a while.

'With Mark?'

'On my own. I wouldn't bring *him*.'

Harriet smiles into the darkness.

'Don't you get scared?'

'No. I like it here. It's got a good atmosphere.'

'My brother's buried,' Harriet finds herself saying. 'Traditionally Johnsons get cremated but Mum couldn't bear that for Stephen. So he's in the vast city-centre cemetery with a three-lane road outside. She and Dad visit him every week. She carries a trowel for the weeds. Keeps it so tidy, that I can't imagine him there.

'It wouldn't be so bad if he were buried here. It's wilder, more alive. It's like the gravestones have just grown up out of the ground.'

She recalls the shift of the leaning stone under her hand.

'I think the dead do walk in a way,' she says, 'draining the life out of the living.'

Radical words. If Mum heard she'd be terribly hurt, if Dad heard he'd be furious.

Iquis's lack of reaction is reassuring. Harriet doesn't actually want a response. This is safer, like burying things in a secret location where they will stay hidden.

It frees her. There's something she's needed to confide for years, yet never dared. Won't dare now if she hesitates. She starts in the middle, knows Iquis will catch up.

'Can you dream noise?'

'I don't know.'

'I don't think you're meant to, but I do. The scrape of metal on stone, the shift of falling soil, the blood beating in my head.'

Iquis turns. '*I have these dreams, nightmares really...*' she quotes Harriet's blurted confidence – given weeks ago, when they hardly knew each other.

'It always starts with me digging,' Harriet says. 'I don't want to dig. I know something bad will happen if I do. But someone's making me. Someone with absolute control over me. They stand behind me and if I turn round I'll recognise them, but they won't let me turn round.'

She grasps a breath.

'I'm digging gingerly, terrified of what's underneath. *They* get impatient and force me to dig harder and faster. The handle of the spade grows slippery with my sweat. My hands slide and burn. The soil flies up into my face. It smells of decay.'

She's talking faster, there's no time to breathe in between the words.

'There's a massive hole. It tries to suck me down. I'm fighting it. But *they* step forward and shove me. The ground tears away and I fall. I feel their fingers denting my back, riding me down. In the last moment before I hit the bottom I realise what I'm going to find and it's so terrible that I know I won't survive it.

'Then I wake up and I can't remember what I was going to find. And that's the worst thing. Because I *need* to know.'

She's out of breath. She gasps like she's been running. Dimly aware of Iquis placing a hand on her heaving shoulder and squeezing.

As soon as she can, Harriet reaches for the bottle and swigs. Her throat is raw and the wine burns against it. Having started, she wants to keep talking. Wants to tell Iquis what happened at Decadance when Glyn showed her the video. Wants to tell her about him posting it to her afterwards, about there being no escape.

If I told her, she might make it safe. Maybe we could watch it together and at least I'd know whether I was hallucinating, or whether I was mad.

But I can't tell her. I'd have to admit that I've hidden things from her. Hidden the fact that Glyn and I communicated far more than she wanted us to. Everything's so precarious between us at the moment, the whole Mark thing unresolved. I can't risk losing what trust she has in me; it's taken too long to build it.

'I haven't had the dream for weeks,' she says. 'At least that's something.'

They sit in silence, their eyes on the distant horizon. Time passes.

*

'My father killed him,' Iquis says. Her hands are round the wine bottle, squeezing so tight that it could almost break.

'Your brother?'

Iquis nods. 'If he hadn't killed him it would all have been different. It was a – how do you say – "cataclysmic act".' She puts quotes around it.

She sounds calm, detached. Only her hands give her away.

Difficult to know what to say.

'How?'

'An accident.'

'Oh,' Harriet breathes with relief. She had thought for a moment...

'Yes. The window was open. The ledge was too low. My father hit him and he went backwards through the window. Smashed into the ground twenty feet below.'

'Your father hit him!'

'Yes. I told you, he killed him.'

'But not deliberately.'

Iquis shrugs. Her face is hard.

'The poor man. How does he live with himself?' Harriet says. 'How tortured he must be.'

'Don't waste your empathy on *him*.'

'But he must feel terrible.'

'Why? He was a tyrant. The only thing he minds is that he didn't control it.'

'You sound like you hate him.'

'I wasn't even born then.'

'Weren't you?'

'No.'

'But you tell it like you experienced it.'

'The others talk. They have to because that's when it all changed. If it hadn't happened everything would have been different.' She drops the bottle on the ground, doesn't seem to notice as the wine spills over her foot. 'I would have been different.'

Then, before there's time to respond, she demands urgently, 'Come to Mark's house.'

'All right.' Harriet concedes. None of her feelings about Mark has changed, but there's a desperation in Iquis that she can't ignore. No matter what the consequences, she's going with her.

*

It's only later that she gets round to wondering what had happened to Iquis's father. Whether he was tried and convicted, punished. She is filled with a curiously strong empathy for this stranger. Iquis was so certain that he didn't feel his crime. But Harriet's convinced that she's wrong; that the self-hatred and suffering is so deep that he can't let his family see, because he can't allow himself to ask for forgiveness.

She wonders, when – or if – Iquis will tell her more.

Perhaps that's how I can help her, and him – bring them back together again. Maybe they need an interpreter. Maybe that's what this is all about. Maybe that's what we've been brought here together to achieve.

Forgiveness.

Redemption.

TWENTY-TWO

Apart from the constant mess in the kitchen, Mark's house has proved surprisingly atypical of student life. It's luxurious and comfortable with deep carpets and grown-up fittings. No wonder parties happen here so often. It's a fabulous den for his friends to settle in after the pub or the uni bar, and in many ways she and Iquis have been effortlessly absorbed.

Harriet, however, is still intent on being the grit in the oyster.

Because we're getting soft. That's what living here is like. Horribly easy and horribly seductive. And I don't like it at all.

In pursuit of Harriet's aim – to be the annoyance, the grit – she's in Mark's shower. He's due back from a hockey match and will expect the shower to be free, ready for his use. He's territorial about these things, which makes it easy to get a rise out of him.

Iquis, in her basement room, has no part in the skirmishes which have occurred frequently between Mark and Harriet in the last three weeks.

The shower has jets which come from all angles, creating a pounding, pleasurable experience which Harriet can't help but revel in, even as she chalks it up as further evidence of Mark's spoilt, rich-kid lifestyle.

Immersed in the protective pod she only gradually becomes aware of the hammering on the door.

'Get out of my fucking bathroom!' he bellows.

Despite provoking this, she's still startled. Mark's CK One shower gel slips from her hand and splashes into the eddy of water surrounding the plug hole.

She wonders if the scent has crept out onto the landing.

So what if it has! He's been hijacking her toothpaste for the last fortnight. She keeps finding it abandoned with its top missing and a thick line of paste oozing out.

She halts the shower, opens the pod, hurls a response.

'What's the urgency? Desperate to admire yourself again?'

Despite her verbal sparring, she steps onto the floor mat, snatches up her towel and wraps it around herself. Enough is enough. Despite its fancy nature, the bathroom lock is less than secure. And on this floor, away from Iquis and the inevitable visitors, her defiance is uneasy.

She scores better in the evenings. Mark cares how he looks in front of his friends, and this gives her an unexpected advantage. He's not as invulnerable as she'd once thought. She can score points and sometimes even win full-on confrontations.

It helps. It's not as bad being here as she'd expected, although there's a constant tension in watching Iquis and Mark circle each other and anticipating them getting together. Yet it never quite happens and sometimes Harriet doubts if it ever will.

Their abrupt, rather aggressive flirtation has quite an audience, and it's unpredictable. There's the evening Iquis claimed she could cut hair, then pretty much scalped Mark in the lounge while everyone watched. Mark had wanted to dispense with the audience, but Iquis refuses to be alone with him. And it's this that causes every night to be a party.

When Mark gets too close Iquis seems to recoil, often covering this by making a show of being deliberately anarchic, changeable. Harriet thinks it's more than this. There was the way Iquis had tensed last night when Mark grabbed her hand. Her forearm had tautened, ready to pull away, and her face had stayed frozen as Mark turned her hand over and stroked one finger over her palm.

Harriet, next to Iquis, had sensed fear and excitement, and had been unsurprised when – moments later – she'd made an excuse and retrieved her hand.

But why did Iquis *need* an excuse?

Inevitably, the more Iquis backs off, the more Mark pursues. He's not used to failing to get what he wants. He's even invited Iquis to go to Australia with him at Christmas so he can teach her to surf.

He'd thrown the invitation out like a joke, so that she didn't have to answer him unless she chose to.

'Of course,' he'd added, 'I'll have to spend a bit of time with my father and the step-brat. But I can fit that around the surfing. Dad knows that's part of the deal, that if he doesn't buy it I'll just stay in England with Mum.'

Harriet had called him a spoilt bastard who was being mean to his real mum, taking her for granted. He'd shrugged, but she thought she'd struck home.

There'd been no talk of the step-mum, no teasing from Paul about MILFs or about Mark being drawn to the unobtainable. Funny that.

'If you don't get out now, I'll break the door down!' Mark yells.

'No you won't.'

There's a loud thud and the door shudders against the flimsy lock.

Fuck! Perhaps he would. 'Okay, I'm coming. Keep your hair on,' she yells then adds, 'what's left of it.'

No time to dress. She secures her towel more tightly around herself, grabs her clothes and unlocks the door.

Framed in the doorway, in T-shirt and shorts, Mark looks huge and very dirty. There's a streak of mud on one cheek, his hair is sweat-spiked, his eyes angry. There's a bruise forming on his forearm, and a hard-edged look to his mouth.

A surge of pure physical fear makes her want to bolt. But she won't give him the satisfaction. 'Lost, did you? No need to take it out on me.'

That strikes home. A hot flush inches up his skin. She thinks he's going to lash out in retaliation, but then he reigns his anger in.

Slowly he scans her up and down. His gaze lingering on the nakedness of her legs, then the narrow peaks of her shoulders. Her towel becomes an inadequate shield.

The slowness of his appraisal forces her to absorb him in return. Her resistance is suddenly absent, so that she has no choice but to acknowledge the way his recent, radical haircut has honed him, has burnt away the previous hint of softness. It is impossible, in this moment of trapped awareness, to ignore how fit, how dangerously sexy he is.

She catches her breath.

For a moment there is something new in the hallway with them. Something that both heats and chills her all at the same time.

'Trying to tempt me?' he says, his eyes studying her.

Seeing her.

The hairs on the back of her neck stand up. She recognises in herself the panic which she has glimpsed in Iquis and finally begins to understand something of what causes it.

She swallows. A trickle of water, improperly dried, begins to crawl down one leg. In a minute she will have to breathe but she's not sure she can remember how.

He laughs suddenly. 'Don't bother. I wouldn't shag you if you were the last woman on earth.'

It's as sudden as being slapped. A stinging release which brings with it a flooding relief. Her legs are shaky. She needs to escape, to hole up and regroup.

'Let me out,' she says, her voice tight. 'Look, do you want the fucking bathroom or not?'

*

Back in her bedroom she towels and dries angrily. She starts planning tonight's retaliation, knowing she has to go on the offensive fast to get things back to normal.

Wouldn't it be great if Iquis and I could just take off to the river or the woods? she thinks, wondering what her chances of persuading Iquis are. Pretty low, she suspects. She's convinced that Iquis regrets her graveyard confidences and is avoiding any situations where Harriet could press for further revelations.

The only time they've spent alone since that night was the two evenings immediately following. At the time Harriet had been happy to back off and give her some space, expecting to learn more once Iquis was ready to talk. Instead she'd concentrated on convincing Iquis that they should whitewash her room before they left.

'But why?' Iquis had argued. 'They can't do anything.'

'Maybe not, but I don't want those women to know I lied to them.' Harriet had shifted uncomfortably. 'Listen, you're not going to get this so stop trying. How's about *you owe me*? And this is how I want to be paid.'

In the end it had been fun. Harriet had covered Iquis's room in second-hand sheets, bought from Oxfam, and they'd spent two long nights applying coat after coat of paint.

At first Harriet painted slowly and carefully, full of a nostalgic sadness about covering over Iquis's artwork. It marked the end of something. Although Iquis could paint whatever she liked on Mark's walls, this particular backdrop had been unique, unrepeatable.

Iquis painted rapidly and soon Harriet caught her rhythm, slapping the paint on at top speed, not caring that it was going everywhere, splattering over the sheets and her shoes, landing in wet splodges on her face and hair. Curiously, Iquis was entirely unscathed.

How did she do that?

Unfair, Harriet decided, as she lowered her paintbrush into the can to reload. She glanced at Iquis and then impulsively flicked her loaded brush in her direction. An arc of paint sprayed across the room and showered Iquis who retaliated instantly, her eyes gleaming as she scooped a handful of paint and flung it. Harriet was laughing too hard to take defensive measures. It hit with a gloop on the crown of her head, and slid down over one ear.

After that it was all out war. They darted between the paint cans, scooping and flinging, taking what cover there was – not to avoid getting coated, for there was no real avoidance, but just to prolong the pleasure. They scrabbled for the last few handfuls, then finally, when they could scrape no more out of the tins, landed laughing on the floor.

It had taken five coats of white to cover Iquis's art and even then the room would never be the same as the others. A hint of wildness lingered, an unevenness to the painted walls, echoes of disturbance seeping out to haunt the room.

Like Iquis, Harriet thinks. *She may be masked now, but it's not that easy to keep things concealed.*

Her gaze is jerked unwillingly to the chest of drawers. In the gap, under the bottom drawer, lies the DVD which Glyn had sent. Unable to abandon it or destroy it, she'd brought it with her, unwillingly. Finding a hiding place for it had been her first action, after Mark had finally allowed her into her room.

She'd thought he was never going to let her take possession. He'd kept her at the top of the stairs for the best part of an hour, while he listed the house rules. All of which she could have paraphrased for him in two sentences.

'Keep out of my way. Act like you don't exist.'

Well, tough.

She gives the chest of drawers an uneasy glance, then turns her back and continues dressing.

'You better watch out, Mark,' she murmurs, for her memory of Iquis's room has restored a sense of power. 'You don't know what's underneath the paint.'

TWENTY-THREE

It's the last night of term and something is going on in the kitchen. Everybody knows it, but no one seems to want to investigate. Not even Harriet. She's curled into a sofa, watching idly as Mark stokes the fire. They've just returned from the pub, a noisy mingled mob of Mark's friends plus Harriet and Iquis. The lounge air is filling with the warm scent of exhaled alcohol.

It's Marcia and Jenna who are barricaded in the kitchen. They have been heady with secrets all night, leaving the pub early with scant explanation and mysterious expressions. Harriet is relieved to see them so excited. As Iquis's friend, she feels a curious responsibility for Marcia's happiness. If Marcia is getting injured in the crossfire between Mark and Iquis, then she, Harriet, ought to intervene.

But how can she? It's not like she knows what's going on in Iquis's head. Far from it.

Marcia had been conspicuously absent when Iquis and Harriet first moved in. But as the weeks passed and the simmer between Iquis and Mark never quite ignited, she'd started to reappear, first in the lounge with everyone else and then, within days, going upstairs with Mark at night and re-emerging for breakfast.

Iquis, who seemed to share Mark's casual attitude to ownership, was indifferent to all this. He should have been pleased, but he clearly wasn't.

Harriet – coming down in the mornings to find Marcia cleaning out the grate, "because Mark doesn't like to", – felt that what was happening was unfair to Marcia. Yesterday, she'd learnt without surprise that Jenna felt similarly.

'But I can't do anything,' Jenna had said. 'If I point out that he's using her and she shouldn't let him, it will only aggravate things. It always does. Despite being twins – or maybe because of it – she hates it when I try to interfere. We think alike in so many ways – and yet...'

She seemed to struggle for words. Harriet, unable to find a response, had murmured encouragement and reached into the cupboard to lift out the coffee.

'There's a side to her which I don't share. It's like being a twin confines her, like she can't be properly wild and reckless because I hold her back. We've got this incredible closeness, and I love it, I couldn't bear to lose it. But Marcia...'

She shrugged, pulled a face, then turned and busied herself spooning coffee into mugs. 'I have to let her make her own mistakes,' she'd added.

'You think her relationship with Mark is a mistake?'

'Don't you?'

'Maybe. But then I'm not a fit judge. You know how I feel about Mark.'

Jenna nodded, a slight twist to her mouth. 'I think everybody knows how you feel about Mark.'

'Yeah, well...' Harriet was torn between pride and discomfort.

'Marcia thinks she can handle Mark,' Jenna said. 'But

she's not as tough as she makes out. Sooner or later, I think – and I hope I'm wrong – that there will be consequences.'

'What sort of consequences?'

Jenna hesitated. 'I'd rather not say. Nothing that bad really, just – well, it's hard waiting for her sometimes, waiting for her to come back. I mean she always does. God! What do I sound like? The worst kind of possessive parent. It's not like that, really it's not. You know, there was a point when I suggested that we went to different universities. I wouldn't have minded. In a way it might have been a relief.

'But that's the funny thing, Marcia went very quiet when I suggested it and in the end I dropped the idea.'

Nothing more had been said, but Jenna's words had stayed with Harriet, making her anxious on Marcia's behalf.

So tonight, it's good to hear them giggling; the noise slipping out of the kitchen along with the smell of baking chocolate. Though why their cooking needs to be surrounded by such secrecy is unclear. Even Mark – idly constructing one of the ubiquitous joints which always start circulating at some point – doesn't appear to know what's going on.

Not that he's bothered. Tonight he's expansive with good humour and cockiness. He leaves for Australia in the morning, and it seems nothing can dim his good mood. Even his exchanges with Harriet lack any real hostility.

'I just hope they do my washing up while they're in there,' Mark says. He points his forefingers at Harriet and Iquis with the speed of an outlaw drawing his guns. 'Honestly, you two never seem to notice what state the kitchen's in, never feel compelled to clear up after me. It's not what I'm used to! Don't you cook?'

It's deliberately provocative. But for once Harriet doesn't rise.

Mark sticks the joint in his mouth, flips open his Zippo lighter and sparks it. A look of deep concentration comes over his face as he lights up, taking a deep drag. Holding his breath, he quirks an eyebrow at Iquis, who nods and takes the joint from his fingers.

Harriet turns away. She's always said she'll never smoke, but there have been times in these last three weeks when it's been hard to resist. Getting stoned seems so much the norm here, and it's one more way in which she feels the outsider.

Tonight, when she's all mixed up about going home in the morning, the temptation is sharper. She pushes abruptly to her feet and goes and stands looking out of the window. After a moment, Iquis joins her there and they stand, side by side, looking out into the night.

'I don't want to go home,' Harriet blurts, ashamed.

'I know. Me neither,' Iquis responds.

'Then why did you say no to Australia?' Harriet has wondered about this, suspects it's because Iquis is not ready to commit.

'I don't think I have a choice,' Iquis says. 'There are things I need to know. Things that only my family can tell me. And perhaps... perhaps only by going back,' she shakes her head slowly, 'can I understand where I'm going. How to get there.'

'What do you mean? Get where?'

Behind them the lounge door bursts open and Iquis turns, obviously relieved at the interruption.

Marcia, flanked by Jenna, comes in carrying a plate of chocolate brownies. Wisps of steam are still rising off them. She walks across to Harriet.

'Hash brownies,' she whispers conspiratorially. 'Made them for Jenna. She doesn't really like smoking, refuses to inhale which rather spoils the effect. Anyway, you tempted? Thought you might be.'

Harriet hesitates. Iquis is watching her, waiting to see what she'll do.

A beat of nervousness. They all make it seem so normal. It makes it hard to ask for reassurance. 'How strong are they?'

Marcia shrugs, 'I don't really know. It's all a bit random.' But her eyes are shining. She's part of the building excitement in the room, and suddenly Harriet wants to be too.

There have been moments, late in the evening, where the rambling, rather stoned conversations have reminded her of the easy companionship with the goths. And although she's tried to resist this, on the grounds that with the goths it meant more, it's been hard to swallow down her desire to belong. Now, on this last evening, she decides to succumb.

She reaches out and picks up a warm chocolate slab.

'Thanks,' she says, beaming at Jenna and Marcia. She edges a corner into her mouth and starts to nibble at it. It tastes good, but there's a weird aftertaste which has her reaching for her beer to wash away the flavour.

'Well?' Iquis asks. She picks at a couple of crumbs, then waves the plate away.

'I don't know,' Harriet says.

Iquis laughs.

Outside the window a street light is yellowing the night. 'It's not raining,' Harriet comments. 'In fact, it's a perfect night out there. Don't you think?'

'Perfect for what?' Iquis asks.

'The river?' Harriet says, with a rush of longing.

'Great idea,' Mark says, appearing out of nowhere and throwing an arm over Harriet's shoulder. He's chewing cake, and his breath smells of chocolate.

Shocked by the unexpected gesture, Harriet shrugs him off. But she can still feel the imprint where his arm had rested. He laughs, and turns to grin at Iquis. Tonight nothing can mar his good nature. It's a curious sensation. If he was always like this, Harriet might actually like him.

Jolted, she turns to glance across the room to where Jenna and Marcia are circulating with the fast-emptying plate. The dense cake is sweating gently in her hand. Nothing extreme seems to be happening to her. Cautiously, she lifts the brownie to her mouth and takes another bite.

*

Stephen grasps Harriet's wrist and ankle and spins her like a starfish through the vast green brightness of the garden. There are dazzling smears of colour. His fingers clasp so tightly that although she screams she has no fear of him letting go. But screaming is so much fun.

Half-crazy with dizziness and pleasure she tries to shout, "I love you Stephen", but this splinters the vision.

She knows she never said that. Stephen would have made puking sounds. She can't change the past. She can only try to hang onto the remaining shards... the smell of cut grass, the feel of the sun, the spinning vertigo, Stephen...

But she can feel the cold sneaking into her front as she lies pressed into the riverbank, and that's real. Her sense of loss is so huge that it seems to punch through her back and out through her chest; a stake through her heart, burning and tearing.

She's never felt like this; she shouldn't have eaten that... Got to get this under control. She plunges one hand down into the river seeking distraction. The water slides and wraps around her fingers, lapping at her flesh. Let go, it seems to say, let it float away...

Behind her she hears the murmur of Iquis and Mark's conversation and tunes into it, as if to a play on the radio.

'I dream about it,' Mark says.

He sounds strangely soft. Is this because he thinks only Iquis is listening?

'What do you dream?' Iquis asks.

'You and me, *together*,' almost a whisper.

'Sex is penetration.' Iquis's voice is abrupt. 'The man dominates, the woman yields. We studied it in psychology.'

'You didn't have to study it,' Mark says. 'I could have shown you.'

Harriet pulls a face and pushes her hand deep, reaching to the riverbed. Further down, the water seems to thicken against her skin. She slides forwards, feeling the rasp of the earth against her front, then her hand touches down, grasps, surfaces.

A tiny city of stone and mud, trapped in her hand.

'I don't like to be dominated,' Iquis says.

'You can go on top,' Mark offers.

Her hand open, Harriet trawls through her catch, feels the way the mud wriggles away from her probing finger. She lifts the hand to her face, presses it to her cheek, a myriad of tiny scratchings. She rubs her hand gently back and forwards.

'Can I tie you up?' Iquis says.

'But then I wouldn't get to touch you.'

Touch. Yes, that is everything, isn't it?

Harriet presses herself into the earth and it presses back against her thighs, her breasts. *Like a lover*, she thinks and nearly giggles, but prevents herself before the sound emerges. There is too much power in her silence.

Her attention is in several different places at once. She is a complex being, full of complicated thought patterns. Omniscient.

'Are you afraid?' Iquis's voice.

'No.'

But you should be, Harriet thinks. She's had too much of this conversation. It's nearly as sickly as those funny-tasting brownies had been.

Jerkily, she levers herself to standing. Balances on fragile, newly born limbs. In front of her the moon carves a path along the river, the water ripping disruptions through its papery light. Dark peat stains which tear and heal, constantly changing, constantly repeating.

She needs to get closer. Needs to join that glittering road. Needs to journey with it.

Tonight, I can do anything I want, even walk on water.

They still haven't noticed her.

She reaches one foot forwards until it dangles over the edge, then rests it on the surface. For a moment she truly believes that it will support her weight. The night hisses with the potential for magic.

Then it opens to let her through. She feels the river soak into the leg of her jeans and lurches forwards as her foot pitches down, jars against the riverbed and settles into the mud.

Carefully she raises her other leg.

I'm doing it, walking on water, following the path.

It's so beautiful, so powerful, so free, that she finds herself laughing out loud. The sound is glorious in the night. More confident now, she wades forwards, revelling in the rush of water against each leg. The river is shallow here, but when she rushes through it, she can make it splash up above the knees of her jeans where it clings and soaks. She loves the feel of it.

'Oh, god! Look what she's doing!' Mark's voice disrupts the night. Disturbs her fantasy.

'Harriet, get out of there!' His voice is stern, angry. He appears on the bank, his arms stretching out towards her.

'Why did you have to bring her?' He turns his head to address Iquis who remains stationary, a dark figure perched on a fallen tree stem.

For a nasty moment Harriet feels normal, and foolish.

But he can't diminish her just like that.

'Spoilsport!' She turns away from him, surges forwards.

'Harriet!'

Why won't he go away?

She spins back, raising a finger towards him in defiance. As she twists the stone beneath her foot gives way. She pitches forwards, lands full length in the river. The water splashes up, then falls back, laps around her like a lover. Lying on her back she abandons herself to it, lets it support her.

'Here's rosemary, that's for remembrance.' She projects her voice gloriously up into the night sky.

She could be on stage. She wishes she had long hair to flow and swell around her. She wishes she knew more of the words.

'Leave her, she's enjoying herself,' Iquis says. 'It's shallow enough.'

'Don't be fucking stupid! It's the middle of winter!'

He disturbs the water with his presence, grabs her roughly.

Bastard. She struggles against him as he half carries her to the bank, strides up onto it and hauls her after him.

'Let me go!'

He's solid. Stronger than her. He holds her while she pummels. He starts to laugh. It seems that all her fury cannot harm him.

It tears at her. She wants to go on beating against his warm flesh forever. There's a sob trapped in her throat. She wants to cling to him, hold him. 'I'm sorry, I'm sorry,' she wants to say. He's so much stronger than her – and she's finally safe, contained.

There's a howl trapped in her throat. Choking her. Terrifying her. Where has all this emotion suddenly come from? She doesn't know.

Gradually, she stills.

'Take your coat off,' he says unbuttoning it for her, then shucking it from her arms, 'and your jumper.' She's like an obedient mechanical doll, lifting her arms, doing as he tells her, beginning to shiver as the cold air hits her.

'Put this on.' His fleece is in her hands, still warm.

'Quickly!' he snaps.

She struggles into it and he zips her up.

'Let's go,' he says. 'Come on. We're running home.' His hand grasping hers, pulling her along as their boots pound against the stone-studded track. Her breath exits in gasps; and all the while the howl is still there, stuck like a knife in her throat.

Somewhere behind them Iquis follows.

*

Later, alone with Iquis in her basement room, Harriet feels quietened. The dip in the river combined with the night run home has stripped away the more extreme effects of the dope and what is left is a slightly blurred feeling, as if the river water has got in. Despite her change of clothes, this feeling lingers. She's appropriated Iquis's long purple velvet dress from her wardrobe. She loves this dress.

'I'm going to miss you,' Harriet says. She knows that this is goodbye. She'll be off long before Iquis surfaces in the morning. Yet some of the urgent need to connect with Iquis which she's felt in the weeks since the move to Mark's house has worn off. What is left is a fatalistic acceptance of the inevitable, and a growing longing to see her parents, which takes her by surprise.

'I'll write you a poem,' Iquis says. 'Like the one that Lucien wrote. But for you, about you.'

'*You* don't write poetry.'

Iquis shrugs. 'Don't I?'

'Well I've never seen you.'

'So?'

Harriet puts on Iquis's abandoned cloak. The huge basement room is always several degrees colder than the rest of the house. 'You will come back, won't you?' she asks, almost casually.

'If I can.'

'Of course you can.' Harriet's startled. She'd expected easy reassurance, not ambiguity. But Iquis looks serious. Harriet has a sudden instinct, that if she asks questions now she'll get answers. 'Why don't you want to go home? Is it because of your father, because of what happened?'

Iquis starts to unthread the wet lace from one of Harriet's discarded trainers. 'That's part of it.'

'What did they do to him?'

The lace comes free from the trainer and Iquis discards it, starts on the other one.

'*They* did nothing. My older brother, who'd just turned seventeen, beat him into a pulp.'

'What!'

'He was so angry he didn't think about it. He lost control and couldn't stop. He'd have killed him if my mother hadn't pulled him off. It would have been better if he had.'

'You don't mean that.'

'I do. Better for everyone.' Iquis's voice carries total conviction.

Harriet is aghast, not sure she wants to hear any more, but Iquis is on a roll.

'My father crawled away, rasping out that he'd get his revenge. He was gone for nine weeks, and when he came back he had found a new source of power. Something so potent, so terrible... I can't explain.'

And yet, something makes her try. 'A kind of unholy Grail if you like, a cup from which he had drunk, a cup from which he made my whole family drink. Something so strong that it even affected me, in my mother's womb. It changed all of us. Forever.'

Now she looks at Harriet. 'Sorry,' she says, and it's the first time Harriet has heard her use that word. 'You wanted a plain tale and I gave you a myth, a legend. But it's better like that. I won't ever tell you the truth, you know.'

'Great! So you've just fed me some story? That's not what I want. Don't you trust me?'

Iquis hesitates. 'I make sense to myself.'

'Well, good for you.'

Iquis looks so defeated that Harriet calms down. Somehow she still feels that Iquis is trying to communicate, despite the bollocks she's just spouted. 'Was the first part true? What your brother did?'

'Yes.'

'And your father going away?'

Iquis nods.

'Do you mean he went to prison?' That's something a myth might have been built around. To hide the truth from outsiders, or maybe even from Iquis herself.

'No. Not that. No one knew he was responsible for my brother's death.'

'Your family covered up for him?' Harriet is shocked.

'It was... it seemed... irrelevant.'

'Irrelevant!' Harriet's voice is accusing, angry. 'He should have been punished.' And then, 'It won't be over until he is.'

'I wasn't there.' Iquis sounds defensive.

'But you're there now.' Harriet is unable to control her own reaction.

'You don't understand. You judge, but you do not know.'

'And you wonder why?'

Iquis shrugs. She looks pale and somehow thinner, vulnerable.

Harriet is full of a tangle of confusion and fear. She'd wanted to know, but she doesn't know what to do with the knowledge. It's more than she'd bargained for.

But I can't let it be.

'Let me come with you,' she says. 'Take me to your family, then I'll understand. I promise.'

Iquis laughs, but there's no real humour in it.

'And maybe,' Harriet continues, 'I'll be able to change things, to make them all right.'

For a moment Iquis's laughter threatens to get out of hand, as if what Harriet has said is hysterically funny.

Yet when she looks at Harriet her eyes are frightened.

'No,' she says. 'I'll never let them near you.'

TWENTY-FOUR

The house looks exactly the way it always has. Harriet, who had half-expected to see the windows ajar, isn't sure whether she's relieved or disappointed. It's hardly the weather for open windows, and yet even so she's –

I've pictured them so many times.

She stops outside the house, drags in a breath. She's walked from the train station, told Dad it was fine, that she's used to making her own way now.

Truth is, she'd wanted to meet them both together.

Home looks little different, but I do.

She's wrapped in Iquis's cloak, the cold drizzle is landing on her crow-black hair and there's the itch of heavy mascara on her eyelashes.

Oh yes, she looks different, and she's a bit worried about it. How is Mum going to react? Harriet's got a good idea how Dad will react: he'll lose his rag. That's okay. But Mum –

"You've got such lovely hair. Why don't you grow it long?" Harriet's lost count of the number of times Mum's said this, the number of times she's added, "The way it was when you were little", nostalgia and sadness mingled in her voice, a yearning for a time she will never get back. Mum keeps pictures of Harriet with long hair on the mantlepiece; Stephen is always in the frame too.

Harriet raises a nervous hand to the still-rather-dry black strands which touch the nape of her neck, then she knocks.

Dad opens the door, blinks, then ruffles her hair. 'It makes you look peaky,' he complains.

Is that it? She'd expected something more... explosive.

Dad throws an arm round her shoulder and steers her inside. 'Look who we've got,' he says.

There's a sudden lump in Harriet's throat.

Mum is in the hallway. She eyes Harriet doubtfully for a moment and then steps forwards.

'It's vital Harriet finds a way to express herself,' she says.

She presses the air between herself and Harriet. It's an odd gesture, over earnest and intense. She sounds like a self-help book.

Dad turns away to hide a sardonic expression, twisting back towards the street. And Harriet is thrown. The windows aren't ajar, but *something's* different.

*

Three days into the holiday Harriet returns from seeing friends and stumbles on her parents having a row in the hallway. Well, maybe row is a bit strong, but even so...

'I'm not going,' Mum says. 'That's final!'

Dad directs a look of bewildered entreaty at Harriet. *What do you want me to do?* 'Not going where?'

'Granny and Granddad's,' he says, 'Christmas day.'

'But we always go.' The traditional visit to Mum's parents has existed as long as Harriet can remember. Dad's parents died years ago.

'The group says...' Mum starts.

Dad utters a bark of laughter then immediately looks guilty. 'Sorry.'

She glares, then continues with visible effort. 'The group says I need to do what's right for me, that I should stop putting others first.'

Dad never loses his temper with Mum. His voice is always gentle, careful, its robustness reigned back. He doesn't shout now, but Harriet recognises the anger in him.

'So what do Harriet and I do? Go without you?'

'If you want.'

He draws in a sharp breath, walks across to the wall and back.

'It's not about what I want.' Frustration escapes into his voice. 'It's about what's right. We always go there on Christmas day.' He shakes his head. 'They're your parents. They'll want to see you.'

'Why? They never have before. The only time I was worthy of notice was when I had Stephen, when I was Stephen's mother. You know only boys matter in that household.'

Harriet is stunned by the concentrated bitterness in her voice. Mum's never said anything like this before.

Harriet's always found the Christmas visit a bit boring, but never thought to challenge it. Dull hours sat quietly in the lounge beside Dad. Mum occasionally with them, but normally busy in the kitchen. Granny Bee standing sentinel at the tall window, gazing dotingly at the running horde of grandsons in command of her garden, or conversing eagerly with whichever of her sons remained inside, an intense concentration on her face as if every word was precious.

Those interminable games of football lasted all afternoon, the long garden full of shouting, running figures, her cousins, who were having *all* the fun.

You wouldn't let me play, she thinks looking at Mum. *Why not? Because you knew Granny Bee would disapprove? Or because you didn't want me to find a way to fit in, to be one of the boys, the way you never were?*

I wanted to be one of them. Just the way I wanted to be included when Stephen...

The doorbell interrupts her thoughts.

'That'll be Becca. I've got to go.' Mum doesn't even try to hide her relief.

'Go where?' Dad demands.

'I told you.' That hint of irritation again. 'It's our Christmas get-together at Becca's house.'

'But we haven't finished.'

Mum turns away, starts to collect her things.

He places a hand lightly on her shoulder.

She shrugs it off.

'Listen. It's okay,' he says, almost pleading. 'We won't go. We'll do something different for Christmas day. Just the three of us.'

Harriet throws him a startled look. Mum's abandoned the kitchen, and Harriet and Dad are taking it in turns to cook: frozen pizza, sauces out of jars, simple stuff. It's been pretty odd, given that they were only ever allowed in to wash up until now. It had always been Mum's domain, the place she spent hours crafting elaborate meals. Harriet, like Dad, feels totally inadequate in there. *Are we really going to attempt Christmas dinner?*

'We'll go out,' Dad says. 'I'll find a hotel. I'll tell your parents, they'll understand.'

He's taking control the way he always has, being the strong one who makes things happen.

Mum bites her lip, then nods abruptly, 'Fine.' She doesn't look particularly pleased. 'I must go.'

She heads quickly for the front door.

Harriet, watching carefully, can only detect a trace of her usual uneasiness as she reaches for the handle. She takes a deep breath, settles her shoulders down, swings the door open and walks out.

Father and daughter look at each other in silence for a while. For someone who's never taken up much room, Mum seems to leave a surprisingly large gap. Their eyes meet across it. There's that trace of confusion on Dad's face again. He doesn't know what he's done wrong.

Neither does Harriet, and it makes her uncomfortable. She's about to make some excuse to go up to her room when he comes to a decision.

'Sod this,' he says, not explaining what "this" is. 'Let's go to the pub.'

She avoids showing surprise.

'Why not.' She can think of plenty of reasons. Like how awkward it might be. Like the fact that his usual way of communicating with her is to ask about her studies. But despite this she can't help being pleased, excited even. They've never done this before.

*

But they don't discuss her work and it's okay. The beer helps. Harriet talks about Cumbria, surprised to find herself willingly sharing the details of her discoveries with him. She leaves out all references to her companions, and in particular to Iquis.

'One of my favourite parts of the country,' Dad says. 'You probably won't remember, but we went there when you were small. The last family holiday we had. We hired a cottage by a lake filled with fish and lived off the land all week. You loved it there. I always wondered whether that was why you chose that university.' He looks at her interrogatively, but she can't recall the holiday he is referring to.

The pub is nothing special. A dark, dirty looking building with a pool table and small clusters of drinkers, talking casually, mainly men.

'My local,' Dad had said when they arrived, nodding acknowledgement in several directions across the room.

Now, made confident by the ease of their conversation and the pleasure of his attention, she asks, 'How can this be your local when you never go out?'

'I haven't been for a long time,' he says. 'At least till recently.'

'Too damn right, Harry.' A large, dark-haired, once handsome man halts at their table. 'We'd decided he'd left the country,' he says to Harriet, then turns back to her dad. 'This your new young lady? She's a bit of all right.'

'My daughter, Harriet.'

He sounds proud. She squirrels the tone of his voice away, in the hoard where she has stored other such moments through the years.

'By heck, don't they grow fast,' the other man comments.

'Don't even think it,' Dad says.

The man laughs. 'So what're you having then?'

*

When he returns from the bar he brings his friends with him. They settle round the table, laughing and joking.

'How do you know them?' Harriet says, rather stunned at being swamped by this group of cheerful, beer-swilling men, who all seem to display a benign, almost avuncular attitude to her. Well, mainly avuncular.

'I used to play rugby with them, before...'

He breaks off, but they both know what he means.

Before Stephen died.

Harriet had forgotten that he used to play rugby. Memories surface.

'You said I could watch when I was a bit older.'

'Yes. Stephen came once or twice, till he got bored. He never took to it. Always preferred football.'

'And you didn't?'

'I wasn't built for it. Rugby suited me better.'

She thinks of playing hockey, of how badly she'd wanted him to watch her. Of how he'd never been able to.

'Do you play now?'

'No. Too old.' He sounds matter-of-fact. What does he really feel?

'Hey, stop monopolising her! You can talk to her any time,' a round-faced, vaguely familiar man interrupts. 'Remember me, Harriet?'

She nods, not really sure whether she does, but happy to please him.

'You were this high, last time I saw you.'

His hand is the same level as Harriet's knees, and only centimetres from them.

'Are you still as cheeky?' he asks.

'Was I cheeky?' Harriet is pleased, though surprised at this image of her.

"Course you were. Used to order your dad around something rotten.'

'He never seemed to mind though,' one of the other men chimes in. 'Don't think he minded anything you did.'

Harriet finds that hard to believe. 'Well, he does now.'

The men laugh.

Harriet finds herself looking at Dad, capturing a strange expression in his eyes. She can't work out what it is.

To escape from it, she asks, 'Was he any good?'

'One of the best, your dad. Once he got the ball, that was it. He was unstoppable.'

'A powerhouse.'

Harriet's father directs a firm look at his beer, but she can sense that underneath he's pleased.

They stay all evening. Dad doesn't say much but he looks relaxed. It makes Harriet realise how tense he always is in the house with her and Mum.

*

'Best if we don't mention this to your mother,' Dad says, as they arrive home to an empty house. 'She might not like it.'

'But *she* went out,' Harriet says.

Dad half laughs.

'Yeah. Old habits I guess.' It's the closest they've got to discussing what happened earlier. Again, Harriet senses that confusion in him. As if all those years of being leant on have bent him into a particular shape. So that now, despite the release of pressure, it's too late for him to spring upright again.

She thinks of Iquis saying, "You have to allow people to change", considers repeating it to Dad. But the evening has been too good, she doesn't want to risk spoiling it.

*

It's while they are walking to the hotel on Christmas day that they see Graham.

Graham, who had been Stephen's best friend.

She still thinks of him as a boy, although it's no longer true. He's older than any of her friends, older than Paul and Mark. It hits her with a jolt; Stephen would be grown up by now, not frozen in time the way he's become.

Everyone halts.

Harriet's parents draw together. It's the first thing in days that has unified them.

'Your fault.' It's Mum who speaks. Dad is just a menacing presence at Harriet's side.

Graham can't have heard, Mum's voice was too quiet, but a twitch runs through his frame. He balls his fists, and his gaze locks onto Harriet. She drops hers, finds herself looking at his crotch. He's wearing old, battered jeans. The zip has given slightly, so that the top teeth curl away from each other.

She jerks her eyes away, down.

The black tarmac is puddled with water. It glistens darkly. A pair of large white trainers are planted there. They mar the perfect black expanse.

He's wearing trainers. Inevitable. He always did.

She has a sudden vision of Stephen and Graham wrestling on the grass, of the sun shining, the tousled nature of Graham's hair, the freckles on his face. She recalls the occasional careless attention that he paid to her and how much it meant.

Graham's trainers are muddy and battered and... is that a rip?

She can't actually see, and yet she's picturing him sliding through white mud, his foot catching against hewn stone. There's an urgency. He's moving too fast, moving towards something, doesn't even notice the damage.

A wound, a gaping tear, in one side of his trainer.

Dad grabs her arm and propels them past. His face turns so that his gaze remains on Graham the whole time, pinning him down, holding him in place, motionless.

Dad's body is taut with repressed anger. Harriet is shrinking into herself, making herself smaller and smaller. She is afraid, but she knows she must draw his anger towards her the way she always does, provoke him until it's out in the open. Exploded. Made safe.

But she can't do it yet. She's too busy swallowing.

TWENTY-FIVE

Harriet's first back; there's no Iquis and no Mark. She's got the house to herself. And there's only one room she's never been in.

She flings the door open. First thing she sees is the bed: an immense double with gleaming, dark-aubergine covers. It totally dominates the room, which is –

Well, typical Mark, really. All show.

She crosses to the window. The view is fabulous. She can see right out to the Lake District. A range of purple, green and grey peaks and ridges which merge into the cloud-smudged sky, subtle colours, beautifully lit, constantly changing.

It's the best view in the house. If this was her room she'd never close the curtains. She'd want to wake to those mountains.

And yet, can they be seen from the bed?

She glances at it. It gleams, as cocky as Mark himself.

There's only one way to find out if she can see the mountains from there. Of course, he'd kill her if he found out.

That in itself is a dare.

She swan dives onto his bed, her face landing in his pillow. It's silky, smooth and still smells faintly of his early morning musk, his lemony aftershave. She rolls away, onto her back, her head falling into the central gap between the two pillows. She stretches her hands back to grasp the wrought-metal bedhead.

Can I tie you up?

The jolt of memory is uncomfortable. That overheard conversation between Mark and Iquis had been more negotiation than flirtation. It had been odd, disturbing – unfinished.

What will happen this term? She *so* doesn't want to find out.

And yet, she'd seen a different side of Mark that night. In his own way he'd been concerned about her, Harriet. His interference unnecessary but well meant.

He's still a bastard though, still treats Marcia like shit. Nothing's actually changed.

The sound of a car drawing up outside is a shock. She leaps from the bed and is halfway to the door when she second guesses, glances back.

There's a Harriet-shaped imprint in the middle of the bed.

She grabs the pillows and bashes them into shape, snatches up the duvet and shakes it out. It's the best she can do. There are creases, but hopefully Mark won't notice.

The sound of a car door slamming, too close to be a neighbour.

She's gone, closing the door behind her and sprinting across to her own room. She sidles over to her window, peers out.

Mark is lifting suitcases out of his boot with careless strength. He looks fit and tanned from the Australian summer.

Spoilt!

What was she doing in his room?

She remembers him pulling her from the river, remembers beating her fists against his chest, and the memory is awkward.

Maybe it's best to avoid him until Iquis gets back.

*

Iquis stands in the wild rain and waits for Harriet to speak. The wind tugs her hair into spikes, raindrops edge her eyelashes, water builds up around her shins.

Harriet wades towards her.

"Teach me to dance," she says, as the storm grows stronger.

Iquis reaches towards the stereo, releases a lightning crack as she switches it on. The light hisses across the water. A blackened burning smell fills the room as the music begins to play. Iquis moves towards her as the lights fuse and the water climbs.

A wall of water hits Harriet and carries her with it. Branches of rosemary bruise themselves against her, flooding her with their scent.

She's in the Eden river, Iquis and Mark on the bank.

Big waves rear above her – foreshadowing, then breaking, crashing down onto her head, plunging her down to where there is only water, only the sound of water. She twists in slow motion like a doll in a macabre dance, like a spiralling cork pulled from a wine bottle. Then, with a sucking sound, she surfaces, bobs on the river's skin and laughs.

She laughs so that Iquis will know that this is okay, that she can take it, that she is determined to go on.

Stephen intervenes.

He is strangely huge. A vast hand swallows her upper arm. A bruise broods sullenly on his forehead. His expression is grim as he tugs her from the water.

She wants to kick against him. To tell him to leave her be. To tell him that she knows what she's doing. But something, some fear, some terror, holds her back. She stays inert, like a rag doll, as he drags her faster and faster.

She can only just hear Iquis's voice, distant and fading. 'Leave her, she's having fun.'

But she's travelling backwards through time, away from Iquis. Away from that voice.

The water sheers off her, as she grows smaller, younger.

Bright sunshine.

His hands. One around her wrist, one around her ankle. Her body splayed out like a starfish as he spins her round and round.

She catches glimpses of his face. The bruise on his forehead. His face intent, not quite friendly.

She begins to feel frightened. She tries to call to him to let her go, but he shows no sign of hearing.

The whirl of green and blue sickeningly fast. Like a car without brakes.

"Mark. Stop! Stop!"

She starts to struggle and feels his hand clench against her wrist.

The golden tan of his face blurs with the green and blue.

Her struggles grow wilder, fear lends her a strength that

she ought not to possess, so that suddenly one foot is free. She kicks out. Deliberately. Wanting to hurt him.

Her anger defies centrifugal force. Defies logic. So that her foot flies, not away from him, but towards him. So that all the force that has been building with this spinning, implodes towards his centre. Like an arrow her foot pierces his chest, embeds itself.

And then he is falling, they are falling...

*

'Wake up.'

A hand shaking her shoulder. She flees back into the dream. Falling...

'Wake up, you daft bint.' Mark's voice.

'What are you doing here?'

'You were screaming.'

'Just go away.'

'Is that all the thanks I get?'

'Just fuck off, Stephen. Just get out of my fucking room. Out of my fucking head. I don't want you here.'

'I'm going. You are losing it big time, Harriet.'

The door slams. He's gone.

TWENTY-SIX

A week passes and Iquis doesn't return. Harriet worries. She keeps going over that last conversation, and each time it seems worse. *Was Iquis asking for help? Should I have stopped her going home? Have I failed her?*

Is she all right?

Finally, on the evening of the second Monday of term, she sits down at her laptop and struggles to write to Iquis. It's such a pathetic action, but it's the only one open to her. She has no idea where Iquis's family live, not even whether it's north or south. Her only hope is that someone in the admin office will be prepared to forward a letter.

But the letter itself is hard to write. Impossible to risk putting her fears into words, in case Iquis's father reads it.

As she deletes the latest attempt, she hears a motorbike prowling along their street. Something in the tone of the engine – or just a need for distraction – draws her down to the front door. The bike is idling outside their house, an unmistakable figure on its back.

Iquis!

The motorbike is huge with gleaming black and purple curves and large don't-mess-with-me tyres. Iquis holds it upright without apparent effort, legs splayed straight on each side of its vibrating torso and arms forked forwards onto the handlebars.

'Thank God! I was so worried.'

Harriet lets the front door bang behind her and rushes across to Iquis. A black impenetrable shell turns towards her. Within the helmet the gap of Iquis's face is both revealed and shadowed by the nicotine-stain light of the street lamp. Under its distorting gaze, she looks unhealthy and compressed.

Harriet has a bad feeling. She tries to ignore it. 'What kept you?'

Iquis flinches. The bike engine is idling with a deep-throated growl. Iquis's hand is taut on the throttle. At any moment she might power the bike back into movement and take flight.

'What's wrong, Iquis? Was it your father?'

Iquis jerks her gaze away from Harriet and across to the lighted windows of the house. 'I shouldn't have come back.' Her hand tightens, causing the bike engine to rev in punctuation.

'Yes, you should,' Harriet says. 'Of course you should.'

Iquis blinks, and looks down at the dial of the speedometer. 'What am I doing here?'

Before she can bolt, Harriet reaches for the ignition key and twists it. The engine falls silent.

'You're returning. That's what you're doing. The way you were meant to.'

Iquis's eyes avoid her.

'Did he hurt you?' Harriet asks. 'If he did I'll kill him.'

'I hurt myself,' Iquis says, and laughs – a horrible, bitter laugh. 'Don't feel sorry for me,' and then, again, she says, 'I should go. I shouldn't be here. I didn't mean to...' She trails off.

The silence stretches. Harriet doesn't know what to say. After a while Iquis glances at the house once more. Looking for Mark?

'He's out,' Harriet says tensely.

But Iquis just looks relieved. She slides from the bike and pulls it backwards onto its stand.

'So how did you acquire the bike?' Harriet tries for a neutral topic.

'My brother arranged it.' Another silence. Iquis fiddles with the tips of her gloves.

'Iquis.'

She looks at Harriet as if deciding something.

'Do you like me?' she asks.

Such a strange question. It throws Harriet. She doesn't know what to answer. Doubts she was unaware of rise to the surface.

'Iquis, I'm confused. Let's go inside.'

A shudder across her face.

'No, not yet. Come for a ride?' A pleading look.

*

It's better on the bike. Harriet clings to Iquis with locked arms. Despite what's gone before, it's impossible not to enjoy this experience. There's a thrilling newness to it. The heavy leather which bulks her out. The weight of the helmet against her head. The rush of speed, like flying. The roughness of the night as they burst through it, abrasive yet sensuous.

Before they left, Iquis had unlocked her panniers and drawn out a full set of protective clothing in Harriet's size. This had been reassuring. No matter how it looked, Iquis had planned to return.

Twisting roads lead them steeply through the Lake District.

At last.

A whole term and we never made it this far, only lurked on the edges always intending to come further. Yet in the end it's better to arrive this way. Like conquerors riding forwards in a blast of power, a blaze of glory.

Only Iquis's brittleness keeps Harriet from pure exultant happiness.

The first time Iquis had tilted the bike round a sharp corner, Harriet had screamed. A scream composed of a mixture of fear, exhilaration and more than a touch of melodrama. The bike had leant so far over, that Harriet had believed – or had chosen to believe – that they might not recover.

In front of her Iquis's shoulders had narrowed and locked. Only then did Harriet become truly afraid. Iquis had seemed welded into place. Immobile. There was nothing and no one to control the bike. Nothing to stop it falling into a skid, crushing their legs beneath it as it travelled along the gravel-studded road.

Despite her impulse to scream even louder and harder, Harriet had forced herself into silence, biting down on her lip and willing Iquis to recover. A split second stretched impossibly, full of images, then Iquis creaked back into movement, lifting the bike upwards by sheer willpower. Harriet had drawn in a shaky, prolonged breath, as with a slight twist of her arm Iquis slowed the bike to a sedate crawl.

It had taken time to relax and overcome her nerves, but gradually Iquis had increased the speed and Harriet, recognising that Iquis was back in control, had learnt to keep her reactions to herself. Silently enjoying the increasing speed and the adrenaline hit at each corner.

*

'Why do you trust me? You shouldn't trust me,' Iquis says.

It's the third night. The third of these long, dark rides.

Harriet's limbs ache constantly from the clinging, from the tension and vibrations of being on the bike. She welcomes it, loves the perpetual reminder of motion and speed which she carries within her body like the after-effects of a drug.

There has been little conversation. Their stops have been brief pauses to shake feeling back into locked limbs, to touch rock, splash boots into streams or to just gaze into the dark scenery falling away beneath them.

But now it seems Iquis is ready to communicate.

There is too much adrenaline rushing around Harriet's body for caution. 'Okay, then,' she says, 'leave me here. I'll walk home.'

They are two thirds of the way up a mountain. Their breath is creating tiny mist clouds in front of their faces. The only light comes from the muted beam of the bike's headlight, burning and disappearing into a dried-out bush.

Iquis doesn't laugh.

Harriet feels the first surge of impatience.

'Look! This is me, Harriet, remember? From last term? Your friend?'

Iquis concentrates on the burning bush.

'What kept you?' Harriet asks, determined on breaking through to Iquis. 'Wouldn't your family let you return?'

'No. It wasn't that.'

'So what was it?'

'It was after I left them. I couldn't come back. I just rode and rode. I wanted to shake it off, to move so fast that it fell away from me. Impossible really.' That hideous desolation in her voice again. So that Harriet finds herself filled with a desire to flee before it, not sure that she can cope. 'I think maybe I shouldn't have come back.'

'So you keep saying. But you did return and I'm glad. Not just glad, relieved. If you hadn't come back, I'd have been terrified about what might have happened to you.

'Iquis, you told me stuff last term which I can't forget. Then you come back like this, and I can't help imagining really bad things. Surely it would be better if you just told me, let me help you.'

'No it wouldn't,' Iquis says. 'Look, Harriet, I've seen how you deal with things you can't face, you pretend they never happened. Why not allow me the same dispensation?'

'I don't know what you're talking about!'

'Yes you do.'

A moment of stopped awareness. Harriet doesn't even want to think about this. She wriggles uncomfortably, changes position on the hard ground. After a moment, to prove she's got the point, she asks, 'So where did you go?'

'South,' Iquis says, 'to the sea. To the Quadrophenia place.'

'I thought that was a film.' Not that she's seen it, just heard of it. Something to do with mods and rockers.

'It's a cliff. In the film he goes there on his moped. It looks like he's going to ride over it, but in the end he leaps off and lets the bike fall. It's meant to be symbolic.' As she speaks, Iquis is regaining her usual sardonic tone. 'I was anticipating a suicide's Mecca but it's not like that. It's crowded with tourists. There's an enormous pub with a kids' play area. People stop there for lunch, then wander over to the cliff afterwards.'

Her voice is full of irony, yet she sounds confused.

'But I kept on catching fragments of conversation. There was a couple near me at one point. The man said, "My dentist jumped off here," and his companion peered over the edge. "Look how smooth the rocks are," she said. "Do you think that's where he hit?"'

Harriet feels a snatch of vertigo.

Iquis continues, 'Then she said that the landlady of the pub keeps an eye out for those who are likely to jump, so she can talk them out of it.'

She summons up a look of mischief, with visible effort. 'I had a great idea for a competition between us.' She pauses, looks properly at Harriet for the first time. 'We both go into the pub, at the same time but separately, and we see which of us can convince the landlady we're about to jump.'

Harriet thinks about it, torn between commenting that it seems a bit mean and seizing the opportunity to heal something within Iquis. Inevitably, her desire to help Iquis is strongest.

She plunges into the game, tries to imagine what she'd be feeling if she was going to jump.

'I could do it,' she says, 'make myself believe it so much that she'd believe it too. It's what I'm good at.' She pauses, stares out into the night, no longer seeing it.

'Okay, this is me. I'm in a corner – the furthest corner from the bar – and I'm just staring down at my glass. Inside, I'm a whole mix of feelings: an abrupt sense of freedom, anticipation even, knocking against the fear which underlies everything. I toss back my drink, and only then notice the way my hand is shaking.

'My eyes are drawn against my will towards the bar. They meet the landlady's stare and skitter away. The empty glass in front of me is like a beacon, drawing her towards me, a bottle of whisky in her hand, a careful look in her eyes.'

Harriet blinks twice and the pub is gone.

'See,' she says, strangely exhilarated. She laughs, holds out her hand. 'I'm glad you're back. It was dull without you.'

Iquis hesitates, then brushes the tips of her fingers against Harriet's.

TWENTY-SEVEN

In the middle of the Lake District the darkness is full of the weight of mountains and the crash of falling water. Few words are necessary in the girls' perfect, trance-like existence. Time halts, every night is the same and yet different, just the welding of girl with bike, the leaning curves and the sense of perpetual motion.

Mark is not included.

Harriet does her best to avoid him when she's in the house, but the noise of his presence intrudes. It has the essential loudness of someone determined not to be ignored. And yet, Harriet's only guessing what his reaction is to his sudden exclusion.

The only clue – the only time when she saw past the boisterous mask – was when one evening, on leaving her room, she spied him in the shadows by Iquis's door.

'Iquis! Stop playing games!' His voice, directed into the thickness of Iquis's shut door, sounded full of a false confidence.

Poised at the top of the stairs Harriet studied him. He was too intent on what he was doing for there to be much risk of him looking up.

The night he came into my room he brought with him a faint light and yet I can't remember him clearly, don't even remember what he was wearing, whether he was dressed... the only thing I remember is his hands around my ankle and wrist as he span me...

From the top of the stairs she could see him clearly, could take in every detail, could ground him back in the real. There was something seductively powerful about watching him knock, then wait, then knock again, with only silence as a result.

As far as Harriet knows, Iquis has not even seen Mark this term.

The bike rides provide a growing certainty. There is no part of the Lake District that they cannot reach in the course of a night and there are many small roads to explore.

The journey is all. *It's like we're trying to escape, and in the act of fleeing we feel whole and at peace.*

*

Dr Drake's letter therefore comes as more of a shock than it should.

'She wants to see me!' Harriet thrusts the letter at Iquis, her fingers holding it wide to display the marching print which parades the page, stiff-backed and unambiguous.

'So she does.' Iquis is unmoved.

'It means I'm in big trouble.' Harriet watches Iquis carefully. She needs her to at least try to understand.

Harriet had always been the good girl at school, had never been in trouble with the teachers. Now a void has opened up between who she was and who she is, and it makes her dizzy and frightened.

Iquis frowns slightly and folds the paper back into its enveloped shape.

'The woman's a sadist!' Harriet says, still trying to involve Iquis. '13th of February! That's almost a week away.' It's also the day before the Dark Island concert, but she keeps that reflection to herself. 'She's deliberately drawing it out. Making me wait.'

Iquis hands the letter back to Harriet, all blanked out and contained.

'You still think Dr Drake matters. You haven't yet worked out that she isn't important, she can't harm you.'

Harriet snatches the letter from Iquis and pushes it angrily into the narrow hip pocket of her leather trousers.

'Can't she?'

'No.' Iquis's voice is uncompromising. 'Come on, let's go out.'

Yes, of course, the solution for everything.

*

But the trance is broken. Real life travels with them, clinging tightly to Harriet's back like some leathery demon. She feels let down by Iquis, and finds fury rising. *I've been so careful of her since she returned, and yet she can't seem to understand why this matters, why it makes me feel so insecure, so lost to myself.*

And with the fury, come all the suppressed feelings from last term. The weeks when she had watched Iquis and Mark flirting. *Why did I accept that so easily?*

It's the same answer: *because she was vulnerable and I was looking after her.*

It's very familiar. Her thoughts flicker to Christmas, to the self-help group that had taken up so much of Mum's time.

All those years I spent trying to make her better, and I never managed it. Wasn't I good enough? Is that why she turned to them?

As Iquis steers the bike off the road and up a rough footpath, Harriet's resentment builds. *Just wait till we stop,* she thinks, as the bike judders and skids.

There's a rumbling sound in the air. At first she thinks it's the bike engine, straining, then she recognises it: a waterfall.

Iquis steers them onto a flat square of concrete and stops the engine but leaves the light on. Its beam widens to reveal shattering diamonds, constantly falling and fracturing against the stark black of the cliff face. High above, water pours endlessly over a lip of rock. The sound is immense.

For a moment the trance pushes back at her, but already Iquis is off the bike and heading across the rocks towards the cliff.

Huh! Can't be bothered to wait for me.

Normally it wouldn't matter, but tonight it does.

Dumping her helmet, Harriet climbs over the barrier which edges the viewing platform and lowers herself down. Despite the thrust of her anger, she can't match Iquis's pace. The rocks are balanced precariously and some of them are huge. In daylight it would be difficult, but in the semi-dark it's an accident waiting to happen.

By the time Harriet reaches the cliff face which abuts the waterfall, the stones are wet and treacherous, and her progress is very slow.

Cold spray soaks her. In front of her eyes the rush of water is so fast that it mesmerises.

'What kept you?' Iquis says.

Harriet ignores her, concentrates her gaze downwards towards the basin where the water pummels, churns and writhes. Gashes of dirty yellow foam well up from the maelstrom and appear ugly in the edges of the bike-light beam.

Is that what it was like when the little mermaid became sea foam? Not a slow dissolving like I've always imagined, but instead this relentless pounding into oblivion.

I wonder whether she too was angry, at the last moment, when it was too late.

Harriet shivers, edges one foot back, and turns to Iquis.

*

But Iquis has moved on.

I thought there was nowhere to go, Harriet thinks, with frustration. *Am I to spend the whole night chasing her?*

Iquis is suspended on the cliff just above Harriet's head. Booted feet and white hands move crab-like as she heads left towards the thick fall of water. A new sound joins the others as chunks of water start to batter against leather.

Iquis twists to look back at Harriet.

'Come on.'

She is slick with water. One shoulder is edged deep into the fall, diverting it to flow past her, landscaping her own small cascade. Below her is a long fall into the basin.

Inevitably, part of Harriet wants to respond to the dare. It's funny how difficult it is to lose her temper. How easily she allows herself to be distracted from it. How easy it would be to just swallow it all down. But there's so much unsaid, and she's tired of it.

'No, it's dangerous,' she says, to provoke one of Iquis's mocking dismissals.

This time she'll be ready.

But instead Iquis swings around to face her fully, so that only one hand anchors her to the rock.

'You want to stop?'

'Yes. No. That's not the point!'

Nothing changes. The water continues to fall unceasingly. Iquis continues to hang above her like an icon.

'You never took me to a psychology lecture,' Harriet says. Her words are puny, frail manifestations of what she wants to express. They lack the power that she knows is dammed within her, ready to smash through, if they can find a weakness.

'You said you would, but then we moved and it never happened.'

Iquis laughs. A flash of white, which matches the splashing water. 'I didn't go to any myself. It had stopped being important.'

'Yes, everything stopped being important once Mark was on the scene!'

'Psychology didn't have the answers.'

'No, and I suppose I didn't either.' Another stone breaks from the dam, flies through the air.

'Yes you did! Of course you did. Why do you think I asked you to come with me when I moved?'

'I don't know. So I could watch you and Mark playing with fire?'

'I was wrong.'

It halts her. Reinforces the dam, just when...

'I thought you were never wrong.'

'So did I. But I was wrong about Mark.'

'Oh right, so you're wrong. Is that just for today that you're wrong about him?' She steps back to get a better angle on Iquis and nearly loses her footing. 'Why should I trust you about Mark? Why should I trust any of this? You can't even come down and talk on the same level. Who do you think you are?'

Iquis works her way quickly back along the cliff towards Harriet, then she simply lets go.

She lands next to her, balled like a black leather cat, feet lost somewhere between two jutting rocks. She is right on the edge, yet she doesn't even falter. Just draws herself up and turns all her attention onto Harriet. Waits for her to continue.

But Harriet just shakes her head, wrong-footed again. *Why do you keep on appeasing me when I don't want you to?*

'But...' Iquis sounds hesitant, 'you didn't fight it... you didn't hold me back.'

'You've said that before. As if it's an excuse.'

'Why did you just accept it?'

'Because it felt familiar.'

'What do you mean?'

But Harriet is silent, staring at the rushing water. 'I wasn't enough for you,' she says at last, 'just like I wasn't enough for Mum. She always wanted Stephen. You wanted Mark.'

Iquis is silent. There's an ache in Harriet's throat. She can feel the energy of the waterfall in the air – feel the spray of it trickling down her face.

'Mark is history,' Iquis says. 'I can't change anything about your family, but I can change that.'

'Yes, but for how long? I saw you last term. That intensity. The way the two of you talked that last night by the river. You expect me to believe that that has all just gone?'

'Mark...' Iquis is close beside her, but her gaze focuses on the turbulent water. 'He was so warm, so alive. I couldn't help being fascinated by him. He made me hungry. For a while that greed, that hunger, blinded me. I didn't recognise it for what it was until after I was away from it. Until after I went home, and saw, really saw, what was in me. What I could be.'

She kicks at the stone that she has been resting on, until it breaks away from the cliff edge and plummets down.

'I sicken myself.'

Her foot hangs over the gap she has made. Briefly she's like a cartoon character suspended over air. Then she retracts abruptly and once started continues moving, retreating across the rocks towards the bike.

She walks fast and without caution. At one point she stumbles, falls, then pushes herself roughly back up, all without breaking pace.

Harriet hurries after her and catches her by the bike, moments before she slots her helmet on.

'Iquis, wait!' Harriet reaches a hand up to where the helmet is suspended above Iquis's head and tugs it away. 'I don't understand.'

'There's nothing to understand. It's over.' But Iquis sounds cold and scared, the same way she'd sounded when she returned after Christmas.

There's a strange, underlying atmosphere between them. A tension, like the electricity of a storm.

'The fascination is still there,' Harriet says, realisation dawning slowly and unwillingly. 'You'll give in to it in time. It's inevitable.'

Iquis drops her hand abruptly, so that the helmet now hangs at her side like a bowling ball.

'Then stop me.'

'How can I?'

'Because you have to. Because you're the only one who can.'

'No one can stop you once you make your mind up.'

'So you won't even try?'

Harriet is silent, staring half at Iquis and half at the backdrop.

Iquis frowns, then digs a hand into the back pocket of her trousers. She holds a mortise key out to Harriet.

'It's for the door between me and the rest of the house,' Iquis says. 'The door between me and Mark. It's locked at the moment. You can be the only one that uses it. The only one that has control over it.'

'But this won't stop you,' Harriet repeats.

'So it's symbolic. By taking it, you're making a commitment to keep me away from him.'

Harriet laughs uneasily. 'Iquis, this is crazy.'

'Is it? Then why are you so afraid of taking the key? It was you who wanted reassurance. Now when I offer it, you won't take it. What do you want?'

'I don't know.' It's true, Harriet no longer knows. *I thought it was for this to go on forever, but secretly I always knew it couldn't.*

'Take it,' Iquis says. Her voice is quiet, yet there is a hint of desperation that Harriet can't ignore. She reaches out and takes the key, but inside she's thinking of the little mermaid and the pounding water.

TWENTY-EIGHT

'It seems I have failed to make an impression on you.' Dr Drake's tone is more caustic than ever.

Harriet stands in front of Dr Drake's desk. She hasn't been offered a chair. It's a small thing, but it tilts the see-saw of defiance and fear down towards defiance.

'You made an impression.'

'I'm glad to hear it.' Dr Drake gives her a quick glare, then glances down at her notes. 'Indeed, when it comes to attendance at lectures, I have been singularly favoured, so perhaps I did make *some* impact. Although, as for the last week...'

You shouldn't have made me wait. Did you really think I'd be in your lectures with this hanging over me?

Dr Drake leans forwards. 'Do you think you can pass this course without attending lectures?'

As always, there's only one right answer. Harriet chooses not to give it. Instead she shrugs, an Iquis shrug.

'You may believe we have nothing to teach you. But if so, isn't it time you displayed some of that knowledge in your coursework?'

Silence.

'What there is of it.' Dr Drake pulls a sheet from the open file on her desk. 'This is a list of your missing coursework.' She hands it to Harriet, who can't drag her eyes from Dr Drake's long enough to look at it.

'My colleagues are concerned. They want to know what happened to the keen student who started the year.'

She stares at Harriet, who stares back.

'So?' Dr Drake sounds impatient. 'What happened?'

For once the correct answer is not implicit in the question. Harriet is not sure she can provide it. "I don't feel like doing it any more," is not an adequate answer and yet it's the closest she can come.

Dr Drake sighs and shifts slightly in her chair.

'Why did you do this course?'

'I wanted to build bridges.'

'And now? Is that no longer true?'

Harriet thinks of Iquis and the Lake District, the power of the bike, the solitary feel of the night. 'I want to cross them.'

A wry smile from Dr Drake.

'Very pat,' she says. She perches her chin on her fingers and studies Harriet carefully. 'How much of this has to do with the girl who came to my lecture?'

'Iquis.' The name is jerked out of Harriet by surprise. *I shouldn't have let her come with me. Dr Drake sees too much.*

'You can't afford distractions,' Dr Drake says decisively.

But Harriet isn't listening.

Iquis happened, is that the answer? When did it start? When she kissed Dad? When I saw her burgundy lipstick tangled in the black hairs of his hand? Yet that wouldn't explain everything that's happened in the last months.

Stephen was involved somehow too, growing away from him, letting him go.

Maybe I just don't want to be the good girl any more.

'I know that the people you meet at university can be very seductive,' Dr Drake sounds pensive, 'can seem to offer you different...' She trails off. 'But you have to be strong,' she says, regaining her usual force. 'Have to shut them out, maintain your focus. It's the only way.'

Yes, strong, rigid, inflexible, just like you, Harriet thinks, and finds Iquis's voice in her head. *"She should get a life".*

'Maybe that's not what I want,' she says, and then finds herself admitting, 'maybe it's got nothing to do with Iquis. Maybe it's got nothing to do with bridges.'

Behind Dr Drake's head the Telford Suspension Bridge spans the width of the wall. Harriet almost expects it to crumple at her words, to cave in like the Tacoma Narrows Bridge had. Or, more realistically, for Dr Drake to accuse her of blasphemy.

But she just waits for Harriet to continue and, under her analytical stare, Harriet finds that she wants to talk, to puzzle it out.

'You asked me why I chose this course,' she says. 'Maybe, it was because it was what Dad would have wanted Stephen to do.'

'Stephen?'

'My brother. He died.'

Dr Drake blinks her eyes closed briefly, then reopens them.

'When Stephen died,' Harriet says, 'they all watched me.' His friends, who had mainly ignored her up till then. 'All those glances, waiting to see how I was reacting. Sometimes

I felt like they didn't even see me, that instead they were looking for something of him – an essence. I was just his carrier, his memory.'

It was as if I didn't exist.

'Work was the only safe place. I shut everything out, just as you're suggesting I should do now, concentrated only on my studies. The teachers loved me. Yes, I know what you're talking about. But that's not what I want any more.'

Dr Drake exhales slowly, and leans back in her chair.

She is silent, yet it feels like a respectful silence, like the only reaction that Harriet could tolerate.

I've told her because I don't think she'll react with sympathy, she realises, *or any of that touchy-feely stuff I hate.*

Finally, Dr Drake temples her fingers together and presses them against her lips. 'So you're having doubts about the course, about your motivation.'

'Yes.'

'I see.'

They seem to be at an impasse.

'I wonder whether I'd have been better off doing psychology,' Harriet says, more as a means of moving them on than because this is a deep-seated idea – although she's wondered about it. When Iquis talked she'd been intrigued, had wanted to learn more, had thought that she might understand other people and herself better if she studied it. But then Iquis had lost interest and Harriet too had largely forgotten about it.

'Too late now, of course,' she says.

'It's never too late,' Dr Drake says, taking Harriet by surprise. 'Of course you're right in one way, it is too late for this year. But there's nothing to stop you restarting next year, once you've worked out what you want. It's far better to do that, than to spend the next four years doing something that's wrong for you.'

For a moment the thought grabs Harriet. *I could do it,* she realises, *could change direction, could take the time to think about who I am, what I want to do – maybe psychology, maybe something else, there could be lots of things.*

No, it's crazy, what would Dad say? It's his money that keeps me here. He didn't want me to get a student loan, said that's what they'd saved for over the years, originally for Stephen as well and then – only for me.

I couldn't. He'd be angry. But then, when isn't he? I'm not really afraid of his anger, she realises, *it's too much like mine. I understand it.*

'I've obviously triggered a train of thought,' Dr Drake says. 'Perhaps you want to think about it and get back to me.'

Harriet nods, eager to leave.

'But,' Dr Drake continues, 'think fast. This decision is going to make itself if you don't make it soon. If you want to go on with this course you've got to start catching up. Otherwise you'll pass the point of no return. Do yourself a favour, make your own choices, take control.'

TWENTY-NINE

The lake seems to have the majority of Iquis's attention. Harriet's words make no ripple.

'Well, what do you think?' she asks.

'You see, I said she couldn't harm you,' Iquis says and continues to stare moodily into the lake.

'Is that it?' Harriet says, with some exasperation. 'Okay, maybe Dr Drake can't actually harm me, but I can't dismiss it that casually. Sooner or later I have to deal with it. If I decide to study something else, there'll be no point in me continuing this year. I'll have to go home.'

We might lose contact. I don't trust you to still be here next year.

'Don't go,' Iquis's voice breaks over her thoughts.

'I might have no choice. I don't know how long I can stall Dr Drake. She wants a decision.'

'No, not that. The concert tomorrow.'

'Iquis! Haven't you been listening to me?'

'You don't have to go home. You don't have to do anything you don't want to do. You worry too much. We'll sort out Dr Drake. That's not important. What matters is the concert tomorrow.'

'It's not that simple.'

'Yes it is. Trust me.' She skims a stone across the water, watches it bounce three times, then sink. '*Now*, about tomorrow, why don't we go to Decadance?'

'Because I'm going to the Dark Island concert. Anyway, I thought you didn't want to go back, thought it had bad memories for you.'

And for me. The music video. I still haven't watched it. It's part of why I need to go to the concert so badly. To get back my sense of Dark Island, to get past what happened at Decadance. Because somehow, since then, there's been a distance. They haven't been able to reach me in the same way. I still play their music, but I feel disconnected. Tomorrow night will be different, because they're going to be real.

'We go to Decadance tomorrow or never,' Iquis says.

'Never then,' Harriet says. 'Look, Iquis, I'm going to the concert, just get used to it. You don't have to have everything your own way, it's not good for you.'

'I just don't want you to be disappointed,' Iquis says. 'To have your view of them tarnished. Wouldn't it be better to keep your fantasy version of them, rather than risk being disillusioned?'

'No, it wouldn't.' Yet Iquis's words are persuasive. She can't quite shake the memory of *that* video. 'You don't get what they mean to me. Just how important they've been.' For a moment, she's back in the record shop, hearing them for the first time and that compulsive longing is back, stronger for having been tamped down. 'I have to see them.'

She'd tried to reach into the speakers, felt like she could reach them that way. Of course, that couldn't really happen, no matter how strong the sense of bond. But at the concert it could.

She and Marcia are going to be at the front. They've already agreed this.

If her fantasies are meant to come true, Dark Island will pick her out from the crowd and recognise she belongs to them. They'll stop the music, beckon her on stage, hand her a microphone and she'll sing Circe's lyrics, as easily as she sang them in the woods.

Iquis leans her head back, hovers the neck of the wine bottle over her face and tilts it slowly. Red wine splashes down into her open mouth, catching in one corner.

'It might be dangerous,' she says, lowering the wine bottle. 'People get hurt at concerts like this.'

Harriet laughs.

'You're worried about the danger! After all the risks we've taken.'

'I've always been there to protect you before.'

'How bloody arrogant! And untrue. What about when you wanted me to climb that cliff face last week? You were ahead of me. You wouldn't have been able to catch me if I'd slipped. And that's not the only time.'

'Okay, so sometimes I don't realise. But I stopped when you said, didn't I? I wouldn't deliberately put you in danger.'

'You don't think it's dangerous to climb up a wet cliff face in the middle of the night, but going to a concert with a group of others is likely to be fatal and Dr Drake can't harm me! Iquis, you have a warped sense of perspective.'

'Maybe I do. But you should trust me on this.'

'But you told me not to trust you.'

'That was weeks ago.'

'So?'

Iquis butts the wine bottle against the ground. The remaining wine sloshes around inside it.

'I'll be with Marcia, Paul and Mark. If I need looking after – which I don't – they'll look out for me.'

'Mark,' Iquis says. 'So it's okay for you to see him. I have to keep away, but you can get all buddy buddy and swan off to concerts with him.' She sounds angry, frustrated.

'It's not like that,' Harriet says. 'We'll probably not even speak to each other. He's just keeping his word.'

She fingers the curt note in her pocket.

Be ready to leave at 2:15 tomorrow.

It had been under her door when her alarm clock woke her at midday. The note was unsigned but Mark's writing was easy to recognise. She'd been relieved.

'You're fascinated by him,' Iquis says. 'I used to watch you fighting with him last term, and you were so intent you didn't even realise I was looking.'

'Only because I hated him.'

'You always knew where he was in the room.'

'So?' Harriet shifts uncomfortably.

'And the way you fought with him when he pulled you from the river; so much passion. There was nothing else except him.'

The crushing rosemary. His hand around her ankle, spinning her round.

'Is that why you wanted me to keep away from him?' Iquis says. 'So that you could have him?'

'No. It's not like that. You think I fancy him or something – I don't.' Harriet's words spill out, as Iquis's jibes cause her to feel things, to make connections. It's like being given the key to a complicated puzzle. 'It's just...' She's scared, she knows she's going to say something that she doesn't want to admit, the dream is flooding her mind, spinning her around, faster and faster, 'that...' and then, thudding to a halt. 'He reminds me of Stephen.'

She feels strangely empty. *How long have I known? How long have I been denying it for?*

'It's stupid,' she says. 'I worshipped Stephen. I hate Mark. And yet there's something...' she frowns. 'There's the obvious things. They're both blonde and they're both competitive, sport mad.'

She flashes through images of each of them flushed and sweaty, filled with excitement and triumph, surrounded by friends, confident in their right to lead, to win.

'But that's it. Nothing else.'

Iquis is silent.

'It doesn't make sense,' Harriet says. 'I don't understand why a smug git like him can remind me of Stephen. It's wrong. He's not fit. It's like insulting Stephen's memory.'

Yet I'm looking forward to seeing Mark tomorrow, to sparring with him, to trying to get the better of him. I've missed it. Things have been a bit flat without the competition between us.

I better not let Iquis realise.

'Maybe you didn't always like Stephen,' Iquis says.

'Don't be stupid!'

Iquis traces a geometric pattern in the mud with a stick which has mysteriously appeared in her hands while Harriet was wrestling with her thoughts. It's disconcerting, in the same way that a jump in a film would be.

'Perhaps I'm scared,' Iquis says.

'What!'

'That if you go, you won't return.'

Harriet is jolted away from her thoughts of Mark/ Stephen. Iquis couldn't possibly know about her fantasy of being adopted by Dark Island at the concert, could she?

'That's daft,' she says. 'Of course I'll return. I came back after Christmas, didn't I?'

Iquis's stick slows against the mud, continues to trace, but very slowly, very gradually.

'Look... there's something...' Unusually hesitant.

'What?' Harriet says, leaning forwards.

Iquis scribbles out the patterns with a swift movement.

'Share blood with me.' She whispers the words. Harriet can only just catch them.

'What do you mean?'

Iquis's expression is intent, unnerving. She doesn't answer. Just waits, the stick stilled in her hand.

Harriet chases images in her head. At first she sees only a cold, metallic, rusty darkness. But then a memory surfaces.

'You mean like the goths were talking about that time when they mentioned human vampires? People who believed they'd inherited something from fiction, that they'd developed a craving. And what Lucien said: that there were others who thought it was an honour to feed them, who willingly donated their blood, only tiny amounts... sherry glass quantities... but even so... ugh! That's sick.'

Iquis flinches. 'No! That's not what I mean. I would never... I'm saying this wrong. I mean like kin, but chosen kin.'

Hesitant at first, she gains conviction as she speaks.

'I want us to make ourselves like family. I want the same blood to run in our veins. So that we belong together. So that however far apart we are, we will always have this bond.'

She gazes directly into Harriet's eyes. Her own eyes are wide, hypnotic.

'Be my blood sister?'

And then the fever is in Harriet – she must have caught it from Iquis. She is filled with urgency. Influenced by her encounter with Dr Drake earlier, and the talk of change, she feels compelled to snatch this opportunity.

I've never had a sister, a sense of belonging, of being chosen. I want...

Even so. 'Let me think about it.'

'No,' Iquis says. 'There's no time. Do this tonight and I'll let you go to the concert.'

'You couldn't stop me.'

'Couldn't I?'

Something in her face, some certainty, makes Harriet doubt her own assertion.

'You want to go,' Iquis says, 'I wish you didn't... but...' As she speaks she raises the half-empty wine bottle and smashes it against a rock. The wine spurts out over the rock, the jagged neck remains in Iquis's hand. 'If you do this, then I know that I'll be there with you, protecting you. That no harm can come to you.'

Unexpected superstition. Iquis sounds so serious, like she really believes it.

The edges of the bottle stand upright like three fingers of a hand, only sharper.

The fever is still there. 'Tonight then,' Harriet says.

Iquis traps Harriet's hand and smooths the pad of skin over her thumb. It tingles as the blood rushes around, evading the pressure.

A brief hesitation.

'Get on with it then,' Harriet says, nervous. 'Don't give me time to change my mind.'

The bottle pushes down; its narrowest point pierces her skin, pulls away. A second of shock, and then blood and pain well up together.

Iquis locks hands with her. Presses her thumb to Harriet's.

Harriet has missed seeing Iquis slice into her own hand, was too busy staring at the dark wound on her thumb.

Their blood is black in the moonlight as it mingles. It spills in rivulets down the trunks of their thumbs.

Her blood burns and pulses as it passes into me, as it mixes with mine. Like a chemical reaction. Like fire. Like ice.

What have I done?

'Did it have to be so deep?'

'Yes,' Iquis says. 'Keep still.'

There's a lack of ceremony. She'd expected more than this simple, almost brutal act. But what? Even Iquis handing her the key last week seemed more symbolic and redolent of occasion than this. If anything, this has had a practical feel. Iquis has had the air throughout of a competent surgeon, albeit one forced to use makeshift tools.

What do we do now? Harriet wonders.

For some reason, the stickiness of the blood as it dries on her skin reminds Harriet once more of the dark stain of lipstick on Dad's hand.

'Why did you kiss him?' She finds herself asking. Not with heat, the way she once would have, but with a curious detachment.

I really don't understand her. I keep on thinking I do, but I always find I'm wrong.

'Your father?' Iquis says. 'Why not?'

She's still holding their thumbs welded together.

'Would you rather I kissed you?' she says.

The edges of her lips in the dark look as sharp and dangerous as the shards of glass littering the ground.

'Not like that.'

But something, a gesture to seal this thing, would be nice.

We're not the sort of people that hug. We're too angular and spiky and cold for that. That's why we need to make the grand gestures, because we're incapable of making the small ones.

THIRTY

Clustered and androgynous, they wait. A long column of disparate height. Forced into line by the brick wall of the concert venue and linked by anticipation. Girls in corsets. Men in dresses. Heavy make-up and dark jewel costumes.

As the sky darkens, they find their setting.

On the other side of the road a young child looks fascinated. 'Mummy, why are they dressed like that?' His mother hushes him, hustles him on, then glances back, drawn by the same fascination.

Marcia's head nods, as she calculates how many people are ahead of them in the queue.

'I wish they'd keep still. I keep losing count.'

Harriet's not counting. She's just absorbing the scene, full of a blissful sense of belonging. It makes her realise how much she still misses Lucien and the others. Mark's friends are okay, but she lacks that sense of natural fit which occurs here.

Ironically, it's Harriet's companions who look out of place, even Marcia, who's dressed the part but somehow doesn't quite convince.

'We should have got here sooner,' Marcia says.

'Chill.' Mark's bored. 'It's taking forever as it is.'

'If we don't get to the front my outfit will be wasted.'

'He won't see you.'

'Won't he? *Anything* is possible.'

Harriet suspects that the radical change in Marcia's appearance is really aimed at Mark, rather than Loki. It's a kind of game-playing.

'We're not far from the head of the queue,' Mark says, 'and Paul and I are good in a scrum. I doubt if this lot are. You stick with us; we'll get you there.'

Harriet, watching Mark, thinks he's indifferent to Marcia's claimed interest in Loki. All she senses is the exuberant battering of his tamped down energy, which has him constantly moving: taking tiny bouncing steps, counting off bicep curls or chain punching the air. It must be hard for someone as active as him to be stuck in one place for so long.

Just like Stephen. He never liked to keep still.

She keeps on doing this, transposing Stephen on top of Mark. It's like a bad habit. Like holding up an identikit picture.

Yet it doesn't fit as well as I expected. When I was home this Christmas I kept looking at pictures of Stephen and thinking: but wasn't he broader? Wasn't he more filled out? More like Mark is what I meant, but I didn't realise it then.

When he was alive Stephen filled my vision. It's only now that I can see clearly. And in my new vision he's left behind, a child, slight and insubstantial compared to Mark.

These thoughts hurt, but she can't stop picking at them. She itemises the differences. Stephen was thinner, his chin more pointed and his face more elfin. He had delicate ears, with one semi-healed piercing in his left lobe. Mark's ears are untouched. He has no patience with jewellery, won't even wear a watch.

Stephen had had the same hole re-pierced several times. Each time he grew irritated with the stud long before the hole had sealed and took it out. Typical Stephen, leaving things half finished.

'Harriet.' Marcia's voice drags her from her thoughts.

'What?'

'Come for a walk?'

A drag of unwillingness.

This is addictive. I want to stay, want to keep dredging things up. Looking at Mark reminds me of details I'd forgotten. I'm seeing Stephen properly for the first time in years. I hadn't realised how much I'd lost until now, or how much he'd changed in my remembering. And yet there's something about this that seems dangerous, as if stirring up the past is asking for trouble.

'Sure,' she says.

'What about us?' Mark asks.

'You can keep our places,' Marcia says. 'Gives you a chance to bond, without us girls getting in the way.'

Mark considers Marcia, then turns towards Paul. Catching him unaware he grabs him by the shoulders and spins him around to face the wall. He splays him into the criminal-being-arrested pose.

'Like this you mean?' Mark pretends to grind his hips into Paul's buttocks. There is too much space between him and Paul to make the pretence convincing.

'Get off me!' Paul begins to struggle.

Wrestling, they roll along the wall and cannon into the quiet, dark-dyed boy ahead of them. He exchanges a brief collusive smile with Harriet and moves gently out of their way.

'I think they're bonded enough already,' Harriet says in a distracted tone.

She's surfing another memory. Stephen and Graham wrestling on the grass, turning over and over, first Stephen on top, then Graham.

A flash flicker of wounded trainer; Graham's eyes at Christmas. She winces.

The boys break apart and lean against the wall.

'I quite agree,' Paul gasps, grinning acknowledgement at Harriet. 'Don't leave on our behalf.'

'I'm not.' Marcia directs a significant look at Harriet. 'Come on. Let's go.'

*

'Do you think we should get back to the queue?' Harriet asks, twenty-five minutes later. 'They'll be wondering where we are.'

She and Marcia are crammed, jostling for position, in the crowd waiting at the back of the venue for Dark Island to arrive. She hadn't suspected Marcia's intentions until they got here. Then it had seemed obvious.

'No.' Marcia shakes her head and the stark black strands of hair fall in witchy clumps across her thin face. Harriet is struck again by the sheer vandalism of what she has done. That shimmering fall of white blonde had been magical, it had been what made Marcia so stunning. Her look is too delicate to suit stygian black. It drains her.

I just hope it's a rinse and not permanent.

The driveway, where they are waiting, is blocked by a solid gate. Tongues of green paint peel away from it to reveal greying wood. Above their heads a camera monitors their movements.

'They're cutting it fine,' Harriet says, watching as two more people abandon the wait and sprint back up the street, towards the corner. 'The doors are due to open in five minutes.'

'They always do,' Marcia says. 'We're just going to have to leg it as soon as we've seen them. You don't really want to go now, do you?'

No, she doesn't. This is her best chance of actually meeting them. But at the same time she doesn't want to miss getting close to the front.

She shakes her head, raises a hand to flick back her hair.

'What happened to your thumb?' Marcia demands.

The cut, which is sealed inside a fragment of Iquis's scarf, throbs hotly. Iquis had ripped the scarf with her teeth, bound it tightly in place. 'It happened last night, in the Lakes.'

'An accident?'

'Yeah.'

Somewhere behind them a cheer starts up. The crowd starts to shift.

'They must have arrived,' Marcia yells.

The crowd parts just enough to allow the long black limos to nose their way forwards towards the gate. The car windows are mirrored. There are two cars, almost bumper to bumper. The camera eye swivels towards the cars. The gates start to open.

'Come on!' Marcia grabs her arm, jerks her forwards through the gates. They're not the only ones. The press of people force the gates wider.

Harriet's laughing. People are throwing roses at the cars.

'We should have thought of that,' Marcia says. Harriet nods.

The cars barrel through the centre of the crowd and pull up in the courtyard. Harriet is level with the second car. Ideal. She's sure this will be the one *they* are in. It's logical. She crouches and tries to look through the black window. She sees her own eyes mirrored back, nothing more.

But *they'll* be able to see her.

She is flushed with excitement. Time has slowed down into this intense moment of connection. Any second now she's going to hear the door handle click, then...

She's so caught up she doesn't notice what's happening around her until she's jerked abruptly sideways by the crowd. The movement is uncontrollable, scary. An elbow hits her in the face, and she starts to fall towards trampling feet.

Just in time, a hand reaches, catches her, and drags her upwards.

'Thanks!' She doesn't have the chance to see who rescued her, everything's moving too fast. They're being forced backwards towards the gate. Her feet keep losing contact with the ground as she's dragged along. She snatches glimpses of what's happening: the doors of the first car wide open, a jostle of panicked faces, a barrage of vast men in black T-shirts encircling them, driving them back.

'Resist!' Marcia grabs her hand, yanks her to an arm-wrenching halt. The goths surrounding her are sucked away. The solid flesh of the minders hits them like a wall, forcing them towards the peeling green gates.

'Wait!' Marcia digs her heels in and pushes delicate hands against a vast chest. She levers her upper body backwards until he can see her.

A temporary hiatus.

His granite face stares unblinkingly at her. Then he bites his lower lip and slips his gaze rapidly down and up, taking in the skimpy transparent top, the pale flash of goose-pimpled flesh, the long slit skirt. He licks his lips hungrily, one hand hovers ready to snatch, then a wary look enters his eyes.

He glances at the other minders to see if they are watching, and Harriet thinks she detects fear in his expression. Then he snaps his gaze back into impassivity and shoves Marcia away. Linked by Marcia's grip on her arm, Harriet falls with her, hits the ground. The green gates close onto their legs, forcing them to scramble out of reach. Then, they are shut out.

On bruised knees, with a flake of cold green paint on one cheek, Harriet stares at the ground.

'We wouldn't have hurt them,' a girl says, her voice choked with tears.

'I only wanted to see...' The speaker kicks a stone along the ground. 'They didn't *even* get out of the car.'

'That was...' a small, timid-looking girl, '... unnecessary.'

Murmurs of agreement.

Someone starts to rationalise it. 'It can't have been their fault. They're probably not allowed to get out – it will be in their contract. I bet they're really shocked, and doing something about it *right now*.'

'That doesn't help us.'

'Perhaps they'll make an announcement in the concert.'

'Yes. Say something to make it all right.'

'Of course, that's it, and they'll be talking to *us*.'

'Harriet. Come on! We've got to run, got to get back.' Marcia grabs her, and drags her up. She rises stiffly from the ground. She doesn't feel part of the spreading hope; she feels cold, detached, let down.

Even so, she succumbs to Marcia's imperative yank.

THIRTY-ONE

"'*Dark child you can't forget us.*'"

No, and wherever she is she should be able to hear them as well at this volume. Far back in the black safety of the stage Medea's mouth widens and the sound is picked up and blasted at Harriet.

"'*And we can't lose, can't lose, can't lose... you.*'"

Medea's voice, an alto fuzz, shrieks at her with a harshness more usual to a bad soprano. The level of noise is painful, stunning. Harriet's been to concerts before, expects them to be loud, knows her ears will probably ring the next day. But not like this. This has to be a mistake. She can't hear the music for the volume, can't connect with the songs, even though they're playing "Bleeding for Strangers", the song whose promise travelled the Pennines with her when she first came to Eden.

They've changed the words, though; they're more threatening. It's less of a "goodbye" message, more of a "You can't escape", and the volume just serves to drive that home.

"'*Dark child, when you're bleeding for strangers*",' on the big screen Kali's snake mouth stretches impossibly wide, "'*just remember how sweetly they break*".'

Harriet is not happy. There has been no explanation, no apology for what happened earlier. In fact, Dark Island seem to have no interest in talking to the audience. The stage itself is off-putting. Long black bars front the stage, stretching up from floor to ceiling. Behind them the group act like dangerous animals, resentful of their capture, skulking at the back of the stage a lot of the time, only prowling forward when the need to lash out becomes too strong.

It's a ridiculous image, but it's what Harriet feels. She remembers Dad at the zoo when she'd stood in front of the lions' enclosure. "Don't get too close," he'd warned, and there'd been fear in his voice, because he'd known their potential.

Harriet's always believed the implicit violence in Dark Island videos was a pretend thing, just part of the story. But tonight, this close to them, she has a real sense of menace and can't shake it. How much of this is because of what happened earlier she doesn't know, but for once Mark's presence next to her is reassuring rather than irritating, and she's relieved that they'd managed to catch them.

It had looked doubtful. They'd sprinted up the moving queue, frantically scanning faces as they ran, and had only just caught the two boys as they were handing their tickets in. Marcia had been upset and an argument between her and Mark had only been prevented by the surge forwards into the venue. Mark had grabbed Harriet's hand and towed her through the stampede. She'd caught glimpses of Marcia on his far side, and known Paul was there too. Somehow all four of them had managed to stay together and, as Mark had promised, to get to the front.

It feels ungrateful to wonder whether they'd have been better off further back. Harriet hates herself for thinking it.

※

An hour in, the barrage of noise stops abruptly. Harriet gasps with relief. Kali slinks towards the front of the stage.

'Circe couldn't make it.' The snakes painted on her face seem to come alive as she speaks, quivering with pre-strike tension. 'But we've got *something* of hers here.'

There's a cheer. Loki walks over and takes the microphone from Kali. 'This is a song she wrote recently.'

The cheers get louder, and Harriet joins in rather tentatively.

Sauron and Medea are at the back. Their shadowy figures edge towards the stage drapes, merge into them and disappear off the stage. Kali slithers away. There is only Loki left, plucking almost idly at a quiet pattern of bass notes, his head tilted to watch his fingers, the big screen blank and unlit.

Circe's recorded voice, when it joins in, is slightly husky. It's like she's talking to herself, recording for herself. The song doesn't sound intended for an audience. Loki's notes follow Circe's voice, making no attempt to harmonise. They are just a thrumming background, a punctuation for her words.

> *"Heavy water diverging round you*
> *crushes the flowers in your hair.*
> *Bereft, I summon Charon, but he*
> *cannot take me where you are.*

Broken sister, broken daughter; you
seem now the source of my despair."'

The song has an archaic feel both in how it is written and in how it is sung. The soft pauses between lines, the meditative, sad slowness of the delivery. And there's something unfinished about it, something slightly awkward about some of the lines, as if Circe was still in the middle of working on it.

Yet that, to Harriet, increases its charm. It's flawed, imperfect, and therefore touchable in a way that nothing else in this concert has been.

"'Ophelia.
I do not know how to say this.
Do not know how to do this.
Ophelia.
Be like a river to me.
Take me, tumble me, hold me, release me.
Ophelia,
use me anyway you like.
Ophelia,
leave me not upon this bank."'

Then silence. Loki's guitar has faded out with the voice.

This is what I've been missing. If Circe was here, the whole concert would be different. I'd have felt different. Maybe she left them because she didn't like the direction they were going in.

The song and her thoughts give Harriet a sense that all is not lost. She still has someone left to believe in.

*

Another hour of noise, and then a final reprieve. Once more the sound is lowered and Loki comes to the front in seductive mode.

> *"For a brief inhuman hour*
> *like a butterfly caught in a net*
> *let me watch the way your wings flutter*
> *let me catch your fading breath."*

He raises one arm in a commanding gesture and the stage lights swivel to face the audience. The lights are hot and intense. Harriet, exhausted and full of a simple uncomplicated desire to go home, wants to back from them, but she's trapped where she is by the press of bodies.

> *"Do you want to be my muse?"*

The viola lifts his voice and sends his cry deep into the audience.

As the note dies away, Kali grasps the bars and shakes herself against them. Her eyes dart over the audience. Harriet wants to duck. It seems a lifetime ago that she had pressed her face to the car window, wanting to be seen.

> *"Pure pilgrim, with your barefoot stride,*
> *lay yourself upon the altar,*
> *rest your neck upon the blade,*
> *lose yourself for me."*

Then Sauron struts out of the darkness and Harriet forgets about Kali.

"'Do you want to be my sacrifice?'"

It's more of a shout than a sung lyric. He thumps the tribal drum balanced on his hipbone with his knuckles to reinforce his words.

The audience remains silent.

There are spiders on his face. They have big, jagged legs underneath tight menacing heads. They look like they've been tattooed rather than painted.

'No I don't, you fat bastard!' Harriet wants to shout, with the same instinctive resistance towards bullying that used to get her into precarious situations in school. Sauron isn't fat, but the word goes some way to capturing the hugeness of his presence, though not the menace of it.

"'Let me hear you',' Sauron demands of the audience, who respond with a mutter.

Medea breaks in with the viola. A soothing, softening slide of notes.

"'Let me hear you scream',' Sauron demands, unsoftened. *"'The way you've been screaming all night. Let me hear you call my name.*

'Do you want to be my sacrifice?'"

And finally, some of the audience start to give him what he's demanding, but not all of them. It's isolated voices.

'Yes,' they call. And then his name, and the names of the others. Harriet hears Marcia's voice, yelling Loki's name over and over. And then Sauron's questioning, and they're responding like a chorus.

It sickens Harriet. Sauron seems to swell with their responses, seems to feed on what they are offering him. On what he has demanded.

'Aren't you listening to what you're saying?' she yells furiously at the people around her. 'I'm nobody's sacrifice!' She projects it at full volume at the stage and sees Sauron's eyes suddenly fasten on her.

'The gates are broken!' she yells at him. Not meaning to. It just comes out.

His nostrils flare. His gaze pierces her.

He is seeing her and she doesn't want him to. He terrifies her. It's like he's sucking something out of her – drawing closer, despite the bars.

Then something registers on his face. There's a moment of fury. She sees his fist slam into a bar, making it rattle. Then as abruptly as he had sought her out he dismisses her. She sees herself fall from his attention, sees him start to focus on the people around her, and despite her relief she feels empty.

Horribly, horribly empty.

> *"Live for me.*
> *Die for me."*

The chant is dying down. It sounds like an anticlimax now. The conclusion has already happened.

'"*Barefoot ghost from a stranger's place*",' Loki sings.

A string on Medea's viola snaps with a magnified pinging sound and the lights go out.

Silence. All she can hear is breathing and the humming of her ears. Then the inevitable applause. Shouting, stamping. 'Encore! Encore!'

But the lights come on and the stage is empty. They do not come back.

THIRTY-TWO

As the cries of the audience die down, Harriet knows she doesn't want to discuss the concert with the others, doesn't even want to think about it. Instead she focuses on material things: her imminent release from being jammed against other people, her longing for the cool night air and how good it will be to climb into Mark's car and be driven home.

The space eases slightly, like an apple press being untwisted and Marcia wriggles across to her.

'Wasn't that something?' Marcia says. 'Do you think the string breaking was deliberate?' And then, lowering her mouth to Harriet's ear, 'Are you coming?'

'Marcia, it's over,' Harriet says.

Marcia tugs her sleeve.

'Marcia, it will be the same as before. What's the point? Let's just go home.'

Harriet has made no attempt to lower her voice. This time Mark hears her.

'No way, Marcia! You were gone for ages last time. We almost went in without you.'

'You wouldn't have done,' Marcia says.

'We fully intended to. What did you expect?'

'I don't believe you.' Marcia sounds hurt. 'Anyway, it won't be as long this time.'

'No. We're going home.'

'But it's my last chance to see him. Surely that's worth...'

As people start to push past them Marcia grows agitated. 'We'll miss them if we don't go now.'

'You won't see anything anyway,' Harriet says. 'You know what it was like before.'

'I will. I've got a tame minder,' Marcia claims.

Harriet recalls the look on his face. 'There was nothing *tame* about that minder!'

Marcia glares. 'That's not the point. I *have* to see him. I can't come all this way and not see him.'

'Quit the groupie act,' Mark says, losing patience. 'We're going home.'

'You're jealous!'

'Of you getting mauled by some fat minder who claims he can get you access to the band? I think not.'

'Oh, fuck the lot of you! Don't bother waiting. I'll get a train back.'

Harriet has never seen Marcia angry before. Before any of them can react, she strides away from them and into the crowd. Taken by surprise they watch her disappear.

Recovering, Mark curses and plunges after her. He barges his way through groups of people with an impatience which no doubt helps to ease his annoyance. It seems to Harriet, however, that Marcia's quicksilver weaving is far more effective than his brute force approach.

He returns empty-handed a few minutes later.

'Couldn't find her.'

'You're such a bastard at times,' Harriet says, aware that she is using him as a convenient and uncomplicated target.

'Me? What did I do?' He looks at her blank-faced with surprise.

She shrugs her shoulders. She's not going to explain the complexities of his relationship with Marcia. Let them play their own games.

'Where's the stage entrance then?' Mark asks.

They walk rapidly, talking little.

'You okay?' Paul looks at Harriet's tired face with concern.

She nods.

The crowd is dispersing, converting back into subdued-looking individuals who fade into the night.

It doesn't take long to reach the side street. As they turn to walk down it a pair of black stretch limos travel towards them, pause at the corner and then are gone.

'She was right. They were quick,' Harriet says.

She looks down the street to the driveway where they had waited earlier, but it's empty, devoid of fans.

How unusual and how sad. They may have got what they wanted on the stage when Sauron demanded it. But this says something different.

'So where is she?' Mark demands. He pulls his mobile from his pocket with an angry gesture. 'I'll give her a ring. Tell her to stop messing us around.'

While they wait for Marcia to answer they walk up to the gate which is firmly shut. Just in case there is anyone trapped inside, Harriet knocks on it. No response. She hadn't really expected one.

'It's ringing but she's not answering,' Mark says, snapping the phone shut. He sounds less angry and more worried.

They walk back to the main entrance, scrutinising the small groups who remain leaning against walls or wandering slowly by. None of them contains Marcia.

Back in the concert hall, the crowd has been replaced by cleaners and security men. When asked whether they've seen one stray female, they look at them in disbelief.

It's like wandering around after a party has finished, eyeing the debris.

They trace their route to and from the concert hall through emptied corridors, their feet echoing away into stillness, then linger outside the closed drink and food stalls.

They return to the faded green gate, hammer on it.

Still no answer.

Back at the entrance the doors have been shut and locked.

'Let's go home,' Mark says. 'She must have meant what she said about getting a train back.'

They walk moodily to the car. Harriet mulls over Mark's tone of voice. He had sounded subdued, as if he was unsure what he had done wrong but felt guilty.

Serves you right, she thinks. *It's about time you started thinking about how you affect people.* But she says nothing, just concentrates on the feel of the pavement below her feet.

THIRTY-THREE

Once they are out of Newcastle and speeding along the deserted motorway, Mark passes his mobile to Paul. 'Try Marcia again.'

Moments later a tinny salsa starts up next to Harriet. She jerks, then fumbles in the side pocket of the door. Her hand closes around something flat and smooth. Marcia's mobile. She pulls it out and holds it up, so that Mark can see it in the mirror.

'That's not going to work then,' Mark says. It's impossible over the sound of the engine to gauge his reaction.

Paul disconnects and the salsa halts.

'Why don't I try Jenna?' Harriet suggests, glancing at her watch which reads twenty to one. 'It's late, but Marcia might have contacted her. Although, without her mobile...'

'Do it,' Mark cuts in.

Harriet presses the phone to her ear to block out the noise of their journey. It rings three times.

Jenna answers. 'Who is it?' she sounds groggy, but somehow alert.

'Were you asleep?'

'Harriet! What's wrong?'

'You were asleep, weren't you?' Harriet stalls for time, as she thinks about how to explain.

'It doesn't matter. Just tell me.'

'It's probably nothing,' Harriet says. 'It's just that Marcia's coming home separately, by train. She and Mark had a bit of an argument. Marcia wanted to go to the stage door and the rest of us didn't. We just wondered whether she'd spoken to you.'

'No,' Jenna says. '*Listen*, don't worry about it. She's done things like this before and she's *always* been okay. There's no reason why she won't be this time.'

'Right,' Harriet says uncertainly. If it's that straightforward why does Jenna sound worried? 'Is there anything we can do? We did try to find her, but she'd already gone.'

'No. It's just a case of waiting,' Jenna says. 'Look, I think I'll go now if you don't mind. I'll talk to you in the morning, let you know whether she's back.'

Harriet feels a jolt. 'But she will be, won't she? I thought you said it would be okay.'

Jenna sighs. 'I'm sure she'll be okay, Harriet. I'm just not sure whether she'll be back tomorrow. Sometimes, when she goes off on her own, she stays away a bit longer than that. Look, I really don't want to get into this tonight. Just tell the others not to worry. Marcia isn't your responsibility. We'll talk in the morning. It's going to be okay.'

She keeps saying that. I'd feel more convinced if she said it less. But what can I do? She obviously wants to go.

'I'll keep the mobile on, in case you want to ring back at any point.'

'Thanks,' Jenna says, sounding distracted. 'Maybe tomorrow. Have a safe journey.' She disconnects.

'What did she say?' Mark demands, turning towards Harriet.

'Watch the road,' Harriet says sharply.

He doesn't have a lot of choice. He turns to face front.

'She said it would be okay,' Harriet informs the back of his head.

*

'Marcia first ran away when she was fourteen,' Jenna confides to Harriet the following afternoon, once Mark and Paul have left. 'She was gone for three weeks.'

The boys are on a round trip to Mark's house to check his answerphone for messages from Marcia. Harriet suspects that they've also gone in order to get a break. They've been holed up together in Jenna's room for hours.

Marcia hadn't returned overnight. This morning, the four of them congregated at Jenna's in a worried huddle. They've been here ever since. Earlier, she had explained about Marcia's history of disappearing for days, sometimes weeks. Her explanation had been stilted, and it was clear she felt compelled to tell them; that she'd rather have kept it private.

'The important thing,' Jenna had said, several times, 'is that she always gets a message to us within twenty-four hours, to let us know she's okay.'

'Well, when she does,' Mark had said, 'can I talk to her?'

Jenna shook her head. 'It doesn't work like that. She never phones direct. There's an organisation that passes on

"Safe and well" messages for missing people. She uses them. She won't speak to us because that would drag her back.' Jenna had seen Mark watching, and her face had shuttered. 'I'd rather not talk about this any more.'

It's been a funny sort of day. The four of them together, waiting for the phone call to come. Harriet and Mark haven't bickered once. It's the most civilised time Harriet has ever spent with Mark. He and Paul have been surprisingly sensitive to Jenna's mood, working hard to keep her distracted by a mixture of banter and tall stories.

Now they've gone, freeing Jenna to confide in Harriet.

'Do you know why she does it?' Harriet asks carefully.

'The closest I can get is that it's like a switch being flipped. Something gets triggered and she needs to be on her own, separate from us.' She hesitates, then continues, 'Whenever she tries to explain to me why she runs away, she always ends up saying she needs to know what it's like not to be a twin, who she is without me. And it hurts, Harriet. I know I should be more grown-up, but it's just that we've always been so close, always understood each other, and then there's this door which only she goes through, and I don't even get any warning, just suddenly she's not there and it's partly my fault for existing.'

Her face suggests anger and tears warring for expression but neither get let out.

'That's why I suggested different universities,' she says. 'I thought it would be a way for this to get resolved. I also thought it would give me some control. I get tired of being run away from, rejected. I guess I wanted to do some of the rejecting myself.'

'Oh, Jenna.' Despite feeling awkward, Harriet reaches

forward and clasps one of Jenna's hands. The hand quivers. 'You always seemed so strong, so content.'

She recalls her first impression of Jenna and Marcia. She had thought they had it all, had seen them as part of the confident set, untroubled by problems. *Maybe we're not as different as I think.* The realisation is huge, confusing, but she can't think about that now.

'We are most of the time,' Jenna says. 'That's what I mean about the switch. The rest of the time we're really close.'

'Has Marcia ever seen a counsellor?' Harriet puts the question in a tentative tone. She'd hated it when it was suggested to her.

Jenna laughs. 'She's been to all sorts of therapists and child psychologists. My parents made sure of that. It never seemed to make a difference. Although, the first time, I think it did help her to talk. Then, at least, there was an obvious cause. She'd been secretly involved with a nineteen-year-old. He finished with her very abruptly and that was it, she just disappeared.

'That time the police found her, and when she realised how worried we'd been she cried for ages, kept saying sorry, and that she wouldn't do it again. And she didn't for a long time, best part of a year. Then something happened and she was gone. The only difference was that this time she got a message to us.'

'You were talking about this last year, in the kitchen,' Harriet says, as something clicks into place. 'When you said about waiting for Marcia. I didn't realise you meant literally. It must be so tough.'

A flicker crosses Jenna's face. 'It is at times,' she says carefully, 'but then, I tell myself I'm overreacting. I mean, she's an adult now – that's what the police say. But what if we stopped taking it seriously, and then she got into something she couldn't control? I'm convinced she doesn't tell me everything she gets up to when she's away. It all sounds so safe, the way she tells it.

'According to her, she never hitch-hikes, never sleeps rough, never meets up with anyone dodgy. But she always comes back exhausted. "Burnt to the socket", that's what Mum calls it. And what I want to know is, how does she get that way if all she's doing is safe stuff? I just don't believe it.'

Harriet swallows uncomfortably. Not for the first time she replays the image of the minder eyeing Marcia up. It feels dirty and threatening.

Earlier the four of them had discussed the possibility that Marcia might have gone with Dark Island. It seemed highly unlikely. The whole set-up had been so keep off. She probably couldn't get near them. And even if she had, they would have known it was trouble to take her with them. Yet Harriet has a hard time feeling logical about the concert and even Jenna hadn't ruled it out.

'I could see her doing that,' she'd said, frowning. 'If the phone call doesn't come, we'll mention the possibility to the police when we talk to them.'

'And if it does?' Harriet had asked.

'I don't know. I'll see what my parents say. We've learnt that the less fuss we make, the less often Marcia feels compelled to do this.'

Harriet doesn't like thinking about Dark Island. The disillusionment of the concert has shaken her in a fundamental way and Marcia's disappearance in the same time frame can't help but seem ominous. Logic doesn't come into this. What does is an instinctive need to see Iquis, to tell her that she was right and get her advice.

She pushes the longing away, concentrates on trying to ease Jenna's anxiety. 'She is going to be okay, you know.'

Jenna smiles. 'Thanks,' she says, and then, 'Do you want another coffee?'

'Yes, please.'

Jenna pauses on the way to the kettle to switch on the light. 'It's getting dark. I expect the phone call will come soon.'

Harriet nods. She wishes there was *something* she could do. She's better at action than words.

Five minutes later Jenna's phone rings with the same salsa tone as Marcia's. Jenna grabs it.

'Yes?' Pause.

Harriet listens to the one-sided conversation.

'Yes.' Jenna nods at Harriet, half smiles. 'She is okay? Did she say anything about the concert – about who she was with, whether she'd met up with anyone?' A long pause. 'No, no, of course, I understand. But if you could maybe ask, I'd be grateful.' She lowers her voice, 'Give her my love.'

She listens for a while to the answer. 'I know – I understand,' then after a moment, 'thank you. No, I won't need that, but it's kind of you to offer.'

Moments later she says goodbye and disconnects. She drops the phone on the bed and closes her eyes, lets out her breath in a long, shaky exhalation. She stays like that for a while, with her eyes closed, then opens them and turns to Harriet.

'She's okay. They can only tell me what she asks them to say. She said not to worry. She always says that – as if it's *that* easy!' She sounds exasperated, then just tired. 'And as usual they asked me if I wanted to talk to someone. But what's the point? There's nothing new to say.'

'And Dark Island?' Harriet asks.

'She didn't mention them at all. If she rings again they'll ask, but they can't get a message to her because she doesn't have her mobile. She always has before. I wish she'd taken it. I know I'm being stupid. It just makes her seem further away.'

'It's not stupid,' Harriet says. 'I think you're *so* brave. I just *wish* I could help.'

'You have. I didn't want to say much in front of Mark, not when Marcia is so hooked on him, but it's a relief to spill it out to you. I trust you. I know you won't gossip.'

Harriet blushes, feeling incredibly touched. 'Of course I won't,' she promises fervently.

THIRTY-FOUR

As she cycles round the corner into Mark's road Harriet recognises the sound of Iquis's motorbike engine warming up – almost too late then. She feels guilty about leaving Jenna, but there's nothing more she can do and she *has* to talk to Iquis. She peddles even harder, finding the same hidden resources of energy that she found for sprint finishes during school race days. It's exhilarating to know she can still do it.

Don't you dare go now, she thinks.

The motorbike is on the forecourt with Iquis straddled across it. Harriet aims her bicycle into the widening beam of the headlight, then brakes her feet against the ground and skews to a halt. She abandons her bicycle in front of the larger bike; a deliberate obstacle.

Iquis has her helmet on.

'Don't go without me,' Harriet yells, between gasps for breath. 'I couldn't get here any sooner. Marcia's gone missing and...'

'I know,' Iquis says. 'Paul told me.' She revs the engine softly.

'Well? Don't you want to know if there's any news?' Harriet demands.

'Is there?' There's no intonation in her voice.

'A phone message came through. She's safe.'

'Right,' says Iquis, and then, 'Listen, Harriet, I want to ride a long way tonight. It's better if you don't come with me.'

'No!' Harriet says. 'I need to see you.' She draws closer. 'You were right about Dark Island.'

There's no reaction.

'I need to tell you what happened. All of it. I need your opinion.' There's a pleading note in her voice.

Iquis shifts uncomfortably on the bike. She still hasn't turned the engine off. 'I have to go.'

'Then let me come.'

Iquis hesitates. She touches Harriet's face with her gloved fingers. 'I have to go alone.' She sounds less certain.

'I won't let you.' Harriet shoves her wounded thumb at her. 'What about this? Doesn't it mean anything?'

'Yes, but...'

'But nothing. Wait for me. I'll be three minutes, four at most.'

'Harriet...'

Harriet doesn't give her time to finish, just heads for the front door at a run.

She changes rapidly, tempted to dispense with the thermal layer which keeps her warm through the cold, winter nights. But Iquis said she wanted to travel a long way. She has to wear them. She drags them on first, then her leathers. Grabbing her boots and helmet, she sprints downstairs in her socks. The motorbike tone is constant, but she's not risking being any longer than she can help.

Once she's outside, with Iquis firmly in her vision, she pulls on her boots, helmet and gloves then lifts her bicycle up. She wheels it across to the low wall and leaves it there. She wants to lock it, but Iquis is widening the throttle so that the bike sounds hungry and impatient, and Harriet decides not to push her luck.

At least she waited. She swings up behind Iquis, wraps her arms around her waist. The action is familiar, comforting.

Harriet holds on tight, as the drive speeds away beneath her feet.

*

While Iquis pays at the window of the shop, Harriet paces the forecourt of the petrol station. The shaky stiffness of her legs adds to her general sense of slowness. Compared to the swooping speed of their combined weight pummelling through the night on the bike, her current efforts at locomotion seem feeble. They are travelling faster on these wide, three-lane roads than they have ever gone before. It's both exciting and occasionally terrifying. The rush of air as they pass cars has the thrill of a fairground ride.

It's only now they've stopped that Harriet feels the weariness which sets in after too much adrenaline.

Iquis turns away from the window and heads purposely back towards the bike, sliding her wallet back into the pocket of her leather trousers as she strides. Harriet hastens to intercept.

'Where are we going?'

'North,' Iquis says, tersely, as she starts to swing her leg back over the bike.

Harriet puts a hand down onto the saddle to prevent her completing the manoeuvre.

'Not yet. We need a break.'

Iquis looks surprised.

'Well, I do at any rate. And even if you don't think you do, you should have one. We've been travelling for nearly three hours. Your concentration must be going and these motorways are hypnotic.'

Iquis opens her mouth to argue.

'Look,' Harriet says, 'even if you're not tired, I am. Tired and stiff. I'm likely to fall asleep on the bike if I don't get some coffee and something to eat. And,' she continues, 'it would provide you with the opportunity to explain why we're on the outskirts of Stirling and not in the middle of the Lake District like I was expecting.'

Iquis stares at her hard for a minute, as if computing something, then shrugs.

'Okay,' she says.

*

The overhead heater just inside the swing door of the services blasts heat downwards, as the jangling sound of arcade machines hammers towards them. Stunned by the instant contrast with the outside, Harriet brakes to a halt.

Iquis heads for the payphone.

'Go into the restaurant. I'll catch you up,' she calls over her shoulder.

'Who are you phoning?'

'The speaking clock!' she says, with obvious sarcasm. 'Go on. Go and get something to eat. We've not got much time.'

Harriet raises one eyebrow then shrugs, an Iquis shrug, and heads for the food service area. She glances back once. Iquis's back is turned to her and her head is lowered, trapping the receiver between her chin and neck. One booted foot kicks the wall as she pushes coins into the slot.

*

Five minutes later Iquis slides into the chair opposite Harriet, who looks up from her burger and chips. 'If only you'd let me bring my mobile phone, you wouldn't need a payphone.'

'I prefer it this way.'

'I know, but why?'

Ever since Harriet's phone rang halfway up a mountain, Iquis has refused to let her carry a mobile on their night-time rides. The reason had seemed obvious then, but tonight Harriet is questioning everything.

'I mean, what have you got against them? And why don't you have one? Wouldn't it be more convenient?'

'I don't like people being able to contact me.'

'Typical!'

Iquis pulls a portion-size bottle of red wine out of her pocket.

'Is that all you're having?' Harriet asks, but she's not really surprised. Iquis never eats much when they go out, seeming to subsist mainly on chocolate and red wine. Harriet, who has a fast metabolism but little interest in food, tends to carry cereal bars and bananas – food which Iquis turns her nose up at.

Iquis shrugs.

'I have to tell you about Marcia,' Harriet says.

Iquis shakes her head. 'I told you, I don't feel like talking.'

'Is this about me going to the concert? Are you angry with me?'

Iquis wrings the bottle's neck to open it, her action accompanied by tiny clicking sounds as the thin metal strands snap. 'No.'

'I don't believe you.'

Iquis shrugs. She swigs the wine straight from the bottle.

'Don't you care about Marcia?'

Iquis lowers the bottle and looks at Harriet, but her eyes seem far away. In the harsh glare of the strip lighting she is even paler than usual. 'I care,' she says, but there is nothing in her voice.

It's like we're conversing via satellite tonight, complete with that gap between sentences where we wait for the communication to catch up.

'Where are we going?' Harriet asks, giving up on the more complicated stuff.

'Sometimes the journey is the destination.'

'Don't even try to quote philosophy at me,' Harriet says, snagging the salt pot in her left hand and upending it. Salt spills out onto the table. 'When do we stop at the mountains?'

'We don't.'

'Listen, Iquis, I'm feeling really out in the cold here. Don't I mean anything to you?'

Again that gap, and then, 'I'm going to keep riding until the sea stops me.'

'I see. Highly romantic.' Harriet thinks about it. 'In what direction?'

'I told you.' Iquis ploughs a finger through Harriet's salt mountain, traces an arrow, then tops it with a squiggled N.

'There's an awful lot of Scotland in that direction.'

'I know.' Iquis presses her fingers into the salt then lifts her hand and examines the embedded grains.

'It would take all night.' Harriet clasps both hands around her coffee cup. The polystyrene yields little heat. 'Are you serious?'

'Yes.' Iquis starts to pick out the grains of salt. 'You should stay here. You're tired. I'll get you a room. Pick you up on the way back.'

'Right. So either I do what you want or I get left behind. Thanks.' Harriet swigs her coffee back with an angry gesture. 'Just what is it with you? Do you really think the world revolves around you, or is it just an act you assume whenever you get bored?'

Iquis leans forwards until her forehead rests against the table. She remains hunched over for several seconds. Harriet's veins hum with irritation.

'Cut the dramatic gestures.'

Finally, Iquis pushes herself back up and looks at Harriet with shadowed eyes. 'It's not that simple. You can't go all the way with me. And I can't explain any more than I already have.'

'Call that an explanation?'

'I shouldn't have brought you, but you didn't really give me much choice.' She sees the furious look on Harriet's face and continues, 'Well no, it's not that really. I guess I wanted you with me. But it doesn't make sense. Not for you. Like I said, they do rooms here. I'll get you one. The best they've got. I'll pick you up when I return.' There's a pleading note to her voice.

'And when will that be?' Harriet says, but she's a little mollified by Iquis's words and tone. 'You can't possibly make it back tonight.'

Iquis looks stuck for an answer.

'No,' Harriet says. 'I'll come with you.'

'Further?' She sounds tentative.

'All the way?' Harriet says, to test Iquis's resolve.

'Not possible.'

Harriet shakes her head. 'Why do I put up with you?'

'I'm sorry.'

Harriet jumps slightly. 'I'd forgotten that was in your vocabulary.'

'It's not often.' She looks at her with uncharacteristic meekness. 'Further?' she asks again. 'If you want to? It helps to have you with me. Makes me less alone.'

As soon as she's said it she slams her gaze down to the table and keeps it there.

She'd deny saying that if I ever quoted her, Harriet thinks, watching the other girl with an aching mix of amusement and tenderness. She sighs. 'If I can't go all the way,' and she'll argue that point further when they come to it, 'I'll go as far as I can.'

'Thanks.' Iquis continues to look at the table but the angle of her shoulders softens slightly.

Harriet has a curious urge to reach out and enfold her in a hug, the way you might a child. Instead, she turns her empty coffee cup over and places it on the table as a kind of punctuation. 'We better get going. We've got a long way to go.'

*

By Pitlochry Harriet starts the "five minutes" game.

There's a prearranged signal which the girls worked out weeks ago; three taps against the leather of Iquis's jacket. It means stop. When they're in the Lakes Harriet uses it sparingly, aware always of Iquis's impatience with any form of weakness.

Just five more minutes, she promises herself, *then I can give the signal.*

When we stop, I'll have another coffee.

She remembers the half-full mug of coffee she abandoned in Jenna's room and wishes she could reach out and snatch it from the past. It was the best coffee she'd had tonight, and she hadn't appreciated it then.

Is it getting colder? Her visor makes a small cocoon for her face, but the air which filters in seems icier now and despite her layers she longs for the warmth of inside.

The sound and vibration of the bike is so ingrained that it feels part of her, symbiotic. She loses herself in it for what she hopes are vast stretches of time.

Just five more minutes, she tells herself whenever she surfaces from her trance.

*

Even the stops start to blur into one another after a while, marked only by the increasing number of coffees that

Harriet lines up for herself and counterpointed by Iquis's quick dispatch of bottled wine, which she consumes in small but regular quantities. It's one of the reasons Harriet tries to keep going as long as possible before each stop. For, despite the fact that Iquis never seems affected by wine, Harriet feels responsible for keeping her under the legal limit.

While it's only one small bottle every couple of hours she should be legal. Harriet wishes Iquis would consume something other than wine, but tonight Iquis won't touch food, not even chocolate.

Each time Harriet consults her watch it's disappointing. The elapsed time never matches her experience. The night is stretching. At this rate it may be endless.

Yet some of Iquis's single-mindedness has affected Harriet, for she refuses to consider Iquis's offer of accommodation. She's not getting off this ride voluntarily.

*

The snow sneaks up on them. A different texture to the air, a glare of white as they corner and then it's surrounding them – lying low in the dark and thickening as it accompanies them north. A subtle presence, which in its own way is as powerful as the bike.

Harriet's first reaction is to feel warmer, as if, now that the evidence of the cold lies all around her, she doesn't have to feel it so much.

Or maybe the cold has spent itself in birthing this low, white mass – which stretches away from them like an ice cap.

After the immense mountains which have accompanied them for most of the journey, this low terrain seems out of character for Scotland.

Maybe we've left Scotland behind, Harriet thinks – ignoring the clear, tarmac evidence of the road and the approaching lights of the next village – *maybe we're heading out across frozen water, with nothing except ice between us and the distant horizon.*

After the first hours of the journey, Harriet had given up calculating minutes. Now, resurfacing from her fantasy, she watches the miles as they count down on passing signs. In particular, after a while, she starts to watch the gradual nearing of the one village that she believes may betoken the end of their journey.

John O'Groats 25 miles.

The furthest point in Scotland. That has to be where Iquis is heading.

"North, as far as I can go, until I hit the sea," she had said.

Trust Iquis to be so literal.

I'm still here, Harriet thinks very quietly to herself. *She hasn't abandoned me yet. Maybe she's forgotten.*

I wonder whether tonight I will solve some part of the mystery that surrounds her. There must be a key in this wild ride, an explanation that I can't even begin to guess. Even she wouldn't do something like this just for the hell of it.

Or would she?

*

John O'Groats 5 miles.

Harriet keeps very still.

*

They pass a sign which indicates a right-hand turning to a village. Harriet feels the twist of Iquis's arm and knows that she's just hit the indicator. The bike slows rapidly. Moments later, Iquis turns the bike east into the village.

The bike prowls along the narrow street. Iquis's head scans from right to left, then fixes. She pulls up by a cottage.

Harriet climbs shakily off the bike and starts to stretch the stiffness out of her limbs. The cottage has an illuminated B&B sign, showing vacancies. There are a couple of cars parked in front of it. Unsurprisingly, the interior of the cottage is in darkness.

'Here's where I leave you,' Iquis says, propping the bike on its stand and heading for the garden gate.

'You can't.' Harriet grabs her arm to stop her. 'It's four in the morning. It would be outrageous to wake them.'

'It says vacancies.'

'That's not an invitation for us to hammer on their door in the middle of the night.'

Iquis looks doubtful and Harriet seizes the advantage. 'Take me with you.'

'I can't,' she says, with absolute finality. 'We have to wake them.'

Harriet's not really surprised, but that doesn't stop her being desperately disappointed. 'How long will you be?' she asks in a subdued voice.

'An hour, maybe two.' Iquis doesn't sound very happy either.

'I could help, with whatever...'

Iquis shakes her head. 'Come on,' she says, her hand on the gate, her expression urgent.

'No.' Harriet's gaze is on the small glimmer of sea to the east. 'Not yet. I'll walk down to the bay first. I need to see some part of this land before I go in, after travelling all this way.'

It's in Harriet's favour that Iquis is oblivious to the doubts that would beset most people when leaving a girl alone in a strange place at night.

Not that this small windswept village looks particularly threatening.

'You go on,' Harriet says, slotting her helmet into one of the bike's panniers with a casualness born of habit. 'I'll wake them once I've had a look at the sea.'

Iquis's urgency is obvious. She hesitates only briefly. 'You'll be okay?'

Harriet nods, and Iquis swings herself back onto the bike.

A slight pause as she takes in Harriet's face.

'Wish me luck.' She kicks away the stand.

Harriet stands back as she rides away. The sound of the bike fades, then is swallowed by the nearer sound of the wind and the faint undertone of sea breaking against shore.

Harriet starts to run.

The wind sweeps in from the sea and blows her back the way they have come. She reaches the main road fast and can just make out the faint beam of Iquis's bike as it heads towards, then becomes lost in, the larger brightness that is John O'Groats.

Less than five miles.

Without further consideration Harriet turns in that direction and continues to run.

THIRTY-FIVE

It's weeks since Harriet has run properly and these are not ideal conditions. Running in leathers is absurd: she's hampered, burning and sweating with effort. She yanks in mouthfuls of icy oxygen, which sears her lungs. With such a mix of sensation she doesn't even know whether she's hot or cold.

Her mouth is full of the taste of ice and she's scared.

The first mile was okay. The pleasure of running, after so much sitting, was intense. But gradually, as her isolation increases, primitive fear takes over.

The moon is bright and the sky cloudless, the road a straight dark line bisecting the snow fields. Ahead of her John O'Groats beams like a beacon, drawing her forwards. Behind her lies safety. Every mile she runs takes her further away.

Once I reach the town I'll be safe, she tells herself. But she doesn't believe it. For a start there's Iquis – she's going to be furious, or even worse, not there. But there's something else. It crept in from Iquis's attitude on the journey: that sense of her going unwillingly forward, like a sacrifice.

I don't think I'm going to like what I find.

The trickling, settling sound of snow and ice accompanies her. It seems constantly in motion, melting and freezing like a glacier or a living entity. However, as she gets closer to John O'Groats, a choppy, mechanical noise overrides it. At first she thinks the town is the culprit. Then, as the noise amplifies, she recognises it from films and looks upwards.

The helicopter heads towards her from beyond John O'Groats, ripping the night apart with its sound. It's so low in the sky that she feels like it's coming at her and looks round for somewhere to hide. But the land is too flat.

Get a grip, she tells herself. *It's not as close as you think.*

She slows to a walk, watching it. It is pretty close though. It seems to be hovering now, just to the right of the town, scoring the ground with a searchlight. It must be coming down.

The realisation is disturbing, though she doesn't quite know why. She puts it down to her general jumpiness. For a second, she wonders whether she should just turn round and go back. But now that she's stopped running, exhaustion is setting in. Her legs are trembling with it and her ankles ache. She doesn't have another five miles in her.

The helicopter comes down so fast she half expects it to bounce. As soon as it's down the lights are switched off and the noise silenced. Harriet stares hard at the point where it's landed but can see no sign of it.

Ten minutes later she reaches the start of the street lamps, and hesitates before stepping into the pool of light. She feels for her key ring and wedges the long mortise key – the one for Iquis's room – between her second and third fingers. It's a pathetic weapon, but it's all she has. Well, that and her boots. If necessary she will kick out.

But of course it won't be necessary.

She plunges into the light. Her boots creak as she walks, she hadn't noticed how loudly until now. Every step announces her presence to the waiting stillness. She tenses. Nothing.

There's not much here. Just a few buildings and a couple of well-lit car parks. She sees Iquis's bike, marooned and friendless, in one of these and for a moment she's relieved. Iquis is here. But the sight of the bike forces a disturbing realisation to the surface.

The vast car parks are empty. There are no cars parked outside any of the unlit buildings, no cars anywhere. It's like walking through a ghost town.

Could it be that there is nobody here except her, Iquis and whoever arrived in the helicopter?

She must be passing it by now. She glances right and thinks she can discern its shape against the skyline, thinks too that she can smell cigarette smoke. Is someone standing, smoking, and watching?

There's no cigarette glow to confirm her suspicions and she's too far in to bolt. Her best bet is to get to Iquis. In front of her the road terminates and an icy path leads towards the sea.

Iquis said she was going all the way to the sea; perhaps she meant exactly that.

Harriet runs along the path, relieved to be leaving her escort of street lamps. As the darkness thickens she slows, then stops abruptly as she hears voices ahead. She ducks down.

There are two people standing at the end of a long jetty. As her eyes acclimatise she recognises Iquis. The other one – tall and narrow – is unnerving. He looks lean and dangerous. He and Iquis circle each other with the shifting stance of fighters, searching for weakness.

Harriet's impulse to go to Iquis falters. This is a duel. There's a balance here which her presence could disrupt.

What sort of person chooses a venue like this, arranges to meet in the middle of the night, and then fights? Harriet has a sinking feeling that she knows the answer. Someone like Iquis. A member of her family.

Not the father though. She's convinced that he's a heavy-set bully, a nightclub bouncer of a man. Iquis's opponent is light on his feet, as feline as she is.

The jetty the pair are on has a shorter, stubbier counterpart, a short distance to the left. At the end of this second jetty there's a boxy, uneven tower of what look like fishing crates. If Harriet could reach them, she could hide and listen.

The wind direction is in her favour, sweeping across from their jetty to hers. Any sound she made would be carried away from them. Immersed in their conflict they seem oblivious to their surroundings. It's possible she could get there undetected. But there's no cover for the full length of the jetty; if they turned while she was moving, they'd see her.

She's come too far to back out.

She draws in a slow, deep breath, crouches low and starts to crawl along the path. The ice melts through her gloves, chills her palms and outstretched fingers. Time slows. She can't look where she's going because she has to watch them. She bruises her knees, but the pain just sharpens her attention. Short gusts of words reach her as she draws closer to the stack of boxes.

'Think of it as a reminder,' he's saying. 'A hint.'

'Go burn!' Iquis says. 'I don't need reminding.'

'Yes, you do.' His voice is uncompromising. 'There's no place for you there.'

'You can't know that.'

'You find it dull, flat. You miss what we have to offer.'

Harriet reaches the boxes and ducks behind them, missing some of the conversation. She sucks her stinging fingers and examines her cover. She'd guessed right. She's behind a stack of fishing crates composed of wooden frames and rope nets. She peers through.

'You can't control me any more,' Iquis is saying.

He laughs. 'Then why are you here?'

'*Burn* in the hottest furnace, ever.'

'Frustrating, isn't it?' He sounds genuinely amused, has got all the cool detachment which Iquis is losing. The balance is tipping.

If I could tilt it back, I'd do something. But I need to know more.

Harriet edges round to the side of the crates to get a closer look at Iquis's antagonist.

He's taller, but apart from that, the two of them could have been created using the same film-noir mould and the same batch of hardened steel.

'You don't even know what you're looking for,' he says. 'Do you really think that travelling around with your little friend each night is going to save you?'

Harriet is jolted. *He can't mean me, can he? How does he know? What does she tell him?*

At a less scary time she'd resent the "little".

'She's not like the others,' Iquis says.

'No. Not now she's not. Father's not pleased with you,' he says, taking Iquis's chin in his hand and forcing her face close to his. 'I don't see why I should protect you this time,' he adds casually.

Iquis jerks her head away.

'You chose. Why can't I?'

'No. I did what was right for the family. I kept the balance. That wasn't choice.'

'More choice than I ever had. At least you knew what you were giving up. I never had a chance to learn.'

'That's why you had the last few months. That's why I supported you in having them. But you knew you had to come back.'

'I'm not ready.' It's a plea. She turns from him for the first time, faces out to sea.

'There is no other way.'

Iquis remains silent.

'You need us, Sis. You're not like those people. You're like us. Don't tell me you're not hungry for what only we understand. Don't tell me you're not tempted with every step you take, with every encounter you have. And the resistance hurts, doesn't it? The not having hurts. You're walking on razor-thin knives whose edges slice into your flesh. It's a constant thing, weakening you. You're bleeding out. If you stay too long, you'll lose yourself.'

His voice is hypnotic. Harriet is permeated by a sense of sadness, inevitability. And Iquis, on the pier, flings out her arms and shakes her fingers, as if to get free of his words.

He grabs her flailing arms, wrenches her around to face him; stills her.

'What do you think you'll find out there, someone who can change your fate? That's not how it's written.'

'I hate you.'

'I'm the only one on your side.'

No way! Harriet thinks, with angry sympathy. *This* is not being on Iquis's side.

'After what you've done,' Iquis says, 'your claim to partisanship is hollow.' She's trying for detachment. Harriet clenches an encouraging fist.

'You know the rules. It was our territory *and* she was willing.' He pauses, and when he speaks again he sounds like Mark, '*Extremely* willing.'

What does he mean? Harriet edges forwards. *Has this got something to do with me? But how can it?*

She knocks into the crates. They shift, only a little, but it draws Iquis's attention. For a moment Iquis's face is directed towards her, pale and very still in the moonlight.

Harriet freezes, but this in itself won't hide her. She knows Iquis can see her.

With a rapid motion Iquis turns to the harbour wall, swings herself onto it and pushes herself upright. Her brother, taking this as a challenge, also leaps onto the wall. They balance there, face to face, like two tightrope walkers meeting halfway across a chasm.

Harriet edges back into concealment.

'Is this really what you want for me?' Iquis says. 'Can you truly tell me what you have is better?'

He doesn't answer her at first.

'It has to be, doesn't it?' he says finally.

'And what if I think that what you are is wrong?'

He laughs, yet it sounds the way the ice had sounded earlier when it was snapping under Harriet's feet.

'It makes no difference.'

Iquis stands motionless, staring out to sea. 'And the girl?' she says finally.

'It's all connected. It's what happens when the balance isn't kept.'

'You're threatening me.'

'I'd prefer to say it's an example. But call it a warning if you like.'

Iquis's voice quickens, 'Just a warning?'

'It could be.'

The fencing has speeded up. Any minute now there will be a result.

But Iquis doesn't respond.

'Father wants to see you,' he says, 'and Mother. She said you'd be hungry, said she'd sacrificed the fatted calf.'

This time Iquis laughs, but with even less humour. 'I ate on the way.'

It seems a puny kind of defiance, yet Iquis's words have some impact. 'Did you now?' He sounds uncertain for the first time. 'I need you, Sis,' he continues. 'We're not the same without you. We need your vividness and your contrast to complete us.'

'But if I did what you wanted that wouldn't be true. I'd be just like the rest of you.'

'How can we know? You've always been unique. Who knows what would happen, what you would become? Aren't you curious?'

Iquis backs slightly from him, glances at the sea, then leaps down from the wall and lands, catlike as ever.

'Curiosity,' she says, 'destroyed the cat. Come on. They'll be waiting. Let's get it over.' She prowls back along the length of the pier, her profile sharp against the night, and in a second is twinned as he joins her.

Their silhouettes merge into the waiting lights of John O'Groats.

*

Harriet sits on the edge of the jetty with her legs dangling off the end listening to the sea working away at the stones. Under normal circumstances it would be soothing. These aren't normal circumstances.

There's a faint, faraway light across the sea. A ship? She watches for a long time, but it doesn't move. Perhaps there's land out there, islands or something.

The thought is comforting, as is the mantra, *Iquis will come for me*, which she keeps silently repeating.

After a long time she hears the helicopter start up. She doesn't turn to look, just listens to the changing sounds of its departure. It flies straight over her head and she ducks, even though she knows she can't be seen. It shrinks in size and sound, until it's just a blinking light in the distance, then gone.

Harriet edges along the jetty until she is clear of the crates and visible. Then she closes her eyes and lets the tension seep away.

Already the night feels safer.

So tired!

The crunch of ice breaking, snapping steps heading towards her. She turns. Iquis! She is giddy with relief.

'I'm glad you came back. I was worried.' An understatement. 'Are you okay?'

'I'm okay.' Iquis's voice sounds smoke roughened.

Harriet staggers up, and can't help groaning at the pain in her bruised feet and aching legs.

'Let's get out of here,' Iquis says.

They walk in silence. There is a strange brilliance to Iquis which makes Harriet uneasy. It's like she's full of static electricity, buzzing with it. Harriet had expected her to be angry or defeated or triumphant, had expected to read the conclusion of Iquis's encounter in her actions and mood.

But nothing doing.

Iquis is as far away now as she was on the other pier.

As they reach the lights Harriet turns to look at her. Iquis's face is unusually flushed, there are red blotches high on each cheekbone and her lips are darker and thinner than ever. But what unnerves Harriet most is her eyes. There's only the thinnest trace of cloudy-grey around the huge, jet-black-glare of her pupils.

Iquis jerks away from Harriet's scrutiny and strides onwards.

Subdued and worried, Harriet struggles to keep up.

When Iquis kicks the bike off its stand and it falls over Harriet's panic increases.

'You aren't fit to drive.'

Iquis shrugs.

'What have you taken?'

Iquis stares back at her blank-eyed.

'We're not going anywhere until you come down.' Harriet snatches the keys out of Iquis's hand and hurls them across the snow-patched car park.

Iquis glares at her, then turns without a word and walks to where the keys are. When she reaches them she kneels down, picks them up and tilting her head back dangles them down her throat.

'Iquis, what the fuck?'

Harriet rushes towards her, but before she arrives Iquis leans forward and retches. Keys and what must be regurgitated wine pour together from her throat to puddle in the white snow.

Harriet swallows down an answering nausea. She's not good with these things, and the brutality of it shakes her.

'Iquis. Are you okay?'

A short answering nod.

'What are you trying to do to yourself?' Harriet says angrily.

'Nothing.'

'Looks like it. Come on, let's go walk, calm you down some.'

'No, I'm okay now.' Iquis sounds surprisingly composed. She kicks the keys through the snow to clean them, then stoops and picks them up in her gloved fist. 'Let's go. I promise I'm in control.'

Harriet is unconvinced.

'Please, Harriet, I need to get out of here.' She says it with such conviction that Harriet finds herself following her back to the bike.

Iquis hefts it up, checks for damage. 'It's fine.' She climbs on, waits.

'You'll stop if I give the signal?' Harriet asks, approaching warily.

'Yes. I promise. But don't worry. We'll be fine.'

THIRTY-SIX

Harriet jerks awake just as she's about to fall off the bike. It's an abrupt awakening. It would have saved her life if she'd really been on the bike. But she's not. She's clinging to a pillow like it's Iquis's back, her whole body acting out the bike ride. She straightens her legs, unclenches her hands. She's stiff, must have been hanging on like this for ages.

A faint shadow of daylight creeps through the curtains and lightens the air. She glances over at the other bed where Iquis is lying still and silent.

How did I get here?

Her recall of events is dreamlike.

Riding away from John O'Groats. Iquis passing the village with the B&B without pause. Harriet full of exhaustion and a desperate need to sleep. That's where the dream comes from. It had been ages, or seemed ages, before Iquis had pulled up at this anonymous Travelodge. She'd stumbled down long corridors after Iquis, then into this room with its smell of cleaning products and its tepid warmth. Turning the heater to full before stripping off, falling into bed, shivering herself to sleep – aware of Iquis's silent presence in the other bed.

She doesn't want to be awake, particularly not on her

own with nowhere for her thoughts to go except round and round. She closes her eyes, concentrates on thinking of something soothing. The river back in Cumbria. Just the flow of it, on and on.

*

When she wakes again it's full dark and Iquis is perched on the edge of the other bed, already dressed.

'You're awake then.' Iquis's voice is quieter than usual, tentative.

'That's right,' Harriet mumbles.

'Want to head for the mountains?' Iquis looks down as she asks this, avoiding Harriet's gaze, and the question wobbles in the air.

'More than anything if I had the energy,' Harriet says, in an awkward tone. 'But I'm wiped out, Iquis. I need a bath and something to eat, and, if I'm being perfectly honest, I'm not sure I can face the thought of ever getting on that bloody bike again.'

There, that's more normal.

Harriet shuffles to the edge of the bed, then, suddenly aware of her nakedness, says, 'Chuck me a towel.'

Iquis complies, then turns away as Harriet twists it round herself and gets up with a suppressed groan.

She aches everywhere. There are bruises on her knees, and sore red patches where the leather trousers have chafed her legs. Then she sees the heap of discarded clothing on the floor and panics.

'I haven't got anything to wear! There's no way I can put these back on, they're... minging.'

It's funny how it's always the little things that undo her.

'It's okay.' Iquis's voice is calming. 'Have your bath. I'll go and get you something to wear and something to eat.'

'But where? The shops will be closed, won't they?'

'I'll find somewhere.'

Finally Iquis sounds more confident, more like herself. Harriet, hobbling across to the bathroom, is a little comforted.

*

Later on, when Harriet feels more human, they take a taxi to the foothills of the mountains. Harriet is dressed in soft jeans, fleece top and a pair of trainers. The clothes have a worn-in feel. Iquis won't say where she got them and Harriet doesn't really care. She's just glad they're comfortable.

They walk slowly, letting the air and space work its magic. Harriet practises questions in her head.

After about twenty minutes, the slope they're ascending dips into a large snow-filled hollow. It's untouched and they pause, unwilling to break its purity. Harriet grabs her courage and turns to Iquis. 'They want you back. Are you going to go?'

'Last night,' Iquis says, 'you shouldn't have come.'

'I know,' Harriet says, *and I wish I hadn't. But it's done now and we have to deal with it.*

'I'm sorry. It was wrong to break your trust. But – But maybe now I can help you. I didn't understand much...' She searches for words, studying Iquis's face carefully. 'But... he threatened to hurt someone and... tried to make you do things you didn't want to do and then... succeeded?'

Iquis doesn't respond but her eyes are on Harriet's face.

'That's what I thought happened. It was... horrible.'

Iquis ducks and scoops up some snow, starts to press it into a ball.

'Who was he threatening?' Harriet asks. 'I thought it was me, but it didn't make sense. So was it your mother? Your sister?'

Iquis shakes her head. She hurls the snowball over the side of the mountain.

'You said your father was the really dangerous one, not your brother. And yet...'

My brother beat him to a pulp, Iquis had said. It's believable, now.

'You can't let them do this to you,' Harriet says. 'There's people we can go to for help, organisations – the police even. I'll be with you, every step. We can sort this.'

'Harriet, I love you,' Iquis says.

'Oh.' It totally silences her. What does she mean? There was no inflection in her voice.

Iquis starts to press a narrow corridor through the snow, placing each heel in front of the toes of the other foot.

'Why?' Harriet asks warily.

'For believing that something can be done. For believing in the force of law and order.'

'So you will let me help?'

'No. No police. No organisations. Believe me when I say they *can't* help.'

'But... ' Harriet is about to argue further.

Iquis turns angrily, 'I mean it, Harriet.'

'But you're not going to go back to them. You can't.'

'Harriet, today I know nothing.'

'A bit like me then,' Harriet says, nonplussed. 'Are you going to tell me what it's all about? I mean I know so much, surely it's about time you told me the rest. I won't judge you.'

'Harriet, will you promise me one thing?' Iquis twists to face her.

'What?'

'Never follow me again.'

'No.'

Iquis sighs, then shakes her head. 'I don't know what to do about you. D'you remember refusing to follow me up that cliff face, complaining that it was dangerous?'

'I was mad with you at the time.'

'You had better sense then, than now. Maybe you should stay mad.'

'You're not going to tell me anything, are you?'

Iquis shakes her head, and turns another corner in the snow. She's making a maze, Harriet realises.

'Not even what they gave you last night?'

Iquis ignores her. All her concentration seems to be on crafting turns and twists into the snow.

'You were on something when you came out, I could tell. You weren't normal, far from it. Is that why you made yourself throw up?'

A slight duck of Iquis's head. Harriet chooses to accept it as confirmation.

'What can I do? How can I help?'

Iquis backs away from the current leg of the maze, leaving a dead end. She walks over to Harriet. 'Learn to dance.'

'What?'

'I want to teach you to dance.'

But that's about me, not you, Harriet wants to say. But she can't because she's remembering her dream. "Teach me to dance", she'd said, and the river had broken its banks.

'I don't dance.'

'Maybe it's time you did. I want to give you something.'

'So why this?' *Why this thing that frightens me?*

'Because dancing is part of all the things you won't face, part of what holds you back.'

Hell – Iquis understands too much. 'Thanks. I'm not the one with the psycho family,' she says, defensively, then feels guilty. She shouldn't have said that.

'You might as well be,' Iquis says, her voice hard. 'You let Stephen hold you back from beyond the grave. Do you really expect me to believe that you've buried him?'

'Not all brothers are like yours.'

'I worshipped him, you know,' Iquis says. 'Before I left I thought he had all the answers.'

Harriet is silent, contemplating the depth of disillusionment Iquis must feel. It would be like finding out that Stephen wasn't as wonderful as she remembers.

It doesn't bear thinking about.

She takes a deep breath. 'Teach me to dance.'

And underneath the snow she thinks she hears movement, the rushing of water, a sudden flood. But she stays silent and the ground stays steady under her feet.

THIRTY-SEVEN

'A ceilidh!' Harriet exclaims, as they enter the hotel ballroom to the sound of fiddle, pipes and drum, to the sight of people circling each other, clapping hands to the beat, laughing.

'See,' Iquis says. 'It's like dancing by numbers. You just follow the instructions. What could be safer?'

Not to dance at all.

Even so, there's relief. This looks manageable.

Harriet is wearing a red silk dress which Iquis had brought back from a solitary reconnoitre earlier in the evening.

While she was gone, Harriet had phoned Mark's house in Cumbria for news of Marcia, but he had been out. Without her mobile Harriet couldn't remember Jenna's number and she'd never had Mark's or Paul's. She left a message saying, "I'll ring again". It was all she could do. There was no point in leaving the Travelodge phone number. They wouldn't be returning to it after the dance; were moving on, destination unknown.

Well, Iquis might know. Harriet doesn't.

The floor is cool against Harriet's naked feet as she

walks towards a tiny corner table, while Iquis heads across to the bar. Trainers would have ruined the look of the dress and for once this matters.

She's never worn anything like this before.

The red silk flutters against her as she moves, releasing a subtle rose scent. She's a butterfly, delicate and vivid.

'Where did you say you found the dresses?' she asks as Iquis returns.

Iquis is wearing an off-the-shoulder burgundy column dress. Definitely not her usual style, but even though she looks angular and rather edgy she gets away with it. 'I didn't.'

Iquis's gaze settles on two boys leaning against the bar. She waits until they notice her, then gives them a wide, dangerous smile. It acts as a summons. The boys walk towards them.

'Wanna dance?' the lead boy asks.

'Yes.' Iquis glances commandingly at Harriet. You choose, the look says.

The blonde boy is the least intimidating. He's hanging back, the way Harriet would. His face is softly undefined, and his long, grey sweatshirt looks comfortable and well worn. She edges towards him, leaving the more chiselled boy for Iquis.

Harriet's hand trembles slightly in her partner's clasp, as they listen to the instructions. She is troubled by a sense of déjà-vu. She has stood like this before, but when? She scrunches her face up in an attempt to remember, but it's gone.

Then the music starts up and they're moving, slowly at first then gathering speed. It's not difficult.

In fact, thinks Harriet, as she spins – hands clasped tight with those of her companion – *it's kind of fun.*

*

'I found a beer called Dark Island!' Harriet lands her pint glass on the table to demonstrate. 'It tastes brilliant.'

Iquis eyes the near-black liquid without enthusiasm, then glances pointedly at Harriet's wine glass.

Harriet is unquelled. 'It had this picture on the pump handle, standing stones against a background of sea and sunset. Apparently it's a real place: The Ring of Brodgar. It's on one of the Orkney islands, just north of Scotland. "A wet and windswept place", the barman said.' Her eyes gleam with excitement. 'Do you think it's connected to the group?'

'You've given them up,' Iquis says. 'Don't forget how you felt after the concert.'

Harriet pulls a face. 'Perhaps they weren't always like that. Glyn said they were corrupted by their success. And the image on the pump handle was so beautiful, so golden and dramatic and full of promise. I thought maybe the Orkneys were their lost world, that maybe they strayed too far from that world and in doing so lost sight of who they were.'

Iquis sighs, 'Look, Harriet, stop trying to resurrect them. You don't need them. And anyway, they're not Scottish. They've probably never heard of the beer, or the island.'

Harriet bites her lip. Iquis is right, of course. It's just hard to forget what they had meant to her. She tilts the beer and drinks, losing herself in its flavour. 'You can taste the island,' she says, then, to change the subject asks, 'Why aren't you dancing?'

'I'm tired.'

'You don't look tired, just sad.'

'I can't dance tonight,' Iquis says.

'Then we should go.'

'No. I want to give you this. I want you to have some happy memories, of something normal.'

This scares Harriet.

'Iquis?'

'Not now. Don't let anything spoil tonight.'

Harriet bites back on the questions. 'If there's anything I can do,' she says awkwardly.

'I know,' Iquis says, and for a moment her fingers brush Harriet's, then she gestures towards Harriet's dancing partner who has come to reclaim her. 'You're wanted. Go, enjoy.'

*

'It's Harriet.'

'Harriet! Where the fuck are you?'

Harriet winces and edges the earpiece further from her ear.

'Well?' Mark demands.

'Scotland.'

'Why didn't you tell us?'

'I left a message last night.'

'Two days after you disappeared!'

'We didn't disappear. Well, it didn't feel like that. We just went for a ride. I didn't think you'd notice.'

'Didn't you?'

'No.' Harriet feels guilty but doesn't quite know how to apologise to Mark. She hadn't meant to worry anyone. 'Any news of Marcia?'

'She's back.' He says it blankly, with none of the relief that Harriet expects.

'That's fantastic! Jenna must be so relieved. Where was she?'

'You'll have to ask her when you return. See whether you can make head or tail of it. So when are you coming back? Or don't you know that either?'

'Oh, fuck off, Mark, you're not my dad.'

'No, funny that, 'cause he wants to talk to you too. He phoned the house earlier today when he couldn't get through on your mobile. I told him you were away with a friend, but you better phone him, Harriet.'

'Okay, I will.' Harriet's confused. Even though Mark is giving her a hard time, there is something about this whole conversation that makes her feel strangely touched. She hadn't thought he'd care. 'Look, I've got to go,' she says, 'before Iquis wakes up and wonders where I am.'

Silence at the end of the line, then, 'Harriet,' sounding a little rushed, 'are you okay?'

What a strange question. 'Yeah. Totally fine.'

'Right, sure.' This sounds more like Mark – careless, indifferent. 'So whereabouts in Scotland?' he asks casually.

'The far north. We're travelling around.'

"Following the dancing trail", Iquis had said. She has made plans, has selected a venue for tonight but remains mysterious about where and what. Another ceilidh?

Harriet hopes not. She'd thought "dancing by numbers"

would be safe, but first there'd been that déjà vu feeling and then, last night, another dream, another strangely shaped encounter with the past, with Stephen and Graham.

'I better go,' Harriet says.

'Wait! Do you have a number we can contact you? In case...'

In case of what? 'No. Look, I'm sure we'll be back soon. We're just having a break for a few days.'

'Okay.' But he sounds reluctant and it's Harriet who hangs up first.

*

'I dreamed I was dancing with Stephen and he was being mean to me,' Harriet says, as the saxophone dips and swerves and the trumpet player arches his back and blasts a series of notes upwards.

'Only I don't think it was a dream. I think it was a memory.'

She and Iquis are seated at a small table, absorbing the atmosphere and studying the dancers. On the walls, pictures of jazz greats abound. In front of them, on a raised platform, a six-piece band burns its way through long, intricate and unpredictable melodies.

Iquis lifts her gaze from her inevitable glass of red wine and stares at Harriet.

'Stephen was trying to make Graham laugh. He was jerking my arms up and down, throwing me off balance, making me look stupid: gawky, like I couldn't control my own limbs. "Look at her," he called to Graham. "Dancing like a stick insect!"'

Harriet sucks in a breath. 'I was far too thin when I was a kid and I hated it, hated people talking about it, asking Mum if I was ill.'

Another breath. 'Stephen knew how I felt. Which is why...'

It was such a betrayal. Particularly when—

'Things were different with Graham then,' Harriet says.

No reaction from Iquis to this. Not surprising, Harriet's never told her about the Christmas encounter.

'I know you don't know who Graham is, but he... mattered.'

'In what way?'

The dream prompts her. She chooses words carefully.

'I kind of liked him. A lot. He was kind to me. Okay, he'd tease me, too, at times. But it was the best kind of teasing. He'd be grinning at me, making me laugh, and he'd got such light in his eyes.' She stops, recalls his face at Christmas, swallows.

'He was just kind,' she says, knowing she's repeating herself. 'He was just... nearly always... kind.'

'Unlike Stephen?'

'It *was* just a dream.'

'I thought you said it wasn't.'

'Yeah. Okay! I just don't know!' The feelings remain though: humiliation, fury. She'd wanted to lash out, to hurt Stephen. And she doesn't like that. Doesn't like it at all.

Iquis raises a surprised eyebrow.

'Sorry,' Harriet says. 'Look, I *think* it happened. I've got a half memory. I suspect Stephen didn't actually want to dance with me, suspect Dad made him. Because...'

She stops, but in her head she can hear Stephen saying,

"Tell Dad you don't want to dance any more," as he lets go of her hands; her face is hot and her arms are sore from where he's been jerking them around and... she can't look at Graham.

She snatches up her beer, fixes her eyes on the trumpet player's red shirt, examines the way it balloons away from his torso, the deep red of the sweat marks under his arms.

Iquis said she used to think her brother had all the answers.

But that's different!

'No one's perfect,' Harriet says, defensive. 'Come on, let's dance. You've been nagging me long enough.'

'Yes, because it'll be easier once you take the plunge.'

Harriet is unimpressed. 'That's the sort of thing Dad would have said.' Once.

And it's not always true. What about yesterday? 'What if I...?'

'You'll *like* this,' Iquis says. 'Just relax.'

They squeeze through the dancers, find the middle of the dance floor, equidistant from each of the two big speakers. This thick into the crowd no one can see her, and it helps that everyone around is moving, and that the music itself is so complex, so seductive, so full of fascinating rhythms. And *so* unfamiliar. She knows she's never tried to dance to anything like this before. The flurry of piano notes, the sexy sway of the sax, the deep, dark sensuality of the bass. The muscles of her back quiver, as she starts to open up. She wants... *this.* Her eyes close and she yields.

*

A boy snags Harriet's attention. Longish hair, sulky lips, lean body. He's dancing around an older couple, weaving loose patterns which only just acknowledge their existence. He's exploring the music, lost in its intricacies.

And yet, not so lost that he doesn't notice Harriet watching. He stares back with a wide-mouthed smile, teeth glinting. Arrogant, like Mark. Only she finds she doesn't care.

She turns back to Iquis, who raises a questioning eyebrow. Harriet shrugs. Clarinet notes flutter through her, small persistent fingers rubbing against each vertebrae. She is full of sensation, caught in the remembrance of all that she'd once felt for Graham. All those hours spent daydreaming about him, not knowing quite what she wanted, but feeling all shiny inside with it. Because he made her feel different, special. Awake.

Just like this music does.

If only she could share this with Iquis, could find a matching excitement. But Iquis is distant, unresponsive to the music. Although she moves she does not let go. Seeing her, it is hard to believe the way she had danced at Decadance, the whole dance floor her territory.

She's just going through the motions, Harriet thinks with a pang of sadness, *still not recovered from that encounter with her family. What will it take?*

Somehow, not long after, the boy is dancing with Harriet and Iquis, weaving patterns and riffs. There's sweat on his face. His body is close to Harriet's, matching her move for move.

The music seeps away into silence. A whisky-soaked voice drawls into the microphone. Iquis puts her arm around Harriet and pulls her backwards towards her.

'I'm going to sit down,' she tells Harriet. 'Enjoy yourself.'

Harriet panics. 'I'll come too. Remember, I don't know how to dance.'

'You're doing fine.' Iquis's voice is low and urgent in Harriet's ear. 'Just relax, let it take you.'

Harriet grips the arm that is slung round her. 'Don't leave me with him.'

'Why ever not?' Iquis laughs. 'I'll be watching. You'll be safe.' Her arm tightens, then it's gone, and Harriet's alone with the boy.

The whisky-voice falls silent, the saxophone releases a ripple of notes. Harriet stares into those confident eyes, sees the gleam of reflected lights.

He grabs her hand, his fingers hot yet surprisingly delicate. The beat quickens and the room whirls as he spins her.

＊

Harriet, who should have little energy left for climbing mountains, is running on exhilaration. 'When it was over I just said thank you and bolted,' she repeats. 'But I stayed until the end. And it was like the biggest dare ever, and I did it!'

Only she's glad Iquis had been there to run back to. It was enough, more than enough, for one night.

The cold biting at her face and fingers contrasts fiercely with the heat and excitement inside. She is eager to share these feelings with Iquis. She is grateful, and wants their moods to match. But although Iquis listens, patiently, she does not lighten.

'I stayed till the end,' Harriet says again. 'I didn't run away,' and then more slowly, quietly, 'and nothing happened.'

This sobers her. She has let something significant into the night. *A prohibition*, she thinks, and something twists inside.

'But why didn't you dance?' she says. 'Why didn't you dance the way you did at Decadance?'

'I...' Iquis starts again, 'I couldn't.'

'Yes, you can. If I can, you can. Why is it any different?'

'Because,' Iquis says, 'I daren't risk losing control like I did at Decadance.'

Harriet is silenced. She thinks of the goths' rejection and it is shadowed by what she saw in John O'Groats. The words of encouragement die on her lips.

'Leave it,' Iquis says shortly.

A sticky silence.

'I rang Mark,' Harriet says. 'Before you woke this afternoon. I meant to tell you earlier.'

'Oh.'

'Marcia's back.'

'Good,' Iquis says, but she shows no curiosity, displays no relief.

'Mark didn't really say where she'd been. I couldn't get much out of him.' Still no reaction. 'He asked when we were coming back.'

It hangs there like a question.

'I must admit,' she adds, after a while, 'I'm pretty intrigued to find out where Marcia disappeared to.'

It all seems so long ago and I miss them. I miss the casual communication, the liveliness of them, even miss fighting with Mark. I didn't think I fitted and yet somehow, surreptitiously, this familiarity has built up.

'When are we going back?' Nothing short of direct is going to get an answer.

'Do you want to go back?' Iquis says. 'Wouldn't you rather just keep riding? We could go anywhere; we've only just started. A different place every night. A different dance hall, a different type of dancing. We could be explorers.'

'But of course we've got to go back,' Harriet says. 'Don't you want to see the others?'

'Not really.'

'Iquis, we can't just run away.'

'Can't we?'

'No. What would Mark and the others say? What would the university say? What would Dad say?' This last, she realises, is actually the most important. Although she'd phoned home after she'd spoken to Mark only Mum had been in. She thinks of the pub at Christmas, that tentative rapprochement. 'I can't do that to him.'

'It was only a thought.'

THIRTY-EIGHT

Iquis stands at the window looking out into the Glasgow night, watching the storm. She's been there for ages, arm outstretched, holding the heavy curtain out of the way – motionless. Her arm ought to be aching by now. The play of the storm is reflected on her face. Moving shadows, rapid changes of light, an impression of heaviness.

Harriet waits. She's been ready in her red silk for over an hour. It's faded now, from repeated washings in hotel-room basins, but it's still her dancing dress.

They'd come to Glasgow to complete Harriet's education – Iquis's words. To seek out the huge, subterranean nightclubs, with their ambient, compelling, consuming sounds. Harriet had danced, drunk water, danced. She hadn't even wanted to bother with beer.

In the low-ceilinged undergrounds there's an intensification. Harriet's part of an immense tribe of dancers. She plunges into the crowd each night like it's a river or an ocean, moving en masse with the others until no part of her is separate. She's like that girl in the red shoes who never stops dancing.

And, like that girl, she's hooked but not entirely happy.

She's worried about Iquis, who seems to slip further and further away from her, and she's having mixed up dreams which are too vivid for comfort.

I dream of dancing with Graham – of kissing the jazz boy – of a hundred hands reaching towards me, holding me, spinning me. I wake frightened and look across to where Iquis is sleeping in the other bed. She sleeps so still. I feel that even if I cried out to her I could not reach her.

Iquis turns from the window. 'You won't need that dress tonight, we're going back.'

'To Mark's house?'

Iquis nods.

What do I feel? Relief? Disappointment? Hard to tell.

'What about the storm?'

'What storm?'

'The one you've been watching for the last ten minutes.'

'I hadn't noticed.' Iquis looks at it vaguely. 'It will pass. And if not, we'll get wet.'

'What if I don't want...? What if I said now that I'd come with you? That I'd keep on running.' A quickening of her heartbeat, a dizzying fear.

Iquis turns and looks at her.

'You asked me why I kissed him,' she says, at last.

'Kissed who?' Harriet asks, thrown. 'You mean Mark? I didn't know you'd kissed him—'

'Not Mark, your father.'

The shock of it comes back: the burgundy lipstick tangled in the black hairs on Dad's hand, his humiliation, her fury.

'Why?' Almost aggressive.

'He wasn't your father then,' Iquis says.

'Yes he was.'

'No, what I mean is, you weren't you then. I didn't know you. He was just someone in my way. I didn't know he was real, had significance. It was just a game,' she pauses, turns her head to look through the window, but the heavy velvet has fallen back into place, blocking out everything outside the room. 'Do you remember facing me down? Do you remember how angry you were?'

'Yes.'

'I think that's when I first began to notice you.' Finally, she turns to face Harriet.

'What are you trying to say?'

'Just that now he is your father. You don't want to keep on running.' It's not even a question, just a statement. Iquis doesn't wait for a response, just strides over to her bed and starts to pull her bike leathers on.

∗

The storm chases them out of Scotland. They are driven ahead of it, hurled along the wide, dark surface of the motorway. At first there is lashing rain but gradually they outpace its fury and travel ahead, like forerunners. Harriet can't see the dial of the speedometer, but she knows Iquis is speeding.

They arrive breathless at Mark's house, shortly before nine. The lounge curtains are drawn, but a blur of light leaks out through the edges. It's strange to be back.

Her bedroom window is dark. She thinks about what's up there: messages on her mobile, files and textbooks on her desk, letters that could be waiting. Dr Drake comes striding into her mind, "If you leave it too long, you won't make the choice, the choice will make you."

But I still don't know what I want.

Iquis is staring up to where the clouds coil and rumble in bruise-like hues above her head. Such a weight of water pressing down. Does she feel it?

It seems to Harriet that she does. That she is at the centre of this imminent storm. She seems smaller, less powerful, even a little frightened.

'So what do we do now?' she asks Harriet.

'But I'm not the leader,' Harriet protests, 'you are.'

I'm worried about you, she thinks, and it's a relief to admit it. She can't avoid recalling how Iquis had been when she returned after Christmas. It's not encouraging.

This is what her family do to her. Each time they see her, they erode a bit more.

In January, when she came back, I thought I could make it better. I thought I was making it better. But now I realise that she never fully returned, even then. She's never been back into the house, hasn't mixed with the others, hasn't been to college. All we did was flee to the Lakes each night. It was just a miniature version of Scotland really.

Iquis stirs beside her. 'We could go to the river.'

'We could,' Harriet says. 'But if we did, we'd still be running.'

'I know.' Iquis kicks moodily at the front tyre, causing the bike to rock.

Harriet puts a hand out to steady it. 'Careful.'

Iquis pats the seat of the bike as if in apology. 'So what do we do?'

Harriet swallows. 'Your room first. So we can change,

and then let's go upstairs. I want to talk to Mark, find out the details of Marcia's adventure, see who else is up there.'

And, she thinks, *build you a proper bridge this time if I can – so you can reach the others and maybe begin to feel normal. The way you once told me you wanted.*

Above them the sky shimmers with tension, the shadow of its mood crossing over Iquis's face. Harriet expects her to protest, to propose a different plan. But she says nothing, just turns towards the basement.

*

Once inside, Harriet changes fast – pulling on the long purple-velvet dress of Iquis's, which Harriet has worn so often it feels like her own. The familiarity is comforting. Despite her best intentions, the idea of bringing Iquis and Mark together is making Harriet uneasy.

Iquis doesn't change, doesn't talk, just stands waiting.

'Shall we go?' Harriet says.

Iquis nods.

Unlocking the door connecting them to the rest of the house is a symbolic act. The key is heavy, the lock stiff. And yet, once it's unlocked the door swings open easily. The warm woodsmoke scent of the house engulfs her.

Iquis's boots make scuffing sounds on the steps as she follows. Her leather jacket is zipped up. Her face wears a closed expression.

Harriet opens the lounge door. Mark's sprawled in an armchair, a tumbler of whisky in his hand. She's never seen him drink whisky. He always drinks beer, straight from the bottle. His head turns and she jerks her gaze away, scans the rest of the room.

It's emptier than usual. There's only Jenna and Marcia, who share a sofa by the settling fire.

Harriet is shocked by Marcia's appearance. Her hair is a pale washed-out grey and – despite Mark's presence – she isn't wearing make-up. She's thinner, and the grey hair makes her look old and brittle.

Harriet senses Mark looking at her and turns, only to find that he's looking past her at Iquis. His gaze is hard, aggressive.

'You're back then.' He takes a large slug of whisky. His eyes detour to check out Harriet and she wants to thump him. But not for the usual reasons; more because, for a moment, the memory of the jazz boy – of moving and flowing with him – is uppermost in her senses.

Jenna is a welcome distraction. 'About time,' she says, moving towards Harriet. She's smiling, but she looks tired and drawn.

'That's right,' Harriet says, and then rather awkwardly, 'Sorry about going away, in the middle of...' she trails off. In Marcia's presence she's not sure what she should and shouldn't say. She glances warily at Marcia, but she is gazing into the fire, paying no attention.

'That's okay,' Jenna says. 'It's not your problem.'

The present tense surprises Harriet. She'd thought it was over.

Perhaps for Jenna it never is.

'When did she come back?' she asks Jenna.

But it's Mark who answers, rising from his chair. 'Five nights ago, at four in the morning. I was asleep when the bell started ringing on and on. I grabbed a towel, went down. She was leaning against the bell.' He crosses towards Marcia, and stops in front of her, pulling her round so she is forced to look at him. 'You were in a right state, weren't you?' His tone is harsh, confrontational.

Harriet stares. What's going on?

He drops his hand and turns back to Harriet. 'She didn't move when I opened the door, the bell just kept ringing. I had to pull her away from it. The sleeve of her jacket was wet. All of her was wet. Like she'd been walking through the rain for hours. There was no one else there – no explanation for how she'd returned. I asked where she'd been and how she'd got back, but she wasn't answering. So I pulled her inside, shoved her in front of the fire and called Jenna to do her Florence Nightingale act.'

Jenna pulls a face. 'Hardly that.'

'Hot drinks. Hand-feeding her. Cocooning her in blankets and watching while she sleeps. What else would you call it?'

'She was ill!'

'She made herself ill. How much sympathy am I supposed to have?'

'Look, I know you're fed up,' Jenna says, 'but can't you please...'

Mark sighs, 'Not with you, Jenna.' He turns back to Marcia and hunkers down in front of her. 'But I just want to know,' and his voice is gentler now, '*when* you're going to snap out of this.'

Marcia's face turns sulky.

'Snap out of what? I don't understand,' Harriet says. 'Why won't somebody tell me what's going on?'

'Ask Marcia.' Mark pushes himself up and crosses back to his chair. 'See how far you get.'

'Marcia?' Harriet's tone is a mixture of interrogation and bewilderment.

She draws closer to Marcia, and senses Iquis moving along behind her, keeping pace. Iquis has been very quiet. Harriet wants to turn to see if Iquis is okay, but she can't be everywhere.

Marcia's expression is dull and there are shadows under her eyes. She says nothing.

'Where have you been?' Harriet perseveres.

No answer.

'What about Dark Island, when you went back stage, did you get there in time? Did you see Loki?'

A gleam of interest. Marcia stirs, then shakes her head. 'I was too late. They had already gone.' She looks over Harriet's shoulder, towards Iquis, and a hint of cunning enters her expression. 'So where did you go?'

'We went north,' Harriet says, pleased that for the first time she's captured Marcia's attention. 'We went to the very tip of Scotland, all in one night.' She draws breath, intending to continue, to breathe some life into this encounter. Iquis's hand lands on her shoulder with an arresting thud.

'We went all over the place,' Iquis says, 'ended up in Glasgow.' Her tone is abrupt, forbidding. Subject closed, it says.

Harriet bites down on her sudden irritation with Iquis. *Can't you see that this is important? Can't you for once relax the secrecy a bit? I wasn't going to give anything away.*

She shakes her shoulder free from Iquis's hand but Marcia has lost interest.

Something in this whole encounter is horribly familiar to Harriet. For nine years her mum had carried a weight of depression so heavy that it hung around her like a visible shroud. Harriet, battling to make contact through it, had felt its edges – cold and damp and fog-like.

'But I'd love to know where you went, Marcia,' Harriet says, and she can hear the pleading tone in her voice. 'Won't you tell me?'

For a moment, it is not Marcia but Mum in front of her. There's that familiar pain in her throat, a sadness so sharp that it hurts to swallow. She reaches out and takes one of Marcia's hands – the nails are pale, translucent, and the hand itself feels limp.

Marcia shifts uncomfortably. 'There was a man,' she says, in a faraway voice, 'he was very beautiful – he made me dream in colours – but it ended too soon – before I saw...'

Harriet is struck by her words, frightened by them. Marcia sounds enchanted, trapped under a spell. What does she mean? She glances at the others, but Mark just looks disgusted and Jenna withdrawn.

Iquis pushes past Harriet to tower over Marcia. 'Before you saw what?' she demands. She sounds angry, even angrier than Mark.

Marcia flinches away from Iquis, pushing back into the corner of the sofa.

'Before you saw what?' Iquis repeats, more quietly.

But the sulky look has returned to Marcia's face. 'Someone interfered,' her voice is dull, 'and I couldn't stay.' She closes her eyes and turns her whole body away from Iquis.

For a moment nobody moves. Then Iquis slowly backs away. Again she passes Harriet, this time to walk to the window. She parts the curtains and pushes through them. Harriet has a glimpse of her resting her forehead against the pane of glass, then the curtains fall back around her.

Silence.

Jenna breaks it. 'I'll make some coffee.' She turns and heads for the kitchen, without enquiring who wants what. Harriet glances at the dark hump of curtained Iquis, then hurries after Jenna.

THIRTY-NINE

Jenna is standing totally still. She jumps when Harriet comes in, then quickly starts opening and closing cupboards.

'Looking for clean mugs,' she says. 'Not that I'm going to find any.'

Even so, she keeps searching.

'What's going on?' Harriet says. 'What's wrong with Marcia? Why's everyone so weird?'

'If you want to know why Iquis is weird,' Jenna's voice is sharp with anger, 'I suggest you ask her.'

Harriet flinches – so much for bringing Iquis in from the cold. 'She's dealing with some stuff.' The words are inadequate, and yet even saying this feels like a betrayal. 'But what about all of you? Is it always like this when Marcia comes back?'

'No.' Jenna starts rinsing mugs under the cold tap. The stack of unwashed dishes in the sink makes this difficult, but she doesn't bother moving them.

'What then?' Harriet says. 'Did something bad happen to her?'

Jenna hesitates.

Harriet stares at the clutter on the counter: a bottle of vodka, several pans, two shopping bags spilling contents. Jenna usually restores order when she visits, but today she makes no attempt, just shoves things to one side and dumps the mugs down. 'We think it's drugs,' she blurts. 'There's a couple of needle marks and some fading bruises in the crook of her elbow. That's why Mark's angry.'

'Shit,' Harriet says. She doesn't know what to say. 'But Marcia's not like that!'

Jenna concentrates on unscrewing the jar of coffee. There are no clean spoons, so she pours the coffee granules straight from the jar.

'Have you asked her?' Harriet says.

'She denies it, says she gave blood while she was away, says she just saw the van and went in. But I don't believe her. I mean, why would she? And when I asked to see the stamp on her donor card she said she'd lost it.'

'It's possible,' Harriet says. She wants so badly for everything to be okay. But she can't help hearing Marcia's words in her head. "... *there was a man – he made me dream in colour...*"

'Normally,' Jenna says, 'we slot back into rhythm with each other pretty fast. This time is different. Our shorthand is missing. I have no sense of her, and that frightens me.

'And Mark's right. She was a complete mess when she came back – pale and weak – she could hardly stand without support and she was really, really out of it. She looked like she hadn't eaten or slept since she left.'

The kettle boils. Jenna starts slopping water into mugs.

'I kept nearly calling the doctor in – but then – well, I don't want to get her in trouble.'

'Have you talked to your parents?'

'I can't – can't tell them this.' She pulls a plastic chopstick out of the drawer, uses it to stir the coffee. 'I *know* there are drug lines I could phone for advice. I've even got as far as phoning the number and hanging up. I can't do it. She'd find out. She always did know when we were taking advice. She heard it in our voices, read it in the way we acted around her. She already thinks I'm the enemy. If she knew I was talking to strangers there'd be no trust left.'

The milk muddies the coffee as Harriet pours it in. 'But you're talking to me. Won't she realise that's what we're doing in the kitchen?'

'You're a friend. That's different.'

'What about Mark?'

'He's trying. But he doesn't get self-destructive behaviour, it's totally alien to him, so he's not all that sympathetic. He tries to shake her out of it, gets frustrated when it doesn't work. But he isn't giving up. He's intent on keeping an eye on her, making sure she doesn't... go looking... for whatever...'

She bites her lip, gathers two mug handles into her right hand with a clink, reaches her left hand towards a third mug.

'We've agreed that that's all we're going to do for now, just keep her safe and give her a chance to pull out of this. She doesn't need *this* on her record. The running away stuff is bad enough. I don't want to make this whole thing permanent, and I can't help feeling with Marcia that it's our reactions – mine and Mum's and Dad's – that perpetuates it. That actually, the less we react, the less reason she has to keep on doing these things.'

She lifts the coffee mugs. 'Come on, let's take these through.'

＊

Harriet stands alone at the front door watching Jenna and Marcia trudge towards their car. The clouds are lower now and the wind sounds angry. Jenna steers Marcia into the passenger seat, then fights to open the exposed driver's door, squeezes in. The door bangs on her.

Something more than the storm is building.

Back in the lounge, Harriet finds Iquis and Mark arguing.

'Stop trying to get out of it,' Iquis says. 'What are *you* going to do about Marcia?'

'None of your business!'

'It has to be.'

'Then you do something!'

Iquis laughs, but it's the way she'd laughed on the pier, without humour.

'I just walked into this,' Mark says, 'and you know who I feel sorry for? Jenna. But you know something else, Iquis – Marcia isn't my responsibility.'

'Of course she is,' Iquis says. 'She's far more your responsibility than she is mine.'

It's a nonsense thing to say; Harriet can't keep quiet. 'Of course she's not your responsibility. What are you trying to do, Iquis, pick a fight?'

Iquis turns, and something in her face silences Harriet.

Iquis pivots back to Mark. '*What* are you going to do about Marcia?' she repeats, in a dangerous tone. 'You've hardly said anything to her all night. Why don't you do what you'd normally do, take her to the pub, then bring everyone back for a party?'

'She doesn't want to go.'

'Have you asked her?' Iquis snaps.

'Will you give this a rest?' Mark slumps down in his chair, picks up his whisky and glares at her. 'Of course I've suggested it.'

'And how long did you spend trying to persuade her, trying to capture her interest?' Her voice is rising. 'Where's the Mark magnetism gone?' she demands.

Mark is silent, his face a mixture of conflicting emotions.

'She's your responsibility,' Iquis repeats again, with greater force.

'Fuck that! You are so out of order.' Mark jumps to his feet. 'You bugger off for months on end. Then you come back and start interfering in something that's none of your business. It's not as if you ever cared about Marcia before.'

'She wasn't in trouble before.'

'It's that obvious?' Mark looks shaken, then something primitive seems to take over. 'Find me the dealer and I'll act.'

There's such violence in his voice, his posture, that for this moment Harriet believes he could kill, would kill. It terrifies her.

Will things ever be normal again? The emotion that surges in is far too familiar. She's nine and the earthquake has just hit, destroying everything stable, everything safe.

Stephen. Her despair is immediate, raw.

She only dimly sees Mark stepping towards Iquis, putting his hands on her shoulders.

They're still arguing, but she misses the words. She sees Iquis knock Mark's hand away with a vicious swipe. Everywhere, there is violence. She forces herself to concentrate.

'She wouldn't need to go chasing shadows,' Iquis says, 'if you paid more attention to her.'

Something changes in Mark's face. 'Listen, you don't interfere with me and Marcia, and I won't interfere with you and Harriet.'

'Don't bring me into it,' Harriet says.

Mark's other hand is still on Iquis's shoulder. He drops it. 'What happened, Iquis?' His voice is harsh. 'One minute we're negotiating, and I feel like I'm getting somewhere. I break off to pull Harriet out of the river, and then... nothing. What changed? Was it because I intervened when *you* said Harriet was fine? I know how you like to be *in control*.'

'You pulled Harriet out of the river because you were worried about her.' Iquis seems to have backed off a little. 'I thought you were overreacting, but it's possible you were right. Maybe it was too cold.'

Mark ignores this. 'Or was it because I called your bluff and agreed to your conditions? Perhaps you were afraid to go through with it. You'd find that hard to admit, wouldn't you? Maybe you're one big fake. Maybe this concern with Marcia is just another obstacle to throw in our path. You never gave a shit about her before.'

'Neither did you,' Iquis snarls, 'and I wasn't the one having sex with her.'

Mark flinches.

Iquis takes a step forwards so that her leather-jacketed front is pressed against him, her face inches from his. 'All that charm. All that sexual energy.' Something seems to flare between them, which is more than anger; something that looks like lust. 'How much of that have you directed at Marcia since she came back?'

Harriet walks over to the whisky bottle and picks it up, weighing it like a weapon. It gives her a sense of power and she needs that. She, too, has to be able to act.

'Don't be sick,' Mark says hoarsely.

'I'm not,' Iquis says. 'What's sick about it?'

'I'd be taking advantage of her.'

'Bollocks,' Iquis shouts. 'You're just afraid that if you wake her up she'll be your responsibility. But she always was. You just wouldn't admit it.'

'She wasn't my responsibility,' says Mark, edging a step backwards. 'She knew the rules. We all knew the rules.'

'Don't you realise that there aren't any rules? Not for Marcia. Not for any of us.' She's talking very fast, emphasising nearly every word. 'You've got to grab her attention. Give her a reason to want to return.'

'But she's back.'

'She may be back physically, but mentally she's still there, still with him. You've got to win her back.'

'I don't have to do anything,' Mark says flatly, turning away.

She grabs his shoulder and jerks him back to face her. 'You never want to get involved, is that it, Mark?'

'Iquis!' Harriet says sharply. She's remembering the encounter on the pier. Iquis had been as scary as the stranger. She's chosen to forget that, but is reminded now.

Her words don't get through.

'I offered to get involved with you,' Mark says.

'You stupid fucking wanker!' Iquis grips his shoulders, driving her fingers into his flesh.

Harriet drops the whisky bottle on the carpet.

'I offered to get involved with you,' Mark repeats levelly.

Iquis explodes. She shoves Mark across the room and into the wall. The cracking sound of Mark's head hitting the wall impels Harriet across the room.

'Maybe I should take you up on that,' Iquis says, moving closely in on him. Mark brings his hands up and attempts to grasp Iquis's wrists, but she just presses her hands harder into his shoulders. Her whole body moves towards him.

'Iquis, stop! What are you doing?'

Harriet grabs Iquis's shoulder. Time slows. It's like she's pulling against a powerful current.

Iquis's face jerks towards her. Her pupils are huge black wells of nothingness and there's a terrible hunger in her face. Her shoulder vibrates frantically under Harriet's fingers.

And then the curtains slam down. Iquis's face clears. She shoves her head down, barrels past Harriet and is gone.

FORTY

Battling against the wind, which keeps shoving her backwards, Harriet runs towards the river. Squalls of rain lash across her face, run through her hair and weight her gown.

Iquis is silhouetted against the raging sky.

The rush of the river rises up from beyond Iquis and blends with the howl of the storm. Panting, Harriet pulls up alongside Iquis and stares into the rapid water. It's higher than usual, has started to spill over the bank. A large branch sweeps past and for a moment Harriet thinks she sees a face in the speeding water, but it's only her reflection, which the river is trying to drag away.

'Are you okay?' Harriet asks warily.

'Yes.' Iquis's voice is calm.

She's shut down again, the way she did in Scotland.

'Mark was well enough to tell me to bugger off when I tried to help him,' Harriet says. 'He's not badly hurt. But he could have been.'

Nothing. Harriet wants to grab Iquis, the way Iquis had grabbed Mark, wants to force some reaction out of her. But she daren't. Iquis is too volatile, needs careful handling.

'You can't keep it bottled up for ever.'

'I know,' Iquis says, but her voice sounds distant, untouched.

Harriet can still feel the earthquake trembling under her feet, can still taste her earlier despair, sour and sickening in her mouth. She can't rationalise this any longer, can't haul them back to safe ground. It's too late.

Mark could have been hurt.

But that's because he shouldn't have been there. This disintegration – this breaking down of everything – Harriet's seen it coming, seen Iquis battling against it, sensed her trying to protect Harriet from it.

But she's wrong!

Harriet fears the earthquake – of course she does – but she also needs it.

'I know that hunger,' she says, and her voice shakes with it, 'that vast emptiness which nothing can fill.' In the buckling mirror of the river she sees Stephen's face, cold and still. 'I recognize that hunger,' she repeats, on a rising, raw note.

'No you don't,' Iquis says shortly, 'you only think you do.'

'No!' Harriet yells, and she allows herself to be angry. 'You're not going to shut me out any longer! I'm sick of it only going one way. I make myself vulnerable, but *you won't reciprocate!* You think I didn't realise that all that time in Scotland you were backing away from me? And then tonight, when something does break through, it's with Mark. How can you let him in, when you won't let me near you?'

'I don't.'

'You did tonight!'

'That was a mistake,' Iquis says, dispassionately.

Her tone chills Harriet. Iquis is slipping away from her.

'We were meant to meet, Iquis. Meant to understand each other. We're twin souls.'

'Or the opposite sides of a mirror.'

'Shut up!' Harriet howls. 'You're not listening. We can help each other. We can cure each other's hunger. Don't you see? We're desperate without each other.'

A flash of lightning branches the sky behind Iquis's head and Harriet has a stark impression of Iquis's face in the unnatural brightness. Her jaw muscles are jerking and her face is burning with all the emotion she has kept from her voice.

Harriet slides her fingers inside one of Iquis's cold hands and tightens her grip.

'Dance with me. Dance the way you did at Decadance. You challenged me to face my fears and dance in Scotland and nothing bad happened. Now it's your turn. I can help you, Iquis.'

Iquis laughs, a ghostly, quiet thing that is whipped away from her as soon as she utters it. 'Can you?' she says in a mocking voice, but her fingers tighten on Harriet's hand and she moves forwards. Away from the river. Towards Harriet. 'There's no music.' Her voice is like a child's.

Harriet feels a rush of pure triumph. 'There's the crash of the river,' she shouts, 'and the beat of the rain. We can do this. We can do anything.' She tilts her face up to the sky, revels in the sensation of the rain against her skin.

'This is fate!' she yells.

Iquis strips her leather jacket off and hurls it away. She stretches her fingertips up towards the sky to catch the power of the storm. The rain slashes against the pale white columns of her arms. She starts to sway.

Awe, excitement, fear. Beneath their feet the ground churns as they twist and turn, gathering speed, finding the beat. Lost in a brilliant mass of water, Harriet grabs Iquis's hands and spins her round. The earth and sky tangle up as they whirl through them.

Iquis digs her heels into the ground and tugs hard on Harriet's hands.

'The river,' Iquis gasps. 'Leave me not upon the bank.'

The words are strangely familiar.

Iquis jerks Harriet out of her spin, pulls her to the riverbank. They leap together over the edge, splash down into the dark water. It's deeper than last time. She plunges knee-deep, deeper. The water is around her thighs, cold and pummelling, tugging at her. She grabs out for Iquis in order to keep upright. The water is trying to pull her away. Then Iquis's arms are on her shoulders dragging her upright, pulling her closer and closer until their mouths clash together.

Shock. Is this what she wanted? Is this what she meant to happen? She has no idea.

Iquis's lips are hard against her, hungry and demanding. Harriet's mouth stings – making it real – shaking her control. The roar of the river is in her ears, there's wetness everywhere. Iquis tastes of the storm.

The water welds the heavy skirts of Harriet's dress around her. The river is rising. She winds her arms round Iquis's neck and they fall forwards into the water.

Iquis is all angles, sharp against her. Harriet gulps a mixture of water and air. The rain has suddenly changed, thickened, so that there is little air anywhere and they are spinning, twisting one on top of each other, like seals, like mermaids. The water in her dress drags her down until it's like she could slip away, slip under. And still Iquis's mouth is fixed on her mouth, searching, devouring. They're under the water and everything is dark, everything is green. She wants to breathe but she knows that she can't.

Then, with no warning, she senses it there in front of her, the mud and the rocks ripping apart to make way for it: the gap, the hole, the roar of shifting soil. The water is pouring down into it, dragging her towards the vast mouth which smells of decay. And then she's in the bubble of the vibe room at Decadance with the nightmare breaking free. Bodies press around her, constricting her, and the video is everywhere, inescapable. She sees the knife falling into the grave and the whole room following it.

She's screaming out. Lashing against bodies. Trying to stop herself being sucked down. There's fingers on her arm.

'It's okay,' Iquis says as Harriet gasps air, but she knows that it isn't, knows that she's still trapped in that room, with all those bodies crowding in.

She fights them off. Kicks out. She has to escape. She strikes out blindly until she is free. Sprints against the churning, turning stones, scrambles up the muddy bank. The smell of dirt is everywhere, the gown heavy around her, dragging her down.

Blind in the night, her boots scrabbling for purchase, she lurches onto the bank and flees.

*

Harriet bursts through the front door and stops, panting, feeling the walls of the house enclose her. Her hands are cramped from holding the hem of her dress out of the way while she runs. She unclamps her fingers and the saturated material falls.

She cannot get the music from the Dark Island video out of her head. The jangly fairground wedding march has looped round and round as she runs. Now, with the competing sounds of the storm shut out, it's louder than ever.

The door of the lounge is shut. She stumbles past it and into the kitchen. She wants Jenna to be there, but of course Jenna has already gone. The kitchen is empty.

She sees the vodka bottle and snatches it up. She wrenches at the cap, but her hands are cold and wet and muddy and the metal slips through her fingers. She puts the bottle to her mouth and turns it against her teeth until it gives.

The taste of mud fills her mouth.

She spits out the cap and tilts the bottle; the vodka gushes into her mouth. She swallows, choking and gagging. The burn hits her throat, then her stomach.

'Very abandoned,' Mark's voice, with its ironic drawl, shocks her. She jerks the vodka bottle away, spits out the last mouthful.

His bulk fills the doorway. His face is flushed and his eyes are turbulent. Even from where she is against the counter she can sense his heat. The music backs off. She feels a shaky sense of relief, wants to grab onto him and refuse to let go.

He can save her.

'Where's Iquis?' Mark says. 'We've unfinished business.' He bounces the knuckles of one hand into the palm of the other.

Harriet watches the hand, tries to make sense of his words. But she can't think backwards. She exists only in this moment.

Mark's hand stills. He stares at Harriet, his gaze travelling over her wet, tangled hair, her wild face, before slowly considering the way the water-drenched fabric clings to her.

'There's something different about you.'

He walks slowly towards her, his gaze on the ticking pulse at her throat. She senses his excitement, sees the triumphant gleam in his eyes.

'Your mascara's smudged,' he says roughly.

He lifts one finger and rubs it across her face. His finger is hot, burning against her chilled skin.

Harriet sucks in an audible breath.

He moves closer until his thighs touch against hers.

His hand grips her shoulder. With the fingers of his other hand he tilts her chin back. She watches his face loom towards her until it is so close that it blurs. She feels his breath against her mouth, then the soft touch of his lips. The taste of whisky fuses with the taste of vodka.

After the cold river taste of Iquis's mouth his lips are blazingly hot.

The counter digs into Harriet's back as his weight presses against her. She flings her arms around him and locks her wrists together to manacle him to her. She feels a sweeping sense of relief, and grips harder.

Mark's mouth quickens against hers, moving and dominating, until that feeling is in her again, that strange spiralling sensation.

It is only then that the fear hits her.

I thought he was safe, she thinks, frantically trying to retain her grasp on him. But the smell of decay is all around her, the tiles of the kitchen floor are sliding away from her and it's there, waiting for her, calling to her. She tries to shove him away, even though she knows there's nowhere else to flee. She jerks her head away from his, looks towards the kitchen door.

If I could only cross... Iquis!

Harriet freezes.

Iquis is standing in the doorway. She gleams with water. Her hair is flat against her skull, her pupils narrow pinpricks around which a storm rages. Static electricity crackles off her.

The terror gripping Harriet has been so complete that there has been no thought of what Iquis must have felt when Harriet hit out at her and ran away.

I made her trust me, told her I could take it.

That dead look in her eyes when the goths turned away from her at Decadance. She must think that I...

'But it wasn't you,' Harriet says. 'It was...' A wave of vertigo hits her and the terror tightens its grip, choking off her words.

Iquis isn't appeased. Her fury is palpable. Her eyes rake over the tableau of Mark and Harriet.

'Who?' It's a dagger thrust. 'No. I don't want to know. You – both of you. Betrayed me.' Her gaze strikes Harriet, who flinches. 'And that's dangerous.' A long drawn-out hiss.

Harriet can hear the ground shifting under her feet, the tiny sound of pebbles and dirt breaking away and dropping a long, long way.

Iquis's eyes unlock from Harriet, lock onto Mark. She thrusts out her hand. 'Come!'

Her gaze appears to mesmerise Mark. Harriet feels him slowly sliding away from her, taking all the heat with him. Once he leaves there will be nothing to stop her falling. But what can she do? Mark isn't safe. Just like Iquis isn't safe.

Iquis looks just once at Harriet, but Harriet has nothing to say.

Then they are gone.

Harriet teeters on the edge of the hole. She raises the vodka bottle to her lips, drinks without tasting, not so much swallowing as gagging it down. Perhaps she can outrace the hole to oblivion.

Then, a rising surge of reaction from her stomach transforms itself from near-nausea to defiance.

Why not just step in? It's going to get me in the end.

She hurls the vodka bottle at the hole and braces herself to step after it. But to her surprise the bottle smashes in front of her feet and she sees its shattered fragments bouncing upwards.

For a moment she sees both gaping hole and tiles – like a surreal double vision – then there's only tiles, spilt vodka and glass.

FORTY-ONE

Time jumps.

The doorbell is ringing. She's in her own bed. Brittle daylight filters through the curtains. She's startled, dehydrated, her tongue swollen, her taste buds burnt raw with vodka. And she's full of dread.

She searches physically for the source, twisting her head to look across the room. There's a dark hump in the middle of the floor surrounded by a spreading stain of river water and mud. Her discarded dress.

She closes her eyes against the image. She doesn't want proof that last night really happened. But the knowledge can't be avoided.

She touches her bruised mouth, is flooded with sensations. Iquis's mouth against hers, the press of Mark's body, the greedy tug of the river. Then, knifing through that: terror, loss, Iquis.

What have I destroyed? The thought is too huge to be considered, and besides, the terror still dominates. She hasn't so much slept as been unconscious. The night has worked none of its usual softening.

The nightmare crossed over last night – became real. Either that or she's going mad.

She shakes her head to trigger the vodka hangover, but it doesn't come. The vodka is still in her veins. She's in that nowhere land, that pause between drunkenness and hangover, trapped in a surreal place.

But then, isn't everything surreal now?

'I'm losing my mind,' she says. 'Imagining things.'

Her voice hurts. She sits up, wraps her arms around herself for comfort. Her eyes travel to the white drawer unit where she keeps her clothes. She swallows.

'I don't want to,' she says, in a small child's voice. But it doesn't matter. She is rising out of bed, walking across to it. She lifts one end and swivels it out into the room. Still holding it, she looks down at the exposed patch of carpet. The DVD lies in its case, covered in dust.

This is where it began. In the vibe room at Decadance, watching this music video. It felt real and I told myself it wasn't. But last night it was ten times as real, ten times as powerful. Is this what ignoring it does?

The chest of drawers is slipping from her hands. She lets it go and it thuds down at an angle to the wall leaving the DVD exposed.

If I had stayed in the vibe room and faced it, maybe it wouldn't have got so huge.

Inside the case the silver disk catches the light at a slanting angle. She stoops and picks it up. It feels inert and very square in her hands.

The doorbell rings again. It's a relief. A distraction. She straightens and reaches for her bathrobe. Shrugging it on, she falters, then shoves the DVD into the right-hand pocket. The pocket is deep, the DVD disappears from sight.

*

Downstairs, Harriet can make out a slender figure through the front-door glass. The caller looks unthreatening – but Harriet is too edgy to take anything on trust.

'Who is it?'

'Jenna.'

It doesn't compute. Jenna belongs to a different world, a sane world. Even though Harriet swings the door open, none of it feels real.

'Is Mark in?'

'Don't know.' Harriet's answer is too fast. She's managed to walk downstairs without looking towards the closed door of Mark's room.

'Can I come in? I need to see him.'

Harriet stands to one side. The cool air from outside brushes over her as Jenna walks by, glances through the open door of the lounge, checks the kitchen, puts her foot on the first step.

'Wait!' Harriet calls.

Jenna turns towards her. 'What?'

But there are no words to explain what Jenna might find if she knocks on Mark's bedroom door.

'Nothing.'

*

Jenna is already hammering on Mark's door as Harriet – unable to stay away – reaches the top of the stairs.

'Who's there?' Mark's voice is hoarse but unmistakable. 'Is that Paul?'

Harriet's heart bumps unpleasantly. He's in then.

'No it's not. It's Jenna.'

'Where's Paul?' Mark sounds jumpy, unlike himself.

'I don't know. I haven't seen him this morning. Have you seen Marcia?'

'No.'

The conversation isn't making much sense to Harriet. It's like watching figures in a play – people she knows nothing about. The Jenna character looks worried. The Mark character sounds uncomfortable. But it's got nothing to do with her. Not yet, not unless Iquis...

'Look,' Jenna says, 'can I come in? It would be easier to talk without this door in the way.'

For long seconds Jenna's request is met by silence. Harriet creeps gradually closer.

Finally Mark responds, his voice full of reluctance. 'I guess you'd better.'

Harriet steps back out of sight and watches Jenna go in. She sees Jenna inhale sharply, sees her hand fly up to her mouth, sees her stare disbelievingly at the bed.

So Iquis is there! I don't want... I have to go.

She moves backwards.

'Who did that to you?' Jenna's stunned voice halts her.

'None of your business.' Mark sounds defensive.

The conversation is wrong. Harriet edges towards the door.

'Your poor wrists,' Jenna says.

'Don't make a big thing of it. It was a practical joke by some fool who should have known not to mess with me. I totally plan to retaliate, just as soon as you untie these... er...'

Harriet has to know what's going on. She walks into the bedroom.

Mark is lying in the centre of the bed. He's naked to the waist. The duvet covers the rest of him. His face is dirtied by morning stubble and by the ominous look in his eyes. His arms are stretched up above his head and held there by his own tightly-knotted ties. Iquis's scarf is tied in a jaunty bow around the elbow of his right arm.

Apart from the scarf, there's no trace of Iquis.

Harriet hears again the thud of Mark's head hitting the wall. Mark's pallor shocks her, as does her own complicity. Iquis had been so angry, so out of control. *He shouldn't have been there*, she thinks again, but this time the words are weak, lack the conviction they carried last night.

'Did Iquis do that to you?' Her words are abrupt, sound accusing. But it's not Mark she's judging.

'You didn't tell me Harriet was nearby!' He slams the words at Jenna.

'Sorry,' Jenna says.

'Sorry sucks,' Mark says. 'If either of you *ever* speak of this, I'll...' He yanks at the ties, his whole body struggling with them. It achieves nothing. He swallows, grinds his teeth.

'Just set me free, okay?' he says, eventually, in a carefully even tone.

Harriet finds herself walking forwards. She's on the right side of the bed, Jenna's on the left. She touches Mark's arm. She doesn't want to see this. But she has to. There are red weals around Mark's wrist where he's struggled to free himself and the knots are pulled tight. She fumbles, ineffectually, but nothing gives.

'I can't undo this.' She spots Mark's penknife on the bedside table and picks it up, easing out the longest blade. Turning back to Mark, she surprises a fearful look in his eyes.

'I'll have to cut it,' she says, and drops her eyes quickly back to his arm.

Mark's pulse jumps rapidly under her fingers as she holds his wrist still with one hand. She slices carefully at the material, which frays, then tears.

Once he is freed, Mark sits up and leans his back against the wall with a groan. He reaches for the whisky bottle on the bedside table. There's only an inch of whisky left. Mark tilts it, swigs, grimaces.

The room is uncomfortably silent. Mark's humiliation is tangible. The two girls glance at each other across the bed, but Harriet can't hold Jenna's gaze. She feels guilty, responsible.

'Are you okay?' Jenna asks, at last.

'Sure,' Mark says. He opens his eyes and stares down at his hands as he moves his fingers up and down to stretch out the cramp. 'What were you saying about Marcia?'

'Have you seen her?'

'Since last night?' He lifts his wrists slightly then drops them back on the bed. 'No, I can't say I have.' His voice is casual, but with an underlying irony that makes Jenna flinch.

'No, of course not. I'm sorry. I didn't think.' Jenna glances away from him and out of the window, biting her lip.

'Something's wrong,' Mark realises. 'That's why you're here. How can I help?' He sounds relieved to be out of the spotlight.

Jenna turns from the window. 'It's Marcia. I can't find her.'

'You're worried?'

'Yes,' Jenna says. 'Her backpack's missing, and some of her clothes.'

'Right. Hang on. I've got to go for a slash, then...' As he speaks he's climbing out of bed, wrapping a towel round his waist. He takes three strides towards the door and then stops abruptly as a tremor hits his body. 'Oh, shit!' he says, then pitches forwards, slamming his face down into the ground.

Harriet lunges forwards to try to catch him, but she's already too late. She kneels next to him and places her fingers against the side of his neck. His pulse jumps out at her and she jerks her hand away.

Mark groans, then mutters a string of expletives.

'Are you okay?' Jenna says, from his other side.

'Of course I'm fucking okay,' Mark says, rolling over onto his back, 'I just stood up too fast.' With the back of his hand he wipes away a trickle of blood which emerges sluggishly from one nostril.

'You don't look okay,' Jenna says. 'I think we should get the doctor.'

'No way!' Mark actually sounds panicked by the idea. 'Look – I just drank too much last night, okay? It's self-inflicted.' He catches sight of Harriet. 'And you can fuck off!' he says, with sudden wrath. 'Do you really think I want you here?'

Harriet can't react – there's too much to react to. She's vaguely aware that Jenna is worried about Marcia. But Mark's state is far more immediate, far more frightening. 'Did Iquis do this to you?' she asks again.

But Mark just closes his eyes. 'Please go away, Harriet,' he says, and for the first time she hears weakness in his voice.

The sound makes her want to cry – the emotion so immediate that it cuts through everything else. But she never cries. She daren't cry.

Jenna is shaking her head, gesturing towards the door. 'I've got this,' she mouths. 'You go.'

There's nothing Harriet can do but obey. That's how it feels. She's been told to go and she goes. In her mind she's picking up her bike, cycling away; time is spinning again.

I'm going mad, she thinks, and this time it's closer. This time, it's believable.

FORTY-TWO

Harriet shuts the door on Mark and Jenna and walks downstairs into the lounge. She presses buttons, bringing the DVD player and TV to life. The little tray inside the player slides out, and she places the disk in it.

She hears a creak, a movement from upstairs, but already it's like Jenna, Mark and Marcia are miles away and where there should be concern, there's nothing.

She shivers, feeling the ice penetrate her. Then picks up the remote control and presses play.

Fairground music – lyrics – the bride with the black-hole eyes – the sinister watcher – the whirling graveyard.

She stands there watching it. Taking it. There is nothing but terror.

The bride slashes her wrists and the blood spills out. The knife falls and the camera follows its silver pinprick light. The grave opens up and swallows her. This is the moment she always wakes up – but this time, she's already awake – which means, she's about to face...

But it doesn't happen.

The pinpoint of light is widening to reveal an antiseptic-looking room. There's no familiarity – no déjà vu – this is not the outcome of her dream. The ground is complete under her feet.

And yet, something still disturbs her. She can hardly hear the lyrics now – the sound of the music. Everything's so brilliantly lit, so surgically clean and uncluttered. Then she sees the figure – the unmistakable human shape, covered by a white sheet – lying on a flat surface just big enough to hold it.

A dead body.

There's no blood, just immaculate white.

The door opens and the watcher sneaks into the morgue, locking the door behind him. His face is in shadow, yet Harriet can see no obstacle between him and the room's lights. He crosses over to the sheeted figure and yanks the sheet away. Harriet screams.

It's not Circe lying there. It's Iquis.

Harriet drops the control and throws herself across the room. Her mind is full of the look on Iquis's face last night. She runs into the hall and hammers on her door.

There's no answer. She grabs the handle and shoves it downwards. The door gives, pitching her down the stairs. She stumbles halfway, then catches herself against the banister and stares.

Iquis's bedroom has been trashed. Splintered furniture and broken possessions are heaped in the middle of the room like a vast funeral pyre. There's nothing here to dispel the image on the TV screen. Harriet staggers down the last few stairs. Iquis's stereo, sides smashed and innards spilling, crowns the pyre. Fragments of clothing and broken-spined books are stuffed into the gaps, like kindling waiting for a torch.

The wardrobe is still standing, but empty – its doors broken wide, discarded hangers scattered around it.

With a jolt, Harriet recalls opening the front door for Jenna. A detail she hadn't registered at the time, hits her. She doesn't remember seeing the bike.

But I wasn't really looking.

The basement door to the outside is ajar. She pulls it open, stares up to the forecourt.

The bike has gone.

She runs upstairs, bursts into Mark's room. He's lying down; Jenna's standing by the window talking on the phone. Harriet bangs into the foot of the bed and halts.

'Where is she? What did you do to her?'

Mark shakes his head, wearily. 'Give me a break, Harriet. We're doing the best we can. We've made a list of all the places Marcia might be. Jenna's phoning around Marcia's other friends now, and Paul's on his way over.'

'Not Marcia. Iquis.'

'I don't fucking care where Iquis is.'

'What happened last night? Was it Iquis who tied you up?'

'None of your business.'

'What did you do to her?'

'Piss off, Harriet.'

'Did you kill her?'

Mark looks confused and then furious. 'Don't be stupid. How could I have done anything?'

'Is Iquis okay?' Harriet asks.

Mark casts her a look in which exasperation seems to combine with pity. 'Iquis is always okay. It's about time you realised that.'

'But she's gone,' Harriet says. 'Her bike's not outside and her belongings have been trashed. It looks like there might have been a struggle. And then the video. I saw her and she was dead. You must know something.'

'Harriet, you're talking total bollocks.' His voice has risen, his eyes narrowed, yet there is an exhaustion to him which saps his response of its full power. 'There was no one here last night except you, me and Iquis. As to her room, I heard her crashing around in it before she left on the bike. Didn't you hear her?'

'No,' Harriet says, thinking of the vodka-induced dead time between last night and this morning. She hadn't heard a thing.

'But the video!' she says, even more urgently.

'What video?'

'The Dark Island video. Iquis was in it and she was dead.'

'What video are we talking about here? Is this something you found in her room?'

'No. Glyn sent it to me a few months ago.'

There's a moment's silence as Mark takes this in. Then his face closes.

'Harriet,' he says, in a strained voice, 'shut the fuck up. I don't have the energy to listen to your mental breakdown. I don't want you in my room. I don't want you in my house. And I don't care where Iquis is. I wouldn't even care if she'd crashed her bike and broken her neck. In fact it's the best thing that could happen to her. Now get out.'

Harriet stares at him. *But I need you. I need your strength and your sanity.*

It's impossible to let him see her desperation. 'Fuck you,' she yells, then turns and runs out of the room.

FORTY-THREE

Stopping only to dress, Harriet flees from the house. Outside the air is watery and weak and the frame of her bicycle is damp with condensation.

At first her only thought is to cycle away, but gradually she realises that habit has steered her towards the university. She can find no reason to change course, even though she has no idea what she'll do when she gets there.

In the end the very stolidity of the university brings a kind of comfort. She walks the corridors bathed in the noise of students, clinging to a sense of the familiar. Although it's crazy, on some level she is searching for Iquis.

She rounds a corner and thinks she sees the ghost of Iquis fleeing from her.

She wants to call, "Wait!", but chokes it back, doesn't want to draw stares or worse – questions. Which she –

Just impossible to pretend to be normal.

In the end she leaves, driven out by the same need to keep moving that had brought her there in the first place.

She keeps searching, trawling through the winding streets of the town, eating mechanically outside the chip shop, not tasting the food, just refuelling so she can keep going, keep searching.

Eventually, inevitably, she cycles out into the Lake District through the lowering afternoon light. As darkness overtakes the sky, her journey becomes more of a pilgrimage than a search. Each place she visits stirs memories and echoes of herself and Iquis.

At the same time, she feels the loss of Iquis constantly. Without her the night is unfriendly and full of sinister, creeping sounds. Horrid superstitions force themselves into her mind. She keeps expecting to stumble over Iquis's corpse staring up at her from some ditch or rocky crevice. But when she twists the bike light frantically from side to side she sees only rocks and earth, trees and bushes.

She's crossing the rocks to Iquis's waterfall, her head full of the chaos of the rumbling water, when she admits the truth.

This is pointless. She's not going to find her. Not like this.

But this is how Harriet wants to find her. She's trying to re-enter the past, trying to undo the previous night.

But it can't be done. And sooner or later she has to face it. She has to go to Decadance and speak to Glyn.

*

It's three in the morning when Harriet – exhausted from the cycle back against the wind – reaches Mark's house.

Had Mark meant what he said this morning?

Harriet half-expects to see her belongings packed into bin bags and piled outside the front door. But the forecourt contains only Mark's car and the front door opens to her key. The house is in darkness. She tiptoes to her room and sees the stiffening, purple-velvet dress, still lying in the middle of its river-water stain.

Absolutely nothing has moved.

*

She sleeps till midday, then wakes with a sense of urgency. The house is empty and has never felt more lonely. She powers up the computer, traces the route south to Decadance, calculates the mileage and groans. Over sixty miles and even if Mark was here she couldn't ask him to drive her – not now.

She forces herself to eat, then pulls on her walking boots – her trainers are still wet from the previous night – and loads the bike with essentials: food, water and protective clothing.

It seems ironic to be so sensible, but habit and the memory of how cold it had been last night, takes over.

*

The dark, sleeping-beauty hedges close in on her as she nears Decadance. She looks above them, searching for where the gates poke out. It *can't* be much further.

She passes a wide open driveway, then slams on her brakes, skews the bike to a halt.

Wasn't that...?

She wheels the bike back to the driveway, stares up its length at the unmistakable turrets of Decadance poking into the late afternoon sky, and grabs in a painful, stunned breath.

The gates are missing.

It's like they've been torn from the earth by a giant hand. The mounds which had held the gateposts are ripped and scarred. Scattered stones and dying grasses lie uprooted at her feet.

The nightmare closes in.

*

The big wooden doors which had been wide open last time are all shut up. She raises the huge ring of the knocker and pounds it against the door. There's no response. She hears the knock echoing in an empty kind of way.

Is she too late?

She hefts the knocker again and slams it down, over and over.

Finally she hears Glyn's voice, muffled by the thick wood. 'All right. I'm coming. Stop trying to break the door down.'

There's the creak of bolts being drawn back. The door swings open to reveal Glyn. He's wearing an old coat, with flannel pyjama legs poking out underneath. His hair is loose and tangled, his face grey with stubble. Under rubbed-red eyelids, his bloodshot eyes water as he squints into the day.

'It's true, isn't it?' Harriet says, taking his disarray as further confirmation. 'Iquis is dead, isn't she? Is it cos of what I did?'

Glyn's face is arrested in mid-yawn. 'What?'

'Iquis,' Harriet repeats, her heart racing, 'is she dead?'

Glyn knuckles his eyes, then studies her, his forehead wrinkled in concentration. 'I know who you are,' he says at last, 'you're Harriet, aren't you? You came to Decadance last autumn with Iquis. You say she's... *dead?*'

'Yes. No. I don't know. I thought you'd know. I thought that was what you were trying to tell me. I thought that was why you sent me the DVD.'

Glyn puts his hands on Harriet's shoulders and she realises she's shaking.

'Calm down. You're not making much sense. I know nothing about this. What makes you think she's... no longer with us?'

'Because of this.' Harriet thrusts the DVD at him.

'What?' Glyn stares down blankly at the silver disk.

'It's the music video you sent me. Iquis was in it, and she was dead. Did Dark Island kill her? And if they did, how did it appear on the DVD, and how did you know it was going to?'

Glyn takes a step away from her. There's a wary look in his eyes.

'Calm down,' he says, and then, 'What have you taken?'

'Taken? I don't understand.' Harriet is bewildered. This isn't the comforting teddy-bear Glyn who understands everything without having to be told.

She needs to watch her words. Despite the gates, Glyn appears to be inhabiting the real world, the one she's left behind.

'Drugs,' Glyn says. 'What drugs have you taken?'

'Nothing. Only some vodka last night.'

'Okay.' He raises his hands in a gesture of acceptance, but his expression remains dubious. 'I guess you better come in.'

'Not until you tell me about Iquis. Why was she in the music video? Is she dead?'

'Harriet, the video isn't real.' It's the voice he might use with a child. 'It's a film. Iquis is in it because she's Circe. That's why I wanted you to see it. So that you'd understand. I'd given her my word I'd keep schtum, but I was convinced you ought to know – so you could help her. So I cheated by showing you the video.'

'Iquis is Circe?' Harriet says blankly. 'She's not dead?'

'Not as far as I know.'

Harriet can't take it in. Her head is buzzing with an audible, mechanical sound that she needs to get away from. She staggers down two of the stone steps, then finds that her legs are shaking too much to hold her. She sinks down onto the final step and curls her head towards her knees. The buzzing consumes her. Then just as suddenly it's gone, leaving a huge silence.

She touches the stone step – cold, dusty. Real.

It's all so obvious. How come I didn't see?

'She was so well disguised,' she says. 'Not just her hair and the colour of her eyes – the shape of her face and her attitude, even her height – all different.'

'But that's easy,' Glyn says, 'they can do what they want on film. They're painting a picture, with make-up and clever camera angles, even CGI or prosthetics. It's not difficult to hide an identity.'

But Harriet is hardly listening.

She's back in the record shop, aged twelve, hearing the wounded jazz-rasp of Medea's voice as it reached out to her. "*Whose hand pushed you?*" That instant sense of kinship, as if Harriet were Dark Island's changeling child, so that even as she hears them for the first time they already seem known, significant.

And now – it's possible?

Twelve-year-old Harriet has no doubts.

Me and Circe together, the way it was always meant to be. I couldn't reach her through the speakers, but she found me. We're blood sisters. I'm part of the family. I belong with them: on the stage, in the music, even writing the lyrics. There'll be fans wishing that they could be me. But they wouldn't have what I have, what I've had ever since the record shop, that unbreakable bond which binds us together. Finally, they'll make sense of so much that I...

'No!' Harriet says aloud. 'Stop it!'

Glyn breaks off mid-sentence, looking startled. 'I don't see—'

'Sorry, not what you're saying. I just...' *Can't afford to listen to those thoughts, there's too much... wrong.*

The lyrics of that first song are on repeat play in her head. "*Whose hand pushed you? Is hell too far to fall?*" Harriet knows what they mean now, she can hear Iquis's blurted confidences, "*I had a brother who died*", and then much later, "*My father killed him*". Then there's Iquis on the pier with her brother. "A warning", he'd said, and something about a girl. Not Harriet. Although he knew who Harriet was. "*Little friend.*" And it was all so scary.

And of course, Iquis's brother must actually be... Loki. "He's to die for", Marcia had said. And now Marcia has disappeared, again, and...

'What is it?' Glyn says.

'Marcia,' Harriet says. 'She lied. She told us she wasn't with them. But she *was!*'

'I don't—'

'It explains everything.'

The mad bike ride. The confrontation on the pier. It was Marcia who gave Loki power over Iquis. It's what Iquis couldn't fight! And it's why the return to Cumbria went so disastrously wrong: why Iquis was so odd, so confrontational with Marcia, why Iquis lost control with Mark.

What did she think Dark Island were going to do?

But that's a stupid question, because Dark Island had already done it, already started. They'd given Marcia something, possibly heroin. They'd messed with her mind, made her want more of the same, made it so that they could reclaim her at will, shaken the peace of the entire household.

And they'd done it deliberately.

FORTY-FOUR

'Harriet!' Glyn is in front of her. He's got her shoulders and he's shaking her. 'Snap out of it! You're worrying me. Is there anyone we can call? You're obviously not well.'

'I...'

But she can't say anything. His hands on her shoulders make her think of clinging to Mark. But she can't cling to anyone because she's lost in the nightmare and if she touches Glyn it will spread to him – like it's spread to Marcia and Mark.

Her nightmare.

Iquis's nightmare.

Dark Island's nightmare.

Is it all connected?

I thought it was my nightmare but maybe it isn't. Maybe it sneaked out through the speakers the first time I heard them in that music shop. And then it fed, gaining strength with every contact, until it was ready to escape – first through the music video at Decadance, then in the river with Iquis.

How the hell do I get free?

But she knows. She has to attack the source. She has to find out what the nightmare is and break its power.

'I can't...'

'Don't try to talk,' Glyn says. 'Look, it's bloody freezing out here, let's go inside. I'll make you a hot drink and you can sit in front of the fire and calm down.'

He steers her through the familiar entranceway and into the hugely empty dance hall. He takes her behind the bar, through a door marked private and into a small room, crowded with furniture. He deposits her in a squashy armchair and turns on the gas fire.

'Now, I'll make a drink. What do you want? Tea? Coffee? Hot chocolate?'

'Anything,' Harriet says. Some part of her mind knows that she needs Glyn, that it's vital to convince him of her sanity. Accepting his offer gets him out of the room, gets her away from his scrutiny, gives her thinking time.

The door closes behind him. The fire hisses, releasing a gassy scent into the room. Its flame is half-blue, half-orange.

Is Marcia still missing? Jenna, yesterday, looking for her – she'd been worried. *Had* she found her?

Everything is happening so fast. Could Dark Island have snatched her? Has Iquis gone chasing off after her? And if so, is it to sacrifice herself in exchange for Marcia's freedom?

But Harriet isn't convinced. She recalls Iquis, frozen on the back of her motorbike at the start of term, agonising over whether she should have returned, saying, "*I sicken myself.*" She hears again the cracking sound of Mark's head against the wall.

Just what is she capable of? Could she have taken Marcia to Dark Island for revenge?

It ought to be unthinkable, but it isn't. Not now she's seen Mark with his wrists tied to the bed and that jaunty scarf tied round his elbow.

Oh shit!

That's another connection. The needle marks in Marcia's arm. Could Iquis have drugged Mark? Was that what the scarf was hiding, and why he looked so rough – why he fainted?

No! I can't believe it of her.

And yet, I knew how deep her self-hatred and fear of losing control were. I told her I could handle it. I promised her I would hold her, contain her – then the nightmare broke through and I ran away, leaving her with all that destructive power unleashed.

That's why whatever happened afterwards is my fault, and my responsibility to undo.

*

Harriet sips her hot chocolate. She focusses on its sweetness, its warmth in her mouth, willing herself to an appearance – a surface – of calm.

'Is there someone I can phone,' Glyn is asking, 'someone who could come and get you? A friend? Or maybe your parents?'

'Maybe,' Harriet says, 'but I need to ask you something first.'

'You do?'

'Yes.'

She's quiet for a minute thinking about how to approach this. 'Look, I know I sounded distraught when I came here.

It's been rather a traumatic couple of days. Iquis and I had a big fight and afterwards I drank a lot of vodka. Truth to tell, I'm still very hungover, and not thinking very clearly.'

She can see Glyn relaxing slightly, though he's still eyeing her warily.

'She's gone back to her family,' she says, speaking the certainty out loud for the first time. 'That's why the gates are missing, isn't it?'

He hesitates, 'I expect so.'

She nods. 'I need your help. I have to find her.'

He shakes his head. 'I don't think that's a good idea.'

*

It takes *too long* to persuade him. Time she doesn't have.

She weaves a story from strands of the truth. Iquis and Mark had fancied each other for a long time. For some reason Iquis had held off. Two nights ago she'd caught Mark and Harriet kissing and felt doubly betrayed.

She's chosen well. She can see his nightclub experience colouring his judgement. He can make allowances for the intensity of passion, he's seen it so many times. As she talks, his philosophical, observer side resurfaces. She begins to recognise the man she met last time.

'You sent the DVD because you wanted me to help her,' she says, 'wanted me to keep her away from her family. I didn't understand in time. But I'm ready now.'

'Yes, but—'

'I broke her trust when she was at her most vulnerable. She'll never trust anyone again unless I repair that. And she'll never escape her family without my help.'

Glyn is frowning, shaking his head. It's not enough. She has to tell him about Marcia.

'It's possible she took another girl with her. Marcia would have wanted to go, she fancies Loki like mad, but you said yourself that you wouldn't let a daughter of yours near them.'

'I know, but—'

'She's vulnerable, has a history of absconding.'

She can't tell him about the drugs. He'd want to tell the police, and Iquis's conviction that this wouldn't work retains its power. But it's more than that, involving the police would destroy any chance of rescuing Iquis.

'You know Marcia's gone with Iquis?' Glyn says.

'No, I don't.' She can't lie about this. Marcia might have just gone off for a few hours. 'But Iquis was very angry when she left. She might not have been thinking clearly. She might have done it to make me jealous, not thought about the consequences to Marcia until it's too late.'

'I see.' He looks worried, puzzled. 'I don't know what's best.'

Harriet falls silent, willing him to help her.

'Is there someone we could talk to?' he says. 'Maybe find out whether this Marcia girl is still missing?'

Harriet nods. 'Jenna. I was going to ring her anyway. Find out whether Marcia's back.'

It works. She sees him relax a bit more.

'Will you tell me where they are?' she asks carefully.

'It's not that simple. I don't actually know.'

She's stunned.

'But you have to know. Otherwise why are we having this conversation? You'd have said that you couldn't help me.'

He lifts his hands in acknowledgement.

'So what is it you know?' Harriet demands.

He hesitates, then speaks, weighing his words. 'Dark Island have bought the gates. They were collected this morning, not long after I'd closed Decadance and gone to bed. I didn't check the time but I'd guess it was about eight o'clock. Two removal guys turned up out of the blue saying they'd come to take the gates. Well, I wasn't having any of it, but when I rang Joe – he's the guy I lease this place from – he told me he'd just sold them to Dark Island, that they'd made him an offer he couldn't refuse. I was furious, but there was nothing I could do.'

Harriet's breathing quickens. 'Do you know where the men were taking them?'

'I think so. It's not a certainty.'

'Where?'

'I caught sight of the destination on their satnav. A place called Thurso, right up at the top of Scotland. There was a street name. I can't remember it, but it began with an H. I should recognize it if I saw it written down.'

'North Scotland,' Harriet says, and shivers at the memory of cold. 'That's where Iquis went before. She met up with her family on the pier at John O'Groats, about a week ago. They must still be in the area. Do you have Internet access? We can pull up a map, check out street names.'

He hesitates, 'I'm not telling you the street.'

'You've got to! Otherwise why tell me anything? Please, Glyn, you have to help us.'

He sighs. 'First we talk to Jenna, find out if Marcia is still missing. I'll introduce myself and explain that you are with me, and that you're safe. I'll swap phone numbers with her, tell her she can phone any time, that anyone who wants to check up on me can.'

'But why?' Harriet is puzzled. 'I don't understand.'

Glyn looks at her under heavy brows. 'Because you're still very young and I don't want anyone worrying about you, or thinking that you've gone off with someone dodgy. I want them to know they can trust me.'

'Yes, but why? I don't understand.'

'Look, Harriet, there's no way I'd let you go off searching for Dark Island on your own. But there's something tragic about Iquis that makes me want to intervene despite myself, and there's also the possibility of this other girl...

'I need to see for myself what the situation is. There's a good chance they'll let me in if we can find them. They may want to use Decadance again, or at least to keep their options open. We can find out whether Marcia is there and it will give you an opportunity to resolve things with Iquis.

'But first,' and he gives her a stern look, 'we talk to Jenna.'

Harriet chews on her lip, prey to a confused mix of feelings. The idea of travelling with Glyn, of letting someone older take over, is comforting. And yet, she can't help feeling that she ought to be going alone, that that is the only way to reach Iquis.

Even so, it's a result of a kind, a step closer. She has to take it.

She pulls her mobile out of her pocket. 'Can we just tell Jenna that I'm staying with you for a few days to allow Mark time to calm down? I want to keep it simple. She'd only disapprove if she knew we were going after Iquis. She's very much taken Mark's side over this.'

'Sure.' Glyn's wearing that philosophical look once more.

FORTY-FIVE

Scotland means a return to the snow. A week ago it had been smooth and white, clean and thick. But now it's humped on the edges of pavements, a frozen slush of greyish-brown and brackish black.

Harriet is jittery and strained. The phone call with Jenna had been disturbing, awkward. Marcia was still missing, and Mark... Well, discussing him had been difficult. Jenna had been openly hostile towards Iquis. 'To hurt Mark like that! There's nothing you can say, so don't try.'

'But you don't know what happened,' Harriet had tried, 'there might be—'

'Mitigating circumstances? Don't make me laugh.' There'd been no humour in her voice. 'I mean it, Harriet. She's...'

'Just tell me how Mark is.'

Harriet had longed to hear that he was his usual arrogant self.

'Still not back on form.' Jenna's voice had been clipped. 'Not that he'll admit it.'

'Did he say what happened?'

There'd been a pause. Jenna sounded troubled when

she responded. 'He won't tell me, keeps trying to act like everything is normal, like he can get up and do stuff, then he flakes out and there's something in his eyes which I don't like – he seems... almost panicked. Like he's still scared of something.'

Last night, Harriet had hardly slept.

Now it's midday, and she is full of a grinding hopelessness.

'We're too late,' she says as she stares down the long, straight street which Glyn claims is the one he saw on the satnav. 'They're not here.'

If she'd had control of the journey, they would have travelled all night, would have arrived hours ago while it was still dark. But she hadn't been able to persuade Glyn to work to her timetable. Not only had he insisted on arranging cover for himself at Decadance and finding them a place to break the journey, but he had even wasted precious time strapping Harriet's bike to the roof bars of his car so that he could drop her off in Cumbria on his way back south, afterwards.

Harriet finds it impossible to imagine an afterwards.

The street looks wrong. Except for a nearby pub and a large hotel some distance away it's just a long line of modern, brick-built houses. Harriet can't picture either Iquis or Dark Island here.

The icy north wind blasts along the street, scouring their faces. Harriet rewraps her scarf, pulls her beanie lower, hunches into her coat. It feels colder than last time, the chill harder to resist.

Glyn, reaching into the boot of his car, drags out a vast anorak.

'My spare,' he says, and holds it out to her.

Mechanically, Harriet shrugs it on over her own coat. It reaches her shins. She removes one glove while she zips it up.

'Perhaps this wasn't the final destination,' Glyn says. 'Perhaps the removal men just stayed the night here before delivering the gates today.'

'We've lost them!'

'Not necessarily,' Glyn says with infuriating calm. 'There may be a trail to follow. Let's go and talk to people, see whether any of the staff at the hotel or the pub remember them.'

He's too sane, too rational – they're not going to find Dark Island like this.

'Let's split up,' she says.

I've got to tune in to my instincts, to whatever it was – is – that connects me to them.

'It'll be quicker. I'll take the pub. You take the hotel. Meet back here.'

Glyn hesitates, then agrees.

*

Aware of Glyn glancing back to check on her, Harriet pushes open the pub door and walks into partial darkness. The bar room smells of ancient whisky, and is little warmer than the street outside. A girl with a shaved head is perched on the bar, bashing the heels of her boots against its side. She's the only occupant of the room.

'What're you having?' she asks in a monotone, as Harriet approaches her.

'Just wondering if anyone stayed here last night,' Harriet says.

'No. That it?'

'No,' Harriet says. 'That's not it.' She wants to take the other girl's head and bash it against the bar until she loses her disinterest and tells Harriet what she needs to know.

The sudden violent urge scares her.

'What then?' the girl asks impatiently.

Harriet drags in the peat-smoke aroma of the whisky. There has to be a scent, a trail. This girl is the right age – her age – Iquis is closer here than anywhere.

'I'll have a beer.'

'Right.' The girl swings her legs across the bar and jumps down behind it.

Harriet looks towards the beer pumps. There's a familiar picture on the pump clip, standing stones, framed by a dark bronze and gold sunset.

Dark Island.

Bitter caramel flavour, and herself happy, hot from dancing, and Iquis...

Harriet's no longer interested in placing an order.

The Dark Island helicopter had flown over her head and out across the sea, heading north. She'd been sitting on the jetty, waiting for Iquis and wondering what was out there, then later, the barman at the ceilidh had told her – the Orkneys, source of the beer.

Driving into Thurso today Harriet and Glyn had passed signs for the ferry port.

She's still looking at the Ring of Brodgar on the pump clip. Dark Island would not look out of place in that setting.

'This one then?' The bar girl's hand is on the pump handle.

'No.' Harriet pushes away from the bar. 'I'm out of here.'

'Suit yourself.'

*

Back at the car Harriet moves fast, climbing up on the bonnet and unhooking the straps holding her bike in place. She shoves the bike off the roof and leaps down with it, then flings one leg over the crossbar and freewheels until she is clear of the car and can hit the road. She pedals madly, head ducked, expecting to hear Glyn shouting behind her.

It's not until she's clear of the street, that it occurs to her that she should have left a note.

But there wasn't time.

I'll text him later, she thinks, as she cycles back the way they'd come, searching for the first of the ferry-port signs.

*

Fifteen minutes later she's at the ferry port clutching a ticket and an ordnance survey map of the Orkney mainland. The ferry, the second one that day, leaves in ten minutes. Perhaps the gate men were on the first.

As she freewheels through the concourse towards the ferry the smell of salt and decaying seaweed swamps her. She's breathing fast.

She stops at the ferry's gaping mouth, puts one foot down. There's just time to text Glyn.

She pulls the mobile phone out of her pocket and switches it on. The message envelope is flashing at her. She ignores it. What should she say?

In the end she just types in, *Sorry, got to do this on my own.*

Her mobile starts to ring just as she's pressing send. For a moment her arm tenses, ready to hurl the phone into the water, but something stops her. She can't quite bring herself to break the connection with Glyn.

So instead she switches it off and shoves it into her pocket. Her safety net. She pushes on, up the ramp.

FORTY-SIX

The ferry battles towards a land of snow and ice. The Orkney mainland rises like wide, soft dough from turbulent waters. Most of what can be seen is low lying, as if anything tall has been scoured away.

It's a land of lochs and chambered cairns, of standing stones and burial mounds, of ancient dwellings and solstice-centred architecture – all of which are marked on Harriet's map. Thrown around on deck, she struggles to hold it open and match its details to what she can see: the inlets, the approaching town and, somewhere far beyond and still out of sight, the Ring of Brodgar which lies on the far side of the vast Loch of Stenness.

Good job she's got her bike. She'll need it. In a funny kind of way, Glyn had been right.

They dock, and she cycles down the ramp and through the town. A passing cafe tempts her with the scent of strong coffee, but it's after three and will be going dark in an hour or so. She can't stop. It's over six miles to the Ring of Brodgar which, isolated between two lochs and far from any buildings, is unlikely to be either lit or hospitable after nightfall.

She emerges into the raw, treeless landscape. The wind swipes at her and the bike shakes. Her legs ache as they force the pedals round. The snow isn't deep because the wind prevents it settling, lifting a constant dusting of ice into the air. She breathes and the cold sneaks up her nostrils, concentrates at the bridge of her nose.

The land empties of buildings. She reaches the Loch of Stenness and turns right to follow its edges down and around and along. The ice chill from its vast, sprawling body rises to touch her face. The loch surface is pitted and glacier-like. The sound of children's voices rings from it. There's a boy running out onto the ice, and a group of children playing at its edge, bashing white shattered patterns into it with stones.

Harriet watches as she cycles past, troubled by the boy on the ice – the potential for disaster. Only gradually does she relax, as she comes to trust the ice beneath his feet. The boy calls to her in triumph and she raises a hand briefly in response.

She cycles on, crossing a bridge where frozen loch and lapping sea meet. Looking down she sees the wet ice waiting, treacherous and dark. She thinks about the boy and glances back but already he's out of sight.

She's head-on into the wind now. It sneaks into Glyn's anorak and inflates it like a balloon. Cursing, she grabs one-handed at the zip and yanks it down. The coat spreads out behind her, like wings. She passes a roadside pub and the wings fall against her back in the sudden lull, then are lifted once more as she leaves its shelter.

It's like being a bird, riding a thermal. She's caught in something elemental. But it's no way to make progress. She halts, yanks the coat from her shoulders, bundles it roughly and attaches it to the cycle rack.

The elements are wearing her down. She stands catching her breath and staring across the loch, searching for the Ring of Brodgar.

Directly across from her the shoreline climbs into a series of mounds. Further along, where the land is flat again, there are no standing stones. They must be behind those mounds which look so tantalisingly close. There'd been something on the map about burial mounds near the stone circle; that must be what she's seeing. She could cross the loch here, strike out across the ice, and she'd be there in twenty minutes – or dead.

Tiredness tempts her to recklessness, but she remembers the black ice, and puts her foot back on the peddle. Fighting the wind to travel around the loch will take much longer but she'll get there. Briefly, she hears a distant booming, rhythmic and distorted, from under the sound of sea and wind and wonders what it is.

Then she's shoving off, head down into the wind.

*

She doesn't stop again until she's reached the far side of the loch where the road she wants leads out along the narrow spit of land between the two frozen bodies of water. She only stops then because a barrier blocks her way. It's a hefty wooden plank, supported by two trestles with concrete bases, and it spans the entire width of the single-track road. There's a notice nailed to it: "Road closed for essential maintenance".

Yellow diversion arrows point back the way Harriet has come.

She can't believe it. It's miles round the loch. And she just can't! Weariness hits her.

There's some smaller text at the bottom of the notice: "Ring of Brodgar closed. No access permitted".

No! This is not happening! She's come so far. They can't turn her away.

She fights an urge to slump to the ground, to howl out in misery, fury, pain. It's almost like someone's deliberately trying to prevent her getting through to Iquis!

No, that's stupid.

And yet, it's another coincidence, like the gates being missing.

Isn't it?

The thought stiffens her legs. She's not done yet.

She locks her bike to the barrier and ducks beneath it, strides along the narrow strip of land between the lochs. She hears the discordant scream of a guitar, then catches the profiles of five standing stones on the land to her right and is absorbed, walking forwards along the road, but staring at the stones.

'Not enough,' she reluctantly concludes. The Ring of Brodgar, with its full circle of stones, must still be ahead. She swings her attention back to the route, then freezes.

The road ahead goes over a bridge and there's another barrier on its hump, but this time there's a heavyset man standing forbiddingly behind it.

'Road's closed,' he announces. 'Turn back.'

The barrier spans the whole width of the bridge and beneath the bridge there is only frozen water.

'I can't turn back,' she yells, quickening her pace. 'It's too far round. Can't you let me through?'

'No.'

His ill-fitting blue uniform with its legend "*Satellite Security*" looks unconvincing, like he's dressed for a part. And he's oddly familiar. Could she have seen him before? But where?

She shakes her head, steps onto the bridge. 'Please. I'll be careful. I won't get in the way.'

The man swings one huge leg upwards until his booted foot rests on the top of the barrier. He leans into it, tensed like an animal ready to spring. 'I told you to go.'

Harriet takes an involuntary step back and the action triggers a memory. She remembers being shoved backwards by the panicked bodies of other goths, sees the line of men shoving, advancing. Recognition hits her.

'Marcia's minder!' she exclaims.

'What?'

Oh shit! Shouldn't have said that aloud.

'Nothing.'

He sways backwards, then lunges forwards over the barrier. Harriet doesn't have time to run. He grabs her. Shakes her.

'What did you mean by that?'

'Nothing. I meant nothing by it. Look, I'm sorry, I'll go. I didn't expect anyone to get so wound up about a load of roadworks. I just didn't want to have to walk around. It'll be dark before I get there.'

'But you said...'

'I was rude. I'm sorry. I know you're just doing your job, I shouldn't have... I'll get out of your way.'

He's staring at her, his expression hard and suspicious. She schools her face to ignorance.

I didn't say what you thought I said, she tells him with her eyes, *you're just being jumpy*.

He holds her gaze for what seems like a long time. Then finally he drops his hands. 'Get out of here and don't come back,' he growls.

Harriet obeys.

*

She cycles fast, returning the way she's come, along the side of the loch. Finally she has the wind behind her; finally she has certainty to boost her fading energy. She's found Dark Island and she knows how to reach them. She'll go over the ice. After all, it was strong enough to hold the boy, surely it will hold her, too. Won't it?

She reaches the pub and sense intervenes. She's running on empty, needs a break from the fierce cold and powerful wind. Besides it's not yet dark and she'll need the dark to conceal her approach.

When she walks inside the heat stuns her. Her face flames and her eyes sting. She leans on the bar for support as she orders whisky and the house special and gets her water bottles refilled.

The barman is young and friendly. She's tempted to confide in him, has to quell the impulse.

She tosses back the whisky and orders another, then drags herself away from the bar to sit by the fire. She opens the map, revising the terrain on the far side of the loch until she has it by heart. Her food arrives quickly and she bolts it without tasting. Her body is trying to go to sleep, but she can't let it.

It's time to go.

Despite the settling dark she doesn't switch her bike light on as she cycles the final half-mile back to where she had stood gazing across the loch searching for the Ring of Brodgar. Last time she stood here the land had felt totally empty, but now she notices the lights of a nearby cottage and becomes cautious.

She hides her bike in some scrub and after some hesitation leaves her map and bottles with it. She pats its saddle then walks away, finds herself a place low on the shoreline and crouches, waiting for the darkness to become absolute.

But it doesn't. The sun has been below the horizon for a while, but the sky behind the ridge of burial mounds retains its sunset glow. There's a powerful source of light over there.

She watches for a while, but the light doesn't alter. She's beginning to stiffen in the cold, and urgency is pulsing in her. She daren't miss them by waiting too long. She stands up.

Near the shore the ice looks dark and dangerous, but further out the surface gleams with those far-flung traces of light. Even though she'd seen the boy running on the ice, it's hard to take those first steps. The ice is slippery and uneven and her instincts try to force her back. She resists, continues to step out – hands sweating inside her gloves, eyes stretched wide. She listens hard for warning creaks, but hears music instead, heavy metal, coming from the other side. Once noticed it seems to grow louder, loud enough to mask any subtle creaks, any early warnings of thin ice.

Don't think about it.

Even though the shore behind is growing distant, the illuminated ice ahead seems no closer. It's like chasing a mirage. The ice is inconsistent and blackly unknowable, sometimes so slick that she struggles to keep upright, sometimes an obstacle course of embedded debris. Each step requires her to push through fear.

Then at last she's in the fake twilight of the illuminated ice and she can see her way to the shore. She stumbles forwards faster, skidding and slipping but not caring. She reaches stones which give under her feet, pitches onto her knees. Her face is soaked with sweat, her fingers aching from being clenched into fists.

She made it. She's safe.

Exhilaration makes her want to cry out with triumph, the way the boy had earlier. Despite the music – which is loud enough to mask any sounds – she resists. She can't take chances, not if she's going to get to Iquis.

She starts to make her way upwards to where the crest of the slope is clearly defined by the blazing light from the other side. The ground is rough, pitted with ditches and stumpy with frozen clumps of stalks. She keeps low for concealment, half-crawling, which makes progress far more difficult. As exhilaration seeps away, exhaustion replaces it.

She closes her eyes – just for a minute – breathes and listens. The current track is grinding to a halt, and as it does she hears a familiar throbbing. Her eyes jerk open, her chin lifts. Up in the sky a helicopter searchlight sweeps.

She presses into the ground. Even though it's ahead of her, beyond the crest, she's not moving. It's John O'Groats all over again. She watches as it lowers, sinks, disappears beyond the crest.

And once again her tiredness is overridden by a surge of energy. This is her chance, while any sentries are – *hopefully* – distracted. She wriggles fast up the slope like a commando, flattens herself just below the ridge and peers over into a white glare. Bright lights, white snow – their glare just like in the *Cold Ethel's Lover* video, in the morgue scene.

She catches her breath, deliberately calms herself. *Just study it*, she thinks.

It's an astounding sight. Film lights surround the stone circle and glare inwards to where the Decadance gates stand upright at the epicentre of the standing stones. The gates are wide open, waiting.

There's no sign of the helicopter, it must be beyond the ring, but there's plenty of people, plenty of action. There's cameras and men behind them, people setting up microphones and a man with a clipboard who looks like he's giving orders. In the centre of the circle wheelbarrows of fresh snow are being dumped and raked, then smoothed. Everything is fast, urgent.

Briefly she is awed, excited even. She's remembering the record shop, and is stunned that the connection is so *real* that she's made it here, that she's found them.

Then she notices the minders, lurking on the edges – constantly vigilant – powerful and threatening.

She sobers. She thinks of Marcia, of Iquis, of how she has to take the minders by surprise and break through before they can stop her. And then, she thinks about how angry Iquis had been the last time she saw her.

The circle empties, leaving a perfect expanse of snow. Sauron strides into it. He's dressed in white robes which look wrong on him, but his black boots, churning and dirtying what had been pure, seem more in character. The vast chain from the *Bleeding for Strangers* video is clenched in one fist. He's swinging it, so that the massive padlock at its end thuds and scuffs the snow.

A woman with a basket of snow sidles towards him. Her shoulders are hunched, her head bent and tilted. She's like a nervous animal watching a threat out of the corner of its eyes. Sauron is by the gates now. She stoops in front of him and he swings the chain more vigorously. Harriet catches the rattle of it, carried by the wind, and realises that the heavy-metal music has ceased.

The arc of the padlock nears the woman's head, causing her to fumble as she fills in the footstep closest to Sauron. She smooths it hastily and backs away to the next one with obvious relief. She works rapidly – returning the snow to perfect evenness – then reaches the edge of the circle and disappears.

Harriet exhales.

The first strains of an unknown intro lift into the air. It's a stark, repetitive mix of tribal drum and plucked viola string which reminds Harriet of the *Sacrifice* song from the concert. An ominous groundswell of organ music joins it. Low notes throb uneasily through Harriet's stomach.

A small blaze of red on the edge of the circle: *Circe!*

Burning ember-red hair drapes her back. Harriet struggles to connect her with Iquis. Circe's in a simple white shift, pale feet sinking naked into the snow. She is slight, ethereal. Iquis has never been that. And yet, isn't there something familiar about the length of her step, the height of her? She's far taller than she looks in the videos.

Iquis is already halfway to Sauron. Harriet pushes herself up, a racing start into a sprint. Heedless of the rough ground, she hurtles down the slope.

'Iquis, stop! I have to explain. It was the nightmare. That's why... Why... everything. You don't have to do this.'

She dives between two of the stones, boots smashing into perfect snow, and the blinding morgue light pinions her.

She stumbles.

Arms lock round her ribs. She's slammed back into something solid, a body. The pressure tightens. Her breath comes in gasps, ribs pressing painfully against her captor's arms.

Her eyes adjust.

Circe is looking at her, blue eyes innocent and expressionless inside a painted mask. This close the red hair is clearly a wig but even so it's hard to believe she's Iquis.

'I think you'll find I do.' The stranger's voice is soft and musical. 'I am Circe. Only Circe.' There's a gentle authority. 'You must go now. I have a job to do, lines to follow. You're interrupting the shoot.'

Harriet had been prepared for Iquis's indifference – knew what it could hide – but this softness, this non-Iquisness, she can't see what's behind it.

But she has to keep going, keep battling at the walls, say what she came to say.

'I'm sorry, Iquis. Sorry for running, and for Mark. But it never meant what you thought it meant. It was the nightmare I ran from. Not you. Never you. It reared up out of the water and I couldn't think, couldn't face it. But I'm ready now – ready to face it – ready to do whatever it takes to rescue you.'

Behind Circe, Sauron watches with impassive eyes, the chain stilled in his hands.

Circe smiles, a tiny smile, not big enough to disturb her heavy make-up. 'You're forgiven, entirely and absolutely forgiven. Now go.' She tilts her head, addresses the man holding Harriet. 'Escort her offsite, far enough away that she can't walk back until after we finish, but gently. *Don't* harm her.' And in the last three words there's the first sign of steel.

The minder's grip shifts.

I'm running out of time. Not getting through.

'What about Marcia? Is she with you? Did you take her for revenge?'

A shiver of reaction. 'No.' She sounds uncertain, jolts a look beyond Harriet. 'No.' She's staring beyond the circle of light.

Harriet's captor hoists her into the air and reverses. The gates fall away.

'Are you sure? You don't sound it. If she's not here, where is she? *Iquis? Iquis?*' But the figures in the circle are as still as stone, and the desperation in Harriet's voice is that of a person caught in a current, swept away, powerless.

'STOP!' A childishly high voice, from the darkness behind the lights.

Harriet's captor freezes on the edge of the circle.

'Keep her there.'

A small, cloaked and hooded figure darts into the circle and over to Sauron. She tugs on his sleeve and he stoops to listen. She's gesturing, demanding with her hands. Circe glides across and takes her arms, eases them down to her sides. A kind of silencing.

Kali? It has to be.

Then Loki, also hooded but recognisable from the pier, strides over to join them.

The minder shifts his grip. Harriet slips a couple of inches lower, but still can't touch the ground. A hiss of sound. She turns her head. There's a hooded figure within breathing distance, jet-black eyes glittering.

Medea?

'You shouldn't have come,' the woman hisses. Then she too turns and walks into the circle.

The snow is all messed up. For some reason, Harriet finds herself thinking about how long it's going to take to scrape more snow from the sparsely covered ground.

None of this is real.

In order to prove this she pats at the thigh of the man holding her, feels the jump of muscle as he reacts.

It terrifies her.

This *is* real. Why is she not doing anything? Her mouth is free. She ought to be calling out, influencing events.

But she's frozen – too bewildered to do more than watch.

Kali prowls towards where Harriet is being held. Black curious eyes in a white face stir an odd sense of déjà vu in Harriet. An uneasy memory, lying just under the surface. Kali curls a beckoning finger at Harriet's captor and he crouches down. She hisses instructions into his ear, then turns another piercing stare on Harriet before disappearing back into the shadows.

Then the man is carrying Harriet away and – *far too*

late – she's struggling, crying out, attempting to look back.

The minder pauses, swings her over his shoulder and clasps her legs tightly into his body to prevent her kicking. She feels the jolts as he crosses the rough ground, hears the crunch and skid as he steps out onto ice, then, over this, the sound of rotating blades.

He's taking her to the helicopter.

She turns her head and starts to scream.

'Stop that!' he commands. He drops her to the ground, and she realises with increased panic that she and the helicopter are standing on the surface of the other frozen loch.

It could break at any minute with that weight on it.

The man starts to search her pockets. She tries to protest.

'Shut it!'

He pools her belongings in one vast hand, picks out the mobile phone with satisfaction and pockets it.

Glyn!

'You can't do this!'

'Can't I?' He shoves the rest of her belongings into his other pocket and swings her back up. She starts to scream again, but her voice is batted away by the whirring blades of the helicopter. He ducks under the blades and she feels their buffeting, as he pushes her though the entrance and climbs in after her.

Holding her against him, so close that she can smell the rankness of his sweat, he rummages in a locker and pulls out a roll of duct tape. Forcing her arms behind her, he wraps the tape round and round, until her forearms are bandaged tightly together like a sticky, splinted double limb.

She sees the pilot, his profile impassive as he toys with his controls, completely ignoring what's going on behind him.

'Help me!' she calls. 'I'm being kidnapped.'

No reaction.

You bastard!

The minder pushes her into a chair and straps her in. His head is shaved, his face narrow and slightly lopsided. Harriet's trapped arms are pressed between her and the seat. They hurt. The hurt and the fear dominate, but she's not going to let him see it.

'Where are you taking me?' she demands. 'And where's Marcia?'

He pauses for a moment, then takes one more piece of tape from the roll and wraps it over her mouth.

FORTY-SEVEN

Exhaustion makes her sleep. Fear jerks her awake. A jabbing, sweating terror that has her sitting up wide-eyed in the four-poster bed, hyper-aware of every inch of her prison: cold stone walls, solid oak door, narrow arrow-slit windows with deep-set, grimy glass. This building has clearly been built to withstand siege. Her early attempts to escape – yanking and tugging at the locked door, pressing and pushing against the stones – had been pointless.

How long till morning?

She's lost all sense of time. She doesn't know how long the helicopter journey took or where she has been brought, just that it is isolated, the building itself a squat, fortress-like shape on top of a low hill, the entire area in darkness. No sign of other buildings, just an encircling of wide-shouldered mountains in the distance.

Since being dumped in here by the minder – who had paused only to slice apart the tape binding her arms before leaving – she has shouted herself hoarse and received no response.

Could Marcia be locked away somewhere in this

building as well? Surely they couldn't have given her this treatment. She'd seemed enchanted, not terrified.

If Marcia is here how do I get her out?

Harriet weighs the metal water pitcher in her hand. There is some reassurance in its weight. Early on, she had searched the room for a weapon and found only the chamber pot beneath the bed and the pitcher of water beside it. She had needed the chamber pot too desperately to sacrifice it, so she's going to use the pitcher when the time comes.

But the time isn't coming. The night appears endless. Everything is so vivid, her thoughts so disjointed, her sleeping and waking such a frantic pattern. There's a battle going on in her body – so many chemicals flooding it that she isn't in control any more. The terror climbs and peaks and then something shuts it down – shuts down all her thoughts – and she's slipping away from consciousness, sleeping like one in a coma. But never for all that long before the terror jerks her back awake, hurling its agenda at her.

I have to get out of here, have to rescue Marcia and – if possible – Iquis, have to contact Glyn. I was such a fool! I should have phoned him earlier, should have told him where I was going. But I never thought... Never expected...

✳

She jerks awake. There's a man in the room. The door is ajar. Light streams in from the corridor, gleams off slicked-back blonde hair.

She snatches for the pitcher, finds only bedclothes and screams. But her voice is hoarse and she hasn't the breath to make much sound.

'Hush, it's okay.'

He's younger than the other minders, his face softer. Perhaps there's hope.

'Have you come to rescue me?'

He shakes his head, looks awkward. 'I've come from them. They said to reassure you. They said they might have given you the wrong impression. But they don't mean you any harm.'

'You weren't there! You didn't see – You have to get me out of here. Or take a message. I'll give you a phone number.'

'No. They want to see you.'

The denial hits her first – the flatness of it. Then his words sink in. 'They're here? But I didn't hear them arrive.'

'They've been back a while. They had to feed, but now they're ready for you.'

He gestures with his hand to the door. There's something relentless in the way he does it.

She drags herself to the edge of the bed, bends forward to pull on her boots. Her fingers are clumsy. She can't tie a bow. In the end she knots the laces several times. She couldn't care less about how she's going to get them undone.

The pitcher is on its side on the floor. Spilt water darkens the slats of heavy-resined wood even further. Her mouth is dry. She snatches the pitcher up – there's a tiny cache of water still inside. Her hand is shaking, she tilts her head back and spills the water into her mouth, swallows. Her mouth seems to parch instantly.

She tightens her grip on the empty pitcher. The man has stepped back into the corridor and is waiting. She walks slowly towards him. Allows him to escort her downstairs, trying not to let his respectful behaviour mess with her mind.

'Is Marcia here?'

He shakes his head. But whether this is anything more than a refusal to answer is impossible to tell.

They reach the stone-flagged entrance hall and she braces herself for whatever room is coming, but the door he opens reveals dimly lit stone steps plunging downwards. A dank earth smell rises: compost, compression, rot.

Harriet wedges a foot against the door frame. 'No.'

But there are firm hands on her shoulders, pushing her forwards and down, and there's no resisting. Her leg buckles and her foot slips from the frame. It's like she's falling down the stairs, only just aware of her feet landing on steps. At the bottom she stumbles, throws hands forward to catch herself against a black-stained wood door. It feels cold and damp under her hands.

'They're waiting for you.'

The door screeches open and the scent of rotting earth increases. A low-ceilinged vault of a room, lanterns on the walls with misted glass, and four pairs of eyes gleaming at her in the dim light. Medea, Loki, Kali and Sauron, standing, legs splayed, shoulders nearly touching. Somewhere behind them there's Circe – a strand of fake red hair, a corner of pale forehead.

Is she distancing herself from me? Or have they placed her there?

She tightens her grip on the metal pitcher, hauls in a stinking-earth breath.

'Right,' she says, and her voice is more defiant than her heart. 'You've got a lot of explaining to do. *Why* am I here?'

Not a single blink.

Harriet swallows to moisten her mouth. 'People know

where I was going.' She delivers the lie with conviction. 'And they know about Marcia. You've been totally out of order: having me kidnapped, having me searched and manhandled. And yet – for Circe's sake – I'll forget about it. You can just let me go. Marcia, too.'

If she's here.

'And I'll say nothing.'

Is that even true? As long as *they* believe it.

There's no immediate response, just four pairs of glittering eyes directed at her. Medea is in a dark red velvet gown, Loki and Kali in black tunics over skintight leather trousers. Sauron is still in his white robe, but it's got dark red stains on it now.

Wine? Or something from the filming?

This close they ought to seem more normal. But they don't.

They seem to crackle with energy and power. They're moving, a restless, jittery action, barely perceptible and yet somehow ominous.

'We apologise,' Loki says. 'Time was rather tight. The film, you see. The minor details may have been a little *crass*. But you're here now which is what matters. We can make it up to you.' His voice is light and tuneful, soothing and hypnotic. She's reminded of the way he'd taken the tension down on stage.

He slinks towards her as if he's still on that stage, a performance just for her. There's mischief and acknowledgement in the quirk of his mouth, an enjoyment which she finds both fascinating and terrifying. What is it about him? He's close now, filling her vision, and it's like he's reached out a hand and lifted her onto the stage beside him: paint and make-up and electricity. He's the brightest thing in the dimly lit room. There's a black-water glow in his eyes, a summoning depth. She's tilting forwards, like she could fall into them, and then he smiles; it's huge, consuming – welcoming.

He's wide open to her in a way that Iquis – who was always guarded – never was.

"I'm the only one on your side," he'd once told Iquis. And Harriet hadn't got it then. But now she's beginning to.

He drives back the scent of soil, replaces it with the scent of himself. It's musk and metal and something... something... feral. She's inhaling harder, so that it catches at the back of her throat, and she's not sure she likes it, but she can't stop drawing in those deep, giddying breaths.

And he's even closer, so that she asks him in a whisper, '*What do you want with me?*'

He holds out his hands like he's presenting a gift. 'Sing with us,' he says. 'Write with us,' he says. 'Perform with us.'

There's love in his voice, inclusion in his voice. The tug of it is the tug she's always felt. She's been wasting so much time running away, when she could be running towards. When she should be –

No! Stop. Don't. Remember.

She's hurling these thoughts at herself, repeating them till they register. She spits out, 'Why?'

He shifts onto one hip. A wry smile, hinting of respect, fleets across his face. It's replaced with a sad sweetness. 'Because,' he says, and his voice is achingly sad, 'we've lost something and you have it.'

'I... do?'

It's hard not to believe that everything before was just miscommunication, misunderstanding.

They just don't know how to explain their need. Just like I –

'We need you to complete us,' Loki says.

It's a wrong note. More effective than a slap.

'You've said that before, to Iquis.'

On the pier.

'So surely now, you're complete.'

'I'd hoped we would be,' he says, 'but when she crossed over she lost... we lost...'

He shapes something in the air and lets it fall, an abrupt widening of the space between his hands, a jerk of his head towards the ground. An invisible shattering.

'So now,' he says, 'we need you. You're the only one who can—'

'Lost what?'

There's a finger under her chin and it's cold, as cold as Iquis's fingers always were.

'Our innocence,' he whispers.

'I...'

'They want you to replace me,' Circe says. Her voice comes from a long way away. 'That's why you're here.'

'Are you leaving?'

'No, not that. Just—'

'She's nothing special any more,' Kali says, and there's triumph in her tone.

'I'll handle this,' Loki says. 'Talk about herding cats!' He winks at Harriet, who shivers. 'We're offering you what you've always wanted. We know it's what you've dreamed of. We heard it in the woods when you sang *Monster Song*. Your voice was just like Circe's, every intonation the same.

You were full of longing, of yearning,' he leans closer, whispers, '*for us.*'

She can't easily breathe. There's a lightness, a brightness, in her head. His eyes are so wide, so huge, so...

'No!' She steps back. 'Wait!'

There's something in what he said that's – *wrong*. What is it?

'The woods,' she says. 'You weren't there.'

He laughs, lightly, full of mischief and enjoyment. 'Oh yes I was.' More laughter. 'We all were.'

Your little friend, he'd said on the pier.

'No!' Harriet says. 'People don't do that sort of thing. It's creepy, it's...' She can't find the words, shuts her eyes to block out his gaze – *the sort of thing serial killers do*. No. She's not saying that. '... worse than creepy.'

'We were keeping an eye on Circe, that's all.' There's impatience in his voice, and it makes her open her eyes. 'You just caught our attention. Even then, before you had the blood, you held a fascination hard to explain. Now that you have it, you belong to us.'

The scar on Harriet's thumb throbs. She finds she's rubbing its raised ridge. It feels angry, hurt – confused.

'It's true, that I'd hoped for a different outcome from Circe's first time,' Loki says. 'She had to cross over, had to join us fully. That teetering equilibrium, that walking on knives, could only be maintained for so long. But I'd hoped that somehow...' He gives a slow, sad headshake. 'It wasn't to be. We lost the infinite, on the cusp, caught between two worlds thing that made our music catch fire. Lost it, and then found it again when you ran into our circle of stones. It was meant, Harriet. Think what you can give to the music. Think what we can give to you. You want this. You know you do.'

His words are a torrent: mesmeric and fluid. His eyes are wide and deep and dark.

'Who will you be without us, Harriet?' he asks in a deceptively gentle voice. 'Aren't you afraid that you won't even exist?'

He's too close – too near to understanding.

She drags in a breath, pushes out a hand to hold him off, fights for words.

'I can't trust you. You creep around in the dark. You surround yourselves with thugs. And...' What else? She struggles to remember. Of course, Marcia. 'And you hurt Marcia. Where is she? What have you *done* to her?'

'Nothing. We don't have her.'

'Why should I believe that? She disappeared after your concert. You blackmailed Iquis with her on the pier.'

'So we're not the only ones who go sneaking around after dark.' Loki's eyes glitter. 'You're more like us than you realise, Harriet.'

'Stop this!' Circe – or is it Iquis? – intervenes, her voice abrupt. She's still far away, half concealed by the others, and yet, even so, it's like being thrown an anchor.

Loki can't sweep her away, now. Can he?

'Marcia was here after the concert,' Iquis says. 'But only ever that one time. The deal on the pier has not been broken. Marcia is safe, will always be safe.'

'Satisfied?' Loki says. 'Now let's talk about you.'

'No, let's not.' Harriet's confused, doesn't know what she wants or who to trust. She's playing for time as much as anything else when she adds, 'I want proof. I want proof that Marcia is okay.'

'You don't believe Circe?' Kali, a voice taunting from the background. 'You must be slipping, Sis.'

'Shut up!' Circe and Harriet together.

'Let me phone Mark,' Harriet says to Circe. 'You know I won't betray you, won't let on where I am. Let me just ask him where Marcia is.'

'Then will you go?' Circe asks.

Harriet hesitates.

'That's not a deal you can make, Sis,' Loki intervenes. 'I'm the casting vote, remember? There's three of us who would welcome her here.' He turns those eyes back onto Harriet. 'And Circe too, in time, would be glad. Don't you think?' Those eyes. Harriet feels the anchor slipping. 'If we let you phone Mark and gain reassurance about Marcia, will you, then, *listen*?'

'No,' Medea says. 'Don't trust her. This is messy enough. No calls to outsiders.'

'She won't betray us. She'd lose too much.' His certainty is unsettling. 'Anyway, Mark's not entirely an outsider, is he? And I for one am curious; after all, he was our Circe's *first*.'

'Yes!' Kali says. 'Oh, yes. Me too. I'm curious. Circe has been downright stingy with details. Ring him!'

'Block the number and speaker-phone it,' Sauron says. 'Hand over disconnect. Break connection if she—'

'She won't,' Loki says. Then shrugs, and it could be Iquis shrugging, so similar is the gesture. 'Whatever makes you happy.'

He lifts the receiver, taps in the digits to prevent the call being traced, and looks towards Harriet.

But her brain won't supply the number of Mark's house. It ought to be automatic, but it's gone. She starts to panic.

Then Circe's voice breaks in, reciting the number in an empty tone.

Circe has dropped even further back behind the others. Her fake blue gaze flickers towards Harriet, then away. Her face is more mask-like than ever – but something is moving beneath it – something fragile.

The ringing tone fills the entire room. The receiver is light plastic in Harriet's hand. She presses it to her ear and hears a smaller, tinnier sound. She counts: one, two, three, four. The ringing stops. The hum of connection is magnified into the room, echoed into her ear.

'Hello.' Mark's voice.

He sounds normal. She can't entirely believe she's reached him.

'Hello?' he says, again. 'Speak or bugger off.'

He sounds healthy, undamaged – strong once more.

'It's me. Is Marcia there? Is Marcia okay?'

'Harriet!' Mark's voice jumps at her, loud and urgent.

'Yeah.'

'You okay? You with Iquis?'

'I'm fine. I'm on my own. I'm okay.' She wishes she could tell him the truth. 'What about Marcia?'

'She's all right. Your mate, Glyn, discovered her looking out to sea on the John O'Groats pier. He was trying to find you! He's driving her back here, says she's fine, says he's far more worried about you. And *he* doesn't know the half of it. Stop looking for Iquis, Harriet. She's dangerous. She's seriously off her head, criminally insane. You mustn't find her.'

'Don't be ridiculous,' Harriet says. 'She's not.' She tries to look at Circe, but instead catches sight of Kali moving forwards, an avid look on her face. And don't the others seem closer? Everyone except Circe. The circle of them tightening around her.

'Believe me,' Mark says.

'I don't.'

He groans, clears his throat, an awkward, embarrassed sound. 'Don't do this to me, Harriet.'

'Do what?'

'Make me... Oh, fuck it. She drank my blood, okay! That's why I blacked out. She took a penknife and... cut me... and then... drank.'

Circe is staring at the ground.

'No,' Harriet says.

'Yes,' Mark says. 'And don't get me wrong, it wasn't messing around. It was...' The sound of him swallowing is magnified into the room. 'It was like she was starving. She was totally out of control. I didn't think she was going to stop. I thought I was going to... die.'

Silence, except for Mark's breathing, which is ragged.

Sauron, Kali, Loki and even Medea are so close to her now that she can hardly breathe. They are watching her – and, absurdly, watching the phone – with rapt attention. And there is no surprise in their faces.

Then Circe looks at her and despite the contact lenses, despite the painted face and the white mask of a dress, she can see Iquis – a thin figure breaking free of the false imprisonment of her Circe persona and stepping forwards. And it's the river – Iquis clutching at her – the water spinning her around.

Dimly, distantly, she can hear Mark calling to her – trying to demand her attention, to call her back – but it hardly touches her. Then his voice disappears, and she realises that Loki must have cut the connection.

FORTY-EIGHT

Sometimes when I sleep the night terror reaches me and swallows me. The dirt bunches up under my fingernails. The palms of my hands blister against the grimy handle of the spade. The presence behind me takes control of me – like a puppet-master. So that I jerk and dig, jerk and dig.

Digging up what I most want to leave buried.

'It's a shock,' Loki's voice drags her back towards him, 'but you had to know, for the music.'

'I don't care about the music.' Her body is still under water.

'You don't mean that. You're just in transition – once you understand us fully it will be different.'

'I don't want to understand.'

'Mark's reaction to Circe is atypical. It tells you nothing of the bond which forms when we drink.'

'Shut up!'

She needs him to stop talking, but he ignores her.

'With Marcia it was beautiful, sensual, a shared ecstasy. That's why she wanted to stay with us, why she still yearns for us.'

That gets through to her. The river vanishes. 'You did that to Marcia! You drank her blood!'

'Marcia loved us. We – in our own way – loved her. We tasted Marcia – she runs in our veins.'

The pride in his voice chokes her.

'Circe and Mark could have been like that, Harriet. I taught her how to seduce – to give pleasure. It was her first time – her changing time – but she'd watched me many times. She could have wrapped Mark in such sweetness, in such honeyed softness, that he would have been like Marcia, desperate to find her, desperate to return.

'But she chose not to. Want to know why?'

'No. I don't want any of this.'

But there's no stopping him. 'You know what we are, don't you?'

She doesn't answer. He can't mean –

'We weren't always. And change, any change, is difficult – painful. Particularly a change you haven't sought. A change that was thrust on you.'

He's looking at Sauron, who stands unmoving, head lowered. A bull-like figure.

'There was a time,' Loki says, 'before we came to value what we are, to understand our new powers, that Circe seemed like our only hope. Born to a mother freshly turned immortal, turned vampire by Sauron – the way we all were – Circe straddled the world we'd left, the world we'd entered, and we – *I* – needed that.

'It all began when our brother had his life taken from him.' Something bleak in Loki's expression, a hard line to his jaw. 'I meted out an inferior justice and—'

'Enough!' Sauron holds up a palm in a policeman's "Halt!", steps towards Loki.

'Whatever,' Loki says. 'Things happened. Sauron went away, came back, bringing...'

"An unholy Grail," Iquis had said – back in the basement room, last year – adding, "You wanted a plain tale and I gave you a myth," saying, "It's better like that. I won't ever tell you the truth."

But is this the truth?

'None of them will die now,' Sauron says. 'I made recompense.'

'There can be no recompense,' Medea says, and her voice sounds the way it did when it emerged from those speakers in that record shop so many years ago. A jazz-rasp of pain and anger.

The stone-chilled air of the room grows colder and more set. The scent of rot and earth strengthens.

'I was everything to her then,' Medea says, with frenzied energy. 'I fed her from my own body, blood filtered and made safe for her. Blood that let my half-human child thrive and grow. *Such* a powerful bond.'

She's looking at Circe, who is *not* looking back.

Harriet swallows, bile and acid flushing her mouth.

'It kept what had been human in us alive in Circe,' Loki says. 'Allowing us – through her – to create the music that led so many to us, that led you to us.'

Harriet is beyond denial, beyond disbelief. 'Mark,' she says, clinging to the last voice she's heard which makes any kind of sense. It's not a question. But Loki takes it as one.

'Yes, Mark. Exactly.' Loki gives her a soft, fingers to palm, round of applause. 'Her first. A necessary loss. Like the breaking of a virginity it marked the end of her unique childhood. When she drank his blood – she grew up.

'Perhaps it had to be the way it was, with that violence, with Mark bound and fully conscious. She, Circe, must have known what was right for such a transition, such a coming of age.'

He stops, but the words are still performing a giddying dance in her head.

'You make me sick,' Harriet says, and it's true. A physical swelling of revulsion from her stomach. She swallows hard. Her saliva tastes of sweat.

'You're crazy. All of you.' But she's trying to shut out the images which his words conjure up.

Iquis cutting Mark's arm, Iquis lowering her head and... No.

Iquis puking in the John O'Groats car park. Iquis hating herself with so much ugly ferocity – and yet, returning to this. Returning to the very thing that she hated.

She looks at Iquis, who jerks her gaze away. Another pair of eyes intrude, locking onto her.

Kali.

That face. There's a split second of realisation. Something she should have known sooner.

It had been Kali in the graveyard. By the risen stone – terrifying her – convincing her that something inhuman had climbed up out of the ground. Then Iquis had been at her side, shouting defiance and she had dismissed it – forgotten it.

But now – those eyes, so familiar. Huge black-hole pupils, feasting on her reaction.

She takes a sharp breath. Because Iquis too had had those eyes, those dilated pupils. She'd come marching towards her on the pier after seeing her family, crackling with energy. The same energy that's present here emanating from all of them.

'Drugs,' she says, giddy with relief. 'You're on drugs, aren't you? That's what this is about. That's what you give to your...'

Marcia, Mark. Some sort of hallucinogenic which convinces them...

'... victims.'

'What drugs?' Loki asks, laughing. 'We don't need any drugs. The blood is better – purer – than any drug.

'You fail to appreciate us,' he continues. 'We're gods, Harriet. The modern version anyway. People get bored with their dull little lives. They need us. Those that come to us are hungry, are searching for something. We satisfy them. We take them to extremes that they never had the courage or the imagination to reach for themselves.'

'You're crazy.'

'You've said that. Repeating it won't make you believe it, any more than you already do. And you're not sure, are you, Harriet? Not sure of anything.'

No, she's not. In the vacuum where her answer should be, Kali starts to sing – quietly at first, then gaining volume.

> '"*Live for me. Die for me.*
> *Live for me. Die for me.*
> *Live for me. Die for me.*"'

Over and over. The chant from the concert. The building menace of it striking Harriet afresh. Panicking her.

The wide snake mouth – stretching and hungry – the glittering eyes.

'Is that what you want with me?'

Kali laughs.

'Are you going to kill me?'

The fear has been in her all along, but it's only when she says it that it becomes real. A possibility.

Iquis is at her side. 'No.' Her voice is abrupt, harsh. 'They can't touch you. You have the blood – they can't harm you.'

'I don't understand.'

Iquis touches a finger to the scar on Harriet's thumb. It's a fleeting touch, gone as soon as it's there. 'You were set on going to the concert. I did it to protect you. We can't prey on our own kind, our instincts won't let us. It was the only way to keep you safe.'

'I'm safe?'

'You're safe.'

It's some comfort, even though she's not sure she believes her. Another thought strikes her. 'Does that make me, make Marcia…' She can't finish the sentence.

But Iquis knows what she means. 'No, it would take much more than that to make you like us. Don't ask,' her voice raw, 'you don't want to know.'

That raw note hits her. She steps backwards, horror and distaste impelling her to plant a space between them. 'I don't know you any more. How could you come back to this?' She sees Iquis flinch but what else can she say? Iquis is part of something monstrous.

Why can she still feel her pain?

'Was it because of Marcia? Is that the deal you made? That you'd return if they let Marcia go? Did you come back to save her?'

That at least she could understand.

'There was a deal. But it didn't matter. I would have come back sooner or later. There was no point in running.' There's resignation in Iquis's tone. 'It's what I am, Harriet. All the time – in Cumbria – that hunger never left me. I kept it pushed down. But it took all my strength.'

Harriet is shaking. 'And I – was that what you wanted from me? Was it my blood you wanted?'

'No. Never! Not after that first week.'

That first week?

The night in the kitchen, Iquis backed in the corner like a spider, that terrible hunger, that compulsion. And me, telling her about my –

'... nightmare,' Harriet says. 'What about the nightmare? How does that fit?'

How did you all drag me into it?

'It doesn't. Forget it.'

Harriet is about to protest, but Iquis turns purposefully to Loki. 'Have you spotted how futile it is, yet? Harriet can't stomach this. She won't collude in it the way I did. You're wasting your time. You can't recreate me.'

'You forget, I have the majority.'

'So what? Sauron and Kali don't care about our lost past, don't even care about the music. To them Harriet is just entertainment – a toy. They'll get bored soon enough. They prefer the music you're making now. They like the way it spreads fear. They like the way they can dominate and bludgeon with it.

'You're running out of arguments, Loki. Let her go.'

'But she wants to be with us. She's drawn to us.'

'No, Loki, she's not.' She speaks firmly, yet there is an unusual compassion in her tone.

Loki seems to deflate. He rests his head on her shoulder, slumps down towards her. She puts one foot behind her, to steady her as she supports his weight, then tightens her grip. Her face is hidden somewhere in his chest. His arms wrap round, trapping her long red hair against her back.

FORTY-NINE

'Come on,' Iquis says to Harriet, 'I'll take you to the helicopter.'

Harriet stares round the empty room. Is that it? The room is vast now that only the two of them occupy it. 'Where did they go?'

Iquis shrugs.

Medea had been the last to leave. 'She must depart before sunrise,' she'd said to Circe. And she'd picked up a large hourglass from a wall embrasure, turned it over. Sand had started to trickle.

'Do you think they're listening in?' Harriet eyes the shut door.

'No,' Iquis says.

'Come with me.' Harriet has to say it, but her voice carries no conviction, only grief.

And Iquis just shakes her head. She's tugging Harriet towards the door – not with hands, just with the movement of her feet, the expression in her eyes.

'What about the nightmare?' Harriet says. 'I can't just forget it, the way you said.'

'Maybe not, but it has nothing to do with us.'

'Of course it does,' Harriet says, shocked. 'Dark Island gave me the nightmare when I first heard them – it crossed over to me from the speakers of a record shop, and then they kept feeding it: *Cold Ethel's Lover*, this cellar...'

Even the river and you. But she won't say this.

Iquis stares at her. 'You really believe this?'

Mark kissing me – the ground had slid apart then, too – which doesn't...

'Yes.' But there's an uncertain feeling low in her stomach.

Iquis glances at the falling sand – nearly as much heaped below as above – and seems to come to a decision. 'Are you sure the music was first?'

Harriet bites her lip. Her brain's foggy – full of incipient loss and a directionless anger.

'You started it,' Iquis says, and for the briefest second the corner of her mouth quirks upwards in amusement. 'Okay, wait.'

She takes her contact lenses out, flicks them away across the room. Harriet seems to catch a faint blue shimmer in the air as they fall. Then Iquis's eyes hold her steady. They are storm grey. They are the colour of the Orkney sea. They are as familiar as Harriet's own.

She swallows against the terrible ache in her throat.

'Get on with it then,' Iquis says. 'Tell me about the first time you had the nightmare.'

'I can't...' But she can. The memory is rushing in on her like a freak wave. 'I'm trembling, awake, terrified of what I've just dreamed... I do what I always do when I have nightmares – I scramble out of bed, intent on making it to Mum and Dad's room – to safety. They'll drive it away, let me climb in with them, make it better. I get to the corridor. I'm scared but I'm okay, until I see the open door of Stephen's room. *He's not there any more. He's dead.*

'I'd forgotten. I kept forgetting. It kept not being real. But it's real now and I'm stuck, shivering in the hallway, because I can't go to Mum and Dad any more. There's no safety to be found, only brokenness.

'I stand frozen in place and the fear creeps out from my bedroom and wraps itself around me, promises never to let go.'

Iquis's gaze pulls her back to the present. 'Just after he died?'

Harriet nods.

'So you were nine.'

'That's right.'

'And the Dark Island music?'

'I was in a music shop looking for a birthday present. I was twelve.'

'Three years after the nightmare started, Harriet.'

'Yes, but...'

It ought to be clear. Iquis certainly seems to think that it is, but something is nagging, surfacing.

'In the music shop,' Harriet says, 'there was something...' She hesitates, plunges on, 'It was already familiar. I already knew the words.'

She shocks herself. It's so obvious now, yet she'd always believed – always chosen to believe – that she discovered them then, in the music shop. These new memories are sickening, frightening. 'I can't trust myself.'

'Hush,' Iquis says, as if to a child. Like the shushing of the sea on the shore.

But Harriet can't hush – it's spilling out now. The lyrics shaking through her, the tune scraping away below: '"*Whose hand pushed you – is hell too far to fall?*"' The memory is shoving into her mind. She's in Stephen's room. No need to fear that he will come back and catch her rifling through his CDs, catch her pushing this particular CD into his stereo and pressing play.

Stephen won't come back and find her. Stephen can't be angry with her any more.

"*You're on my territory*", his voice echoing in her ears, aggressive and terrifying. But it's a memory voice. He'll never again resent her intrusion. And her parents are out, at the doctors yet again. They'll come back with more pills for Mum, but it won't make any difference.

'It was Graham's fault,' Harriet says. 'I only went into Stephen's room because he made me. I wasn't supposed to talk to him. Mum and Dad hated him. Wouldn't speak to him. Wouldn't allow him to be at the funeral. Slammed the door on him, the only time he called at our house.

'I knew they blamed him for what happened to Stephen. Knew it was his fault. Just didn't understand why. None of it made sense.

'I wanted to hate him too, but he wouldn't let me. Forced me to see him.'

She remembers him looming over her, his face unfriendly, his eyes hurting. "*You owe me this*," he'd said. He hadn't touched her, not even to hold her there, but his words had compelled her. He'd stepped back from her. Shoved out his arm, with the list jutting towards her face and she'd reached up a shaking hand and taken it.

'He gave me a list: CDs he and Stephen had bought together at the music shop.'

"*I want something to remember him by*," he'd said.

'And in Stephen's room,' Harriet continues, 'I got stuck looking at that CD. Something about the cover – that falling figure in the darkness – so that I had to play it, had to hear it.'

She trails off – more confused than ever – what was the question she was supposed to be answering?

Iquis moves fractionally closer to her – still not close enough to touch – or to threaten.

'Why, Harriet?' Iquis asks. 'Why did you do what Graham wanted? What hold did he have over you?'

Her words send flashing images though Harriet's head. There's white stone all around her. She's clambering over it and the stone is huge, except that somehow she knows it's not huge, that it's like the garden when Stephen span her round in it. The garden wasn't huge. She was small.

'I don't know,' she says. But the smell of stone dust is in her nostrils. Clean, weathered stone dust, not like the dank shut-in stones that comprise this fortress. She can feel the stones shifting, and she knows that if they shift far enough there'll be a gap and she'll see through to what she doesn't want to remember. She glimpses Stephen's hair – slightly too long, ready for a cut – flying in the air. Blonde hair – tossed – and then gone. Empty space.

From somewhere she hears Graham's voice saying, 'What have you done?' and then – the nightmare is shaking her awake – and she's standing in her parents' corridor at home – frozen and stuck.

Iquis is watching her.

'The nightmare came first,' she says, fighting an urge to deny it. She wants to go on believing that Dark Island are responsible, but she can't. 'Before the music. Before I went into Stephen's room, because Graham told me to, because Graham...'

She breaks off – she can't! She can't breathe. She feels dizzy. Everything is being shaken – the Dark Island house is falling around her – and she's running away from the falling stone.

Falling.

Stone.

'Help me!'

'I can't,' Iquis says, and her voice is very steady, very gentle. 'You can't save me and I can't save you, Harriet. I never could. You have to find your own redemption, in your own world.'

Iquis sighs and opens her hands as if releasing something. 'It's over,' she says, and even in the midst of her turmoil it reaches Harriet.

The pain of it. The severing of that bond.

She tries again to reach Iquis because she has to try, even though she has no firm ground from which to throw a lifeline. 'What you're doing is wrong, Iquis. Give it up. Walk away.'

'I'm not Iquis, Harriet, I'm Circe.' The answer is still so calm, so settled. Nothing can shake her. 'And the hourglass is empty.'

Harriet doesn't look at it. 'But you're not Circe,' and this at least is something that she can say to Iquis, can mean. 'You may think that you are. But it's your voice that I hear now, Iquis. It's your eyes that I see. Whatever happened –' *best not to think about that* '– we can find a way to make sure it never happens again. We can keep riding, the way you wanted. We can outpace it.'

'No, Harriet,' Iquis says, and there is finality in her tone. 'It's Iquis's ghost that you're hearing, nothing more.'

Harriet shivers. There's a certainty here that she can't avoid.

'I haven't quite gone yet,' Iquis says, 'haven't quite slipped into sea foam, but that's where I'm going. That's where I want to be. It's only you that's keeping me here. Let me go, Harriet. Let me taste and touch and be the foam on the sea. There's only pain here, Harriet, there's only ever been pain.'

Harriet looks deep into the storm-tossed eyes and loses herself. There is no choice, the eyes tell her, and something more, something that she doesn't understand – but she sees it, pure and clean, like steel. A determination, a knowing, a destination.

'Iquis,' she says and there is everything in her voice, everything she can't say. In her memory she sees Iquis the way she was the first time she saw her. Sees Iquis, clinging to the cliff beside the waterfall, the water splattering against her leathers. Iquis persuading her to dance. Iquis in front of her on the bike, while ahead of them the curving road stretched out into the distance.

Then she opens her hands, in a gesture that mirrors Iquis's earlier gesture and lets everything slip away.

FIFTY

In the pale light of morning, Harriet is back on the Orkney mainland, and it's hard to believe that the dank fortress and the words she heard were real. Perhaps she never left. Perhaps she just wandered all night, ending up lost, far out in the snow-covered moors, her mobile for some reason out of charge, her map and bike left far behind, on the other side of a frozen loch.

But her body knows better. There's a soreness in her ribs where the minder had clasped her, a sting of skin where the tapes had been. There's the imprint of the harness they'd used to lower her, spinning and twisting in the icy down-draft from the helicopter blades. And there's a jittery, stunned feeling – the shakiness of leftover fear, leftover dread.

It's like the morning after the tiles slid apart in the kitchen and she saw down into the earth. And although there's no vodka in her bloodstream, no incipient hangover waiting to crawl out, no guilt for her own actions – *at least this time I did my best* – there's the same loss of Iquis to contend. There'd been a finality which –

No, they can't be vampires. Just because they made me believe it last night, just because Iquis –

She believes it. There was no doubt in her. And I –
Yes, but vampires don't exist. They can't!

What would Dad say? He'd say there was no empirical evidence. He'd say, "Did you see proof of immortality?" He'd point out that "Your friend" – *or would he even call her that?* – "used a knife". He'd suggest drugs as the obvious explanation. And so what if they denied it? Of course they would, because they believed their own myth. "Group hysteria", he'd say, and he'd talk about cults – and about how people rescued from them had to be deprogrammed because they'd learnt to believe totally in the world they'd lived in.

She tries to think of Iquis being deprogrammed, but can't imagine it, not when she recalls Iquis's certainty.

It's the death of Iquis's brother – that's what did it, isn't it? That sort of loss, well it can do strange things to the mind. It can destroy families. Can't it?

She shivers.

It's so cold here, colder for the thought of how far away shelter is. Whatever the truth – *You're not sure, are you?* – Dark Island have bought themselves time by leaving her here, with white moors in every direction, and no means of contacting anyone.

*

It had been Loki who handed Harriet's belongings back to her, and she hadn't thought to check her mobile for charge. She'd been standing with Iquis by the open helicopter, and he'd come loping across the snow. His stride was as self-sure as ever and yet Harriet sensed little amusement in him.

He'd tilted her chin. 'You might as well keep quiet about this,' he'd said, 'because no one will believe you. We've kept our tracks well covered. You and Marcia are the only exceptions. And she won't be saying anything.'

What about Mark? Harriet had thought. *What about his evidence? And there's Glyn, who knows that Iquis is Circe. He's heading to Mark's house with Marcia, isn't he? And I could –*

Loki's fingers tightened into a pinch. 'We're more powerful than any force you can set against us. So don't try. You'd only damn yourself for seeking to betray Iquis. And you don't want to do that, do you?'

Iquis had stepped between them, and his fingers had dropped away. She'd pushed a bag towards Harriet. 'Food,' she'd said, adding, 'It's not been tampered with. Chocolate and sandwiches and water. Enough for several hours, perhaps longer. As long as it takes for you to find your way.'

She'd gestured at the helicopter and Harriet had started to climb.

Under the whir of the helicopter blades and the thrum of the engine, Loki's voice had carried in waves to her, 'And anyway, we'd just disappear...'; 'Perhaps it's time to reinvent ourselves...'; 'The music's not the same...'

*

Just walk in a direction, any direction.

Harriet turns towards the sun, pale and low in the sky. That will do for a compass. The wind blasts across her, and she shifts one foot, then the other. The ground is dazzling in its whiteness, and the moor is not easy to cross. It's full of dips and ditches, pockets of deep snow where she flounders, sinking and recovering, over and over. Her steps drag.

"*They cut her head off. Stuffed her mouth with garlic. Thrust a stake through her heart.*" Iquis, standing in the graveyard beside the tombstone she'd claimed was Lucy's, speaking with a bitterness Harriet couldn't then understand.

"*They said they loved Lucy but they did this to her.*"

Harriet thinks of putting down the phone after telling Glyn everything she knows, thinks of sirens, thinks of Dark Island not yet fled, not actually believing that she... Handcuffs and a police van and flashbulbs, because somehow the press would have already found out, and baying – baying for blood.

What will they do to Iquis, the modern-day authorities: police, social workers, the courts? Would they help her, see her as a troubled teenager, or would they see a criminal, something monstrous? Would she end up behind bars? Trapped.

"*Imprisoned her here, never to rise again.*"

Iquis by the window –

Always needing to get out: into the night, under the sky. "This place constrains me."

*

Do I have to do this?

Harriet's stopped again. This snow-heavy moor and battering wind is draining her, and when she looks back her footsteps wander. She'd have crossed this field in half the time if she'd walked straight. She's dizzy, weak – not quite there. She forces herself to reach for the food, the drink. Can't keep going without it.

"*It's not been tampered with.*"

Iquis shouldn't have had to say that! As if it's us and them. As if it's always been us and them, throughout history.

If Loki is to be believed, perhaps Iquis can't be held. Perhaps she'd bend the bars of her prison and climb through them. Only if she could, they all could. And there'd be a new fortress. Another Marcia. Another Mark.

Harriet remembers the missing girl at that ages-ago party, long sleeves drenched in the flow of water. She'd been as hostile to Iquis as Marcia had become. Was she too...?

Unthinkable. But Harriet's thinking it: remembering a missing poster, an argument under a willow tree, and Iquis storming off into the night.

I didn't see her for three nights.

Was there another wild ride? Another rescue of someone who didn't want to be rescued?

And who will rescue the next girl? Now that Iquis –

*

A blue car cuts across the landscape in the distance, and Harriet's startled, almost unwilling. But she forces herself to take note. The car was maybe a mile away, maybe more.

"*They were her friends. They'd given their own blood to her. Yet in the end they killed her.*"

Harriet can't stay out here forever, lost in the circle of her thoughts, the circle of her feet. She's no Frankenstein's monster loping across the ice. She's human, and she's weakening. Despite her gloves, despite her hat and her double layer of coats, she's growing numb inside.

She heads towards where she saw the car, stumbling over the rough ground at an increased pace. She's still forced to detour, along stone walls and beds of streams, around deep ditches and up and over hillocks, but now there's a direction to regain each time.

Another car passes, and this time there's the soft vibration of its wake. Soon after she finds a rough track, and it brings her to a gap in the wall, and she stumbles through it onto a road.

She turns right. Her footsteps chime, and she sees a huddle of buildings some distance away. She draws closer. There aren't many, but there's more than she needs. There's a long building to her left, and an old-fashioned, red-metal phone box to her right.

The building is all shut up. It's some sort of a museum, but she doesn't stop to find out what sort. The phone box, with its panelled windows crusted with ice, is unavoidable.

Glyn. There is no choice.

She jams her gloved fingers into the cupped-metal handhold, and fights the wind to pull the door open. Inside, the cold is different, more heavily settled, more dense. It reflects onto her from the metal sides, and without the wind the silence and the stillness is shocking. She lifts the handset. It purrs into life.

This time she has no difficulty remembering Mark's number. She's about to dial, when another memory from last night slips in – Loki preventing the call from being traced, tapping in those numbers. For some reason she does the same.

Mark answers.

'It's Harriet. Is Glyn there? I have to speak to him.'

'Harriet, are you okay?'

'Yes, I'm fine. But I can't talk now. Get Glyn. It's vitally important.'

I just have to close my eyes and act. I can feel it afterwards – not now.

'Your dad's here, too,' Mark says, and Harriet twitches. 'He arrived this morning. He's taking over. I'll get him for you.'

'No! I can't to talk to him.'

Falling stone, Graham's voice, "*What have you done?*"

'I have to talk to Glyn. It's urgent! You must get him for me.'

There's a murmuring of voices at the other end, then the sound of the phone changing hands. 'Harriet!' Dad's voice. 'Can't tell you how good it is to... Well, I haven't heard your voice yet. Speak to me. Are you all right? Where are you? I'll come and get you. I've been... we've been... so very worried.'

Raw panic – she can't speak.

'Harriet? Harriet?'

She hears Iquis's saying, "*the nightmare has nothing to do with us*". There's a tight band around her head.

Silence. A long gap, with just phone static.

'I love you, Harriet.'

You wouldn't if you knew!

The thought burns her. She jerks the phone from her ear and drops it. Her teeth bite hard into her upper lip. The pain helps, but she can still hear Dad's voice – shouting now. She can't pick up the phone – but she doesn't need to – just needs, like Loki, to lift her hand and press the disconnect.

Silence. She backs out of the phone box. The door swings shut. She sees a woman walking along the path, looking at her curiously.

The woman starts to say something – but the words don't register.

Harriet turns and runs, back the way she's come, and then further. Running faster and faster until she can't see for sweat, until her breath is struggling and hurting her, until she has to stop and double over, gasping.

Then, breathing raggedly, she begins to walk again, letting the monotonous rhythm steady the shake in her. Her feet are rubbing inside her walking boots. Her face, wet with sweat, stings as the ice air dries it. She reaches a split in the road and takes the obscure route. A muddy, unmarked track, which leads between fields, and which gradually starts to slope downwards. When it eventually brings her to the sea, it seems inevitable. She turns and scrambles along the shore, over unsteady rocks and through the push and shove of the wind.

An island emerges from the sea ahead of her. It's only a small island, maybe half a mile across at its largest point – maybe less – it's hard to tell. It appears deserted.

The tide is low and a causeway draped in slippery-looking green stuff leads most of the way to the island. She clambers over seaweed-covered rocks to reach the causeway, then walks along it to where a shallow sea still crosses. The water is dense with tossed foam, and she splashes through, not really caring whether she misses the edge and plunges into deep water. Then she's on the island side of the causeway, stumbling up the bank.

She can smell stone dust.

Impossible.

But the memories are here, growing out of the snow and mud of the island.

The quarry – *the rasp of half-rotten wood against her fingers. That single loose board. Grasping it and lifting it aside so that she can squeeze through the fence and into the quarry, after Stephen and Graham.*

The island is a graveyard of snow-drenched ruins. Ragged lines of stone poke up where the wind has scoured, and elsewhere the ground humps into long snow-covered rectangles. She circles the rest of the island, finds nothing else. She's on her own here, can let the memories take over.

She keeps circling, to keep the cold at bay. Her rubbed toes sting.

I only wanted to know what they were up to. She stifles a sob. "Only girls cry," Stephen used to say. He had no use for girls, so she'd learnt not to. Never cried. Won't now.

Despite the bitter cold reflecting up from the snowy ground, and the ice particles in the air, she's feeling the heat of that day – and with it anger and a hot defiance. She hated Stephen. He'd been ignoring her all summer. Not even teasing her or sending her on errands. Nothing.

What had she done?

She'd never complained about being the fall guy in their games, getting bruised when they kidnapped her, being tied up for hours and then drenched in the eventual rescue. She'd never objected to being sent to fetch things. And the number of times she'd got him out of trouble, covering for him with Mum or Dad! Well, mainly with Dad.

It was always Dad who was down on Stephen, Mum on her. Or at least that's how it had been until that summer. Now everyone seemed angry with Stephen and he didn't care. He was far too caught up with whatever he and Graham had discovered. There was something secretive about them, an air of mystery and excitement. They disappeared for entire days, and she couldn't find them in any of their usual places.

So in the end she followed them on her bike when they left the house. It was easy enough. They were walking. She kept thinking they'd turn round and see her, but they only looked back once, and by then they'd reached the quarry and she was able to duck out of sight, behind a red van.

✳

The smell of stone dust is all around her. The sun is dazzling against the dirty white of discarded stone. It's vast inside the quarry – an entire other world. Two long ridges of slag hills sprawl across it, with a stone-strewn channel between them where Stephen and Graham must have passed. The stone clacks under her feet and she freezes in place. Waits. There are no sounds from ahead. The boys have vanished into the centre of the quarry. She starts after them again – moving slowly, cautiously, over the crackling stone.

The stone gradually shallows until she is on a white scraped-clean looking surface – only loosely scattered with stones. She sees the rusted metal corpse of a digging machine and beyond it the water-filled crater of the disused quarry itself. She takes in a deep breath. The scum-covered water swallows the sunlight. The silence of the place is huge.

Where's Stephen?

It's a bit scary here. Abandoned and decaying, like a ghost place.

There's a derelict hut at the far side of the quarry-pool. The door is padlocked but most of the hut's side has rotted away. She shades her eyes. Inside the dusty dark there's movement. She can just make out the boys' heads and shoulders. Placing her feet carefully, she works her way round the pool, edges towards the opening.

They're intent on something: a pale plastic box, containing a rectangle of changing colours and shapes. It's Graham's portable TV, resting on a tower of stacked crates. The atmosphere in there is strange, yet familiar. This is what being around Stephen and Graham has been like recently – something going on that she doesn't understand.

What are they watching? She draws closer, dangerously close.

A woman with a bare bottom and thigh-length boots is kneeling on a metal-framed bed, resting forward on her hands like a cat. She's got red hair and a wide-open, black-red mouth. A man wearing only cowboy boots is standing behind her with his hands on her hips. They are rocking. The springs of the bed are screeching.

Weird. Kind of horrible.

Harriet jerks her gaze from the screen, but the boys have caught the rhythm too. Hips flexing, arms jerking, hands somewhere in front of them.

She's both fascinated and repelled. That action – she's seen it before, earlier that summer. Those fish in the red bucket which Dad had caught, they'd moved like this. She'd stood watching them thrash, compelled by something both primitive and significant. Those jerking tails; the bucket juddering and shifting on the planks of wood. Then Mum had caught her watching. The memory is shaming, the look of disgust on her face. "Put them out of their misery, Harry." Mum's voice cold, tight. The bruising grasp of her hand round Harriet's wrist, dragging her away.

Mum hadn't said anything more, but she hadn't needed to.

At teatime, Harriet had been handed a plate of fried fish, its flesh oily and flaking, its cooked, burnt smell overpowering. She'd refused to eat it and been sent to bed hungry. But when she slept, she'd dreamed of that red bucket, and this time the fish had turned it over and flown off into the sky – and something had leapt inside her.

Now, in the quarry, she's watching with the same fascination. This time she knows what she's doing is wrong. But she can't stop. That strange excitement which is creeping out of the hut towards her is too powerful. It draws her forwards. She thinks she's moving silently, but something gives her away. Stephen turns his head and looks straight at her.

'What the *fuck*! You little...'

The look he's wearing scares her. She turns and flees. He's going to kill her, isn't he?

Is he gaining? She glances back. Her foot hits a stone. Her ankle twists. She lands on her knees, her arm flings out and her hand hits air, not ground. She recoils, curls into herself. She's right on the edge of the quarry-pool. There's empty air behind her.

The legs of the two boys stop some metres away, close enough to grab her if she tries to get up and run. The distance is more threatening than if they had come the whole way.

She looks up the square angle of their bodies. Graham's face is red, sweaty, his eyes darker than usual. The zip of his jeans is only half done up. There's something bulky and awkward about him – something complicated. He's not going to save her, not going to intervene, the way he sometimes does when Stephen bullies her.

She drags her gaze to Stephen. He's pale: teeth clenched, lips drawn back, eyes narrowed, fists all knuckle.

'You don't learn, do you?'

She swallows. Can't find a voice.

'You're on our territory and we make the laws here. There are penalties for those who enter without permission, who sneak and follow and spy.' There's a sing-song note to his voice. Ritualistic, scary.

She doesn't know him.

She rolls backwards to get away and is almost over the forgotten edge before she realises, the lip of the crater cutting into her spine, one shoulder in loose air.

Stephen sprints towards her. To stop her or to push her over? There's no way of knowing.

Her hand finds leverage and she pushes herself away from the lip, starts to roll. She anticipates the collision before it happens and does nothing to stop it. Her hip bashes against Stephen's legs. There's the weight of his body flying over her, then a lightness, a sucking away of air, and he's gone. She's lying on the ground, bruised but triumphant. She's won.

The first time she's ever beaten him.

The elation only lasts for a second. Then she hears the splash.

FIFTY-ONE

The sea is deeper now, the causeway fully covered. The cold ebbs and flows as the waves break against the rocks. The final part of the memory floods in with the tide.

Stephen hadn't died in the quarry-pool. They'd got him out. A frantic business, slipping and scrambling down the side. She'd been scared of falling but hadn't slowed her pace. Graham got there first and pulled Stephen out, landing him like a huge, ungainly fish.

*

Stephen's clothes are clinging to him and his face is surprised. And yet there's nothing obviously wrong with him. Harriet has been anticipating the bruise on Stephen's forehead – that, after all, had been what she'd dreamed a few weeks ago. Stephen in the water – Stephen falling – the bruise. But Stephen's hair is wet and slicked back and his forehead is unmarked.

Harriet is puzzled; but that puzzle is lost in the intensity of the memory which rushes through her like a bore tide.

*

Stephen's not angry. It's more like he's stunned. Maybe he just can't believe she beat him. Harriet wants to laugh with relief. But for some reason she's still too scared to be able to.

They start up the slope. Stephen is heavy with water and his movements are clumsy. Yet, though his progress is slow, his breathing is rapid. Graham drops back to help, pushes him upwards; together they manage it. Stephen crawls over the lip of the crater and slumps onto the ground.

'You all right, mate?' Graham asks.

'Head hurts,' Stephen mutters. 'Head hurts like fuck.'

'Did you bash your head?'

No answer.

Graham runs his fingers lightly over Stephen's head, checking for damage.

'Don't do that,' Stephen says. 'I don't like it.' He sounds petulant, like a young child.

'Stephen,' Harriet says, in a small voice. 'Are you okay? I'm sorry.'

He doesn't turn his head to look at her, but after a moment he mumbles, 'Not your fault. Accident.'

But it was her fault – and there had been that moment when she'd anticipated and not... She has to confess, needs to do penance. But now isn't the time, Graham is looking edgy.

'We ought to move,' he says, 'at least get to the edge of the quarry. Come on, I'll give you a hand up.'

He puts his shoulder under Stephen's arm and lifts him. They cross the flat white plane, reach the edge of the stones. Graham is half carrying Stephen. The stones resume their clacking protest. But this time there's another sound which accompanies Harriet and the boys – a rusty, groaning sound. Stephen's making it, through his teeth.

Graham allows Stephen to drag him to a halt.

'Hell,' he exclaims. 'Perhaps we shouldn't have moved him.'

He looks to Harriet for an answer, but she can't give him one. He frowns, glances at the sliding heaps to either side of them, then stoops and picks Stephen up in his arms. The load staggers him and he slides deeper into the stones. For a moment it seems Stephen's weight will be too much for him, but then with an effort he straightens and starts to push doggedly forwards.

By the time they reach the edge of the quarry, Stephen is starting to retch.

Graham lowers him quickly to the ground. Stephen twists against it and vomits violently across the stones.

Then Graham is saying something about an ambulance, a call box. He's looking towards Stephen for approval, the same way Harriet would, but Stephen doesn't see the question.

Then Graham's telling Harriet to take care of Stephen, and he's running, ducking through the gap, gone. And she's just watching Stephen's shut eyes, his pallid face, counting off the minutes until Graham's back, saying, 'It's on its way.'

Stephen's eyelid's splinter open. 'Not... Harriet... Keep her out of it... Don't let them know she was here... Better that way... Less trouble.'

His eyes close.

*

Harriet helps Graham move Stephen to a clean patch of quarry floor. Then Graham pushes her away, tells her to do what Stephen wants and get out of here. There's a relief for both of them in following Stephen's orders – a normality, which they desperately want to believe in.

Harriet's focus is all on action, as she crams herself through the narrow opening, sprints to her bike, picks it up and straddles it. She cycles fast, like she's in a race, not going in any particular direction, just away.

The sound of the ambulance cuts through the air, but she doesn't see it, only sees the worn tarmac of the road and the vague shadows of parked cars.

*

I didn't know he was going to die. I didn't know I wasn't going to see him again.

'Stephen!'

The wind shakes her, dragging her back to the present. The sea is rougher now. She glances towards the causeway and sees deep waves passing over it.

'Stephen. I'm sorry. I'm so sorry.'

She turns her face into the wind, pushes herself against it until its blast drags tears from her eyes, makes them burn across her cheek. She listens for Stephen's reply, but there's nothing.

She thinks of him as she last saw him, curled on the ground, his head in Graham's lap. The skin around his eyes tight with strain.

My fault. I killed him. I killed my brother.

*

Darkness falls. The sound of the sea surrounds her. There's no way back to the mainland. It would be easy to lie down, easy to sleep, to let go. She knows now what the burden is that she's been carrying, recognises its weight at last. With recognition there comes an immense weariness.

Just like Iquis, I too am damned. The mirror was more accurate than Iquis knew.

And yet – that thought rattles something inside of her. She feels that Iquis did know. Maybe not what it was that Harriet was carrying – but certainly that there was something.

And yet, she still made me dance. She still kept pushing me away from her own darkness and into living. "You have to find your own redemption", that's what she said to me.

But how can I?

If Harriet wanted to, she could walk out into the sea – that would be an action of a kind. But the sea would be cold and rough. She doesn't feel strong enough for that. Easier, perhaps, to just give in to the weariness, to stop struggling. She could just rest against this slump of ruined stone, and let her eyes close. Not a decision, just...

*

Iquis slaps her awake.

'So I was right, you don't want me to die,' Harriet says. She opens her eyes. She's surrounded by sea and night and air.

But no Iquis.

She must have dreamt her, and yet she can still feel the cold imprint of Iquis's hand across her cheek.

She pushes herself upright, starts to move. Iquis doesn't want her to go to sleep.

The darkness seems to go on forever.

Iquis makes her rummage in her pocket for the chocolate bar. It's cold, hard to break. The chewing is rough, full of nuttiness and the grainy fragments of dried fruit. She grinds it down, then lifts the water bottle to her mouth, washes and swallows until her mouth is clean. She finds she is breathing better, less rapidly. There's a flicker of energy inside of her. The walking becomes the tiniest bit easier.

Iquis doesn't want me to die.

She stumbles on. Time passes.

*

Iquis is shaking her again. She's lapsed into a rhythm, a routine that is in itself hypnotic.

'But you're not really here,' Harriet protests. She doesn't want to leave the comfort of her trance.

Iquis just keeps shaking.

'What is it?' Harriet demands, irritably. 'I'm tired. This better be good.'

'I have to go,' Iquis says. Her voice is like the deep movement of the sea.

'No, don't do that. I'll go to sleep.'

'Don't you dare!'

Suddenly Harriet is laughing, not for long – it takes too much energy – but she's back in the night, back feeling the sear of the wind.

'You'll be okay,' Iquis says, and her voice is drifting away. 'Just keep walking and it will all be okay.

'I promise you.' Just the faintest whisper, carried back to her by the wind.

And then she's gone, and Harriet wants to howl with the pain of it. With the cold and loneliness of where she is. Trapped and isolated on this tiny, inhospitable island.

'I'll go to sleep!' She yells her protest at the wind. 'Look! I'm dropping to my knees. You can't just leave me.'

Yet her anger and grief are not hypnotic. Instead they make her more awake. She can feel the cold snow biting into her knees and the sensation is bright and brilliant, with a stinging immediacy.

Seconds later the sky ahead of her blossoms with colour, like a misplaced sunset. Fiery amber, glowing and gleaming, lighting up the night, giving her vision.

She can see. She knows where she is. The island is no longer an amorphous mass – a rugged, meaningless treadmill. She is kneeling at the edge of the island, facing a causeway puddled with water. The sea is gone. The path to the mainland is open.

There's a huge rumbling sound in the sky. A bit like thunder, but closer in somehow. It makes her jump. Then instinct takes over. She pushes herself upwards and sprints across the uneven ground. Her feet hit the causeway and she pounds along it.

The light is fading, fading fast, but she's almost over now. She fumbles the last few steps in the dark, stubs her foot against a rock, feels for it with her hands, and sits. Her heart is banging in her chest – her breath ragged. She feels a little sick, but gradually that passes.

She lifts the water bottle to her lips, sucks at the chocolate bar, lets her eyes adjust to the dark.

For a moment, there's peace, resting. She's okay now, she's going to make it.

She pushes herself up, full of a new determination. She starts to feel her way across the seaweed-covered rocks, heading away from the sound of the sea.

Smoke engulfs her. Acrid, dirty smoke, whipped across her by the wind.

Like a funeral pyre, she thinks, and wonders who it's for, Stephen or Iquis or her.

Maybe it's for all of us. Maybe, it's for the past.

*

Time passes. Hours. She crawls across rocks, grabbing handfuls of slippery, bulbous seaweed to haul herself forwards, casting around for the footpath she'd arrived on. Finally she finds it, and stumbles along it, feet dragging with weariness. She keeps having to stop to rest, or dozing off and stumbling into the low-lying scrub on each side. The walking feels perpetual, endless. Like being in some sort of limbo, or one of the seven circles of hell.

And yet it ends. She's on roads now, turning each time she finds a junction, following pointing signs where there are ones, because surely they will lead somewhere.

And they do. She starts to sense and then see the shape of a village gathering density in front of her. She draws closer. The silhouette of a telephone box jolts her.

She was meant to speak to Glyn yesterday. To tell him about Dark Island. It had been important. It's hard to remember why, hard to think at all. And yet, nothing's really changed, has it? Not in the outside world – only in her head.

She pushes the light button on her watch: 3 a.m. It's still the middle of the night. But the phone box is nagging at her.

She thinks of her father answering and feels totally numb. She doesn't know what she'll do if that happens.

The metal handle of the phone box is freezing. She has to fight to pull the door open against the wind, then she is in and cocooned. Staggered by the absence of the wind, the quiet of it after so long, she closes her eyes – then forces them open again, quickly. Not a good idea. She reaches for the handset, pushes at the numbers, hears the connection being made, the ringing start.

Glyn answers almost instantly.

'Hello? Who is it?' He should sound sleepy – but he doesn't – not at all.

'Glyn?'

'Harriet, thank God you're okay! Do you know? Were you involved?'

There's something in his voice she doesn't like.

'Know what?'

There's a pause. She hears him swallow.

'It's bad news Harriet. It's Iquis, Iquis and Dark Island, they're dead. They died at midnight – just three hours ago.'

'No!' But she isn't surprised. She's a tangle of feelings: wrenched and shocked and in pain – like a wounded animal – and yet...

It's like I already knew.

'Tell me,' she says, and her voice is horribly calm.

'Iquis crashed the helicopter into a cliff. All five of them were in it. No one else. There were no survivors.'

'She was flying it? I didn't know she could.'

'They all could.'

There's a silence. Harriet thinks of the words she was going to say, the betrayal, which now doesn't have to take place.

'It was deliberate, Harriet,' Glyn says, 'she left a note. She meant to do it.'

The metal and glass of the phone box shut out the elements. Harriet's body is warming, releasing the scent of smoke from her clothes and hair. Her nose and throat and mind fill with its pungency.

'Where?' she asks. She closes her eyes and the image of orange-amber flowers blossoming in the sky plays across her eyelids.

'It was one of the Orkney Islands, the island of Hoy. It's the hilliest one, the one with the biggest cliffs.'

"*I have to leave you.*"

I thought I was hallucinating you. I told you not to go but you went. I didn't want you to go.

'Harriet, Harriet, are you okay?'

'I... don't ask.' Her body is shaking slightly, aching. It hurts to stand. Everything is such an incredible effort.

'She left a note, Harriet. I have the wording of it. The manager told me what she'd said. I've been bugging him about you ever since you disappeared. That's why he phoned me after the crash. I haven't known long, less than half an hour. It's still so new that I keep on disbelieving it, having to remind myself it's real. I keep on looking at her message, trying to understand what was in her head.' He hesitates. 'I wondered if you...'

'Yes, read it.'

'Okay.' He clears his throat, she hears the rustle of paper, then Iquis's words, but his voice.

'It is my intention that we crash and burn tonight. No point in explaining why – you wouldn't get it – and the only person who would, already does. We flew too close to the sun – that is all.'

He stops. The silence, the stillness, has a texture.

'*The only person who would, already does,*' he repeats. 'Harriet, do you know why she did it?'

Harriet hesitates. *He's right, she did mean me. Do I understand? Absolutely. But I don't want to.*

'It was the only way,' she says, and stops, horrified by what she's said. Not "*Iquis thought it was the only way*" but "*it was the only way*". By the sense of something terrible and out of control having been concluded. By the awful fact that part of what she is feeling is relief. *I couldn't stop it. But Iquis could. Iquis has.*

'Harriet?'

'Wait.' She's thinking back over that last conversation with Iquis. Revisiting it with the clarity that this new knowledge brings. Recognising the coded farewells that had been in Iquis's words.

She knew then, back at the fortress, that this was what she was going to do.

I wonder when she decided. Maybe it was even before the river, even before what happened with Mark.

That hurts.

'I think she had no choice,' she says eventually. 'I think there were things wrong – terrible things – that she couldn't escape. I think this was the only way she could have any kind of peace.'

'I see,' he says, 'or at least, I think I see some of it. What a tragedy. What a terrible, terrible waste.'

'Don't, Glyn, please. Don't say things like that. I'm not ready to hear them.'

'It's not wrong to cry, Harriet.'

'Don't.' Harriet is struggling to get herself back under control, but there's something wrong with her body. She's cold, shaking, things are beginning to blur around her. *I have to crash. I physically can't keep going any longer.* But she has to make Glyn understand first. Or is it just that she has to speak the words in order to make them real?

Glyn is saying something, but she's not hearing it. She interrupts.

'Glyn, I've got to find shelter... Listen to me. When I saw Iquis she kept talking about redemption, telling me I had to find it in my own way. Now I get the hidden message. What she meant was, "*You have to find your own redemption. Just as I have to find mine.*" She knew what she was doing, Glyn. You have to respect that. She was doing the best thing she could.'

Harriet closes her eyes, leans against the wall. She can't say any more. After a moment, she pushes herself upright, lifts the receiver and replaces it. She leans back against the door and slowly it gives, dropping her into the night.

The icy wind is stronger than ever. As she staggers through it towards the houses, the phone starts to ring behind her. He must have traced her call, must be trying to reach her. But there's nothing she can do about that.

She keeps walking until she finds a B&B sign by a cottage. She stops and presses her forehead against the doorbell, releasing a constant drone which vibrates inside her head.

Sometime later, a panicked woman in a dressing gown opens the door.

'What is it? What's happened?'

Harriet pushes herself off the doorbell. 'I'm sorry,' she says. 'I'm just so cold, so tired. I need to sleep.'

The woman exclaims and pulls Harriet in. She touches Harriet's face, Harriet's hands.

'You're half frozen! What have you been doing, you crazy girl?'

She props Harriet up in an armchair and bustles about lighting a fire, chaffing Harriet's hands, placing her feet in a bowl of warm water. All the time she scatters words over Harriet in a comforting shower. She pushes a mug of cocoa into Harriet's hands.

'Drink this,' she says, 'then you can sleep.'

The cocoa is warm rather than hot. Somehow, Harriet swallows it down to the woman's satisfaction and at last she is steered up the stairs and into a warm bed. Her feet bump into a stinging hot-water bottle. She pushes it away, further down the bed and closes her eyes.

Sleep is like falling. A long, long distance.

FIFTY-TWO

Someone's shaking her awake.

Is it Iquis? Am I still on the island? Maybe I just dreamt...

A woman speaks. 'I'm sorry, I know you need to sleep, but the police officer is here. He just needs to check you're okay. You've been reported missing. He has to see you. He says it won't take long. Then you can go back to sleep. Here, put these on. Your clothes are still drying.'

Soft clothes – trousers and a sweatshirt, purple and black. She drags them on.

*

Downstairs, the policeman is slight and friendly looking. But even so he pulls Harriet's guilt closer to the surface. Caution wakens.

Don't say anything. She wishes he wasn't here.

She lets him do the talking. He is nice to her, in the same way that the woman is. He doesn't ask her to justify anything, just asks if she's okay.

She nods, keeps her mouth tightly shut.

He asks her for identification and she shows him her student rail card. He looks from the face on the card to her face and back again.

For some reason this makes her want to cry. But she's trying not to wake up too much. It's like she's been doped up after an accident – if the drugs wear off it's going to hurt like hell. She tries to let everything soften around her, to make every response minimal.

And yet when he turns to go, she finds that she has to stop him, has to ask, 'My father?' Her voice is husky.

He looks back at her. His eyes are a light blue. 'Is worried about you,' he says quietly, steadily.

Harriet drops her gaze. 'Will you tell him where I am?'

'You're an adult, we wouldn't divulge that information without your permission.' He hesitates, looking at Harriet intently, then continues, 'But he knows where you are. He kept redialling the number of the phone box until the baker's wife picked it up, half an hour ago. She told him that you're staying here. It's too small a village to keep anything hidden.'

'Oh.' Harriet digests this, aware of a nasty, nervous feeling in the pit of her stomach. 'Is he coming?'

Again the officer hesitates, then nods. 'I believe he's on his way.' There's a lilt at the end of his sentence, which makes it sound like a question.

Harriet blinks her eyes shut and then back open again. 'I'm tired,' she says, 'I need to sleep.'

And there's that numbness again, creeping over her like a sleeping pill. She's grateful for it. She yawns, and then he's gone and she's falling into bed, sinking back under.

*

Finally, she can't sleep any more, no matter how hard she tries. She keeps on waking up, and each time it's more of a struggle to slip back under. She lies in the bed and stares up at the ceiling, which is an unusual, pale lilac colour. She lets her gaze slide down to the walls, a soft bluey-purple. She likes the colours.

It's daylight again, although it has been dark sometimes when she's woken. She must have slept through yesterday and into today. She can't hear anyone moving around. She turns over, buries her face in the pillow. It smells of smoke.

She twists away from it, slides her legs over the side of the bed and sits up. She feels weak, exhausted, close to tears. But if she starts to cry she won't stop – may never stop. She needs to keep a bit numb, to move about carefully like someone who bruises easily. The clothes she'd worn to see the policeman are by the bed. She pulls them on; soft, thick black trousers and a purple sweatshirt, and next to them a pair of slippers. They're about two sizes too big. She shuffles in them to the door and opens it.

Her legs feel shaky, knees weak, as she descends the stairs resting heavily on the banister. She opens the door of the room that isn't marked private, sees her father sat in an armchair reading a newspaper and freezes.

He looks up, drops the paper and for a moment just looks at her. Then he levers himself out of the chair, walks over to her and wraps his arms round her, squeezing hard.

Daddy, she thinks, but doesn't say. She closes her eyes and stands inside his embrace. She can feel the heat of it, feel his strength. Her breath feels trapped. What is she going to do?

Her dad eases his arms from her. He seems awkward,

looks older. He gestures at the table, 'Why not have some breakfast?'

He's not shouting at her or demanding an explanation.

She edges forwards and sits at the table. There's a basket of rolls. She picks one up, splits it and starts to butter it. The tear of the soft bread inside the roll is uneven and fascinating. With her knife, she scoops the butter up and over each cresting peak. Her knife dances patterns across the bread. She keeps finding bits where the butter hasn't reached and – with great concentration – starts to cover these bits too.

'Are you going to eat that, or frame it?' Her father asks after a while.

She looks at him, then looks away. She catches sight of his fallen newspaper on the floor. Iquis's Circe-persona stares up at her. She drops her knife and reaches for the paper, leaning far out from her chair and snatching it up.

She scans the paper. Most of it she already knows, but there are small snippets of information that are new and a lot of speculation, which she ignores.

No bodies recovered, she reads, and then, more about the island of Hoy, which has been besieged by Dark Island fans. The newspaper shows a second picture of a mass of people standing on the edge of a cliff. There are flowers floating below them in the water.

The journalist makes much of the fact that the island of Hoy is often referred to as *Darkest Island*. Harriet finds herself smiling slightly at that. How typical of Iquis.

Dad is looking at her. 'I didn't expect...' He shakes his head as if to clear it.

'What?'

'Real danger. Physical danger. You disappearing like that.' He takes in an audible breath, tries to say something, but fails.

And yet the room is suddenly full of what he can't say.

'I'm sorry.' It comes out almost without volume, as if Harriet doesn't even have the right to say this, doesn't have the right to have created this panic in him.

He lifts his shoulders, rolls them backwards. 'It's over,' he says, then hesitantly, 'Glyn thought you knew her,' he gestures at the picture of Circe, 'that you came to Scotland to try to find her.'

There seems no need to lie any more and, besides, she can't. 'She needed me.'

It hangs in the air. The pain of it starts to drill into her. 'I can't believe...' She stops. But amazingly he's nodding. He understands this. Of course he does.

Stephen! Guilt tightens its grip.

Her dad reaches out and touches her hand with tentative fingers. 'No need to tell me. Not if you don't want to,' he says, 'but if it would help?'

She keeps perfectly still – concentrating on the rasp of his fingertips. A sob rises in her throat and she swallows it down. She's not allowed to cry.

'We're not far from the Isle of Hoy,' he says, awkwardly. 'We could go there if you wanted, pay our respects.'

Harriet closes her eyes, looks deep into the stormy-blue of Iquis's. 'Thanks,' she says, and then, 'but no. She won't be there.' She thinks of Iquis's words. 'Sea foam,' she says, 'she'll be in the sea foam, and that's everywhere.'

Silence between them. She leans forward and rests her forehead against the picture of Iquis, breathes in the newsprint scent, then folds the paper carefully and places it on an empty patch of table.

Something settles.

'I did it,' she says. 'I killed Stephen. It was my fault.'

'What?'

She hears the shock in his voice.

'It wasn't Graham. It was me. I was there, too. We lied about it. Graham took the blame, but it was my fault, not his.'

She stares down at Iquis's face. There, it's said. She wonders what Iquis was thinking about as she saw the cliff rushing to meet her. Dad isn't saying anything. He's twisted away, staring out of the window. He looks caged. He looks like he needs to get out of this room.

Then he wrenches himself round towards her and there's bewilderment on his face.

'What do you mean?'

'I was there. In the quarry. I'd followed them there. And they... It made Stephen angry. He ran towards me. I was on the ground, by the edge of the quarry-pool. I rolled towards him and... We collided. I saw it coming and I didn't try to stop it. I don't know whether I could have – but I didn't try.' Her voice is shaking.

Dad looks stunned. 'Why did you never tell us?'

'Stephen told me not to. And then, I blocked it out. Forgot it. I've only just remembered.'

He shakes his head. She's watching him, terrified. She wants him to hit her. That would be okay. That would make it better, not fix it but at least he'd still be connected to her. She wants to say sorry, but it's such a stupid, powerless word.

A tremor starts in his body, beginning in his legs and working upwards like a travelling earthquake. He turns away from her and bangs his head into the wall and then huge rough-sounding sobs are breaking out of him, washing over Harriet, dragging her into the storm so that she too is crying.

She sees the door open and the woman look at them and then back away, closing the door, shutting them in with the storm.

*

At some point, Harriet is aware of her father moving over to her, pulling her into his arms. And then she's sobbing against him and his jumper is rough against her and she smells his smell, which is her smell.

'Don't you hate me?' she chokes out. 'You ought to hate me.'

'Don't, Harriet.' His voice is muffled by her hair. 'He could have died at any time. It was like a time bomb in his head waiting to happen. It might not even have been the fall that triggered it. It could have been something else.'

He takes a deep breath, continues. 'I know we've always blamed Graham, but that was unfair. There were reasons, but even so it's inexcusable. Your mother felt that Graham had taken Stephen away from her... corrupted him... You wouldn't understand – there were... dodgy magazines. She found them in the drawer in his desk. It was only natural, but she couldn't accept it.'

'Oh.'

'They'd always been so close, but they weren't after she found those... She... she couldn't forgive herself for that – for how cold she'd been with him. So she had to have someone else to blame. We both did.'

He pauses. 'I knew it was wrong, but we were just trying to survive.'

He's shaking again. 'I didn't know – couldn't know – that you thought...'

He presses a weighty hand on her shoulder.

'I don't understand,' Harriet says, in a tiny, scared voice. 'What do you mean by a time bomb?'

'The brain aneurysm. We didn't know it was there – there was no family history. No way of knowing.'

'But I don't know what you're talking about!'

Dad stares at her. 'You didn't know?'

'Know what?'

'Stephen died because of something wrong in his head – it's like... a weak artery, it starts to balloon out,' he swallows, she can see him picturing it, there's a catch in his voice, 'starts to balloon out, because it's full of blood. Then something happens – it could be anything – and it bursts.' As he says it, she can feel him feeling it. 'Maybe it was the fall, maybe it wasn't. There was a suggestion at the inquest that something he'd been doing shortly before the fall might have...'

He stops. 'You don't need to know about that.'

But Harriet is reeling. '*Inquest?*'

'Hell,' her father exclaims. 'We've made a right mess of this. You didn't know about the inquest? But then, how could you? We didn't talk. Not afterwards. And at the time...' He stops, frowns. 'Yes. At the time... There was an inquest, and before that an autopsy, and you were only nine. We didn't want to expose you to any of it. It was horrible, Harriet. We were protecting you.'

He stops, paces the room, turns back to face her. 'I'd no idea you'd been in the quarry, that you needed to know any of this. All I knew was that afterwards I couldn't get close to you any more. I thought it was something wrong with me. I knew I couldn't feel properly.

'If I'd known...'

He breaks off. Harriet is crying. He puts his arms around her, and holds her.

She cries for Stephen and for Dad, for their whole lost family. And then, inevitably, she allows her grief for Iquis to surface, cries for the lost girl in the sea foam – cries for the suffering, the walking on knives, that she had gone through.

*

Later, much later, they go out for a walk. The tears and the truth have drained a heaviness out of Harriet. She's so light that the wind could almost pick her up and carry her for miles. She's always felt like a terrible person, always known deep down that she was bad, and now she doesn't. That takes some getting used to.

She feels released, reprieved, forgiven; and yet unbearably sad for Stephen. She doesn't feel completely free of what happened, but then, from what Dad has told her, neither he nor Mum do either.

'We just have to learn to live with it,' he'd said, 'not to let it spoil our lives. That's helping no one. Your mother – it's taken her a long time to begin to let go of the past, but she's doing it and we can, too. We have to Harriet. We have to think of the future.'

And then, they'd actually talked about the future. He'd said that her mother was on her way, travelling towards them with one of the women from her group.

'She's been ill for a long time, but she's getting better now. She doesn't want to lose you, Harriet – she loves you; she just... she just hasn't known how to love anyone – most of all herself – for a long, long time.'

Then, obviously awkward with such confidences – so alien to his usual way of speaking – he'd asked about the course, told her about speaking to Dr Drake. 'She couldn't tell me much, but she hinted that it wasn't what you wanted?'

Harriet had been amazed. Dad was open to the possibility of change. She'd found herself telling him about her doubts, about not knowing what she wanted, about needing to find out who she was first, because only then would she know what it was she wanted to do.

'I think,' she said, 'that I only did the course because it was what Stephen would have done.'

Her father had laughed at that. 'Only if he'd got over rebelling against me first,' he'd said. 'I know it was where his natural talents lay, but he was determined not to follow in my footsteps without a struggle. I think he'd have found something else to do. Something that was just his.'

He'd hugged her again. 'It's all right, we'll work something out. You're young. You've got time. You should take it.'

It had felt funny, talking about such things; like survivors crawling out of the wreckage and beginning to plan how to rebuild.

*

Now, walking by the sea and gazing at the creamy, flecking foam, she feels an incredible peace. There's a pain that she feels for Iquis, for Iquis's life, which she doesn't even try to wrestle with – a candle lit, which nothing will ever blow out. And underneath, an older grief for Stephen, the big brother whom she'd loved and adored and hated all at the same time.

She'd never been able to grieve for him properly, because too many memories and emotions had been locked away. This too will take time to work its way out. But today, in the fleeting warmth of the late afternoon sun – with the retreating snow thawing behind her – she's just enjoying the wind tossing and tangling her hair, and concentrating on the way her arm is tucked through her father's, on the fragile but growing understanding between them.

ACKNOWLEDGEMENTS

Thank you to all my creative writing teachers and in particular to Maggie O'Farrell, Andrew Cowan, Karen Hayes, Patricia Dunker, Tim Pears and Crysse Morrison who have all been significant to the development of this novel. Your expert advice still rings in my ears.

Thank you to Chris Hammacott, Wendy Metcalfe, Carol Westron and Eileen Robertson for being there – for your fabulous feedback, encouragement and enthusiasm; for weekends away, wine and laughter and friendship. Special thanks to Chris, for reading two different versions in their entirety, and for giving thoughtful and constructive feedback on both.

Thank you to everyone at Matador, and in particular Hannah Dakin, Fern Bushnell, Sophie Morgan and Andrea Johnson, for making this journey to publication a less frightening experience – for breaking every step down and always being there with advice and friendly support. Thank you to Hannah Eveleigh for meticulous editing, and to Jack Wedgbury for the wonderful cover design.

Thank you to Sallyanne Sweeney, for reading an early version of this novel and responding with telling feedback. And thanks to Beth Lewington, for sharing your promotional expertise and experience.

Thank you to my family, my first readers. Mum and Dad, I remember being scared when I showed you the start of an early version of this novel. I needn't have been. You encouraged me and sounded impressed. You even told other people about your daughter, "the writer" – perhaps a little prematurely! And later when there was only you, Dad, it meant everything to have you read the whole manuscript and I loved the pencilled comments you left for me in the margins. So glad we had time for that. Thank you Ruth and Uncle Robert, Sandra and Aunty Margaret, Kate, Rachel and Margaret Bryant – for your encouragement, your support, your interest. And thank you Ruth, Margaret B, Sara Leathes and Robert for critical reading and feeding back on early drafts. You were hugely helpful.

Thank you to Dianna Hardy for asking me why I wrote this novel during my final edits and reconnecting me with how it started.

Thank you to Andrew Tees, Denise Ferguson and Abby Kirkham for help with research. Thanks, Abby, for dressing me up in goth clothes and taking me for a walk along the seafront, for introducing me to nightclubs, and lending me music, and just generally helping me to enter your world. Thank you, Andrew, for the "You come in here and say that!" story which I used for the Call of Cthulhu role-play game.

There really is a beer called Dark Island which is brewed on the Orkneys. It tastes fabulous. I did my best to describe it in the scene where Harriet discovers it. That is the only connection it has with this novel. I have no connection with the brewers, and this isn't an official endorsement of their product.

Thank you to my amazing community of fellow writers and performers.

Thanks to everyone at the Portsmouth Writers' Hub, and in particular to Tessa Ditner Amorosi, Will Sutton and Alison Habens for your amazing enthusiasm, warmth and ability to make things happen. Thanks also to Amanda Garrie, Annie Kirby, Tom Sykes, Sarah Cheverton, Karl Bell, Christine Lawrence, Clare Forsyth and Eileen Phyall for all the other writerly opportunities. And thank you to everyone involved for your friendship, knowledge and support.

Thank you, Gail Loose – for everything! You have been such a good friend. I love your enthusiasm, your encouragement. I love sharing this journey with you, love talking about technique with you. And I love that we just keep writing and keep talking. So glad I know you.

And finally, Richard, without whom! Thank you for helping me to grow as a writer, for helping me to play with ideas, explore new angles and try new techniques. For picking me up when I'm stuck and for reading and honing my work – over and over! For being my best friend and my most wonderful writing companion. I love spending days writing with you.